Rose Tremain has known the landscape described in *Trespass* since childhood, and has frequently taken France and the French as subjects for her novels and stories.

Her most recent book, *The Road Home*, won the Orange Broadband Prize for Fiction in 2008. Her novels have been published in twenty-seven countries and have won many prizes, including the Whitbread Novel of the Year Award, the James Tait Black Memorial Prize, the Prix Femina Étranger and the *Sunday Express* 'Book of the Year' Award.

The bestselling *The Road Home* is being adapted for television. Rose Tremain lives in Norfolk and London with the biographer, Richard Holmes.

TRESPASS

In a silent valley stands an isolated farmhouse, the Mas Lunel. Its owner, Aramon Lunel is an alcoholic, haunted by his violent past; his dogs starve and his land is in ruins. Meanwhile, his sister Audrun, in her bungalow within sight of the Mas Lunel, dreams of retribution for the betrayals that have blighted her life. Into this world, from London, comes disillusioned antiques dealer Anthony Verey, hoping to remake his life in France. He looks at properties in the region, but his arrival at the Mas Lunel marks the beginning of a frightening and unstoppable series of consequences. Two worlds and two cultures collide. Ancient boundaries are crossed, taboos are broken — a violent crime is committed . . . whilst the Cévennes hills remain, ever cruel and seductive.

Books by Rose Tremain
Published by The House of Ulverscroft:

THE COLOUR
THE ROAD HOME

ROSE TREMAIN

---◆---

TRESPASS

Complete and Unabridged

CHARNWOOD
Leicester

First published in Great Britain in 2010 by
Chatto & Windus
The Random House Group Limited
London

First Charnwood Edition
published 2011
by arrangement with
The Random House Group Limited
London

British Library CIP Data

Tremain, Rose.
  Trespass.
  1. Alcoholics- -Fiction.
  2. Antique dealers- -Fiction.
  3. Brothers and sisters- -Fiction.
  4. English- -France- -Cevennes Mountains- -Fiction.
  5. Cevennes Mountains (France)- -Fiction.
  6. Large type books.
  I. Title
  823.9'14–dc22

  ISBN 978–1–44480–508–6

Published by
F. A. Thorpe (Publishing)
Anstey, Leicestershire

Set by Words & Graphics Ltd.
Anstey, Leicestershire
Printed and bound in Great Britain by
T. J. International Ltd., Padstow, Cornwall

This book is printed on acid-free paper

For Richard, with love

The child's name is Mélodie.

Long ago, before Mélodie was born, her pretty mother had had a stab at composing music.

Mélodie is ten years old and she's trying to eat a sandwich. She prises apart the two halves of the sandwich and stares at the wet, pink ham inside, and at the repulsive grey-green shimmer on its surface. All around her, in the dry grass and in the parched trees, crickets and grasshoppers are making that sound they make, not with their voices (Mélodie has been told that they have no voices) but with their bodies, letting one part vibrate against another part. In this place, thinks Mélodie, everything is alive and fluttering and going from one place to another place, and she dreads to see one of these insects arrive suddenly on her sandwich or on her leg or start to tangle its limbs in her hair.

Mélodie's hair is dark and soft. As she looks at the slimy ham, she can feel sweat beginning to seep out of her head. Sweat, she thinks, is a cold hand that tries to caress you. Sweat is something strange inside you trying to creep from one place to another place . . .

Mélodie puts the sandwich down in the dusty grass. In moments, she knows, ants will arrive and swarm round it and try to carry it away. Where she used to live, in Paris, there were no ants, but here, where her new home is, there are

1

more ants than you could ever count. They come out of the earth and go down into it again. If you dug down, you would find them: a solid mass of them, black and red. Your spade would crunch right through them. You might not even have to dig very deep.

Mélodie lifts her head and gazes at the leaves on the oak tree above her.

These leaves are yellowing, as though it were already autumn. The wind called the mistral keeps blowing through the tree and the sun keeps moving and piercing the shade and nothing in this place ever ends or is still.

'Mélodie,' says a voice. 'Are you all right? Don't you want your sandwich?'

Mélodie turns to her teacher, Mademoiselle Jeanne Viala, who sits on a rug on the grass a few paces away, with some of the younger children hunched up near to her, all obediently chewing their baguettes.

'I'm not hungry,' says Mélodie.

'We've had a long morning,' says Mademoiselle Viala. 'Try to eat a few mouthfuls.'

Mélodie shakes her head. Sometimes, it's difficult to speak. Sometimes, you're like an insect with no voice, which just has to make a movement with some part of its anatomy. And everywhere around you the mistral keeps blowing and autumn leaves keep falling, even though it's a midsummer day.

'Come and sit here,' says Mademoiselle Viala. 'We'll all have a drink of water.'

The teacher tells one of the boys, Jo-Jo, (one of those who tease and bully Mélodie and imitate her posh Parisian accent) to pass her the picnic bag. Mélodie gets up and moves away from the sandwich lying in the grass and Mademoiselle Viala holds out her hand and Mélodie sits down there, near the teacher whom she quite likes, but who betrayed her this morning . . . yes she did . . . by making her look at things she didn't want to see . . .

Mademoiselle Viala wears a white linen blouse and blue jeans and white canvas shoes. Her arms are soft and tanned and her lipstick is a bright, startling red. She could have come from Paris, once. She takes a little bottle of Evian water out of the cumbersome bag and passes it to Mélodie.

'There,' she says. 'There you are.'

Mélodie presses the cool bottle against her cheek. She sees Jo-Jo staring at her. Bully-boys' faces can be blank, absolutely blank, as though they'd never learned to say their own names.

'So,' says Jeanne Viala in her teacher-voice, 'I wonder who can tell me, after the presentations we saw at the museum, how silk is made?'

Mélodie looks away, up, sideways, far away at the jumping light, at the invisible wind . . . All round her, the children raise their arms, bursting to tell Mademoiselle Viala what they know, or what, Mélodie suspects, they have *always* known, because they're part of this landscape and were born out of its earth.

Jo-Jo says it: 'Silk is made by worms.'

He, like the others, always knew it. Everybody learned about it from their grandparents or great-grandparents and only she, Mélodie Hartmann from Paris, had never ever thought

3

about it until today, until Jeanne Viala took the children to the Museum of Cévenol Silk Production at Ruasse . . .

'Right,' says Mademoiselle Viala. 'Don't all shout out at once. *You* tell me, Mélodie. Imagine you wanted to breed a healthy crop of silkworms, what would be the first thing you would do, once you'd bought the eggs?'

The first thing. She looks down at her hands, which are dirty with sweat and dust — with human mud.

'Keep them warm . . . ' She whispers it. Her voice smaller than the voice of some tiny creature living between two stalks of corn, or underneath a tree root.

'Yes,' says Jeanne Viala. 'Good. And how would you do that?'

Mélodie wants to say: I said my answer. I said it. I don't want to say any more of it. But she just keeps looking down at her muddy hands, clutching the Evian bottle.

'I know!' says Jo-Jo.

'We know!' say two girls, two inseparable friends, Stéphanie and Magali.

'Go on then, Magali, you tell us,' says Jeanne Viala.

Magali's face is scarlet, puffed out with pride and embarrassment. 'My Gran told me!' she explodes. 'You put them in a pouch and you stick the pouch up your knickers!'

As laughter breaks round her, Mélodie gets up. Her legs feel trembly, but she walks as fast as she can away from the huddle of children.

Red-backed crickets jump and flit in her

4

pathway. She snaps off a stick with a brittle seed-head at its tip, and tries to stop the insects from coming near her with this. She hears the teacher call to her, but she doesn't turn. Surely, Jeanne Viala knows . . . surely she does . . . that if you've lived your life in Paris — ten years of it — then you're homesick for the city, for a nice clean, carpeted room in a nice apartment, and you don't want to talk about worms writhing in a pouch under your skirt. Because it isn't as if Paris had been obliterated. It's still there. Your street is there. Your apartment. The room that was once yours. And it's only you who are never going back. Never. Because Papa has been given a 'great opportunity'. Papa has been offered a promotion. He's been made the Head of a Laboratory of Medical Analysis in Ruasse. *Head.* 'It's fantastic,' says Maman. 'You have to understand that it's a wonderful chance.' And all it means is . . . Paris has disappeared. Now there is a house made of stone, way out on its own in a shadowy valley. Mosquitoes whine in the dark, hot nights. The house is known as a *mas*, pronounced 'masse'. In the crannies of its stones, where the mortar has flaked or fallen out, scorpions hide from the sun. And sometimes there is one, black and deadly, on the wall of your bedroom and Papa has to come and . . .

. . . he brings a wooden mallet or a hammer. Blood comes to his face.

The blow of the hammer leaves a mark on the plasterwork of the wall.

'There,' he says, 'it's all right now. It's no more.'

5

No more.

No more walks home from school, past the optometrist's shop and the flower shop and the pâtisserie on the corner. No more winter afternoons when the Paris sky is electric blue behind the shoulders of buildings.

No more ballet class, swimming club, violin lessons. *No more.*

With her seed-head stick, Mélodie flays her path through the grasshoppers.

She opens a rusty iron gate and walks into a tussocky pasture, going towards shade, towards yellowing ash saplings, a place where she will be alone and drink her water. The teacher is no longer calling her. Perhaps she's walked further than she realised? The air is quiet and still, as though the mistral has died.

Mélodie opens the water bottle. Not cool any more, but dirtied by her muddy hands and smelling of plastic. Not meant to smell of plastic, but smelling of man-made plastic only here, where Nature is so . . . determined . . . so . . . *everywhere.* Only here, where Nature fills the ground and the air and the sky. Where it fills your eyes. Where you can taste it in your mouth . . .

Halfway through gulping the water, Mélodie hears a new sound.

People talking on the radio? One of those discussions, far off, about politics or about the life of someone famous? A conversation you weren't quite expected to understand?

She stops drinking and listens. No. Not people. Something gabbling softly like them, but not them . . . unless they're talking in a language Mélodie has never heard before . . .

She looks down to where the pasture seems to end in a line of nettle-green, feathery-leaved weeds. The weeds grow in clusters, so close together it looks almost impossible to find a way through them. But Mélodie is determined to discover the source of the new sound, so she makes her way towards them. She still has her stick. She begins to whip the weeds down. She thinks: This is the way to treat this place, this land of the Cévennes: you whip it! But then it fights back. The stick breaks. So Mélodie begins kicking and stamping a pathway through the weeds with her white sneakers, bought in Paris, no longer white. She takes big strides. She feels the ground underneath her begin to slope downwards. One of the ash trees trembles between her and the sun, like a flimsy curtain drawn above her head.

She's invisible now. Neither the teacher nor the other children can see her any more. They, the others — every single one of them — knew about old women who incubated worms under their heavy skirts, white worms against the white flesh of their bellies, their thighs, but they didn't come here, didn't dare to come and whip the weeds and stamp them down and make a path towards . . .

. . . a curving beach of grey stones and sandy shingle. And there, beyond the shingle, eddying between huge boulders, a narrow sliding stream. Not a river. Still *pretending* to be a river, *talking to itself* in the language of a river, but shrunk by the heat to a streamlet. Dragonflies darting above the high stones. Ash leaves flying off and riding on the surface of the water.

Mélodie crosses the shingle to the stream's edge. She stoops and drenches her hand, washing the mud away, loving the cool, the cold, the almost-ice of it. A thrilling feeling, suddenly. And here she is, invisible in the beautiful tree shade, invisible and safe, as though the dark green weeds had sprung up again behind her, cutting off her way back.

Almost happy, she walks along the little beach, following the stream to where it turns a corner. And she turns the corner and sees the water flowing unexpectedly into a deep, sea-green pool. She stares at the pool. A streamlet trying to be a river again! So even Nature could have a memory — could it? — just as she has a memory, of what she thought she was meant to become and where. For this is how it feels to her, that the stream *longed for the pool*. It was embarrassed by being a rill, a runnel. It might even have been sad, sorrowful, as she is, 'heavy of heart', as Maman calls it. But now that it's merged with the great, deep pool, it knows that it's come home.

For a long time, Mélodie stands still, observing. Then, she's overtaken by a desire to bathe her itchy, sunburnt body in the water. She looks behind her, half expecting the teacher to appear through the curtain of saplings. But no one comes.

Shoes. Jeans. T-shirt. She casts everything away except a little pair of red-and-white knickers, bought at Monoprix in the Champs Elysées. Then she begins to climb the first of the rocks that separate her from the pool. Agile now, she goes from boulder to boulder, towards the highest of them, which stands in mid-stream, and she remembers her instructor at her swimming club saying to the other children: 'Watch Mélodie. This is how I want you all to be when you dive: like a bird, graceful and light.'

So she's going to dive now. She's positioning her bare feet on the edge of the white boulder. She's a moment from a neatly executed dive, a moment from the drenching, reviving cold of the pool, when . . . at the very corner of her vision, she sees something which shouldn't be there. At first look, she doesn't recognise what it is. She has to look again. She has to stare.

Then she starts screaming.

The tapestry ('French, late Louis XV pastoral, by Aubusson') depicted a gathering of stylishly dressed aristocrats, sitting on the grass in the shade of some broad-leaved trees. Approaching the group were two servants, an elderly man and a young woman, bringing meat, bread, wine and fruit.

A dog lay asleep in the sunshine. In the distance ('Some fading evident, texture of weave slightly hardened') was a flower-filled meadow. The border was intricate ('Formal frame pattern: escutcheons, roses and oak leaves') and the colours ('Reds, blues and greens on a neutral ground') soft and pleasing.

On a cold spring morning in London, Anthony Verey stood in his shop, *Anthony Verey Antiques*, warming his hands on a mug of coffee, staring up at this tapestry. It had been in his possession for some time. Four years? Five? He'd bid for it at a private sale in Suffolk. He'd wanted it badly enough to pay more than a thousand pounds over the reserve price of £6,000 and when it was delivered to the shop he'd hung it on a wall at the very back, opposite the desk where nowadays he sat all the time, pretending to do work of some kind, but in fact existing in a shallow state of reverie, keeping watch over his marvellous possessions — his *beloveds*, as he called them — and sometimes peering beyond them to observe the passers-by on the Pimlico Road.

Once the tapestry was in place, Anthony found that he was dismayed by the idea of selling it. The sale-price he put on it — £14,000 — was intended to discourage buyers, but in fact this price only existed in Anthony's mind and wasn't written down anywhere. Sometimes, when people asked him about the tapestry, he told them it wasn't his, he was just looking after it. Sometimes, he announced that the sale-price was 'in the region of £19,000' and waited for dealers to wince. Sometimes, he just said baldly that the tapestry wasn't for sale. It was his: his own Louis XV Aubusson. He knew in his heart that he'd never part with it.

Anthony was a sixty-four-year-old man of medium height, with abundant grey crinkly hair. Today, he was wearing a red cashmere polo-neck sweater under a jacket of soft brown tweed. It was never very warm in the shop because the *beloveds* had a tendency to crack, bulge, fade or split in temperatures above 60° Fahrenheit. But Anthony himself was thin and he feared the cold. By his desk, he kept a heavy old oil-filled heater, which creaked companionably on winter afternoons. He drank a lot of very hot coffee, occasionally spiked with cognac. He wore thermal socks. Even scarves, sometimes, and woollen gloves.

He knew that this inconvenient palaver for the *beloveds* was eccentric, but he didn't care. Anthony Verey had no wife, mistress, lover, child, dog or cat. Across his life, at one time or another, in various pairings and combinations, he'd possessed all these things — all except the child. But now he was alone. He was a man who had grown to love furnishings and nothing else.

Anthony sipped his coffee. His gaze remained on the tapestry, in which the aristocrats sat on the right with the trees behind them and the servants approached from the left. The dog's slumber and the happy expectation apparent on the faces of the people suggested a moment of undisturbed, hedonistic contentment. Lunch was arriving. The sun blazed down.

But there was something else. At the very edge of the scene, to the extreme right of it, almost hidden among foliage, was a sinister face, the face of an old woman. On her head was a black cap. She was directing towards the people a look of exceptional malevolence. But nobody paid her any attention. It was as though they hadn't seen her.

For long periods of time, Anthony found himself looking at this old woman's face. Had she been part of the original design? She seemed insubstantial: a disembodied face, a gnarled hand on her chin, the rest of her hidden by the trees. Had the tapestry weavers ('Probably from the atelier of Pierre Dumonteil, 1732–1787') alleviated the monotony of their work by adding this small but telling detail of their own devising?

Anthony drank the dregs of the coffee and was about to walk over to his desk, to make a half-hearted beginning on his weekly accounts, when something else caught his eye. It was a loose thread in the tapestry.

12

A nearby halogen lamp illuminated it. This black thread hung down over the old woman's brow, as though it might have been a lock of the crone's hair. Anthony put down his mug. He reached up and took the minute silk filament between thumb and forefinger.

The filament was less than a centimetre long. The feel of it was exceptionally soft, and Anthony kept his hand there, rubbing the little thread for a short space of time which could have been a minute, or could have been three minutes, or four, or even seven, but which was in any case long enough for him to come to full consciousness of the shocking and incontrovertible fact about his life that it had suddenly revealed to him: when he died, not one shard or splinter from any one of his *beloveds* would he be able to take with him. Even if some afterlife turned out to exist, which he doubted, he wouldn't have with him *anything* to console him, not even this black silk thread, less than one centimetre long.

The door buzzer sounded and woke Anthony from a trance which, in all the days and weeks to come, he would see as being of paramount importance. A man in a pinstripe suit and wearing a pink tie came into the shop. He looked around him. Not a dealer, Anthony concluded swiftly, not even an amateur collector, just one of the Ignorant Rich, looking first at this thing and then at that, not knowing what he's seeing . . .

Anthony let the ignoramus move towards the most expensive piece in the shop, a marble-topped giltwood console table ('The top assorted

13

specimen marbles within *verde antico* moulded borders, first quarter 19th century, Italian. The gilt frames and supporting standing Atlas figures, 3rd quarter 18th century. Also Italian.'), then wandered slowly towards him.

'Need any help, sir?'

'Yes,' said the man, 'I probably do. Looking for a wedding present for my sister. They're buying a house in Fulham. I'd like to give them something . . . I don't know . . . for the hall, I was thinking. Something everybody will . . . erm . . . notice.'

'Right,' said Anthony. 'For the hall. Well . . . '

He saw the man's eyes bulging in startled appreciation of the gilded Atlas figures, so he moved straight to the console table and caressed its marble top. 'This is a beauty,' Anthony said in a voice which still had about it an unfashionable English drawl he could no longer be bothered to suppress. 'An absolute dreamboat. But it needs space to show itself off. How big is your sister's hall?'

'Haven't a clue,' said the man. 'Haven't seen it. But I really like the gold cherubs or whatever they are. Quite a wow-factor there! What's the . . . erm . . . price?'

Anthony put on his glasses and bent down, searching for a minute label taped to the marble plinth on which the Atlas figures stood. He straightened up and said without smiling: 'Twenty-eight thousand.'

'OK,' said the man, fingering his pink silk tie with a meaty hand. 'Let me have a wander, then. I guess I was hoping to find a bargain.'

14

'A *bargain?*' said Anthony. 'Well don't forget this is Pimlico.'

★　★　★

Pimlico.

No, not Pimlico itself. Still Chelsea. The westerly end of the Pimlico Road, London SW3, Anthony's home, his living, his life for the last forty years, the place where his knowledge, shrewdness and charm had once made him rich. Not only rich. Here, he'd become a star of the antiques world. Dealers said his name with awe: Anthony Verey; *the* Anthony Verey. There had been no important auction, no private sale, no gallery preview to which he was not invited. He knew everyone: their place in the dealer or owner hierarchy, their weak spots, their failures, their maddening triumphs. He was like a spoilt prince in a small but opulent realm, courting *invidia.*

At the height of his celebrity, he'd been able to lull himself to sleep by counting — one by delectable one — the people who envied him.

And now, on this cold spring morning, he'd suddenly seen . . . well, what had he seen? He'd seen how *alone* everything was. Not just the man who'd once been a prince, once been *the* Anthony Verey. But all the *beloveds,* too, all these wonders, made with such care, with such dedication . . . these things which had endured and survived for so long . . . even these were tragic in their separateness and solitude. All right, he knew this was a sentimental thought. Furniture couldn't feel. But you could feel for it.

You could worry about that day when you had to leave it behind, to the mercy of other people's neglect and ignorance. Particularly now, in these times, when there was a universal letting-go of objects like these, seen as belonging to an old, irrelevant world. What awaited them? What awaited?

Anthony was seated at his desk now, on a hard Windsor chair, but with his still-narrow arse carefully placed on a green silk cushion. This cushion, bought at Peter Jones, was moulded so perfectly to the shape of his bottom that he seldom dared to plump it up or shake the dust from it. Nobody else came into the shop. Outside, the day was lightless.

Anthony took down his accounts ledger, put on his glasses and began staring at columns of figures. The ledger was old and thick and worn and was one of seven that contained all he had of a written history: every purchase, every sale, every tax payment, every expense. Ledgers 2 to 5 held all the dazzling figures. In Ledger 6, prices began to fall away and the volume of sales to diminish in a horrible descending curve. And now, in Ledger 7 . . . well, all he could do, frankly, was to avoid looking at bottom lines.

He turned to the Sale Entries for the month of March: an undistinguished portrait ('English School, early 18th century. Sir Comus Delapole, QC, and Lady Delapole. Pastel with touches of watercolour'), a majolica jar ('Ovoid, Italian 17th century, decorated with large scrolling foliage clusters'), a George III silver teapot ('The circular body engraved with a band of

16

anthemions and wrigglework'), and — the only thing of any real value — a Regency mahogany sofa table he hadn't particularly wanted to part with. These things had earned him slightly less than £4,000; barely enough to pay the month's share of the repairing lease on the shop.

Pitiful.

Anthony now vaguely wished that he'd tried harder to sell the peachy Italian console table to the man with the pink tie, who, in the end, had bought nothing and had been seen making straight for David Linley's shop on the opposite side of the road. He knew that not only the price of the table, but also his unconcealed disdain for this person, had driven him away, as it drove many customers away. But that couldn't be helped. The fact was that Anthony enjoyed being disdainful. Disdain — born out of specialist knowledge, or what he thought of as *secret knowledge* — was a habit perfected over forty years, and was now one of the few pleasures left to him.

Anthony put his head in his hands. He clung to tufts of his hair. At least he still had that: he had hair. He might be sixty-four but his hair was fantastic. And of course what he liked most about it was the envy it provoked among his male friends — the few that he had — with all that pink head-shame they had to endure day in, day out. And he found himself admitting, as he could have admitted long ago, that the envy of others — the blessed *invidia* to which mankind is so ruinously prone — had really and honestly been the thing that had kept him alive. This was

17

an outrageous realisation, but a true one. Lovers of both sexes and even one brief wife, Caroline, had come and gone, but the admiration and envy of others had stayed with him, moved with him through his work and his rest, fed and nourished him, allowing him to feel that his life had meaning and purpose. And now that, too, was gone.

Pity had replaced it. Everybody knew he was struggling, that he might even go under. They certainly discussed it round their dinner tables: 'Nobody wants brown furniture any more. Interiors look completely different now. Anthony Verey must be in grave trouble . . . ' And of course there were many who wanted him to fail. Hundreds. If the shop were to close, how triumphant certain people would be . . .

Bitter thoughts. Anthony knew that, somehow, he had to resist, had to labour on. But who or what would help him? Where could meaning any longer be found? It seemed to him that outside the confines of his shop, where the *beloveds* clustered round him, keeping him safe, now lay a heartless wasteland.

His telephone rang.

'Anthony,' said a brusque but kindly and familiar voice, 'it's V.'

An immediate feeling of relief and gratitude rushed like an adrenalin shot into Anthony's blood. His sister, Veronica, was the only person alive for whom Anthony Verey felt anything like true affection.

In that same cool springtime, Audrun Lunel, a woman who had never moved from her village of La Callune in the Cévennes in sixty-four years, walked alone through a forest of oaks and chestnuts.

This forest, a sighing and beautiful thing, belonged to her absolutely by the instruction of her dead father's will (*'To my daughter, LUNEL Audrun Bernadette, I bequeath in its entirety that parcel of forested land designated* Salvis 547 . . . ') and Audrun often came here alone, to feel under her rubber boots the contours of the earth with its carpeting of leaves, acorns and chestnut husks, to touch the trees, to look up at the sky through their branches, to remind herself that this place was hers 'in its entirety'. She had memories of this wood which seemed to go back beyond time, or to be *above* time, or above what people called 'time' with its straightness, its years in a line, its necessities. These memories, in Audrun's consciousness, *always had been.*

She knew she was often confused. People told her this. Friends, doctors, even the priest, they all said it: 'You are sometimes confused, Audrun.' And they were right. There were moments when consciousness or existence or whatever it was that you had to call being alive, there were moments when it . . . faltered.

Sometimes, she fell down — like her mother, Bernadette used to do, fall in a faint when the wind blew from the north. At other times, she went on seeing and hearing the things that were there, but it was as if they were seen and heard through glass, at some oddly terrifying remove, and then, a moment later, she wouldn't know what it was, exactly, that she'd just seen or heard. There would be the feeling of an absence.

Episodes, the doctor called them. Short episodes of the brain. And the doctor — or doctors, for it wasn't always the same one — gave her pills and she took them. She lay in her bed, swallowing pills. She put them on her tongue, like a Communion wafer. She tried to imagine herself transfigured by them. She lay in the Cévenol night, listening to the scoop-owl, to the breathing of the land, trying to envisage the chemical river in her blood. She saw this river as a marbled swirl of purple, crimson and white; the colours drifted in skeins, expanded into almost-recognisable shapes, like clouds. Sometimes, she wondered whether these envisagings were inappropriate. She'd also been told that her mind was liable to fabricate 'inappropriate ideas'. It could imagine terrible things. It could imagine torture, for instance. It could discover, inside the old abandoned wells of La Callune, the bodies of her enemies hanging upside down, their ankles tied with wire. This wire bit into their flesh. Blood seeped from their eyes. The water in the wells kept rising . . .

'*Enemies*, Audrun? You haven't got any enemies,' said the people of La Callune.

But she had. Her closest friend, Marianne Viala, knew who they were. The fact that one of these enemies was dead and buried in the churchyard didn't remove from his hated form the mantle of enemy. It often seemed to Audrun Lunel that the dead, becoming formless, also became agile and could seep not only into your dreams, but into the very air you were breathing. You could taste and smell them. Sometimes you could feel their disgusting heat.

Audrun walked on. Her eyes were keen and never dimmed, except when an *episode* was nearing and objects and faces appeared to stretch and shift. Today, she could capture the signs of spring, clear and sharp and filled with light: pale leaves on the chestnuts, dog's-tooth violets at their feet, catkins on a hazel bush. Her hearing, too, was exact. She could recognise the song of the willow-warbler, be troubled by the squeak of her rubber boots. And now, at the centre of the wood, she stopped and looked down at the earth.

About the earth she knew she was not wrong. About the earth of her beloved Cévennes she never conjured inappropriate thoughts. There was a pattern to how things *became* and she — Audrun Lunel, child of the village of La Callune — understood it perfectly. Fire or flood could come (and often did come) to sweep everything away. But still the rain fell and the wind blew. On the bare mother-rock, tiny particles of matter accrued in cracks and declivities: filaments of dead leaves, wisps of charred broom. And in the air, almost invisible,

21

were specks of dust, grains of sand, and these
settled in amongst the detritus, making a bed for
the spores of lichen and moss.

In one season, the burned or washed
limestone could be green again. Then in the
autumn gales, in the drenching rains falling
under Mont Aigoual, berries and seeds fell onto
the lichen and took root. Box and bracken began
to grow there, and in time wild pear, hawthorn,
pine and beech. And so it went on: from naked
stone to forest, in a single generation. On and
on.

Except there could be trespass.

'People can come and steal from you,
Audrun,' whispered her mother, Bernadette,
long ago. 'Strangers can come. And others who
may not be strangers. Anything that has
existence can be stolen or destroyed. So you
must be vigilant.'

She'd tried never to cease this vigil. Since the
age of fifteen, when Bernadette had died,
Audrun Lunel had followed her mother's
instruction. Even in sleep, she'd felt the long
weariness of the watcher. But it hadn't been
enough to save her.

★ ★ ★

The sun was warm. This was like a spring day
from childhood, when she'd sat on the steps that
led to the heavy front door, waiting for the
arrival of the bread van.

Hunger.

She could recall its power over her will. She

22

was four or five years old. She took the two loaves from the van into the kitchen, which was cool and silent. But she couldn't walk away from the bread. She tried to, but she couldn't. She broke one of the loaves and began stuffing the crusty white bread into her mouth.

Such wonderful bread! But then her older brother, Aramon, had found her, caught her, told her that his father, Serge, would whip her with his belt. She pushed the broken loaf away. Willed it to be whole again. Terrified because it had led her into temptation. And then Aramon had sat her down and told her a fearful thing: that she didn't really belong in this family and had no right even to a share of the bread they had to buy so dearly. Because she was somebody else's child.

In 1945, he said, when she was a few days old — 'a stinky baby' — she'd been wound round with rags and dumped on the steps of the Carmelite Convent at Ruasse by her mother, who had been a *collaboratrice*. But the nuns didn't want her. She was a child of sin. The nuns had gone from village to village, asking, did anybody want a baby, a girl? Would anybody agree to care for an ugly baby with a belly-button like a pig's tail? But nobody wanted her. Nobody in their right minds wanted the baby of a *collaboratrice* with a belly-button like a pig's tail — except Bernadette.

Bernadette was an angel, boasted Aramon, his angel of a mother. And she had persuaded Serge to let her adopt the baby. Adopt. That was the word Aramon used when he told this story. He

23

said it meant taking pity on something that wasn't yours. He said that Serge had screamed and shouted that no, he already had a child — his son, Aramon — and that was all that mattered to him, and what in the world did he want with a mewling girl?

But day and night Bernadette had pleaded with him — God knows why — to let her take in the baby dumped on the doorstep of the Carmelite nuns. And, in the end, she'd won. God knows how. And so they all trooped down to Ruasse and went into the freezing cold convent and heard the baby's cries echoing round the freezing cold walls, and brought her home and she was given the name of the Abbesse of the Convent of the Carmelites: Audrun.

'And that was you,' Aramon concluded. 'Adopted. See? And now my father's going to swipe your arse for eating our bread. Because he never takes pity on things that aren't his.'

★ ★ ★

For a long time, Audrun had believed this story which the brother, Aramon, kept alive.

'I expect you've been wondering who your father is, Audrun. Uhn?'

Yes, she had. She knew babies had to have two parents, not one. Everybody in La Callune had two parents, except those who had 'lost' their brave fathers in the war. So she asked Aramon: 'Was my father one of those 'lost' men?'

'Well,' he said, laughing, 'lost to evil! Lost in

24

Hell now! He was a German. An SS man. And your mother was a *putain de collabo*. That's why you've got a belly-button like a pig's tail.'

She didn't understand what any of this meant, only that she was supposed to feel ashamed. Aramon told her that the people of Ruasse had shaved off her mother's hair (not the hair of her mother, Bernadette, but the hair of this other mother she'd never known, the *collaboratrice*), shaved off her long blonde hair and marched her naked through the market, and the market traders had thrown handfuls of fish guts at her breasts because this was what you had to do to women who 'went' with German soldiers, this was their punishment, this and the birth of deformed children with pigs' tails growing out of their stomachs.

Hunger.

For the bread that day. For closeness to something.

Little Audrun sat in the dust inside the wire pen where the bantams foraged. She tried to clutch the smallest of the hens in her skinny arms. She could feel the terrified beating of its heart, see its gnarled feet, like baby corn cobs, clawing the air. Not even the bantam wanted to be close to her. She was the daughter of a *putain de collabo* and a German soldier of the SS. In nearby Pont Perdu, twenty-nine people had been killed by German infantry in a 'reprisal operation' and their names had been engraved on a stone monument, on a wayside shrine above the river, and flowers were laid there, flowers which were not real and never died.

25

★　★　★

Audrun drew her old and frayed cardigan round her body and walked on through the wood, her face lifted to the warmth of the sun. In another month, there would be swallows. In the hour before dusk, they'd circle, not over her bungalow with its low, corrugated iron roof, but above the Mas Lunel, where Aramon still lived. They'd be looking for nesting sites under the tiles, against the cracked stone walls, and she would stand at the window of her flimsy home, or in her little *potager*, hoeing beans, watching them, watching the sun go down on another day.

She would see the strip-light blink on in the kitchen of the mas — that old green-tinged rod of light — and picture her brother stumbling to and from the electric stove, trying to fry *lardons*, gulping from his glass of red wine, dropping ash from his cigarette into the fat of the frying pan, picking up the bottle and drinking from that, his stubbled face wearing that fatuous grin it acquired when the wine excited his senses. Then, with a shaking hand, he'd try to eat the burnt *lardons* and a burnt fried egg, spooning everything in, with another cigarette smouldering on a saucer and outside in the dark the dogs in their wire pound howling because he'd forgotten to feed them . . .

Upstairs, he lived in grime. Wore his clothes till they stank, then hung them at the window to wash themselves in the rain, air themselves in the sun. And he was proud of this. Proud of his 'ingenuity'. Proud of the strangest things. Proud

26

that the father, Serge, had named him after a variety of grape.

What a brother to have!

Who was your mother, Audrun?

Putain de collabo.

Who was your father?

SS prick.

★　★　★

She went to her other mother, Bernadette. She took a pair of scissors and asked Bernadette to cut off the pig's tail. And the mother held her close and kissed her head and said, yes, it would be seen to. They'd go to the hospital in Ruasse and the doctors would make everything 'sensible and tidy'. But doctors were expensive and life was hard, here in La Callune, and she would have to be patient.

So Audrun patiently asked, 'Who was my other mother, the *collabo?* Did she die? Was she hung upside down in a well by her ankles tied with wire?'

Bernadette began weeping and laughing, both at once, and sat Audrun on her knee and cradled her head against her shoulder. Then she tugged her arms free of her pinafore and undid her blouse and showed Audrun her white breast with its brownish nipple. 'I'm your mother,' she said. 'I nursed you here, at my breast. What's this nonsense about *collabos?* There were none of those in La Callune, and you mustn't use that word. I'm your mother and this is where I suckled you. Feel.'

27

Audrun put her small hand on the bosom, soft and warm to her touch. She wanted to believe this mother's words, comforting to her as bread, but Aramon had warned her: 'Bernadette will lie to you. All women lie. They're descended from witches. Even nuns have witches for mothers. Nuns lie about themselves, about their chastity . . . '

So she took her hand away and climbed down from Bernadette's knee and began to run away from her.

But this upset Bernadette and she came after her and lifted her up and said: 'You're mine, Audrun. My little girl, my darling. I swear it on my life. You were born in the early morning and I held you in my arms and the sun shone through the bedroom window and in my eyes.'

★ ★ ★

Audrun stood now in front of a sweet chestnut tree, moved, as she was each spring, by the sight of the new leaf. In her childhood, the family had fed their pigs with chestnuts and the pig flesh had skin that bubbled up into beautiful dark crackling, and it tasted sweet and had no taint about it.

But now a blight had come. *Endothia*, it was called. The chestnut bark split and reddened and fell and the branches above the reddened scars began to die. All over the Cévennes, the chestnut forests were dying. Even here, in Audrun's wood, the signs of *endothia* were visible. And people told her there was nothing to be done, there was

28

no magician or saviour, as there had been long ago, when Louis Pasteur had travelled down to Alès and discovered a cure for the terrible silkworm diseases. *Endothia* was part of life now, the part that had changed beyond recall, the part that was old and blighted and withered by time. Trees would soon die in this wood. There was nothing to be done except to cut them down and burn the logs on the fire.

Audrun's bungalow had no fire. It had four 'night-storage' heaters, heavy as standing stones. As the winter afternoons drew on, the heaters cooled, the air cooled, and Audrun had nothing to do but sit in her chair with a crocheted blanket over her knees. She folded her hands in her lap. And sometimes, in this deep cold stillness, she would feel an *episode* approaching, like a shadow that laid itself across her, a shadow attached to no solid form, but which took the colour from everything in the room, which bleached her mind and made the furniture stretch and shift behind a plane of glass . . .

Audrun examined the trunk of the chestnut tree. No sign of disease on this one yet, but she said the dread word to herself: *Endothia*. The air was so still that she seemed to hear her own soundless voice. Then, the next moment, she became aware that she wasn't alone and she turned and saw him, stumbling as he did these days — he who, as a boy, had been as agile and swift as an Indian brave — gleaning wood for the fire, putting the fallen pieces into some kind of sling on his back, a sling he'd cobbled together out of an old moth-eaten blanket.

29

'Aramon.'

He raised his arm, as though to prevent her from coming near him. 'Just a bit of wood,' he said. 'Just a bit of wood for the fire.'

He had trees of his own, a dense thicket of holm oaks behind the dog pound. But he was too lazy to take the saw to them, or else knew that he shouldn't trust himself with the saw; the saw would have his hand.

'Just a branch or two, Audrun.'

His hair was dirty and wild. His unshaven face was pallid, almost grey in the sharp sunshine. 'And I was coming to ask — '

'Ask what?' she said.

'I've got in a muddle there, up at the mas. I can't find anything. My *carte d'identité*, my glasses . . . '

She hardly ever went inside his house — the house that had once been kept so clean and orderly by her beloved Bernadette. The stink of it made her gag. Even the sight of his old shirts hanging out of the window to be washed by the rain, she had to turn away when she saw these, remembering Bernadette's laundry chest and all the sheets and shirts and vests white as fondant and folded edge-to-edge and smelling like fresh toast.

'Aramon,' she said. 'Go home. Take the kindling. You can keep what you've gleaned, even though you know it's not yours.'

He let go his makeshift sling and the pieces of wood crashed around his feet and he stared helplessly at them. 'You've got to help me,' he said. 'It's *complicated* up there. You know?'

30

'What d'you mean, 'complicated'?'

'Everything's got jumbled up with everything else. I can't tell one thing from another. Someone has to sort it out. Please . . . '

Her stare was as hard as yew. She felt the poison of him, like a yew berry in her mouth.

'You can have a couple of bantams,' he offered. 'I'll wring their necks for you, pluck them, gut them. You can invite Marianne Viala, uhn? Have a lovely feast. Get the gossip. *Pardi!* I know how you women love to gossip.'

'Have a couple of bantams for doing what?'

He shifted his feet, scratched his neck. His eyes, once beautiful, were still brown and deep. 'Just *help me*. Please, Audrun. Because I'm scared now. I'll admit it.'

'Scared of what?'

'I don't know. It's this mess I'm living in. I don't know where to find the things I need.'

Boys.

They were young men in their twenties, but Anthony Verey had often referred to them like that: 'the boys' or 'my boys'. It had given him power over them to disparage what had, until recently, threatened to overwhelm him and make him weak: their beauty.

The boys he chose were mostly poor, on state benefit or with menial jobs, trying to get into their adult lives, trying to survive in London. He brought them to his exquisitely decorated flat above the shop on the Pimlico Road. Loved the thrill of it — a poor stranger in his bed. Then he took them downstairs and let them see the *beloveds* in the near-darkness. Let them feel, touch, smell the *beloveds*. Smell knowledge, security, comfort, entitlement, money. But he never let them linger. Paid them fairly, but always sent them away without any promises of further meetings, because he couldn't stand the idea of their presumption that he, because he was older, because he was almost *old*, would enslave himself to their virility and youth.

But for a long time, now, there had been no 'boys' in Anthony's bed. Desire for them had gone absent-without-leave. The only boy who visited Anthony — in dreams and in those empty times when he sat at the back of the shop and no customers came in — was the boy he himself had once been.

He knew that this was abject, a sentimental surrender, but he couldn't help it; this was who he yearned to be: himself as a boy, sitting with his mother, Lal, staring at the rainbow colours the sunshine magicked into the bonbonnière on the dining-room table of her house in Hampshire, while the two of them entranced themselves polishing silver, and outside in the garden one of the long untroubled summers of the 1950s went slowly by.

It was more than abject. Anthony told nobody, not even his sister Veronica (or 'V' as he always called her), that what he longed for was to be the child he'd once been. It appeared that V — three years older than he was — was getting on perfectly well with her life, still moving obstinately forward, full of plans and projects, and not even particularly attached to her early memories. If he'd admitted that where he dreamed of being was in the old Hampshire dining room, aged ten or eleven, cleaning silver with Lal, V would have been stern with him. 'Oh for God's sake, Anthony. Cleaning silver! Of all pointless tasks. Have you forgotten how it tarnishes?'

He and Lal never minded about that. When it started to go brown, they just cleaned it again. They sometimes sang as they worked, he and Lal in perfect harmony. While V was known to be safely cantering around the paddock on her bay mare, Susan, or clamped in her room, making pencil drawings, with her nose pressed to her favourite art book, *How to Draw Trees*, they sang show tunes.

33

*'The boat's in! What's the boat brought in?
A vio-lin and lay-ay-dy!'*

The silver object Anthony had adored most in the world at that time was one of Lal's cream jugs. His careful hands traced the complicated contours of its handle, the delicate foliate sprays engraved on its sides. 'Oh yes, that's a poppet,' Lal had cooed. 'Georgian. About 1760, I think. Lovely little hoofed feet. Wedding present to me and Pa. You can have it when I'm dead.'

There had been a hundred other objects in that house which had given the boy pleasure. He liked to press a latticed silver cake-slice against his cheek, open and close the clever silver asparagus tongs. Oh yes, and hear the chime of the grandfather clock ('Wm. Muncaster, Whitehaven, 1871') in the hall, a sound he for ever associated with the school holidays, with a white Christmas tree in December or with a vase of sweet peas in July and the end of Latin and rugby for a long and blissful while. Lal would observe him listening to the chimes of the clock, observe him with her blue eyes the colour of the sky, and touch his face with her hand in its silver-cleaning glove. 'That's so dear,' she would say. 'The way you love the Muncaster.'

And he would smile and suggest another show tune, so that she wouldn't see that he was giggling at the way she, who had come to England from South Africa and still spoke with an accent which flattened vowels and slid numberless sounds in strange and embarrassing directions, used the word 'dear'.

Anthony thought that Lal would have understood his longing to be a boy again. In the last fifteen years of her own life, he'd observed her thoughts returning quite frequently to Hermanus, where her parents had owned a villa within sight of the sea and where, in the South African summer, meals had been served by black servants ('houseboys') on a fifty-foot verandah. She told Anthony that she'd grown to love England, her adopted country, 'but part of me stays South African, you know? I can remember African stars. I can remember being smaller than a Canna lily.'

★ ★ ★

Anthony sat on at his desk as a slow twilight descended over Chelsea, and glared at his address book. He wondered whether, tonight, he was going to be brave enough to call one of the 'boys'. Without enthusiasm, he turned the pages of the book, reading names and telephone numbers: Micky, Josh, Barry, Enzo, Dave . . .

They challenged him. Hungry, vigorous, wild, they were all, he felt, more alive than he'd ever been. The last one to visit his bed had been the Italian, Enzo, with solemn eyes and a lovely pout. He'd worn an expensive shirt, but his shoes had been dusty and down-at-heel. He'd showed off his cock, *presented* it for admiration, ropey and big in his hands, as though offering it at auction.

Then, whispering in Anthony's ear, the boy had begun a stream of dirty talk, a continuous,

35

low accompaniment of smut. Anthony had listened and watched. The light in his bedroom was doused to dull amber and the body of the boy appeared smooth and golden, exactly what Anthony liked, the buttocks fat, almost woman-ish.

His arms went round Enzo. He touched his nipples, stroked his chest. He began to feel it, the first choke of desire, but then the damned monologue drifted into Italian and now had no meaning for Anthony, just became irritating, and he told Enzo to stop talking, but the boy didn't stop, he was a dirty-talk diva, a smut-salesman and he was keeping on going.

The things we do . . .

The desperate things . . .

Enzo lay on the bed. Anthony knelt. He still wasn't hard. But he thought the fat buttocks might do it, if he concentrated on them, stroked and kneaded them, parted the flesh . . . But no, really and truly what he wanted to do, suddenly, was to slap them. Wound the Italian boy. Wound himself. Because it seemed so base, so pitiful, this getting of boys — just to prove that he was still alive as a man. It was ridiculous. He'd moved away from the bed, tugged on his robe, told Enzo to get up and leave. Paid the promised cash, stuffing it into the pocket of Enzo's leather jacket and the boy went out, sulky and offended. Anthony had sat in his kitchen for a long time, had sat without moving, listening to the hum of the fridge, to the traffic on the road, aware that he felt nothing; nothing except rage.

★ ★ ★

Now, he laid the address book aside. The thought of a boy — any boy — in his bed made him feel tired. His body was having difficulty enough with mundane, everyday things. The base of his spine ached from sitting all day at the back of the shop. To walk as far as Knightsbridge made his feet sore. His sight was deteriorating so fast, he could hardly read his own price tags, even with his glasses on. So why on earth did he imagine that it could suddenly be overwhelmed by ecstasy or caught unawares by love?

He imagined it because, somehow, he had to find the means to go on, to persist. And what better thing to furnish the future than love of some kind?

Anthony rubbed his eyes, poured himself a tumbler of dry sherry and began to gulp it. He got up and walked about among the *beloveds* in the near darkness. He caressed them as he passed, his hand reaching out and reaching out again. He knew that he just couldn't, at this moment, envisage a future of any kind. All he could envisage, all he could see waiting for him — for the once celebrated Anthony Verey — was a slow and lonely decline.

He thought about Lal's grave in Hampshire and the beech tree that grew nearby. He longed for the sound of Lal's voice, for the touch of a certain silver cake-slice against his cheek.

He paused beside a gold-framed engraving of an Italian garden ('*Li Giardini di Roma,* one of 30 plates by de' Rossi from the originals by

37

Giovanni Battista Falda, 1643–1678'). He stared for a long time at the ordered alleys and parterres and at the happy sepia people walking at leisure there, with the soft hills beyond.

'V,' he said aloud. 'I need rescuing. I'm sorry, darling, but I think it's going to have to be you.'

Veronica Verey was a garden designer. Her latest project — not yet completed — was a book about gardens in southern France. The book's working title was *Gardening without Rain*.

Veronica lived with her friend Kitty in a fine old stone farmhouse, 'Les Glaniques', in one of those villages south of Anduze, in the Gard, where the 21st century hardly seemed to have arrived and where Veronica went about her life in a mood of robust contentment. She was getting fat (as a girl, both she and her pony, Susan, had been described as 'chunky') but she didn't mind and Kitty didn't mind. They went together to the market at Anduze and bought bigger clothes.

Kitty, the only child of sad parents who had spent their lives trying to run a guest house on the Norfolk coast, was a watercolorist, who made a barely adequate living and who now, in a passionate response to the quality of the light in this part of southern France, was teaching herself photography. Kitty hoped to contribute all the pictorial material to Veronica's book. She had waking dreams about its thrilling title page, with their two names side by side:

GARDENING WITHOUT RAIN
by
Veronica Verey and Kitty Meadows

Kitty felt that all her life, until she'd met Veronica, she'd been a kind of no one, a watery nonentity, her habit of quietness, of self-effacement, formed early, when she'd been told as a child to stay out of sight and sound of the clientèle of the guest house. Now, at last, in her late fifties, she'd become visible to herself. She loved Veronica and Veronica loved her and together they'd bought their house and made their extraordinary garden, and so Kitty Meadows felt as though she was beginning everything again: beginning it better. At the age where many of their friends were giving in or giving up, Kitty and Veronica were trying to start over.

The house was half a mile from the village of Sainte-Agnès-la-Pauvre. From its terrace, looking west, you could see the great blue-green folds of the Cévennes hills, dense as a rainforest. Moments spent on this terrace, sipping wine and eating olives, listening to the swallows, face to face with sunsets of blinding red, were, Kitty Meadows felt, like no other moments in her life. She tried to find a word to describe them. The word she came up with was *absolute*. But even this didn't quite capture what she felt. One night, she said to Veronica: 'Part of me would like to die right now, this is so beautiful.'

Veronica laughed. 'Tell that part to shut up, then,' she said.

They both knew that it was borrowed: the view of hills; even the sunsets and the clarity of the stars. Somewhere, they knew it didn't belong to them. Because if you left your own country, if you left it late, and made your home in someone else's country, there was always a feeling that you were breaking an invisible law, always the irrational fear that, one day, some 'rightful owner' would arrive to take it all away, and you would be driven out — back to London or Hampshire or Norfolk, to whatever place you could legitimately lay claim. Most of the time, Veronica and Kitty didn't think about it, until, suddenly, they found themselves objects of derision, sneered at as *putains de rosbifs* by a group of youths in a café in Anduze, or they remembered the time when the mayor of Sainte-Agnès-la-Pauvre had accused them of 'stealing' water from the commune.

Water.

For the sake of the garden, they'd been too profligate with it, testing to the limit local agreements about the use of hoses. 'You have behaved,' said the mayor, 'as though you believed that, as foreigners, you were not subject to the law, or else pretended that you didn't understand it.'

Veronica — as furious as when she and Susan had been drummed out of a three-day event for cutting a corner on a hurdles course — protested that this wasn't true. They knew the law perfectly well and had kept within it, never watering before eight in the evening. 'I agree,' said the mayor. 'You have kept within it — just — but not within the *spirit* of it. Your lawn sprinklers were overheard to be turning at midnight.'

It was true. They liked listening after supper, to the lawn sprinklers, as to a homely snatch of music, imagining the nourishment this music

41

was giving to the thirsty grass.

Now, they sat in silence on the terrace, sunk in worry, staring at the vivid green, staring at their beloved flower borders until the only points of light that remained in them were the white petals of the Japanese anemones in the purple dusk. Veronica said: 'Well, I suppose this garden will fail now. Half the gardens I've designed in this region will fail. I suppose it was all futile. How can anybody garden without rain?'

It became the question, then, the only one: how can you sustain a garden with such a low rainfall?

Kitty got up and paced about. Then she said: 'There are ways of conserving and getting water that we haven't thought about. We have to explore every one. We have to put certain bits of engineering in place.'

One of the many things Veronica valued about Kitty was her quiet practicality. She herself was clumsy, often confused by how things worked in the modern world; Kitty was orderly and resourceful. She could fix objects that were broken. She could mend the lawnmower and rewire a lamp.

So it was Kitty who set about solving the water crisis. She had their well cleaned and restored and bought a new pump that brought water up from nine metres down. She instructed work to begin on a second well. She installed new gutters, with underground conduits leading to a new concrete *bassin* beyond the fruit trees. New piping conducted bathwater into green plastic butts. Kitty and Veronica laid down heavy mulch on every centimetre of unplanted earth. They took out the thirsty anemones and substituted prickly pears and agavés. When the heavy autumn rains came, they religiously laid out barrows and buckets and bowls on the lawn and tipped every extra drop into the *bassin*. And, as if to compensate them for all this, the following summer was cool and wet, almost like a summer in England, and the new *bassin* filled to its brim. They invited the mayor down to the house and drank pastis with him and took him round the garden and showed him all their arduous work. It seemed to amuse him: all this for a plot of land on which hardly any vegetables were grown!

A quoi sert-il, Mesdames?

A rien, Monsieur. Mais, c'est beau.

But it was clear that they were forgiven. And it was after that night that Veronica announced that she was going to begin her book and she had the perfect title for it: *Gardening without Rain*.

'The English think that gardening's going to be the same everywhere,' she said. 'In India, in Spain, in France, in South Africa, everywhere — but it isn't. So I want to explore how best to make it work here. I'll do it properly, experiment with different varieties of things. See what survives and what dies unless you pamper it with rivers of commune water. It'll be a long project, but who cares? I like it when things are long.'

★   ★   ★

This early spring was warm at Sainte-Agnès. Five or six degrees warmer than at La Callune,

43

in the hills, where Aramon Lunel came cadging wood from his sister, nine or ten degrees warmer than in London, where a light rain was now falling on Chelsea. Kitty took her easel outside and worked at a delicate watercolour of mimosa blossom. She sat in a worn canvas chair she'd owned for most of her life. Sometimes, if she closed her eyes, she could hear the sound of the seabirds she tried to paint long ago in Cromer, sitting in that same comfortable, sagging chair.

'Always sketching away at something!' her father used to complain. 'As though your life depended upon it.' It *had* depended upon it. That was what Kitty Meadows had felt as the years of her childhood and youth went slowly by and she took part-time jobs in a post office, in a chemist and finally in a library. The only moments when she'd been happy — or this was how it appeared to her now — were when she was out under the big, lonely skies, with her sketchbook and her colours, with the salt winds and the shifting dunes and the magnificence of the light. Painting had saved her. It had let her escape into a life she enjoyed. And it had eventually brought her, after years and years of waiting, into the arms of a woman she could love.

★ ★ ★

Now, she saw Veronica coming towards her across the terrace. On Veronica's face was an expression Kitty recognised immediately: chin lifted and set, brow furrowed, eyes blinking

44

anxiously. It made her, in Kitty's mind 'pure Verey', with all the cherished 'Veronica' part of her suddenly missing.

Kitty rinsed her brush, kept staring at the sunlight on the fabulous mimosa tree. She knew that to Veronica's family she was no one, just 'that friend of V's, that little watercolour woman'. She had to fight not to fade back into invisibility. She looked up at Veronica and said, as gently as she could: 'What's wrong, darling?'

Veronica snatched a cigarette out of the pocket of her gardening apron and lit it. She only smoked in times of anxiety or sadness. She walked up and down, puffing inexpertly on her Gitane.

'It's Anthony,' she said at last. 'I couldn't sleep for worrying, after my phone call yesterday, he sounded so terrible. And he just rang me, Kitty. I was right to worry. He told me he feels . . . defeated. He sits in his shop all day and no one comes in. Imagine it! Alone like that and waiting and no one buys anything. He says the whole thing's finished.'

It crowded Kitty's memory, then, making her head ache, that glimpse she'd once had of Anthony Verey's treasure house — all the wood and marble and gilt and glass, the turned-this and frieze-moulded-that — a princely stash of priceless stuff in the Pimlico Road he designated his *loved ones*, or some such sentimental epithet. How could such a mountain of expensive objects be 'finished'?

'I don't understand,' she said.

'I know it's difficult to believe,' said Veronica.

'He's always made tons of money. But it's gone wrong now. I suppose even the rich are reining back on Chippendale.' Veronica stamped on her cigarette and came and laid her heavy arm on Kitty's shoulder. 'I know he's spoilt,' she said. 'I know he's not the easiest guest. But he's my brother and he's in trouble and he wants to come and stay with us. Just for a while. So I said yes. You'll be nice to him, won't you?'

What could Kitty answer to that? She rinsed her watercolour brush, reached up for Veronica's hand. She wanted to ask: How long is 'a while'? But even that seemed selfish. And there was no limit — almost no limit — to the things she would do for Veronica's sake.

'Of course I will,' she said sweetly.

★ ★ ★

Their guest bedroom faced east, over their small orchard and, beyond this, towards fields of apricot trees and vines. It had a white tiled floor and a sleigh bed and a rickety wrought-iron side table. The beams were painted magenta.

For Anthony, Veronica emptied the walnut armoire of the winter clutter she and Kitty kept there, put white cotton sheets on the bed, vacuumed away the cobwebs, oiled the shutters, shined up the bathroom. Then she stood staring critically at her efforts. She saw the rooms as Anthony would see them: too plain and unadorned, too shabby, with a stupid colour ruining the beams. But there was nothing to be done about it. And at least the view from the window was good.

Anthony hated flying. He thought budget airliners should be shot out of the sky. He said he would take the train to Avignon and collect a hire car.

He insisted he would bring them Earl Grey tea and Marmite, even though Veronica told him they didn't need these things. He said he was 'unbelievably grateful'. He said he was sure the air of the south would make everything clear to him.

Clear to him in what way? Kitty wondered, but didn't ask. Because Anthony Verey had always struck her as a man for whom everything was already clear, already decided, judged, categorised and appropriately filed and labelled. What more, in a life as apparently selfish as his, was there left to understand?

Audrun made her way slowly and carefully up to the old house, vigilant every step, alert to all that was there, to all that might be there . . .

You could never predict what Aramon was going to do. One day, he'd chucked out his old television and bought a new one, wide as a wardrobe. Last winter, he'd taken delivery of a pile of sand but never said — never even seemed to know — what the sand was for. Already, weeds had sown themselves in its shifting and collapsing mass; the sand pile and the ruined old television sat side by side on the grass and the snow fell on them in January and the warm breezes blew on them in this new springtime, and Aramon just walked on by them. Sometimes, Audrun noticed, the dogs did their business in the sand pile, cocked their legs against the television. So the screen was yellowish now, a stripy yellow that occasionally took light from the sunshine, as though some old broadcaster were trying to get his faltering signal through.

When Audrun was a child, the Mas Lunel had been a U-shaped house. Now, all that was left of it was the back section of the U. The roofs of the two wings, where once the cattle had been housed and grain stored and silkworms reared, had been damaged in the storms of 1950 and the father, Serge, had said: 'Good. Now we can get to work on them.'

Bernadette had told Audrun that she'd thought that 'getting to work' on them meant rebuilding them, filling the cracks in the walls, attending to the damp, relaying the brick floors, replacing doors and windows. But no, Serge had begun to dismantle both edifices. He tore off the clay tiles and stacked them up in his cart and drove the cart down the old, pitted road to Ruasse and sold them to a builder's merchant by the river. Then he hacked his way through the grey mortar that covered the walls of the two wings of the Mas Lunel and began gouging out the stones. He proudly told his neighbours, the Vialas and the Molezons, that stones were his 'inheritance' and now — in this post-war time when nobody had anything left to sell — he was going to make his fortune out of this, out of selling stones.

Selling stones.

Bernadette had pleaded with Serge: 'Don't destroy the house, *pardi*! Don't leave us with nothing.'

'I'm not leaving us with nothing,' he said. 'You women don't understand how the world works. I'm making us rich.'

But they never became rich. Not that anybody could tell. Unless Serge kept the money somewhere else: in an old fertiliser sack? In a hole in the ground?

On the ground, still, were the ghostly outlines of the former east and west wings of the Mas Lunel. It had been grand, a true Cévenol mas, with space for everything and everyone, with all the machinery kept out of the rain and all the animals sheltered in winter and, above this the *magnaneries*, the attics where, season by season, the silkworms were hatched and where they ate their vast quantities of mulberry leaves and spun their cocoons and were sent down to the last *filature* at Ruasse to be boiled alive as the precious silk was unwound onto bobbins.

Audrun could just remember the old *magnaneries* at the mas, the smell of them, and the chill in the air as you climbed the steps towards the well-ventilated rooms, and the sound of the thirty thousand worms chomping on leaves, like the sound of hail on the roof.

'It was terrible work,' Bernadette had told her. 'Terrible, terrible work. You had to collect bunches and bunches of mulberry leaves every single day. And if it had been raining and the leaves were wet, you knew a lot of the worms were going to die, because the damp gave them some intestinal infection. But there was nothing you could do. Every morning, you just had to pick out the dead ones and carry on. And the stink up there, of the dead worms and all the horrible excretions, was vile. I used to gag, sometimes. I hated every minute of that work.'

Yet, she'd done it without complaining. Still hanging on the wall of Audrun's small sitting room was a photograph of Bernadette with, on her lap, a basket full of silk cocoons and on her face not a trace of anguish or disgust, but only the smile of a tired and beautiful harvester, her labour complete. The picture was faded and brown, but the white of the silk cocoons still had about it an obstinate kind of light.

All the silk in France came from the Far East now. What once had been a flourishing trade, and had kept thousands of Cévenol families alive, had died in the 1950s. When Serge sold the stones of the Mas Lunel, he'd already known that it was finished. The wooden hatching trays were chopped up and thrown on the fire. The last *filature* at Ruasse was demolished. And though Bernadette had been terrified by the violent way Serge tore down the two wings of the U-shaped Mas Lunel, she'd sighed with relief once the *magnaneries* were burned and gone. She told Audrun: 'When that ended, I slept easier in my soul.'

* * *

Aramon slept in the bed where Bernadette had died. On the very mattress. In sheets that had once belonged to her.

Audrun hated going into this room that stank of his encroachment on their mother's memory. Because her brother had never loved Bernadette, not as Audrun had loved her. All her life, his wild behaviour had plagued and punished Bernadette and when she died he just looked blankly at her corpse, chewing on something that might have been tobacco or gum or even a mulberry leaf, because this was the way he was, like a silkworm, with his jaw grinding on something day and night, and in his eyes a vacancy.

Reluctantly, Audrun had agreed to help him tidy the house and try to find the things he'd lost.

51

While he killed the bantams he'd promised her, she began searching among all the clutter and garbage for his spectacles and his identity papers. She put his dirty laundry into two pillowcases, to take down to her bungalow, to wash in her machine and dry on the line in the sun and wind. She could find nothing clean to put on the bed, so she left it as it was, with just the old blankets and the eiderdown airing under the open window. Let him scratch all night. She didn't care.

She doused a rag with vinegar and cleaned the windows. She swept and washed the wooden floor and took the rug into the garden and hurled it over and over against an old mulberry tree. As she slammed the rug against the tree trunk she heard the dogs begin howling in their pound, so she decided to go up there, to see if Aramon was taking care of them or letting them starve to death.

It was then, as she looked up at the house on her way to the dog pound, that Audrun noticed the crack in the wall. It was an immense, dark fissure in the stone. It ran down from under the eaves, like a fork of lightning, skirting a window frame and narrowing as it sped on towards the door.

Audrun stopped and stared. How long had the crack been there?

She felt time begin its peculiar pull between past things and present awareness. Had she looked a hundred times at this lightning strike in the front wall of the Mas Lunel and never seen it — until now? The howling of the dogs grew in urgency. The still-dusty rug in Audrun's arms felt as heavy as a corpse. She walked slowly on.

She remembered sitting with the men who built her bungalow, sitting on the stony earth among the recently delivered slabs of plaster-board while the Camembert the builders were eating for lunch ripened in the sun, and hearing them say that, all over the Cévennes, cracks were appearing in the walls of old stone houses. The taller the house, the deeper ran the cracks.

And nobody knew why, said the men. These dwellings had been built to withstand time. But they were not withstanding it. Time, it seemed, destroyed everything at a faster pace now, at a pace no one had ever envisaged.

'Do you think that the Mas Lunel could fall down?' she'd asked the builders. And they'd all turned and stared up at the big hunk of a house, solid as a *caserne*, tucked in underneath its wooded hill. 'Not that one,' they said, shaking their heads. 'That one should see us all through.'

Audrun had said nothing. She'd just watched the men spreading the oily Camembert on their baguettes and putting the hunks of bread and cheese into their mouths. But, privately, she believed they were wrong. She believed that, if you built a house in a U-shape and then, as Serge had done, tore down the buttressing arms of the U, you left something that was vulnerable. Whatever was incomplete — a cherry tree leaking sap from a torn branch, a well that had lost its cover — was at the mercy of nature.

In the human world, only love was adept at completion.

Audrun went into the dog pen and the hounds clamoured round her. Bred to hunt wild boar, wiry and fearless, they chafed and whimpered in their pent-up life, spent their existence with their noses pressed against the wire.

Aramon still belonged to a hunting syndicate and liked to boast about the boar he'd killed in the past, but he seldom went on the hunts any more, knowing he was too unsteady to manage a shotgun correctly. He seemed to prefer sitting and drinking and staring at the jumpy, violent life on his new TV, where younger people, people with greater agility, tortured and killed and were tortured and killed in their turn. And his dogs were all but forgotten, abandoned to monotony and winter cold, fed chestnuts like the pigs, fed swill and bones. Today, even their water trough was dry. As Audrun filled it up, anger with Aramon made her rib-cage ache, set a vein twitching in her neck. One day, she told herself, all this would be put to rights. *One day.*

★   ★   ★

In the kitchen, scouring his blackened pans, scraping grease off the stove, Audrun said: 'You know there's a fissure in the front wall, Aramon?'

He'd come in with the two dead bantams and thrown them down on the table. Now, he was fumbling with his spectacles, found by Audrun under his pillow, the wire arms bent out of shape by the weight of his head.

'I've seen that,' he said. 'It's nothing.'

Audrun said he should ask Raoul Molezon,

the stonemason, to look at it, but Aramon said no, he'd looked at it himself and it was a crack in the mortar, that was all, nothing to start sweating about. Then he tugged his bent spectacles onto his nose and searched for his cigarettes and lit one and coughed and spat onto the stone floor and said: 'I've had enough, anyway. It's driving me mad, this big shit-hole. It's pulling me down, ruining my health. So I've decided. I'm selling the house. And the land. I'm selling everything.'

Audrun stared at her hands, like root vegetables in the sink-water. Had she heard what she thought she'd heard?

'Yes,' said Aramon, as if reading her question. 'I've had enough. So I've got onto it right away — before someone changes my mind for me. Estate agents came out from Ruasse. I expect you saw them when you were squinting through your curtains! Mother and daughter. Daughter wearing high-heeled shoes, stupid bitch. But they were interested. Very interested indeed. The market's dipped a bit from what it was, but they say I can still get a good price, *pardi*, a mountain of money. Live in clover for the rest of my days.'

Live in clover. Aramon?

In such a scented, green and blameless thing?

'Yes,' he said again. 'Sell to foreigners, that's what the agents told me. Swiss. Belgians. Dutch. English. Plenty of them have still got money to burn, despite recession. And they like these old places. They tart them up with swimming pools, and God knows what else. Use them as holiday homes . . . '

55

Audrun dried her hands on a torn dishcloth. She turned to Aramon and said: 'It's not yours to sell, Aramon. It belonged to our parents, and our grandparents . . . '

'It *is* mine to sell. You had your sainted wood and your bit of land for your bungalow and your vegetables. I had the house. I can do what I like with it.'

Audrun folded the torn cloth. She said calmly: 'How much do you think you're going to get for it?'

She saw him look startled, almost afraid. Then he picked up a used match and with its charred end, wrote a number on his palm, then brought his palm — cupped, as though to hold a bantam chick — close to Audrun's face and she saw what was written there: €450,000.

★ ★ ★

Audrun took her medication and lay down for the night.

She dreamed about the strangers who would install themselves in the Mas Lunel while, some way off, Aramon basked in his clover field.

The strangers attacked the house with a peculiar ferocity, as though they didn't want *this* house, but some other house of their own imaginings.

They rearranged the land. A lake appeared. The colour of the lakewater was pink, as though it had been mixed with blood. They spoke some other language, which might have been Dutch. Their children rampaged around the yard, where

Bernadette had sat in the sunshine, shelling peas. In the night, they cavorted, naked and screaming, in the blood-tainted lake and played rock music. The noise they made bounced and echoed from valley to silent valley.

On the evening before he left for France, Anthony dined with his old friends, Lloyd and Benita Palmer, in their house in Holland Park.

Lloyd was a semi-retired investment banker who, over the years, had bought hundreds of thousands of pounds' worth of furniture from Anthony. Benita was an interior decorator who'd created the rooms where this furniture sat. Her preferred palette of colours ranged from straw to cream to coral. In her downstairs lavatory, decorated in apricot *toile de jouy,* stood an 18th-century snakewood and mahogany vitrine ('The brass galleried top over a flower-painted frieze, the base with two snakewood inlaid doors and parcel gilt festoon apron') worth at least £16,000. In the beige and cream and gold dining room, where they now sat, hung a pair of oil paintings by Barend van der Meer ('Fine example, still life of plums and grapes with vine leaves arranged on a glass dish, 1659' and 'Fine example, still life of pomegranates with African grey parrot, 1659') worth a conservative £17,000 each. The George III silver wine coasters ('The sides pierced with scrolling foliage with waved gadroon rim'), that had come to rest in front of Lloyd's place at the table, Anthony had picked up in a sale in Worcester for £300 the pair and sold on to Lloyd for £1,000 each.

Though Anthony had often teased Lloyd

Palmer that he was one of the 'rich bastard masters of the universe', he'd previously been happy enough with his own role in that universe as the prime arbiter of Lloyd and Benita's taste in furniture and pictures. But now, tonight, when he saw Lloyd, at sixty-five, still sailing triumphantly through his life, despite the economic downturn, about which he complained very loudly ('I've taken hideous losses, Anthony, absolutely bloody hideous!'), but to which his lifestyle seemed strangely immune, with his large but still handsome wife like a sequined spinnaker beside him, whooshing along in the vanguard of all that was most desirable in rich British society, Anthony felt a wounding stab of envy.

The Palmers were a ravishingly fortunate pair. This vast and magnificent ship of theirs, ballasted by numerous children and grandchildren, was unthreatened by storm or by calm or even by corrosion — or so it appeared. Anthony had to express it baldly to himself this evening: Lloyd had always been *ahead* of him and always would be. He was so far ahead, in fact, his lead so manifestly unassailable, that there was no point in Anthony imagining he could ever catch up. And the worst thing was, he could see Lloyd thinking these same thoughts. Even Benita may have been thinking them: Poor Anthony; things are difficult everywhere, but for *Anthony Verey Antiques* it has to be the end of the road. Thank God *we* aren't trying to make a living, in the anarchic 21st century, out of trying to sell what our American friend Mary-Jane refers to as 'dead people's furniture' . . .

These sombre considerations had led Anthony to drink a great deal of Lloyd's excellent wine. Lloyd had matched him, sip for sip, and the two of them now sat face to face, across a choppy lake of glassware, coughing on cigars, slugging cognac and determined, as Lloyd had touchingly put it, 'to get to the heart of the whole ruddy thing'.

Benita had gone to bed. She knew — perhaps because she was more cultured than Lloyd and had read and understood both Ibsen and Lewis Carroll — that there was no 'heart of the whole ruddy thing' and that when men talked about searching for it what they often wound up talking about was cars. Occasionally, she'd noticed, they reminisced in a sentimental way about their past lives, elevating university pranks into myths of universal significance or exaggerating the traumas caused to them by public school beatings. Tonight, as she closed her bedroom door, she heard Anthony say: 'The only time, Lloyd, that I was happy . . . the only fucking time that I was happy in my life was in a tree-house!'

Lloyd's explosion of laughter was loud. Lloyd adored laughing (and people tended to adore Lloyd partly because he laughed so much), but now, tonight, Lloyd discovered that the side-effect of this particular collapse into mirth was a slight wetting of his underpants and this, he thought, as he continued to giggle, was something surprising, something that happened to old men, but not (yet) to him.

'Yes,' Anthony was going on, 'that's the honest truth, old man. In a tree-house.'

60

'Oh God!' said Lloyd, recovering from his laugh and putting one of his meaty hands on his groin, to see if the wet had come through to his trousers, which it had. He thrust a crumpled linen table napkin down there and said: 'So go on, tell me, where was the fucking tree?'

Anthony poured himself more cognac from the William Yeowood decanter. 'In the hols', he said, 'when V and I were kids, I once made a tree-house in the spinney behind the house . . . '

'Barton House, or whatever it was called?'

'Yes. Bartle. Ma's house. Our house. Before you knew me.'

'Well before I knew you, old man. I mean, *well before*. Unless you were still building tree-houses when you were at Cambridge?'

'Shut up and listen, Lloyd. We're meant to be getting to the heart of things.'

'Are you saying . . . are you saying, at the heart of everything . . . at the heart of fucking everything is a fucking tree-house?'

'No, I'm not saying that. I'm just saying . . . I'm just saying . . . all I'm saying is I was very happy when I gave the tea party for Ma.'

'What tea party?'

'Just listen. You're not listening to me.'

'I am listening.'

'I gave a tea party in my tree-house. I invited Ma. OK? I had Mrs Brigstock bake some stuff: malt loaf and brandy snaps. And I got everything ready. Table. Tablecloth. China etcetera. Chairs.'

'Who's Mrs Brigstock?'

'Mrs Brigstock is Mrs Brigstock, Lloyd. The cook-housekeeper Ma had at the time.'

'OK. OK. Keep your wig on! How was I meant to know? And how did you get a ruddy table and chairs up into a ruddy tree-house?'

'I carried them. Up the ladder. I wanted everything to be spot-on for Ma.'

Lloyd was unable to stop himself from breaking out into another spasm of laughter at this point in Anthony's story and when this, in turn, was accompanied by another warm seepage into his pants, he stood up, and bent over, holding his napkin in such a way that Anthony wouldn't see the area of wet on him, and tottered towards the door. 'Back in a jiff,' he said. 'I want to hear the *dénouement*! Truly, I do, Anthony. This is as gripping as Winnie-the-Pooh.'

In the charming *toile de jouy* cloakroom, Lloyd relieved his aching bladder and attempted to dry his underpants with wads of apricot toilet paper.

The snakewood and mahogany vitrine flung back at Lloyd his own unsteady reflection. This little wetting business had sobered him up slightly, but not so much that he wasn't still enjoying the evening, enjoying both Anthony's company and, at the same time, the realisation that his old friend was in some kind of mental turmoil. This turmoil, which — yes — Lloyd was actually *enjoying*, appeared to be connected not only to Anthony's finances, but to something else, some existential something he didn't seem able to express.

In years gone by, when Lloyd had told people he was a friend of Anthony Verey's, he'd often had to suffer — time after predictable time

— their star-struck reactions and he'd always felt the unfairness of this in relation to himself. Because, year by year, he'd made more money than Anthony, probably far more money. But he'd made it quietly, away from the glare of notoriety. People 'knew' Anthony Verey because he was seen at glamorous exhibition previews and gallery openings, often among a coterie of flamboyant actors and artists, and because he had his name on the sign of a smart shop in Pimlico, which no amateur collector dared to enter. He understood a hell of a lot about furniture and pictures, Lloyd had to admit, but he, Lloyd, understood a lot about global markets. Why had art turned Anthony into 'the Anthony Verey' when making money in the city had never turned him into 'the Lloyd Palmer'?

Lloyd stood swaying there. The *toile* milk-maids and their lovers danced on, ageless, on the wall. The lavatory bowl choked up with apricot paper.

Time was getting to everybody of his generation now, Lloyd mused. Even to Benita, whose beautiful upper arms had lost their firmness and sheen. But it was getting to Anthony Verey in a satisfyingly lethal way.

★   ★   ★

Left alone in Lloyd's dining room, Anthony soon became aware that his cigar had gone out. The paraphernalia of relighting it suggested itself as being beyond him at this particular moment, so he laid it down in the heavy glass ashtray and sat

63

very still, doing nothing except stare at the room in all its opulence and grandeur.

Indistinctly, he caught sight of his own face in the giltwood overmantel ('Second quarter 19th century, flower and scroll carved frame with asymmetrically carved cartouche crest') and discovered this face to be wan-looking, rather *small*, more crumpled than it usually appeared. He heard himself sigh. He didn't want to look small and crumpled, when Lloyd was so huge and loud, his skin so pink and bright, the collars of his shirts so stiff and immaculate . . .

And now a new cause for dismay seeped into Anthony's mind: why on earth — for God's sake — was he telling Lloyd Palmer the story of the tree-house? The whole tree-house thing was private. It had been between him and Lal. Between them alone. So why, suddenly, was he blurting out something so personal and precious to a philistine like Lloyd? What was the matter with him?

He realised with a shudder that he was ridiculously drunk. Perhaps this face in the overmantel wasn't really his? It was just a . . . *suggestion* of how he might look to an unpractised eye, to someone who didn't really know him . . . And by tomorrow, it would be gone, that face that no one knew. He'd be far away in France, in a different kind of light, with Veronica, with his beloved sister, V . . .

But he knew that it was stupid of him to have got drunk. It meant he would arrive at Avignon with a hangover. Just when he'd hoped to see things clearly again, his head would be aching, his brain in a fog. And V's friend, that stumpy little Kitty woman — with her watercolour daubs and her shocking habit of saying her thoughts out loud — would know exactly how he was feeling and let him know that she knew, and make the first twenty-four hours hell for him . . .

Oh God, why was everything so tainted and marred, so pickled in misery and compromise? Anthony cleared a space around his table mat, which was not a table mat but a huge papier-mâché gilded plate, and he laid his head down on the plate, rather like an outcast angel, he thought, tumbling down onto its own uncomfortable halo.

He closed his eyes. The house felt silent, as though Lloyd might have gone, not to the lavatory, as Anthony had supposed, but to bed, having tired of him, tired of trying to get to the heart of things, knowing that the heart of things — the true heart — lay far behind you somewhere and could never be altered.

But that was OK. Lloyd wouldn't have understood this anyway, but there were certain things you *didn't want* to alter. Indeed, you had to keep rerunning them in your head, to make sure they stayed exactly the same, stayed faithful to how they had felt. Not faithful to how they had *been*, necessarily — because that was unverifiable, anyway — but faithful to how they had appeared to you. You had, precisely, to protect them from the alteration of time.

He'd had everything prepared. Everything. White linen tablecloth with a heavy border of Brussels lace. White linen napkins. Lal's favourite blue-and-white-and-gold china teacups and saucers and tea plates and sugar bowl and slop bowl and her favourite little bone-handled knives. Blue velvet cushions for the hard chairs. Primroses in a cut-glass vase. He was nine years old.

He kept watch, so that he could help Lal climb the ladder to the hideaway. And here she came, now, through the spinney far below him, wearing a lavender dress, with a matching lavender cardigan and white canvas shoes.

'Here I am, darling!' she called out. And he went to the edge of the platform of the tree-house and made his answering call: 'Here I am, Ma!'

He helped her up the ladder, though she barely needed his help, she was so agile and light. She came in and the sunshine at the doorway behind her made her fair hair shimmer white. When she saw the preparations on the tea table, she clapped her hands with delight.

'Oh this is so dear!' she said. 'I love it!'

He led her to the small window, and showed her how the green of the beech tree, in which the house had been built, came clustering in and how the sky seemed so near and brilliant, it was as though it were his own private sky. Then, he sat her down in one of the chairs and the house swayed gently as the tree moved, and they listened to the wind in the leaves and the afternoon chirruping of the birds and Lal said: 'Magic. It's magic.'

Mrs Brigstock brought the tea and the malted bread and the brandy snaps on a silver tray and

Anthony climbed down and took the tray from her and — this was the moment he knew he would be proudest of — carried it aloft, without needing to hold on to the ladder with his hands. As he set the tray down in front of Lal, his heart was beating like a lover's.

Afterwards, he could never remember what they talked about. All he remembered was the feeling: the feeling that this was perfectly achieved, that it was a work of art, *his* work of art, and that no moment of it was flawed. And that they'd both understood this. He'd contrived an hour of aesthetic perfection.

★ ★ ★

Lloyd came back into the dining room, still clutching his napkin, and found Anthony asleep with his head on a gold plate.

He gave him a prod. 'Wake up, old man,' he said. 'Come on . . . '

But Anthony didn't stir, couldn't stir.

Shit. Lloyd Palmer cursed. Now, he'd have all the ding-dong of getting Anthony into a bed, fretting about him throwing up onto one of Benita's impossibly expensive carpets, arranging breakfast for him, making sure he didn't miss his plane or his train or whatever damn thing he was meant to be catching. And all for what? Some half-baked crap about happiness.

'Shit,' he said again. 'Bloody happiness.'

While Veronica shopped and cooked for Anthony's arrival, Kitty escaped to her studio, in a stone shed behind the house, that had once sheltered animals in its dark recesses. This darkness had been punctured out of it by slabs of skylight and a heavy glass door in its west side. A wood-burning stove heated it in winter.

Kitty stood with her back to her porcelain sink and contemplated her watercolour of the mimosa blossoms, still on the easel. The thing didn't shrivel under her scrutiny, as many of her paintings did; on the contrary, she thought it was probably the best bit of work she'd done for about a year. The colours were delicate, held back from gaudiness, and she'd captured the paradox of the blooms — their individuality and their mass — without betraying the terrible effort involved. Kitty fantasised that even her most revered heroine, the watercolorist Elizabeth Blackadder, might have given this picture some curt but thrilling nod. And she felt confident that it would find its way into *Gardening without Rain:* 'Acacia decurrens, *dealbata*'. Watercolour by Kitty Meadows.

Buoyed up by this, Kitty felt in the mood to begin something else.

In painting — perhaps in all the arts? — success drove success, failure whipped you towards failure. She should capitalise on the achievement of the mimosa and she wondered whether she wouldn't risk having another try at the olive grove. She longed to be able to capture the movement and shimmer of this restlessly beautiful corner of the garden, but all her previous attempts had foundered. She'd made the olives look spiky, when they weren't; the surprising whiteness in the leaf colour had eluded her; in her inexpert hands, the gnarled trunks of the trees had resembled turds.

A flush of shame at her own inadequacy overcame Kitty, obliterating her moment of optimism. Why were these trees so difficult? Perhaps because, at the heart of each tree (expertly pruned every second spring by Veronica), was an unexpected revelation of air and sky, and it was this brightness, this necessary element, which had been entirely missing from every one of Kitty's pictures. She'd reverently tried to depict the gaps in the grey-green foliage, but then the sky had somehow pushed itself through the gaps, stupid patches of solid blue which appeared stuck on from outside, making the overall result shockingly bad.

'Crap,' Kitty said aloud. 'Out-and-out crap.'

She decided with a sigh that now was definitely not the moment to attempt the olives again. In a few hours' time, Anthony would be here, and the thought of trying to paint something so elusive within the range of his appraising eye made Kitty Meadows feel sick.

She resorted, in an aimless, slow-moving kind of way, to tidying her studio. She sharpened all her pencils. She rewashed and regrouped her brushes in their stained and familiar jars. She scrubbed her sink, swept cobwebs off the stone walls. Her thoughts drifted and stumbled from present to past. She soon enough became, in her mind, the lowly, untalented manual worker she somewhere knew herself to be.

She gathered up all her failed paintings of the olive grove, tore them to shreds and threw the scraps into the blue recycling bin. She felt hot and fearful, full of her menopause and her mortal failings. She became again the timid library assistant, trundling her book cart from steel stack to steel stack, as the afternoon darkness came down over Cromer.

★ ★ ★

Dark was nearing as Anthony stepped out of the train at Avignon TGV Station and trundled his suitcases, like two obedient black dogs, towards the car rental offices.

He'd slept in the train, slept off most of his hangover, while the woods and valleys and industrial zones of France hurtled by, unseen. A shame, he thought now, to have missed France — the whole country, almost, from north to south. But that was what drink did to you: it made you miss things. You aimed at this or that grand notion in your delirium and then you missed it.

But now, leaving the station behind, Anthony lifted his face to smell the sweetness of the air. Pines and starlight, things dark and bright and pure: the air smelled of these. Among the lines of

70

rental cars, Anthony set the suitcases down. He stood very still.

I'd forgotten this, he thought: the feeling of arrival; the heart-lift.

He watched dark dragon clouds stretch themselves across the pearly horizon. He felt the last traces of his hangover evaporate.

'Old age,' an actor friend of his had once said, 'arrives in short flurries. Between the flurries, there's a kind of respite.' And this was what Anthony felt he'd been given now: respite. He could even have termed it remission. So he instructed himself not to waste the remission time or tarnish it with unkindness. He'd be a good guest in his sister's house. He'd rhapsodise about her garden, drink pastis with her French friends, conform to her chosen routines. And — just as long as she didn't insult him — he'd be nice to Kitty Meadows.

As he drove the hired black Renault Scenic north-west towards Alès, Anthony felt a radical new idea beginning to form in his mind. He congratulated himself that it wasn't only radical, but also logical: if his life in London was over, then to regain his happiness all he needed to do was to admit that it was over and to dare to move on. He'd never imagined himself living anywhere else but Chelsea, but now he had to imagine it. He had to imagine it, or die.

So, in its essence, the idea was simple and straightforward. He'd sell the flat and wind up the business. From the great emporium of *beloveds*, he'd keep only those pieces for which he felt extreme ardour (the Aubusson tapestry,

71

for instance) and put the rest into the appropriate sales at Sotheby's and Christie's. One or two pieces he might sell direct to American clients over the phone for reasonably stratospheric prices, and then ship them to New York or San Francisco. And at the end of all this, he would easily have enough money to buy a beautiful house down here in southern France, near V, in this kinder and simpler world, and here he would start his life again — a different life.

Anthony drove fast, loving the sight of the dark road blossoming up to embrace the rented car. The orange-lit dash cast enough light on his features for him to be aware of a stubborn smile engraved there. His evening with Lloyd Palmer, with all its complicated feelings of material envy, seemed a world away. Anthony was fully in the present now, beautifully alive. His plans chattered away in his mind like Happy Hour drinkers. Hadn't he subconsciously thought for a long time that it would be good to live near V, near the one person for whom he still felt genuine affection? Because, with V, he could become the younger brother again, yield up some of that oppressive responsibility for his own well-being that he was finding harder and harder to sustain.

★ ★ ★

At Les Glaniques, Veronica and Kitty waited in silence. From the hall, they could hear the familiar tick of the grandfather clock. It was as though, Kitty thought, they were waiting for

72

something momentous, something dangerous and potentially catastrophic, like a NASA launch.

She looked at her friend, sitting in her favourite chair by the brightly burning fire, and she had the sudden and terrible thought that their lives together might never be the same from this moment on. And the awfulness of this — even if it were just a possibility and not a certainty — impelled Kitty to get up and kneel down by Veronica and lay her head on Veronica's knees covered by her newly washed denim skirt.

'What?' said Veronica. 'What, Kitty?'

She couldn't blurt out her worry. It was too irrational and emotional. But she needed comfort. What she wanted was for Veronica to stroke her hair, to say something affectionate and normal. But she could feel the tension in Veronica's body: a tremble in her right leg, an absence of stillness all through her.

'Tell me what the matter is,' Veronica said again.

'Nothing,' said Kitty. 'Stroke my hair, darling, will you?'

Kitty's short hair, dusted with grey, was curly in a thick and tangled way. Veronica laid a hand gently on Kitty's head and picked up this strand and that and held these strands between her fingers. Then she said: 'Actually, your hair is quite difficult to stroke.'

The buzzer at the automated gate sounded at that moment and Veronica had to lift Kitty away from her so that she could get up and go to the gate release. 'He's here,' she said unnecessarily.

Kitty saw the car headlights well up out of the night. Then she heard Veronica's voice at the door, bright and emphatic, as it might have sounded for the long-looked-for plumber or stonemason. And *his* voice: the Chelsea drawl, the way posh people spoke long ago when Kitty was a skinny girl, helping to make beds and prepare breakfasts in the Cromer guest house . . .

Veronica led him into the sitting room, led him by the hand, the adored younger brother still, the charmed and charming boy, Anthony. He was pale from his indoor life, his skin flaky. He approached Kitty with a smile that narrowed his eyes, creased his cheeks in these days of his seventh decade, but which, Kitty guessed, could still seduce when he wanted it to.

He kissed her lightly, with only a trace of fastidious disdain. He smelled of the train, of things marooned in stale air, and Kitty had the peculiar thought that he needed hosing down with salt water, needed abrasion, ice, grains of sand, to bring the blood back to his skin, to make the world real to him again.

He stood by the fire and admired the new rugs and cushions they'd bought in Uzès. Veronica poured champagne, handed round her home-made tapenade. He said he was glad to be there. He said: 'What I love hearing is the silence.'

Four hundred and fifty thousand euros.

This sum of money preyed on Audrun's mind. Had she really seen such a shockingly large figure written on Aramon's palm? Or was it just floating there, a thread of numbers unconnected to anything, in the confused grey mass that was her brain?

She asked him again: 'How much did they say you could get for the house?'

But he wouldn't tell her this time. He gobbed up some shreds of tobacco and spat them out as he said: 'The mas is mine. That's all I know. Every euro of this is mine.'

From her window, moving the net curtains by half a centimetre, Audrun watched people arriving to look at the house. She saw them stand and stare up at the crack in the wall. They picked their way past the pile of sand and the rusty, urine-stained TV. They turned to look back at the view on the south side, which included her bungalow and her vegetable plot, criss-crossed with baling twine hung with rags to scare away the birds, and her washing line, draped with Aramon's tattered laundry. The hounds in their pen barked themselves crazy at the scent of them. They drove away.

★ ★ ★

Raoul Molezon, the stonemason, arrived.

Audrun rushed out with coffee for Raoul and asked: 'Is it true, about the four hundred and fifty thousand?'

'I've no idea, Audrun,' said Raoul. 'I'm just here to fix the crack.'

She told him the crack would travel right through the house and split it from top to bottom, because where the two arms of the Mas Lunel had been, now there was only air. She said: 'The earth calls to the stone walls, Raoul. You're a mason, I know you understand this. Unless they're buttressed, like they used to be, the earth will call to them. I'm sure my mother knew it.'

Raoul nodded. He was always gentle with Audrun. Had been gentle with her all his life. 'You may be right,' he said. 'But what can I do?'

Raoul swallowed the last dregs of the coffee and returned the bowl. He wiped his mouth with an old scarlet handkerchief and began setting up his ladders and wedging them with shovelfuls of sand. In his pickup were bags of cement. So Audrun now saw what Aramon was doing: employing Raoul to patch up the crack with mortar and then to plaster a coat of grey render over the new mortar veins, so that when the purchasers came, they'd never imagine a fissure in the wall — never dream of any such thing. She held the empty coffee bowl close to her and said: 'I'm telling you, Raoul, you've got to tie that wall with an iron bolt . . . '

He was halfway up his ladder, nimble and neat and unafraid of falling, even at the age of sixty-six. Long ago, Audrun could have fallen in love with Raoul Molezon, if Bernadette had lived, if her whole life had been different. She stared at his brown legs, in dusty shorts. She used to think, watching Raoul, you might love a man just for his legs, for the joy of stroking them, as you might stroke the sweet neck of a goat. But that was before love for any man had become impossible . . . forever impossible . . .

She watched Raoul put on his spectacles, which hung from a chain round his neck, and peer at the fissure in the wall. He put his hand into the fissure. Now he would know how deep it went.

'See?' she called up to him. 'It goes right through, eh Raoul?'

He said nothing. His face was close to the wall now, half swivelled round, as though listening to the heartbeat of the house. Then, the door banged open and Aramon came charging out like a terrier, his face flushed with anger and wine.

'You let him be, Audrun!' he yelled. 'You leave Raoul alone!'

He tried to swat her away with the flat of his hand, as he would swat a fly.

She recoiled from him, as she always did. He knew he could frighten her the moment he touched her. She turned and walked away. Almost ran.

She held tight onto the coffee bowl in case she needed a weapon, in case Aramon followed her. She imagined how she would jab the bowl into his face, like covering a spider with a cup.

But he didn't follow and Audrun reached her door — that flimsy thing that had no weight and solidity in it, her pathetic front door. She went inside and closed and locked it, but knowing that the lock, too, was insubstantial, a little nub of weak metal. These things were never meant to be like this. Doors were supposed to have solidity and strength. They were supposed to keep out everything and everyone who could do you harm. And yet they never had.

She sat in her chair. Somewhere in the distance, she could hear the voices of Aramon and Raoul Molezon, carried to her on the wind that was blowing from the north, the wind that sometimes blew into the skull of Bernadette and laid her out cold under pegged washing or on the feathery floor of the chicken coop.

Audrun tried to sweeten her thoughts by remembering the wonderful cures for ailments old Madame Molezon, Raoul's mother, used to brew up in her dark kitchen: young blackberry shoots, dried and stewed and mixed with honey, for sore throats; sage tea for nausea; borage tea for shock. But then Audrun couldn't help remembering, too, that certain ailments had no cure. Nothing from the kitchen of Madame Molezon, nothing on the earth had been able to save Bernadette. In her last days, she'd told Audrun that her cancer was like a *magnanerie* of silkworms and her body was a mulberry tree. Nothing on the earth could deter the worms from ingesting the leaves, right down to their last little bit of green.

And that was when everything changed

— when that last little bit of green was gone.

At the age of fifteen, Audrun was taken out of school and sent to work in a factory making underwear in Ruasse. Her father and her brother stayed home, worked on the vines, the onion beds, the fruit tree terraces and the vegetables. They cared for the animals and then slaughtered them. But Audrun was told she was no good on the land and would never be any good; her duty was to earn money. So she caught a bus at seven every morning, six days a week, and the bus dumped her outside the underwear factory on the outskirts of Ruasse and she spent all day hunched over a sewing machine, making girdles and suspender belts and brassieres. In her memory, all of these oddly shaped garments were pale pink, the approximate colour of her own flesh, the bits of it the sun had never found.

Her father ordered her to bring samples of her work home. Serge and Aramon fondled these pink samples and sniffed them and stretched the elasticised girdles this way and that and pulled on the elasticised suspenders like you'd pull on a cow's teat, and laughed and sighed and shifted in their chairs. Then, Audrun was told to put the samples on, to show them off, to pretend she was a fashion model in a magazine. When she refused, Serge tugged her towards him. He touched her breasts, which, at fifteen, were already large. He whispered that she needed a brassiere for these beautiful breasts, didn't she, and he would buy her one if she would just show off the girdle . . .

She pulled away from him. She saw Aramon,

doubled up in the corner, scarlet-faced with embarrassment and thrill, laughing his hyena's laugh.

She ran out of the house and walked to the cemetery where Bernadette's body lay in its stone catafalque, piled in on top of her parents-in-law, and that was when Audrun began to feel it for the first time in her life, the stretching of everything round her into skeins of un-meaning . . . the breeze like beating wings, the sunlight slippery on the gravestones, like melted butter, the cypress trees like buildings about to fall. She cried out, but there was nobody to hear her. She clutched at the earth and felt it crumbling in her hands, like bread.

Audrun rocked in her chair, remembering: that was the first time.

★   ★   ★

Raoul Molezon arrived every morning for four successive days. He brought his apprentice, Xavier, to help him. They filled the crack with cement, covered it with new render, repointed the brickwork round the windows. Then they did something extraordinary: they painted the render bright ochre yellow.

In the cool shadow of early morning, it looked primrose-pale; in the evening sunlight, it blazed out like a waterfall of marigolds. It no longer resembled the Mas Lunel.

Audrun spent hours standing in her *potager,* leaning on a fork or a hoe, staring in amazement at this yellow apparition. She watched Xavier loading the abandoned TV into Raoul's pickup and shovelling away the sand. She watched Aramon plant a forsythia bush near the front door. She noticed that the dogs were quiet, as though drugged by the fumes from the paint.

She saw the estate agents come back — the mother, and the daughter in her brown high-heeled shoes. She saw Aramon, dressed in clean clothes for once, standing with them in the new warmth of midday, the three of them gazing up at the startling new face of the Mas Lunel. The agents began taking photographs, one after another, from near and from far away. And Audrun knew what they were considering — that this transformation might put up the price of the mas still further.

Half a million euros?

She clutched the area of her heart. Her own little house had been built in four weeks for a few thousand. And it was the only shelter she would ever own.

★   ★   ★

She stopped the agents on the road, waving her thin arms to flag down the car. She stuck her face in through the car window.

'Excuse me,' she said. 'But I'm Monsieur Lunel's sister and that house was once my home. And I saw what was done. He called the stonemason, and now the crack's covered over, but it's still there.'

The agents had round faces, almost identically formed, with pursed little lipsticked mouths. The daughter was smoking, drawing deeply on some expensive mentholated brand and puffing the smoke out of the car window. They both stared wordlessly at Audrun.

'A bit of cement won't stop it widening,' Audrun went on, clutching at the burning metal of the car, 'the earth calls to the stones on either side. It never stops calling.'

'Listen, Madame,' said the mother, after a moment or two. 'I think we have to make something clear to you. We've been asked by your brother to handle the sale of the mas. And that's all. We honestly can't have anything to do with a family feud.'

Family feud.

'Ah,' said Audrun. 'So he told you, did he? He told you how I was treated?'

'How you were treated? No, no. Nothing in the past has anything to do with us. We're just acting as agents for the sale.'

'I'm not surprised he didn't tell you. He pretends none of it ever happened.'

'Well, I'm sorry, but we have to be on our way now. We've got another appointment, a very urgent appointment in Anduze.'

'You should ask him about the crack. Ask him. He called Raoul. And I saw what Raoul did. I'm not lying. He just jammed a bit of mortar in . . .'

But they weren't listening any more. The mother threw the gear lever forwards and Audrun felt the car beginning to move and she had to hop and skip with it for a pace or two, then jerk out her head and watch it accelerate away.

A week after his arrival, hoeing tiny weeds from Veronica's otherwise immaculate gravel court-yard on a warm afternoon, Anthony caught sight of his own reflection in one of her French windows and noticed how the southern sun had already taken away his London pallor and made him look more youthful.

Admiring this new self, his mind blazed suddenly with a new thought:

I *could* love again. After all, perhaps I could . . .

Anthony straightened up and lifted his face to the sky.

Love a woman, even? Why not? He'd loved his ex-wife Caroline in a companionable sort of way. Why shouldn't he lead a comfortable but simple life with an attractive but undemanding woman, for ten or fifteen more years, and be at peace . . .

. . . or then again, this part of France was full of tanned, dark-haired boys and the thought of these, and the way they might whisper to him in French in the hot nights, was now, already, giving him a tentative but gloriously welcome erection.

He returned to his task with renewed energy, determined to root out every last weed from the courtyard. He hadn't looked forward to garden-ing, but now he found that the work produced in him a sweet stillness of mind, in which hope had begun to gleam again, like the sun emerging from round the edges of a cloud.

'You know you've saved me, don't you?' he said to Veronica that evening, as they sipped chilled white wine in the salon.

'What do you mean?' she said.

'London's killing me, V. It literally is. I've thought about this a lot since I've been here, and now I've made a definite decision. I'm going to sell up. I should have done it two or three years ago. I'm going to be reborn in France.'

The moment he said this, he looked for and found — and enjoyed — a flash of terror in Kitty Meadows's eyes. It was such an eloquent flash.

'Don't worry,' Anthony said, smiling lazily at her. 'I won't perch on your doorstep. I'm not that insensitive. I'll look further south — near Uzès, probably. As long as the view's beautiful and I have enough room for a few of the *beloveds*. Nothing else matters.'

Veronica got up and crossed over to Anthony and put her arms round his neck. 'Darling,' she said, 'I think it's a wonderful idea. It's colossal and brave and brilliant! Let's drink to it! We'll help you find the perfect house.'

Kitty sat motionless in her chair. She folded her small hands in her lap.

★　★　★

Anthony telephoned Lloyd Palmer. He began by apologising for his drunken night at Lloyd's house.

'It's OK,' said Lloyd. 'At least you weren't

sick. How's France?'

'Listen,' said Anthony, 'I've had a kind of epiphany. Too long and dull to explain, but I think I might buy a house down here.'

'A tree-house?' said Lloyd with a snigger.

'All right, *touché*, Lloyd. But why I'm calling is, I may be asking you to put in hand the sale of some of my shares . . . '

'*Sell* shares? Is that what I just heard you say?'

'Yes.'

'Are you out of your fucking tree? I couldn't bring myself to do it, old son. Have you checked the Footsie lately? I *could not do it*. Not even for you.'

'If I find a house, Lloyd, I need to be able to move quickly. You can't dilly around here when you buy property. You have to commit.'

'Use cash.'

'I don't *have* any cash. All I have beyond the shares is debt.'

The d-word silenced Lloyd Palmer.

'I'm shocked,' he said at last. 'What happened?'

'Reality happened. Time happened. And selling the flat is going to take more time, so — '

'*Selling* the flat? I can't believe what I'm hearing in this conversation! Have you lost your marbles, Anthony?'

'No. It's over for me in London. You and Benita know that as well as I do. So I'm going to try to make a new start, down here, not too far from V.'

Lloyd let out a long, melancholy sigh.

In the silence that followed this sigh, Anthony

said quietly: 'I'm trying to save my soul, Lloyd, or what's left of it.'

'*Borrow*,' snapped Lloyd. 'It's the only sensible thing you can do.'

★ ★ ★

Rain fell.

Veronica and Kitty sat on old wooden chairs in the stone arch that led to the terrace and watched it.

It was manna: the thing they longed for, month in, month out. They listened to it swishing along the smart new gutters, clattering on the leaves of the Spanish mulberry tree. If the ground underneath the Spanish mulberry was soaked, then it was a good rain, more than what the people of Sainte-Agnès called *deux gouttes*. This was one of the ways they measured it.

They breathed the moisture-scented air. Imagined how, in the million upon million tiny fibres of the roots of the grass, an imperceptible swelling was already occurring and how, if only the rain would keep on and not stop suddenly from one moment to the next, their lawn would be bright green again in thirty-six hours.

The blessed rain was becoming heavy now, the sky above was the colour of slate. The water was beginning to make puddles on the uneven stone of the terrace when Anthony wandered through into the arch.

'What *are* you doing?' he asked Veronica.

'Watching the rain,' she said.

'Watching the rain,' said Kitty.

Anthony looked at the two women. They held themselves so still, appeared so moved and entranced by the falling rain, they might have been spectators at some exquisite performance of *Swan Lake*. So it seemed only right that he join them, that he fetch another chair and sit quietly behind them, as in a box at the ballet or the opera, and watch it too.

So odd, he thought as he sat down, so unpredictable, the things that become precious to us, become *beloveds*. Who would have imagined that rain could be beloved by two middle-aged English women? To Africans, yes. To that parched land. Lal used to remember and evoke for him the arrival of the rains in the Cape Province and how the tracks to her grandparents' farm would become red, beautiful blood murram red, and how nameless flowers would blossom out across the empty veld. But surely Veronica had never thought about rain in this ardent way.

'The thing is, you never know,' he said aloud. 'You just do not know.'

'What?' said Veronica.

Anthony hadn't really been aware of speaking out loud.

'Oh,' he said, 'I was just thinking that it's good, not knowing. Not knowing what's going to suddenly make you feel something.'

'Feel what?' said Kitty.

She was a spell-breaker. That was one of the many things Anthony couldn't stand about her. She was this little pedantic spell-breaker with no imagination. What a comedy that she considered herself an artist! Anthony sighed. After he'd moved down here, he'd find a new partner for his sister.

'Feel *anything*,' he said. 'Rapture, for instance. Or irritation.'

★ ★ ★

The rain kept on for three days. The mimosa blossom turned to a brown mush. The house grew cold. Anthony began to feel that England had followed him here, was trying to pinch at his sleeve, but he struggled to fight it off.

From his window, he stared at the Cévennes, folded in blue mist. Wondered if there wouldn't be something uniquely wonderful about living up there, really high, so that you could feel the ancient grandeur of things, feel closer to the stars. And get the sense that the world was once again spread out at your feet, that you were lord of your domain — as he had once felt himself to be in his glory years of money and success — superior in your way to everything and everyone who toiled below you in the valley.

It looked miraculously lonely among all that pine-scented mist, as though it didn't belong to man at all, but to eagles and silence. And so you would be able just to *be*. At last, you would be able to stop striving and wait for it to flood back to you: the thrill of being alive.

Now, the estate agents' car came and went, came and went all the time to and from the Mas Lunel. The starving dogs barked in anguish. Audrun saw the would-be buyers stand in the driveway, frozen by this animal frenzy.

When she went up there, to take Aramon another pile of clean laundry, she said: 'If you want to sell the house, you'd better get rid of the dogs.'

He was fumbling with a broken flashlight, taking out batteries and putting them in again, banging the flashlight on the wooden table. 'It's not the dogs,' he said. 'They know the dogs will be gone with me. It's your bungalow.'

Audrun laid the clean washing on a chair. She'd been going to put it away in the airing cupboard for Aramon, but now she didn't care to do this. She saw the flashlight suddenly flicker into life. Heard her brother give a snort of pleasure.

'Yes,' he said, shining the torch beam in her face. 'They said your house was an eyesore. That was the expression they all used, an 'eyesore'. So I told them to buy you out. Knock your house down! There's a thought, eh? Or I could do it for them. Have them pay me for doing it.'

He doubled over with his high-pitched, wheezy laugh. Switched the flashlight off and slammed it down and reached for a cigarette.

'People with money,' he said, 'they like old houses. They're in love with stone and slate and fat pieces of timber. To them, a place like yours is worthless, just a blot on the landscape.'

Audrun turned away from him, going towards the door. She was about to walk out into the sunshine when she heard Aramon say: 'Shame for you that you built it so near the boundary.'

'I built where I was told I could build,' said Audrun calmly. 'To connect to the electricity supply and the water.'

'Well,' said Aramon, 'that's all very well, but you strayed over the boundary line in places. I saw you do it, *pardi*! So I'm going to get the surveyor to come and have a look at that — where you strayed onto my land. And anything that's found to be on my ground I have the right to bulldoze.'

There was no point in staying to argue with him. Words never prevailed with Aramon. As a child, only one thing had prevailed: the beatings Serge used to deal out with a belt or a bamboo cane. Now, what prevails, thought Audrun, is money. That's the only thing left.

★　★　★

When she got back to her door, Audrun looked all around her, at everything she could see. Although these two houses, the Mas Lunel and her own bungalow (which had no name), were only just outside La Callune, it was as if they were miles and miles from any other habitation. Apart from the road which ran behind her

90

property, the old driveway to the mas, laid down in schist and brick rubble by Serge, the collapsing stone walls of the vine terraces and her square of vegetable garden, the rest was wild nature, meadow grass, holm oaks, beech, her chestnut wood with the pine-clad hill above and the river beyond. People thought her stupid, not right in the head, because she sometimes lost track of bits of time, but she wasn't so stupid that she couldn't see how lovely these things were and how, if you were a businessman from some ugly, teeming city, it would be these you would want to buy.

She turned and stared at her bungalow. Its rendering was a faded pink and Audrun had painted the metal windows blue, which had been Bernadette's favourite colour but which had somehow always looked wrong next to the pink. In summer, she planted scarlet geraniums in pots on the window ledges, but the pots were empty now, waterlogged by the recent heavy rains. The crazy-paving of her terrace was covered with damp leaves, bunched into odd patterns by the wind. Her stone bird-bath, where she watched sparrows and tom-tits come to drink, was green with verdigris. Her fly-curtain had fallen askew across the front door lintel. Her small Fiat car, parked near the door, was so scarred with rust that it appeared only to be waiting for the metal merchant's grab-iron to snatch it away.

The place looked abject. And Audrun thought how the prospective buyers of the Mas Lunel were right: the bungalow should never have existed. The Mas Lunel and the land around it should all have been hers. She would have sold the dogs to a hunter who would have cared for them and let them work. She would have repaired the crack in the wall. She would have kept everything clean and sanitised and alive.

But, more than anything, she would have looked after the land. Because it was the land that mattered. In recent times, in their mania to make money from their houses, thousands of Cévenol people had seemed to forget their role as caretakers of the land. Diseases came to the trees. The vine terraces crumbled. The rivers silted up. And nobody seemed to notice or care — as if these things would cure themselves, as if nature would do man's work while he sat — as Aramon sat — in front of his vast TV, lasering his brain with kilowatts of meaningless light.

And what about the new people, the foreigners, who were buying up the land? They're helpless, Audrun thought. Helpless. It isn't their fault. They're affected — she knew they truly were — by the beauty of it. They begin by believing they can care for it all by some means. But in fact, they don't understand one single thing about the earth.

Not for the first time, certainly not for the first time, Audrun told herself that Aramon and not Bernadette should have been the one to die in 1960.

He'd be dust now. Exquisite thought: his face, his laugh, the stench of him . . . all would be dust.

And all the Lunel land, acquired more than a

century ago by her grandparents, would be hers, and thriving and forested and green.

* * *

Audrun walked in her wood with Marianne Viala. The river at their backs was high and swift. The sun came and went between puffy white clouds.

'You need to protect yourself, Audrun,' said Marianne.

Protect herself? Surely Marianne could remember that, after Bernadette had gone, there had never been any means of doing that?

'I mean it,' said Marianne. 'You'd better see a lawyer. If any part of your bungalow is on Aramon's land, then he has a right — '

'It's not on his land. It's on my land.'

'How can you be certain?'

'We laid out the drawings. We put lines where the boundaries lay.'

'I guess it's all right, then. I guess you've got nothing to fear.'

* * *

Nothing to fear.

That was what Bernadette had said when she took Audrun to see the surgeon at the hospital in Ruasse. She said the surgeon would cut off the pig's tail growing out of Audrun's stomach and make a nice, normal belly button, like all the other children had. And after that, she wouldn't hear the mockery any more: 'Show us your piggy

93

tail, Audrun! Show us your hog's arse!'

She lay in the hospital bed and she could feel the warm blood gushing out of her wound and sliding down onto her thighs. She tried to call somebody, but the room she lay in was tall and echoey and her voice had no strength; she just made a little strangled noise that went up towards the ceiling, like a trapped bird.

Nothing to fear.

She was eight years old. She wondered whether this hot, gushing blood was normal. It didn't feel normal. It felt like her life seeping away, the precious and only life of the daughter of Bernadette Lunel, sandwiched in between the thin covering and the hard hospital mattress. Moment by moment, she would become thinner, flatter, as all the veins and arteries inside her emptied themselves. She would become as pale as a silkworm.

★   ★   ★

She woke with her arm attached to a bag of blood and a cool hand on her forehead — Bernadette's. Bernadette put her face very near to hers and said: 'It's all right now, my little girl. It's all right. I'm here now. Maman's here. Nothing to fear now.'

★   ★   ★

Audrun and Marianne walked on and when they came once again within sight of the bungalow, Marianne stopped and looked at it and said: 'I've

94

got another idea. Get Raoul to come and put up a wall.'

'What good's a wall?'

'A high stone wall, so that whoever buys the mas won't be able to see your house and you won't be able to see them.'

'How would I be able to afford that?'

'It could be cheap cinder blocks on your side. Just faced with stone on the side they're going to see.'

'Even that. Where would I get the money?'

Marianne stopped and looked back the way they had come. 'Sell the wood,' she said.

Sell the wood?

Audrun shook her head side to side, kept on shaking it like this, like a puppet. She felt herself made weak and limp by all this bad, rotten thinking.

★   ★   ★

Later, she lay in the dark.

'Safe in your bed,' Bernadette used to say, 'now, you're safe in your bed.' But Bernadette had been wrong.

She was trying to remember: had part of her house been built on Aramon's land?

All she could recall was that it had been done roughly, hastily, in a haphazard way, with just a scribbled permission from the mayor's office and no proper plans, only sketches made by the builder: put this here, put that there. Raoul should have been the one to build it, but he didn't want the job; he only liked working with stone.

95

So another company was brought in from Ruasse and it was all decided day to day, moment to moment, in those times when the men sat in the sun, eating bread and Camembert and drinking beer and sometimes peering at this drawing or that, and once wrapping up what remained of their cheese in one of the drawings they said was no longer needed.

No surveyor had ever come back to check on the finished house — had he? No one had ever come back because no one cared a fig about it. All this land belonged to the Lunel family — had belonged to it for three generations. Boundary lines were for the brother and sister to draw . . .

But now a surveyor would come. Even a wall of stone could keep no one out, no one who believed he had a right to be there. She, Audrun, would sit helplessly by and wait for the surveyor to lay a line on the ground with a steel measure. And suppose this line led up to her house and out again the other side, what then? Would she hear someone explaining to her — as they had explained to her all her life — that she'd made an error?

You don't do things right, Audrun.

You don't see the world the way it is.

Audrun lay on her back and stared up at the darkness. Then, she folded her arms by her sides and closed her eyes and tried to slow the beating of her heart. She pretended she was Aramon, lying in his tomb. She waited for the vault that surrounded her to grow colder.

The restaurant terrace at Les Méjanels, a few kilometres outside Ruasse, was perched above a stone bridge over the River Gardon. The water was now as high as it had been in springtime for years. Everybody was talking about this, the beautiful jade-green swell of the Gardon after the snow melt of a cold winter and the recent rain.

Veronica, Kitty and Anthony sat at a table near the terrace edge.

The April sun was warm and flashed cutlass-bright on the swiftly moving river. On the menu were fresh trout, frogs' legs and *omelette aux cèpes*. Veronica ordered a carafe of a local rosé wine. Anthony put on an old cricketing hat. There were no clouds in the sky.

Anthony ordered the omelette, followed by the trout. He ate everything slowly, taking small forkfuls, each one aesthetically perfected by the addition of a few beautifully dressed salad leaves. The wine was very cold and dry and light, and this, too, he drank slowly, not wanting any *gourmandise* on his part to disturb the perfect equilibrium of these delectable moments.

He knew that he was as near to being happy as he had felt for a very long time. Happy. He dared to conjure this Peter Pan word. He felt as pleased with life as he used to feel after a successful auction bid. And these hills, this long, majestic valley with its ancient river . . . these at least, he told himself, had permanence. If he could remake his life in a house here, they'd be his marvellous companions. The beauty he'd create with and for his *beloveds* inside this house would find an echo — day by day and season by season — in the beauty outside its windows.

He turned to Veronica and said: 'This is the place, V. This is where I want to be. I'm going to make a bid for the Cévennes.'

Veronica smiled. Her nose was turning red in the sun. 'Well,' she said, trying to include Kitty in her smile, 'that's OK. That's brilliant, in fact. We just have to start looking for a house.'

Anthony realised another thing. He'd been thinking of a small house, with some modest little curtilage, just enough space for V to design him a neat garden. But this image was altering now. What he'd begun to imagine was something more stately, where the ceilings would be high, where the kitchen would be big, where he could contrive some audacious lighting effects to show off the cream of the *beloveds* collection — as many of them as he could afford to hang on to. And, in the grounds, enough space for a swimming pool. A pool would help to prolong his life. Oh, and plenty of land. He wanted land now. Not so much to protect him from the envious world, but to give that envious world something new to envy.

His plans grew and flowered and multiplied in his head: guest suites, a pool house, a sauna, a knot garden, a wild flower meadow . . . He caught Kitty Meadows staring at him, as though she could read his extravagant thoughts and already had some strategy to crush them. He sat back in his chair and said: 'What d'you think, Kitty?'

She looked away from him, looked far away at the high tops of the hills. She had a snub nose that had probably once been called cute, but which now gave her face the squashed look of a Pekinese.

'Why don't you rent for a while?' she said. 'See if you get used to being this far away from everything.'

Rent? What kind of a wasteful, unambitious idea was that? And what was this 'everything' she was talking about? Kitty Meadows hadn't the remotest idea what was — or had been — important to Anthony Verey, wouldn't even come close to imagining it. And he certainly wasn't going to reveal to her the truth about his 'everything': that it had been straying, apparently irretrievably, along the pathway towards 'nothing'. Because anyway, he was going to grab it back now, he was going to get it all back, and he wouldn't let anybody stand in his way, certainly not Kitty Meadows . . .

'I don't want to rent,' he said. 'I want to find something and commit to it. I want to do it before it's too late.'

'Too late?' said Kitty. 'What d'you mean?'

'V knows what I mean,' he said, 'don't you, darling?'

★ ★ ★

He was talking about time, as Kitty knew perfectly well. He wanted to make some grand new statement about his life before the years ate any more of him away, before he had to lay vanity aside. And this was going to be it, apparently: some expensively restored, immaculately furnished house in the Cévennes. Famous friends would be invited down to worship. He'd spend his days getting everything just so and then showing it off. He'd speak bad French in a loud voice. In the neighbourhood, he'd be disliked by everyone, but never ever be aware of it.

Kitty was already so weary of Anthony's company that she had begun to experience it as a deep unhappiness. He'd been with them at Les Glaniques for ten days, disturbing the rhythm of their life, making work impossible for her, and now he was going to start his house-hunt and this could go on and on for weeks or months to come. It was intolerable.

Intolerable.

As Veronica ordered crème caramels and coffees, Kitty thought how she'd like to march Anthony Verey down to the bridge below them and shackle his feet to stones and tip him into the raging water. He was the last of the Verey men, with all their old snobberies and unjustified feelings of entitlement. It would surely be better — for her, for Veronica, for the world — if he was simply disposed of, if that life he appeared to regard as so precious was brought to an abrupt end.

'What are you thinking, Kitty?' asked Veronica suddenly.

Kitty felt startled, fidgety as a bird. She laid

down her napkin, said she'd changed her mind about the crème caramel; she wanted to go for a walk along the river.

'Oh don't,' said Veronica. 'Wait till we've finished lunch and we'll all go.'

But Kitty got up. As she shook her head, she remembered, with some pain, the thing Veronica had said about her hair being 'difficult to stroke'.

She walked away from the table towards the steps that led down to the road. As she went, she heard Anthony say in a loud voice: 'Oh God, did I say something terrible? Am I a monster?'

Kitty kept on, without looking back. She thought: Every step I take away from him is a consolation. But the fact that she was walking away from Veronica as well put a little twist of agony into her heart. The last time the two of them had been here at Les Méjanels, at the end of the previous summer, they'd wandered down to the Gardon after lunch and sat in the hot sun, playing noughts-and-crosses in the sand, and Veronica had said: 'I'll do the crosses. There you are. That's the first kiss for you.'

As Kitty walked towards the water, she wondered: Doesn't every love need to create for itself its own protected space? And if so, why don't lovers understand better the damage trespass can do? It made her furious to think how easily Veronica was colluding with the unspoken open-endedness of Anthony's visit — as though he was the one who mattered most to her, who had the right to come first and always would, and it was up to her, Kitty, to accept this

101

hierarchy with grown-up grace and not make a fuss.

And of course Anthony knew all this. He no doubt enjoyed the knowledge. Enjoyed seeing 'V's little friend' relegated to second place. It was possible that he'd let his stay drag on into summer or beyond, just to persecute her, to do his best to destroy Veronica's love.

Reaching the river, Kitty turned right and walked along the narrow path above the churning, dazzling water. She saw that the grey beach where she'd sat with Veronica was flooded and would only reveal itself again when the heat of July came back and the river shrank to a slow-moving channel. Boulders that had been stranded mid-stream last year were submerged now, and Kitty could imagine all the newly hatched brown trout beginning their lives in this sheltering darkness, nibbling at the green protein-rich weed that billowed up from the shingle bed.

Thinking about the innocent lives of fish, Kitty found that she was crying.

She stumbled on. She wanted to sit down and cry properly. But there was nowhere to sit. There was only the narrow path, just wide enough for one person, and nothing to do but to follow that, until she felt able to turn round and go back.

* * *

Anthony believed she'd done it on purpose, to spoil his moment of happiness, and this made him all the more determined not to let her ruin

102

the whole day or distract him from his plan, which was now to visit as many estate agents as he could find in Ruasse.

They were on their way there at last, after waiting half an hour for Kitty to show up. Veronica drove and Anthony sat in the front and nobody said a word. Kitty rested her head against the window and closed her eyes.

No doubt, thought Anthony, she wants to go straight home, to stare at her hopeless watercolours and drum up some way of getting rid of me. But I'm not going to let her get rid of me. I'm Anthony Verey and I'm myself again: I'm *the* Anthony Verey . . .

*   *   *

In Ruasse, Veronica parked the car in the market square, under white plane trees just coming into leaf, as the sun began its decline and a suggestion of cold was felt again in the air. On the opposite side of the square were two agents and Veronica directed Anthony towards these, saying she'd catch him up.

'All right,' he said. But he said it wearily, to let his sister know that he disapproved of her pandering to the moods and whims of Kitty Meadows. Kitty, he thought, should have been left to stew in the back of the car while he and V went and looked at photographs of houses. Indeed, this would have been ideal, to strand her in the car, lock her in like a child, while they, the Vereys, got their first glimpse of his future . . .

He strode off across the square, still wearing

103

his cricketing hat, hearing the click and knock of a *boules* game in the sandy gravel, the chime of an ancient clock. Ruasse, he'd been told, had two souls and this was one of them, its old soul, defined by the white plane trees and narrow, tilting buildings with clay roofs and a clutch of expensive shops. But its other soul was elsewhere, on the margins of the town, where high-rise flats balanced on flimsy foundations. If you could keep from coming face to face with this other soul, so much the better, or so V had said.

Now, Anthony stood at an estate agent's window. His heart was racing. He began to stare at photographs and prices. Through the glass door of the premises, he could glimpse two women at work on their computers under cold strips of industrial light. He saw them glance up and stare at his comical hat.

Veronica sat in her kitchen and smoked and listened to the stillness of the night.

In front of her on the kitchen table were half-finished sketches of a garden she was designing for clients at Saint-Bertrand. She wasn't working on the drawings exactly, just moving her pencil around, shading in stands of box and a line of yew buttresses over which the clients had rhapsodised. Veronica knew that these buttresses would take three years to look solid enough to form the architectural shape that had so thrilled Monsieur and Madame, but she hadn't dared to mention this. She got tired of repeating that gardens took time, that they weren't like interiors, that you had to have patience. She knew she didn't live in a patient world. Even here, where life went along more slowly than in England, she could sense the restless agitation people felt to make real and tangible to them the fugitive wonders that flickered into their minds.

Tonight, Veronica's own heart was agitated. The day had begun well, ended badly. She'd had to be severe with Kitty in the car in Ruasse, had to say to her that nothing, no, *nothing* would stop her from caring for Anthony, because he was her brother, and if she, Kitty, expected her to stop loving him, then they were all in grave trouble.

She knew Kitty had been crying and this upset her. Whenever she remembered where Kitty had come from, and allowed her mind to form some torturing image of Kitty laying breakfast tables in the Cromer guest house, waiting on a shabby clientèle who left stingy tips, then toiling off to her lowly job in the library, her heart felt like breaking. She wished she could have changed Kitty's past, retrospectively. But the past was the past. You couldn't change it. And this was what she'd had to remind her in the car: 'You have your past and I have mine and Anthony was a part of mine and I'm never going to push him away. Not for you. Not for anybody. Never.'

Never.

She saw the word have its effect on Kitty. And knew that Kitty still hadn't understood how strong was Veronica's need to protect Anthony — from the world and from himself. So she began to explain it again: how, when they were children, Raymond Verey, the handsome father who was so often missing from home, bullied his son, called him weak, puny, babyish, kept asking him when he was going to 'become a real boy'. Lal, still enslaved by Raymond Verey, had mainly stood silently by when he did this, but she, Veronica, had formed the habit of speaking out for her brother.

'I hated my father for tormenting Anthony,' said Veronica. 'It wasn't Anthony's fault that he wasn't sporty or strong. I was those things, but he wasn't. He was thin and dreamy. He liked doing little domestic pastimes with Ma.'

Veronica remembered very vividly Anthony's

106

obsessive love for Lal. She'd had to protect him from that as well, she explained to Kitty. On days when she saw him almost dying of hurt, she'd had to try to protect him from his own feelings.

'What about you?' asked Kitty. 'Who protected you from anything or anyone?'

'I told you: I was OK,' said Veronica. 'I was impervious to a lot of things. And I had my pony, Susan. I talked to her. Susan and I would go and tear round the jumps and I'd forget everything. I was fine. But when Ma turned away from Anthony, he died.'

She evoked one such day. It had been Anthony's eleventh or twelfth birthday and Lal had driven them to Swanage beach for a birthday picnic. It had been just three of them. Raymond was in London, as usual, living his own distant life. And it was high summer, with a hot sun shining and the sea calm and blue. And they ate the delicious picnic Lal had prepared, everything except the birthday cake, which they were saving for later, and then they went swimming.

Lal, elegant as ever, was zippered into a skin-tight, lime-green bathing costume. But when the swim was over and she tried to get out of the wet costume, the zip jammed, and there she was — with a wind whipping up now and the sky clouding over — getting cold and cross. She tugged and tugged at the zip, then she tried to get herself out of the costume without undoing it, but it was too tight.

Anthony danced about on the sand, his face white with terror. He gave his own towel to Lal,

107

but she tossed it away, saying, 'Don't be stupid, Anthony. That thing's soaking wet.' She threw him the car keys and sent him off over the dunes, wearing his sagging bathing trunks, to get pliers from the tool-kit of the Hillman Minx. He came panting back with the whole toolbox and Lal lifted her shapely brown arm impatiently while he searched for the pliers among the jumble of wrenches and spanners and then found them and clenched the zip head with them and attempted to drag the zip down.

But the zip wouldn't move. Lal was going blue-white with cold, her whole body in a spasm of shivering. 'Come on!' she kept shouting at him. 'Come on, Anthony! For God's sake fix it! Can't you see I'm freezing to death?'

He was freezing too and his hands were shaking. And then he accidentally let the pliers bite into the soft white flesh underneath Lal's arm and she gave a scream and pushed Anthony away from her and he fell backwards into the sand and began sobbing.

He spent his days trying to please her and now, when she was in trouble, when she needed him, he'd only managed to wound her.

'He couldn't bear what he'd done,' said Veronica. 'It traumatised him. To have hurt Lal! To have drawn blood! It was the worst thing he could imagine.'

'So what did *you* do?' asked Kitty quietly.

'Well, I think I put my hanky on Ma's wound and told her to hold it there, or something like that, and then I tried to get them both warm. I got the rug from the car and made them sit down close together and I wrapped them in it. Anthony just clung to Ma and cried and I said, 'That's good, Anthony. Hold on to her very tight and keep her warm.' Then I went looking for some scissors. It took ages, but eventually I found a nice woman with a knitting bag and she had scissors in that and she helped me cut Ma out of the bathing costume. We got Ma dressed, and she drove us home but she wouldn't talk to us. She thought the world should be punished because she'd been stuck in a lime-green bathing costume.'

'Ridiculous . . . ' breathed Kitty.

'I know,' said Veronica. 'But that's just how she was, sometimes. And we never touched Anthony's birthday cake. Ma conveniently forgot all about it. And when he realised she wasn't going to put candles on it or cut it or sing or anything, he sat down and ate almost the whole thing, on his own in the kitchen, then threw up in the garden.'

Kitty was silent when Veronica reached the end of this story. No doubt she was thinking how spoiled and difficult their mother had been, how half a lifetime spent in white South Africa had blinded her to her own selfish behaviour. But Veronica hoped the anecdote about the day at Swanage had driven home to Kitty the realisation that protecting Anthony was a lifelong habit which she would never be able to break.

After a moment, Kitty said: 'I understand it. I do. It's part of why I love you; because you're kind. But you've got to tell me how long

109

Anthony's going to stay with us. Just tell me that.'

'I can't tell you. Because I don't know. He wants to look for a house, now. He's putting all his hopes into that. So I have to help him, don't I?'

'Sure. But he doesn't have to be with us day and night. Why can't he move to a hotel?'

Veronica turned away from Kitty angrily and punched her fist against the steering wheel of the car. 'If you can say that,' she said, 'you haven't understood one word of what I've been talking about!'

★   ★   ★

On the table, underneath Veronica's garden sketches, was a pile of brochures from the estate agents in Ruasse. Veronica moved her own drawings aside and began to leaf through these. She stared at washed-out photographs of big, crumbling, stone houses attached to scant descriptions and large prices. It seemed that Cévenol property owners were bent on getting rich now, along with everybody else in the Western world.

Veronica's eye fell onto a photograph of a tall, square mas, standing with its back to a low hill planted with holm oaks. Unlike all the others, the cement façade of this one had been painted a creamy yellow and this gave the place a kind of unexpected grandeur. The price being asked was €475,000. Veronica rubbed her eyes and began to read the details: six bedrooms, large attic

110

space, exceptional beams, high ceilings . . .

A noise in the kitchen made her look up. Kitty was standing there, wearing the bulky, washed-out cardigan she used as a dressing gown.

She came over to where Veronica sat and bent down and put her arms round her shoulders and laid her head on hers.

'I'm sorry,' Kitty said. 'I'm sorry.'

Veronica pushed aside the house details. She reached up to Kitty and they stayed like that, in an awkward hug, for a long moment.

'I'm sorry, too,' Veronica said at last.

'Come to bed,' Kitty whispered. 'I hate being there without you.'

Whenever a car stopped on the road, now, Audrun thought it would belong to the surveyor. 'He's coming any day,' Aramon had told her. 'Then we'll see how much of my land you've taken! Then, we'll know, ha!'

She stood at her window, waiting.

She saw Aramon walk out early one morning, going towards the neglected vine terraces, bent low by the weight of the metal weed-killer canister strapped to his back. He'd told her that the estate agents had advised him to clean up the terraces, that the kind of purchasers interested in the Mas Lunel would also be seduced by the idea of growing grapes. 'I can't see it myself,' he'd scoffed. 'Bossy cunts of agents know nothing about vines! But *I* know. I know how they break your back. No lazy town-dwelling Belgian or Englishman would put in the work. But who cares? I'll do as I'm told. For 475,000 euro, I'll be as obedient as a whore.'

Audrun followed him, unseen, down to the terraces. She stared at the rows and rows of vines, all unpruned, with the skeins of last year's growth still tangled round them and all the stony earth that nourished them choked with grass and weeds. Standing in the shadow of some ilex scrub, she watched Aramon working half-heartedly with his secateurs, snipping a few cuttings, then stopping and lighting a cigarette.

He stood there smoking, with his nervous, inebriated glance jumping here and there in the bright light and the canister of weed-killer abandoned in the long grass.

Audrun looked at him with her eyes narrowed and hard. She was trying to decide how best to kill him.

★ ★ ★

She went up to the Mas Lunel and began searching for his will.

He'd never married or fathered any children, so everything would be hers if he died before her, unless he'd contrived to will part of it away to one of his old hunting friends. And she doubted that he'd got round to this, ever made the necessary burdensome visits to a notary, but she needed to be sure. If he'd made a new testament just to spite her, he would have hidden a copy somewhere.

She went first to an old mahogany chest in the salon, the most comfortable room in the mas, but where Aramon hardly ever lingered, as though he recognised that the space was too grand for him — for the person he was in his core.

Bernadette had always kept the family Bible in this chest. Over all the years, this Bible had exerted its holy magnetism upon everything that seemed to plead its own bureaucratic importance or sentimental preciousness, such as the letters Serge had written from the Ardennes during the war, then from Alsace, where he was repatriated after France's surrender, and then during his time spent working for the *Service de Travail Obligatoire* at Ruasse.

There were large heaps of these letters in Serge's untidy writing, unread for years. There were also ancient identity cards, bills of sale to the wine co-operative, invitations to marriages, christenings and first communions, mourning-cards, family photographs, newspaper cuttings, letters of condolence, edicts from the mayor, a faded menu from a cheap Paris restaurant in Les Halles ... All of these things had flung themselves in to be with the Gospels.

Audrun opened the chest and took out the Bible. She held it to her face for a moment, picking up — even now — the scent of her mother embedded in its cloth covers, then laid it aside. She stared at the heap of papers, sprinkled with woodworm dust, finer than fine-grained sand. This dust suggested to her that the papers hadn't been disturbed for a long while. Aramon never looked at the past, then, and no wonder. He was afraid to catch sight of himself in it.

Audrun lifted out an armful of letters, cards and photographs. One photograph, of Bernadette, fell out of the pile and Audrun stared down at her mother's face — that sweetest of sweet countenances — as it had once been, when she was young and smiling at the old box camera in the sunshine. How beautiful Bernadette had been! Her hair was parted at the side and swept up into a tortoiseshell clip. Her eyes were wide and sleepy. Her skin was smooth and unblemished. She wore a striped blouse that Audrun couldn't recall.

Audrun put the photograph into the pocket of the old red cardigan she was wearing that day. She returned to the chest. Again, the arrangement of the remaining papers indicated neglect. But it was still possible that Aramon had made his will and layered it silently in, deep down in the complicated *mille-feuille* of what passed for a family archive.

She sifted and sorted, looking for a document that would probably be whiter than the rest, with dark printing. But she found nothing. Reaching the bottom of the chest, Audrun picked up a picture postcard of the river at Ruasse, with the water almost overflowing the banks and washing against the old market stalls that had once stood there and all the patient cart horses waiting in a line. The message, written by her father and dated 1944 read:

My dear Wife,
I pray you're safe and all in La Callune also safe, and the boy and the baby. My work here is not difficult. I am part of our S.T.O. group guarding the locomotives at night against sabotage by Maquisard elements. I am getting fond of these engines. Did you ask old Molezon to repair the chimney stack? Is the boy cured of his cough? We work in the dark and sleep in daytime. I kiss your breast. Serge.

Audrun laid the card back in. Arranged everything as she'd found it.
I kiss your breast.

115

She put the Bible away and closed the chest. She didn't want to think about her father.

My dear Wife, I kiss your breast . . .

She stood up and looked around. Where else was she going to search?

She made her way up to Aramon's bedroom. The window was wide open, freshening the foetid air. Audrun knelt by the bed and ran her hands under the mattress. She tugged out a clutch of magazines of the kind she was expecting to find and as she looked at them she thought that his death should be the right death, the one he'd deserved, and it should not be quick and it should not be painless.

Audrun shoved the pornography back under the heavy mattress. Circling round to examine the other side of the bed, she remembered that there were always bottles and blister-packs of pills on Aramon's night table, and she returned to these. She fumbled for her spectacles and put them on. She stared at the neat pharmaceutical labels, none of which she recognised, but she supposed they were sleeping tablets or anti-depressant tablets or some other oblivion-inducing drugs.

And so she wondered . . . might it be as easy as that, to get him more drunk than he knew and cram pills into his mouth or mash them up and let him swig them down himself with his wine and whisky, and be taken for a suicide?

Or better still, lie him face down on the bed and get out his enema paraphernalia and pump the poison into him that way. For hadn't she read in some magazine that Marilyn Monroe had

116

died like this, from having a river of barbiturates squirted into her colon? And yet, at the time, everyone had believed she'd died by swallowing pills, that she wanted to die, that her life had become unbearable . . . and what nobody had revealed until years and years later was that there was no residue of an overdose in her stomach. None. But still the verdict of suicide had been returned.

Audrun imagined the two scenes, Marilyn's death, past and gone, and Aramon's death, yet to come. She could envisage the softness and beauty of Marilyn's arse, her languid sleeping defenceless body, and the rough panicky gestures of the assassins, shoving and pumping. They made a mess of it, so the magazine article said. The sheets had to be washed in the middle of the night. *Imagine that.* As the pale, famous woman lay dying, as the dawn crept nearer and nearer, the drum of some old American washing machine kept turning . . .

If she, Audrun, was going to kill Aramon this way, she couldn't afford to mess it up like that. Despite the disgust she'd feel, having to touch and smell his arse, to guide the enema tube inside him, she'd have to do it carefully, like a surgeon, wearing protective gloves, and leave no trace of herself behind. No trace.

And she thought that once she'd got the tube inside him, then it might be extraordinary, it might be almost *beautiful* to begin squeezing the bag of fluid, to feel the venom's ejaculation from the tube, feel its infusion into his body.

When she'd filled him up with it, when the

117

fluid bag was empty and he lay unconscious there, she'd take the tube out very carefully and replace it with a cork, an ordinary wine cork, dampened and made soft. Then, she'd bind his arse with rags, to stop the cork from popping out and letting the poison escape. How hilarious, how wonderfully right, to bind him up like that, to stop anything coming out of him! And then there would be nothing more to do; she'd simply wait. And it would certainly be beautiful — that silent waiting, that solitary waiting until he died.

★ ★ ★

She was back in her bed now. *Safe in her bed.* With the sighing of the wind in her wood to comfort her. She'd found no will.

By the yellowish light of an old parchment-shaded lamp, she stared at the photograph of Bernadette. She whispered to Bernadette that she wasn't afraid of the surveyor now — now that she'd decided to kill Aramon. They could come and knock her house down and she wouldn't care, because soon Aramon was going to be in the ground and she would install herself at the Mas Lunel, in Bernadette's bed, made clean and sane once more with a new mattress and crisp new cotton sheets . . .

She turned the photograph over, to see whether there was a date on it.

And she found these words: *Renée. Mas Lunel. 1941.*

★ ★ ★

Renée. They never talked about her. Never. Not even Serge talked about her. Except just one time. One time. When he made her his excuse for everything that was going to happen next . . .

Renée.

Audrun put the photograph face down on her night table.

Less than a year after this photograph had been taken, Renée was dead. Killed by German soldiers in reprisals against the first feats of the *maquisards* at Pont Perdu.

And so Audrun had dared to ask her father, 'What was Renée doing at Pont Perdu?'

He'd sighed and shifted on his chair. 'She was just there that day, *ma fille.*'

'Why? We don't know anybody at Pont Perdu?'

He looked as sad as a mule, with his greying head hanging down, and Audrun had felt sorrowful for him and gone to stand close to him, and then regretted that she had.

He'd rubbed his eyes. 'Women,' he said. 'You have to control them — day and night, day and night. Or they get the better of you. But I wasn't there. I was in Alsace. I couldn't control anything. I was trapped by the war.'

Renée was in her grave by the time he got home. She'd been his fiancée, the most beautiful girl in La Callune, but she was slaughtered before he could begin his life with her. Perhaps she'd betrayed him with a lover at Pont Perdu, but nobody ever talked about it, one way or another. Serge Lunel let a few months pass and then he married her identical twin sister, Bernadette.

'*Continuity*,' Serge had said, with his grey-flecked head in its attitude of sorrow and his hands twisting in his lap. 'That's what a man needs. It's what he aches for in this shit-hole of a life. And I ache as badly as the next bastard.'

Anthony sat alone at the marble-topped table on Veronica's terrace, staring at details of properties for sale in the Cévennes, given to him by the agents in Ruasse. Above him, in the Spanish mulberry tree, a gathering of sparrows came and went with twigs and pieces of straw for their nests.

The photographs printed on the agents' details were maddeningly unsharp. They also had a greenish-blue tinge to them, as though they'd already begun to fade — from languishing in a filing cabinet or from being shoved into a too-bright display window. In most of the pictures, the sky behind the houses wasn't blue, but grey. It looked almost as if a silent, invisible English rain were falling.

Anthony took off his glasses, polished them with his handkerchief, put them on again and returned to the pictures. He thought about the care he always lavished on photographs of his *beloveds* for advertisements in the high-end glossy magazines, making sure that the light was such that patina and texture, detail and colour were all exquisitely, irresistibly captured. In contrast to this, these pictures — aimed at buyers willing to part with more than half a million euros — had been hastily, clumsily taken. And not one of the properties bore any resemblance to the house Anthony saw in his mind. In fact, they frightened him. Although he reminded himself that the gap between an idea and its realisation was sometimes so large that the only human response could be a low cry of despair, he felt this cry rise up in him so strongly, so almost audibly, that he choked and became short of breath.

He was about to walk into the house and dump all the brochures in Veronica's paper-recycling box when Kitty Meadows came out onto the terrace and sat down, uninvited, opposite him.

She smiled at him. This smile, Anthony thought, made her look more than ever like a Peke. But he suspected that she intended something by it, that it was probably standing in for words she couldn't (or wouldn't) utter. An apology, he decided, or rather hoped for. Because, after her sulky behaviour at Les Méjanels, this was what she surely owed him? An apology for having underestimated the power of the family bonds that tied him to Veronica.

The smile vanished as Kitty reached out and picked up one of the house brochures.

'May I have a look?' she said.

'Help yourself,' said Anthony.

He watched her examine a photograph of what appeared to be some kind of stone factory, possibly once producing perfume from lavender or oil from local olives, with a line of narrow windows under its roof and a tall, industrial chimney — a place purpose-built, it seemed to him, for the inevitable suicide of its occupants.

He kept watching as Kitty took in the colossal

122

price of this monstrosity and started reading through measurements and descriptions. Above them, Anthony heard the sparrows suddenly burst into fidgety, ardent chatter and he thought how sublime it had once been, to be part of a garrulous admiring group and how this group had truly carried him on its wings, to all the places where he wanted to be seen and where people said his name with awe.

Again, he looked at Kitty. Pathetic woman, he thought. She would never be able to imagine — never get *near* to imagining — what it had been like to walk into a *vernissage* at a Mayfair gallery, and hear, as he sauntered among the clusters of guests, little admiring silences falling softly like snow all around him. 'That's Anthony Verey. *The* Anthony Verey . . . '

And people turning from the pictures on the walls to make ostentatious greetings. 'Anthony darling!' 'Anthony, what a heavenly surprise!' And, best of all, knowing that his presence there was important to the artist himself, an endorsement without price, and that he could use his power or withhold it, according to his taste or his mood that night. He could whisper in the ears of the rich, in the ears of dealers, in the ears of friends like Lloyd and Benita Palmer: 'This painter is *really* good. Take my word. He's going to be huge a year from now.' Then later, mildly delirious on champagne, see some leggy young woman clacking round on four-inch heels, peeling red stickers from a card and putting them on the pictures. And then at last taking the artist aside and saying, with a curve of his lip:

'I've been telling people to buy. Do a tour of the room. See if it's worked.'

And then leaving early — always ostentatiously early — just to sniff for a second the dark scent of disappointment he left hanging in his wake. Leaving early, because very often he had another party to go to and when he arrived there, it would happen all over again. 'It's Anthony Verey. Gosh.' And his host or hostess would break away from whomever they were talking to and greet him and lead him forward into the throng, on wings of expectation.

Gone, those wings. And his name gone . . .

Kitty put down the details of the olive oil factory and picked up another clutch of brochures. Irritated that he was going to have to sit and wait while she waded through the whole batch, Anthony took off his glasses, rubbed his eyes and said: They're no good. None of them.' He wanted to say: They're no good, just as your watercolours are no good. These things I can tell right away. I really don't need to waste time deliberating about them.

But he restrained himself and Kitty turned the picture she was looking at towards him. It showed the tall, oblong house, painted yellow, that he had, in fact, examined with slightly more enthusiasm than the others.

'This one,' she said. 'Veronica said she liked this one.'

'Well,' he said. 'I wondered about it, for a bit. But I think the shape's too blocky and forbidding.'

'The description says the ceilings are high and

beautiful,' said Kitty. 'And it's got acres of vine terraces. Think of the garden we could help you make.'

He took the picture from her and looked at it again, then up at Kitty, and he saw that her smile had come back, her Peke smile, and he mistrusted it now. It had an intention he couldn't fathom.

At this moment, Veronica appeared beside them, carrying a jug of home-made lemonade. She, too was smiling. 'I've decided to be bossy, Anthony,' she said brightly, setting down the lemonade. 'I've rung the agents and made us an appointment to see that house on Friday.'

Anthony's hands clutched the two arms of his spectacles. He wished he had hold of something more substantial.

No, he wanted to say. No, V . . . '

Because he couldn't lie to himself: he was afraid. Afraid of seeing any of these places face to face. Mortally terrified that, standing out under the sky and contemplating someone else's imperfect arrangement of stone and brick and slate, his fragile vision of his future would be broken so badly it would be like the breaking of a Lalique vase: impossible to repair.

'V . . . ' he began, 'I don't honestly think — '

'It probably won't be right at all. It doesn't matter. But you've got to start looking, Anthony. I said I was being bossy and I am. If you're serious about moving to the Cévennes, you've got to get out there and look at places, so that you have something against which to measure.'

He was silent as Veronica poured out the

lemonade. His mouth was a thin line of anguish. He felt helpless, as though Lal were standing there very close to them all, in the cool shade of the mulberry tree, and had turned on him. Unexpectedly turned on him and told him he was a cry-baby.

★ ★ ★

Kitty Meadows saw it, enjoyed it, almost felt thrilled by it: Anthony's terror. If you'd lived thoughtlessly, hedonistically, as he'd done for more than sixty years, then what could you expect but mortal fear, when the last act of your life approached? But it was fascinating how visible his terror was, like an extreme form of stage fright, or like the panic of a condemned man. It was so fascinating, in fact, that Kitty quite wanted to see it prolonged. She thought she might be able to fall asleep at night, consoled by the thought of it, and that when Anthony next turned his demeaning stare on her work, she would be able to say to herself, or even say aloud to him: All right, as a painter I'm mediocre, but as a human being, I'm in possession of a grand passion that could last my lifetime — and this you've never experienced and never will. And already, before you've looked at a single house, your plans for a life in France are turning to dust . . .

But Kitty was also doing and redoing the arithmetic of Anthony's stay at Les Glaniques. And this, she saw, could mass to a vast number of days, unless or until he found a place he

126

wanted to buy. At that point, she supposed, a line would be drawn. Because then, or soon after, he'd have to go back to London, to wind up his business, raise a sum of money and put in hand the sale of his flat. And from that time on, they'd be rid of him for a long while. Perhaps for ever? Because if he suggested staying with them while he organised all the tedious, expensive refurbishments to his new abode, she, Kitty, would put her foot down and Veronica would just have to accept this foot.

It amused Kitty to remember that Veronica had a weakness for her lover's soft feet, that she liked to caress them with her palms perfumed with rose oil, even let them gently chafe her *there*, where she used to feel the chafe of Susan's saddle and the pony's warmth under her thighs and cling passionately to the horse's neck as she rubbed herself to her gorgeous teenage climaxes. So yes, this is what Kitty would say: 'I put my foot down, darling.' And Veronica would be seduced into accepting it. That would be the word: seduced.

In Kitty's dreams, though, the immediate future didn't go according to her plan. In fact, they weren't dreams; they were nightmares. They could happen when she was wide awake. In these nightmares, Anthony found no house to buy. He just stayed on and on at Les Glaniques, as spring became summer and summer became autumn. He took over the kitchen. The smell of his after-shave corroded the air. And all his conversation — on and on and on — was about the past he shared with Veronica, about the way

127

they'd suffered from their father's absence, and the way, after Lal died, they'd become 'all in all' to each other, because they'd had no one else. And the evocation of this 'all in all', spiced with its private jokes and innuendoes, tormented Kitty to the point where she had to take herself away somewhere, out under the sky, down the long path to the river or up into Sainte-Agnès, where she sat by the communal fountain and bathed her face in the cool water and let the chatter of the village women — about the mayor's new girlfriend, about the list of names for the fête committee, about the loss of the postmistress to a man from Limoges — soothe her back to normality and equilibrium.

Another thing gave her pain: she believed that Anthony listened to their love-making through their bedroom wall. Not only in her nightmares, but in reality: he stood there in his room or in the passageway, listening in the dark. She couldn't see or hear him, but she felt sure he was there. And she knew the same anxiety was gradually taking hold of Veronica. Because, now, it was as if Veronica had become frightened of being caught out in the act of loving Kitty. In bed, where she'd always been so voluble, even unashamedly loud, she began to talk in a tiny little mouse-like voice, as though she and Kitty were children, condemned to silence after lights-out in a boarding-school dormitory. When Kitty tried to kiss her, she often pushed her gently away.

Upsetting as this was, Kitty decided not to make a fuss. She was determined not to let herself fall into the kind of detestable sulky behaviour Lal had clearly been guilty of. So she lay wide awake while Veronica slept and tried to dream up some clever way of getting Anthony to leave Les Glaniques. But she knew there was no clever way. He'd announce that he was leaving as and when it suited him and not a moment before. All Kitty could pray for was that he abandoned his implausible idea of living in the Cévennes (whose remoteness he had not fully grasped and of whose history and customs he knew nothing whatsoever), or else that soon some house turned up that would fire his precious imagination.

While Veronica snored softly, Kitty tried to soothe her mind with the remembrance of Anthony's agitation over the agents' brochures. She tried to picture the condition of his heart, of the actual organ, and she envisaged it as being brownish in colour and dry and pithy and yet with a small pulse inside it, beating with the frenzied little ticking movements of a stopwatch. And she thought that a heart in such a condition couldn't possibly keep a person alive for very long — even somebody as languid and inactive as Anthony Verey. So it was likely that he would die soon. He would die of his petrified heart.

After a while, these imaginings had some consoling effect on Kitty and she began to feel sleepy. She turned over and laid her palm tenderly against Veronica's back. Before she closed her eyes, it occurred to her that it would be enjoyable to go with Veronica and Anthony to see the yellow house on Friday, and to observe — up there among the wild gorse and the dying chestnuts, and the ever-present idea of snakes sleeping in the sun — how far his terror deepened.

Anthony, Veronica and Kitty were driven from Ruasse to La Callune in the agent's car. The agent's name was Madame Besson. She'd left her daughter, Christine, at her desk in the office, closed now at midday, chain-smoking her eight-centimetre cigarettes and talking on her mobile.

Madame Besson knew this corniche of a road very well and she drove it worryingly fast, waltzing into blind bends, nudging up too closely to the traffic in front. Anthony, sitting beside her, bound himself in tightly with his seat belt, but he couldn't stop his right foot from shooting forwards all the time onto an imaginary brake pedal, couldn't put down a silent screaming inside himself.

He felt that dying in a car accident would be a pointless way for his life to end. And the idea that he could perish here and now in an old, badly driven Peugeot, not only made him angry, it made him suddenly, passionately impatient to see the yellow house. He now longed — yes *longed* — to walk in through its front door, to understand how it sat in the landscape, how it coped with the weather. His terror at coming face to face with it — with one actual version of his future — had miraculously vanished, replaced by his fear of dying on the road before he got to it.

To distract himself, to try to diminish his fear, Anthony asked Madame Besson, in his stumbling, imprecise French, to tell him more about the Mas Lunel. The silence that met this request suggested that it took her a moment or two to remember which house it was they were driving to. *Besson Immobilier,* said this panicky little pause, is the smartest agent in Ruasse; you have to understand that we handle hundreds of properties, so we can't always recall . . .

'This is a beautiful house,' she announced at last, letting the car bound up to a slow-moving cement truck and stay clamped there in its sulphurous slipstream. 'Don't be put off by the state of the rooms. They're full of an old man's clutter. But you have to imagine how it will be once all that has gone. With old houses like these, that have been in the same family for years and years and never updated, you've got to use your imagination.'

Anthony nodded. The woman annoyed him. She smelled of nicotine. She drove dangerously. She talked so fast it was just about impossible to understand her.

'Paysage,' he said. 'How is that?'

'*Paysage?* What d'you mean?'

'Paysage. The land near the house . . . '

'Ah, I see. Well, it's overgrown. Nobody has worked the land for years now. Some of the terrace walls have collapsed. But that's nothing. You can repair those. You English have a mania for gardens, I know. And you've got plenty of space here. So.'

The road unspooled on and on, rising, falling,

rising, turning, falling. Anthony began to be tormented by thirst and when he saw a roadside stall advertising Orangina, he asked Madame Besson to stop. They pulled over and Anthony, Veronica and Kitty got out. They stood on the verge, breathing the sweet air. The sun today had a new heat to it. Bees hummed above the yellow gorse. A green meadow below them was shiny with buttercups.

'Summer,' said Veronica. 'It comes early here. You suddenly feel it.'

They walked over to the stall, which called itself *La Bonne Baguette.* When Veronica saw that there was a chiller full of crusty sandwiches on its counter, she said: 'Let's get a sandwich each. It's almost lunchtime.'

Madame Besson got out of the car and lit a cigarette. Anthony offered to buy her something, but she refused, staring pointedly at Veronica's bulky form. 'You English,' said this look. 'You eat junk. And you don't seem to have noticed that it's killing you.'

She paced up and down while the drinks and baguettes were bought.

'Eat them here,' she instructed peremptorily. 'Then I won't get crumbs in the car.'

So they walked down to the buttercup meadow and sat on the springy grass, eating and drinking, with the eyes of Madame Besson on them.

'I guess,' said Anthony, 'she's tired of foreigners. We make money for her, but really she wishes we'd all go home.'

He laughed as he said this and looked over to

Kitty, as if he expected some chiming reaction from her, but she just turned her head away.

In fact, what was preoccupying Kitty was the sandwich filling that Anthony had chosen: Camembert and tomato. It thrilled her to remember that a friend of Veronica's, living not far from here, had died from eating unpasteurised cheese.

★　★　★

Now, there it was at last: the Mas Lunel. Golden in the midday sun; the holm oaks behind it just coming into leaf and, above these, the dark shoulders of firs. Daisies gave the unkempt lawn a dusting of white.

What Anthony liked straight away was the feeling the mas had of being completely on its own, on a sheltered plateau, as though the land had sculpted itself around the building. To the south of it were the vine and olive terraces, descending towards the road. Anthony got out of the car and stood very still, trying to catch the mood of the place, to seize this — its marvellous isolation, its wild beauty — before anything came along to compromise it.

An elderly man came out of the house. He walked with a slight limp. He was skinny, in shabby clothes, and with the hectic, high colour of a drinker. A dark red kerchief was tied around his scrawny neck. He shielded his eyes against the sun.

Madame Besson went to him and shook his hand. Anthony heard her reminding him quickly

134

that these were English buyers she'd brought this time, and he saw the man look over to where he stood, with Veronica and Kitty, and gawp at them, wiping a thread of saliva from his mouth with the back of his hand.

Madame Besson made the introductions. 'Monsieur Lunel. Monsieur Verey. His sister. A friend . . . ' And they all moved to cluster together, to undergo the obligatory handshakes, the good-mannered greetings long ago abandoned in Britain. The dogs, in their wire pound, had begun barking, visibly unsettling Kitty, and Monsieur Lunel hurried to apologise for this. 'Take no notice of the hounds,' he said. 'They're my hunting dogs. We hunt wild boar up in the hills here. But they'll be going away with me. Don't worry. I'm not trying to sell them with the house!'

Lunel laughed at his own little joke and was quickly punished for this as the laughter turned into a loose cough that boiled up from his chest, so that he had to turn away and spit into a rag. Anthony thought: He's selling because he's dying. He wants to cash in before the darkness comes.

When he recovered from the cough, Lunel said he'd go and make coffee. Or tea. Would the *Britanniques* like tea? He had some tea. Lipton's Tea. He said it was probably better if he made the tea and Madame Besson showed them round the house, because he wouldn't know how to describe things. He'd lived here all his life. When you've lived in a place all your life, he said, you don't know how it appears to strangers. You don't know what might worry them or what might please them . . .

They agreed to the tea, then set off, following Madame Besson, and Anthony saw Lunel go down to the dogs and throw them some scraps out of his pocket, to calm them.

★　★　★

'Cévenol houses are dark,' Madame Besson said, as they walked into the large space that contained the kitchen range and a warped and beaten refectory table, 'because the window space is kept to a minimum. This way, the houses stay cool in summer and retain the heat from the fires in winter. You notice how thick the walls are?'

The room smelled of the fire and of cooking grease and onions.

The stone floor was worn down in places by the repetitive traffic of feet in heavy shoes. A vast oak dresser, ('French, circa 1835 . . . ') Anthony guessed, (' . . . overscroll pilasters showing wear and chipping'), was crammed with meat platters, plates, jugs, bowls and blackened brass lamps. In the far corner of the room was a day-bed, covered with a tartan rug and piled up with faded farm machinery catalogues. By this, on the floor, was an old bakelite telephone. A tap dripped in the stone sink. Empty whisky bottles decorated the draining board. On the table were some mouldy apples, a bottle of pastis and a clouded glass.

'I warned you,' said Madame Besson.

136

'Everything's a mess. But this room is a very good size. And now look up. You see the fine ceilings?'

Anthony saw wide, smoke-blackened wooden beams holding up a dense cross-hatching of narrower rafters. Between these, the plaster-work was patched and flaking, but Madame Besson was right, the ceiling was exceptional. It reminded Anthony of the roof in the plain little parish church of Netherholt, where Lal was buried. And he thought: This would be the place to start work on this house, this ceiling like a church roof, with its echo of the past. Restore the wood to its original colour. Re-plaster. Then tear the rendering off the walls and return them to stone. Dismantle the present. Get back to how everything had once been, and flood it with bright light.

They were present in every room on the ground floor, these astonishing ceilings, even in the pantry, with its concrete floor and its ancient freezer, looped up to a trailing electric cable. 'Don't they,' Anthony whispered to Veronica, 'remind you of Netherholt Church?'

Veronica smiled and Anthony saw that it was the kind of indulgent smile she might give to a child, but he didn't care, because he was feeling excitement now, real excitement. It was almost catching at his breath as he followed Madame Besson up the steep staircase to the first floor.

Here, the ceilings were lower and the rooms felt cramped and surprisingly small, but, reading Anthony's disappointment with impressive precision, Madame Besson immediately began tapping at one of the walls and quickly said: 'Partitions. You could take them out. And what I would do is, I would also take out these ceilings, get rid of the attics. You've got plenty of rooms without them, including space for new bathrooms. So I'd let the bedroom walls go right up into the roof. You can insulate, of course. Then you would have exquisite spaces with, almost, a Gothic shape.'

Anthony loved Madame Besson now. He forgave her her bad driving, her disdain for Veronica's fat stomach, her smoking habit. She'd done her job as an agent with intelligence. She'd replaced for him something ordinary with something marvellous. She had, in fact, made the house *one*: a beautiful gem, with its most audacious wonders still waiting to be revealed behind flimsy slabs of plasterboard. He wanted to slap a kiss on her sun-wrinkled face.

He walked to one of the bedroom windows and stared out at the big parcel of land which would belong to him. There was even a sizeable stone barn below the lawn, which could be put to some magnificent use (Pool house? Separate guest suite?), and to the left of this he could glimpse the terraces falling away towards the south. They were overgrown with weeds, but they were planted with vines and olives and what looked like gnarled old fruit trees, sweetly fuzzed with grey lichen. The window was open and Anthony leaned on the sill, hearing nothing now but birdsong. He adored the feeling of being high up. And he thought how, with V's help, this view might in time become so seductive he'd

138

never ever want to leave it . . .

He was on the very precipice of calling Veronica over to him and whispering to her that he wanted to buy the house, that he'd made up his mind already, that he had a sublime vision of what it could be, when Kitty arrived beside him. She'd said nothing so far, but he'd noticed her ferret eyes go peering into corners, seen how, straight away, the dogs in their pen upset her, sentimentalist that she was. Now she stood by Anthony, peering out.

'It's interesting,' she said. 'From inside, and even from here, you feel as if the house is on its own.'

'What d'you mean?' said Anthony. 'It *is* on its own.'

'Well, not quite. There's the bungalow.'

'What bungalow?'

Kitty leaned further out. Anthony couldn't stand the way she cut her hair so short at the back, like a man's hair, as if enticing you to keep noticing the tough sinews of her neck.

'Over there,' she said. 'You can just see it. There. On the bend in the driveway.'

He looked to where she was pointing. Saw a low, corrugated iron roof, the edge of a façade, painted pink, geraniums in what looked like plastic pots.

'Didn't you notice it as we drove in?' asked Kitty.

'No,' he said. 'No.'

And he hadn't noticed it. He'd been staring straight ahead, fixated on his first sight of the Mas Lunel. But there it was. Another habitation, another person's life, with all its mess and clutter, squatting on land he'd been imagining was his.

He cursed silently. He'd believed he'd been looking at a slice of paradise and he'd chosen to forget that there were no paradises left in the world. All the still-beautiful places were blighted by their nearness to some other thing you didn't wish to see or hear or have to think about. And here was that blight again, like the face of the old crone in the Aubusson tapestry, mocking the blithe aristocrats at the very moment when delicious food and wine were being brought to them.

He felt choked, furious with himself. Why hadn't he, who was normally so vigilant about the details of his surroundings, taken in the damn bungalow? He kept staring at it now, as though willing it not to be there. Of course, he thought wearily, it had to be Kitty, it *had* to be her who drew his attention to it, who came and took away his excitement, his incipient joy.

The only question that remained was, did the fact of the bungalow ruin the whole place for him, or might some compromise with it be reached? He knew he'd have to go outside and look at it face to face to be able to answer this question, but he shrank from doing this. He was afraid that its ugliness would send him plunging back into depression.

Anthony called Madame Besson over to him.

'Ah yes,' she said, 'that little house belongs to Monsieur Lunel's sister. But most of her land is on the other side of the road. She just has a bit of

140

grass and a small vegetable garden there. You could easily screen her off. Plant some fast-growing cypresses. Then you wouldn't know anything was there.'

Oh yes, thought Anthony, this was agent-talk of the kind they loved to perfect, but he was Anthony Verey, and he *would* know. Even if he couldn't see it, he would feel it: the hag in the forest, another human existence, with all its distress and noise, all its grinding ordinariness, when what he yearned for was perfect, unpolluted solitude — a kingdom of his own, where he could grow old in style.

Anthony turned to Madame Besson. He was too agitated to try to speak French. 'I love the house,' he said in English. 'The high ceilings, the space. The position, even. But I think the bungalow ruins it. I think, for me, the bungalow makes it impossible.'

★   ★   ★

Out of politeness, they had to drink the tea Monsieur Lunel had prepared.

He sat them down at the kitchen table, cleared of the apples and the pastis. He passed round a plate of stale biscuits.

'So,' he said, 'I'll take you down to the vines when you've drunk your tea. They've got a bit overgrown. I'm on my own here. I've got no son to help me or take over from me, which is why I'm selling up. But it's good land, worked for generations . . .'

Anthony, sipping disdainfully at the tepid

141

brew, said to Madame Besson: 'Please can you ask him how much of the land belongs to his sister.'

'I already informed you,' said Madame Besson. 'Most of the sister's land is on the other side of the road.'

'Nevertheless, ask him please,' snapped Anthony.

When Madame Besson put the question to Lunel, Anthony saw sudden anxiety darken the man's face. He didn't reply immediately, but then leaned over and whispered to the agent: 'Tell them my sister's of no account. She'll be gone. That house will be gone. It never should have been built where it is.'

Madame Besson pursed her lips. She shifted in her chair and began patting her hair as she turned to Anthony and said: 'There is . . . a . . . *suggestion* that Monsieur Lunel's sister may also be leaving. In which case, I suppose that plot with the small house would become available to buy. But I am not certain about this.'

'Audrun owns a whole wood!' Lunel burst out. 'I told her to build there, in her damned wood. That's where the house should have gone. And instead it went on my land.'

'Are you saying that your sister's house is, in fact, on your land, Monsieur Lunel?' said Madame Besson.

'Yes, it's on part of my land . . . part of it . . . '

'Ah. That was not made clear to me. According to the plans I've seen — '

'I'm getting a new surveyor!' said Aramon Lunel, banging his fist on the table. 'Those boundaries are all wrong and Audrun knows it!'

Madame Besson took a notebook out of her handbag and began to write in it. Anthony saw sweat begin to bead at Lunel's temple. His clenched fist was shaking. 'I've told Audrun,' he said to Madame Besson, 'she's in breach of the rules. We're just waiting for the surveyor to come and sort it all out.'

'I think you should have informed us, as agents, about this . . . family dispute, Monsieur Lunel,' said Madame Besson. 'I can't continue to show people round the property while there's uncertainty about boundary lines.'

'No, no!' cried Lunel. 'There is no uncertainty. There is no 'dispute'. You'll see! It's all going to be sorted out. Just as soon as I can persuade the surveyor at Ruasse to get off his arse . . . '

Madame Besson got up and made a sign to the others to do the same. Lunel clutched at Madame Besson's sleeve. 'Don't go!' he implored. 'I like these buyers. The *Britanniques* have money. They haven't finished their tea. Let me show them the vines . . . '

'No, I'm sorry, we have to go,' said Madame Besson, pulling her arm away and consulting her watch. 'We have an appointment to see a house at Saint-Bertrand.'

Audrun was cutting her grass with her small petrol mower when Aramon came limping down the driveway and began shouting at her. She manoeuvred the mower towards him, thinking how extraordinary it would be to run over his feet.

'Turn it off! Turn it off!' he yelled.

But she let it idle near her, like a weapon primed and ready.

He was drunk on pastis. His gaze looped and swivelled all around him. The sun beat down on his wild head.

'I've got a buyer!' he babbled. 'It's eighty per cent sure. Ninety per cent sure. An English buyer, some dealer in antiques, stuffed with cash. But he's hesitating, damn him! He's hesitating because he wants your bungalow gone, and I've told the agents it *will* be gone!'

'You've told the agents — '

'I'm not letting this sale go. It's my due. It's my right, *pardi*!'

Audrun said nothing. She held onto the mower handle. She could imagine the blood and tissue and bone from his feet exploding in a fountain over the grass, the colour of the pink lake in her dreams. Aramon lurched nearer to her. 'Surveyor's coming tomorrow,' he said, shaking a finger at her, almost in her face. 'And I've told him, your house is illegal!'

144

'Leave me alone, Aramon,' she said.

'Didn't you hear me? Surveyor's coming in the morning. And by next week, there'll be a demolition order on your bungalow. And I've told those stupid agents, I'm taking care of it. I've told them — '

He was sick then. He convulsed and spewed up on her cut lawn, clutching his gut. Audrun had to look away, the sight was so repellent, it made her retch. And she thought about where she'd bury him once she'd killed him; not in the family vault at La Callune, where their parents lay, but in some unsanctified place, some unvisited slope of land, among the thorny gorse. And birds of prey would come, smelling his terrible flesh, and pick him clean, as he'd never been clean in his adult life. And all of this was only a matter of time.

She turned her back on him and resumed her mowing, going in wider circles now, without looking in his direction. The scent of the mown grass gradually replaced the stink of his vomit. And after a while, Audrun knew that he'd walked away, going shakily along the drive towards the Mas Lunel. She imagined him crawling up the stairs to his room and collapsing onto his bed. He should have been working on his vines, but he'd be snoring in his pit, with daylight flooding the walls, and she began to wonder, would this be a good time to do the things she had to do . . . ?

She'd seen the English people, heard the sound of their voices, peculiarly loud. And the smaller of the two women had come a little way down the drive and stared at the bungalow. Audrun had watched her from behind her lace curtains. The woman resembled a man. She was short, but she walked with a swagger. And the swagger had made Audrun feel strange, as though this person had mystical power.

She found herself wondering, had Jesus of Nazareth walked along the shore towards the fishermen in this swaggering kind of way, when He summoned His disciples and they'd risen up from their boats and left their nets and all that they'd worked for, to follow Him there and then? Audrun knew this was an inappropriate kind of idea, a blasphemy, exactly the kind of thought which made ordinary people believe she was crazy. But nobody seemed to understand that thoughts couldn't always be chosen. This was one of the confusing things about Audrun's life: *thoughts chose her.* And not only thoughts. She was a vessel, a receptacle for unimaginably terrible actions. And this was what she lived with: the fact that, sometimes, the unimaginable became real in her: only in her.

She sat in her chair, resting after her mowing. She asked herself how long it would take her to snatch Aramon's pills, grind them up and dissolve them in warm water and fill the enema bag and go silently back to his room. Would he wake up too soon, and begin struggling with her? Or would she, even as she worked with the fluid and the tube, be able to calm and reassure him, tell him she was trying to do him good with a special kind of purge that would flush the sickness out of him? And then he would submit.

146

He would submit to his own death . . .

Audrun closed her eyes. Once, when they were children, before Bernadette had left them to lie in the cemetery at La Callune, Aramon had fallen out of an apricot tree on one of the far terraces, and she, his ten-year-old sister, had heard him screaming and found him in a swoon of pain and tried to soothe him and calm him as he writhed on the ground with his ankle broken.

She'd attempted to pick him up and carry him, but the weight of him was too great and she had had to lay him down on a mush of fallen apricots and dry leaves. She told him she was going to run and fetch Bernadette or Serge, but Aramon clung to her. He was thirteen and afraid and he said: 'Don't leave me out here. Don't leave me alone, Audrun . . . '

So she laid his head in her lap and stroked his face and tried to calm him and after a while he was quiet and fell into a kind of trance. She sat there, on the mushy ground, tormented by wasps, holding him and waiting. Not daring to cry out for help, in case she broke his peculiar sleep, proud of the way she'd been able to bring this sleep about.

And only later, after Serge had found them as the light was fading, was she told that she'd done wrong, that Aramon could have died of shock out there on the lower terraces, that she should have covered him with her own coat and run immediately for help. In the night, she heard her father say to Bernadette: 'That daughter of yours has no sense. She doesn't do what's right. God knows what kind of life she's going to have.'

147

God knows what kind of life.

And now, it could go wrong again, that thing she called her life. If she did what she wanted to do, what she knew she *had to do,* wasn't she afterwards guaranteed a miserable end? Because prison would feel like dying, just as working in the underwear factory at Ruasse had felt like dying. She'd spend her days trudging between a freezing cell and some noisy, echoing room, where women laughed and screamed like demons as they went about their ugly work. In this place, her eyesight would surely fail. Her *episodes* would increase, until they joined one to another in a skein of unpronounceable suffering and confusion. And in the nights, she'd be haunted by dreams about her wood, knowing that she'd never see it again, never hear its sighing, never see the glad spring, but only imagine the seasons passing and flying on . . .

Audrun sat on in her chair and the evening darkness slowly visited the room. She realised now that she didn't have it yet, the plan that would accomplish its end and leave no trace. She pulled her cardigan round her. Then she thought: I don't have it yet, but it *will* come. It will arrive in me, unbidden, like a stranger with a swagger arriving at the door. And I will rise up and follow it.

★   ★   ★

She got up early and drank her bowl of coffee and put on her flowery overall and began to tidy her house for the surveyor's visit. She dragged a

148

mop over the tiled floors, watching the pathways of shine its dampness made and wishing that this glimmer wouldn't fade, the way it always did.

She knew the bungalow was a dump, botched together under its tin roof, but now that she was probably going to lose it she felt her sentimental attachment to it increase. It contained all there was of her: her bed, her armoire, her plants, her television, her stove, her rugs, her favourite chair. The walls had sheltered her, kept her pain in one place.

The morning was bright and still. Audrun watered the geraniums on her terrace, pulled up two white onions for her supper, chased a green frog away. As the frog disappeared into the grass, Audrun saw Marianne Viala walking up the road towards her.

'The surveyor's coming this morning,' she told Marianne.

Marianne had brought her a piece of her famous *tarte au chocolat* on a blue plate. She set this down on the plastic table. She shook her head that appeared small, with its tightly permed curls, coloured pale brown. 'Aramon should be ashamed of himself,' she said.

They sat down in the plastic chairs, with the *tarte* between them, uneaten. Whenever a car came by on the road, they turned and stared, wondering if it was going to be the surveyor arriving. After a while, Marianne said: 'If your brother knocks your house down, you can come and live with me.'

Audrun was silent. She knew this was very kind of Marianne, exceptionally kind — if she

149

really meant it — but it wasn't a thing she could contemplate. She'd lived her whole life here, on land that had belonged to the Lunel family for three generations. To find herself in some little shadowy back-room, surrounded by Marianne's possessions, would be terrible. She lifted her head and said: 'I think I'll go and live at the mas.'

'What,' said Marianne, 'with *him*?'

Audrun looked down at her hands, clenched together on the table top.

'The way he's drinking,' she said, 'he can't have long to live.'

★ ★ ★

After an hour had passed, Audrun made more coffee and the two women ate the chocolate *tarte* and they felt the sweetness of it bring their blood alive. And they started on some reminiscences of their schooldays and among these was a memory of how their teacher, Monsieur Verdier, used to bring his mongrel dog, Toto, to Thursday classes because his wife worked in the village shop on that day of the week and Toto was a creature who couldn't bear to be alone.

At break time, Toto would be let out into the school yard with the children and they hugged him and petted him and pulled his ears and fed him sweets and chased him round and round, and some of the older boys threw sticks at him but he kept scampering on.

Then, one Thursday, Toto wasn't there in his basket in the classroom, and Monsieur Verdier set the children a reading assignment and sat at

150

his desk without moving, staring out of the window at the sky.

'Please, sir,' one of the children asked. 'Where's Toto?'

'Toto's disappeared,' said Monsieur Verdier. 'We don't know where. We just hope he's not alone.'

'Did he ever come back?' asked Marianne. 'I can't remember.'

'No,' said Audrun. 'He never came back. The things you love never do.'

Marianne sniffed, as if to say that, really, Audrun's pessimism was wearisome sometimes, and she changed the subject to her daughter, Jeanne, who was a teacher, now, at a school in Ruasse. 'The children there,' said Marianne, 'are far less disciplined than we were. Far less — in the city schools. Jeanne has terrible difficulty. And she told me in her class this term she's got a child from Paris, who's getting bullied.'

'Well,' said Audrun. 'That's not new. Bullying.'

'No. But it's hard for Jeanne. She has to try to be fair to everyone. She hates it when any of them are unhappy, but she says this little girl has been very spoilt. Her father's a doctor, or something like that.'

'What's her name?' asked Audrun. 'In Paris, they give children the names of movie stars, American names.'

'Yes,' said Marianne. 'Her name's Mélodie. *Mélodie*. Imagine calling a child that! And of course it makes another difficulty for Jeanne.'

★ ★ ★

151

The morning went by and Marianne returned to her house, and there was no sign of the surveyor.

'If you're a woman,' Bernadette once said to Audrun, 'you spend a lot of your life waiting. You wait for the men to come back from the war, or from the fields, or from hunting in the hills. You wait for them to decide to mend all the things that need mending. You wait for their words of love.'

Audrun went indoors. She ate some bread and cheese and then locked her front door and lay down on her bed. She discovered that the waiting had tired her. She slept for two hours and was woken by a knocking on her door and she thought from its frenzy that it was probably Aramon, come back to shout at her about something or other, so she took her time answering.

A man stood there, wearing a crumpled grey suit and a tie tugged loose from the collar of his shirt and hanging down all anyhow. Under his arm was a sheaf of papers.

'I'm the surveyor,' said the man. 'From Ruasse.'

Soon after Bernadette died, Serge Lunel had said to his son: 'It's us against the world now, Aramon. You and me against the world. We have to take control. And I'm going to tell you how.'

Aramon stood now near the Lunel tomb in the cemetery at La Callune.

He found that he was holding in his hands a small wreath of plastic flowers, but he wasn't certain how his hands had come by this. Had they taken it from another family's mausoleum? Had they found it lying in the grass?

He told himself that it didn't really matter, that a plastic wreath was the kind of thing nobody cared a fig about, and he set it down distractedly at the foot of the granite tomb that contained his parents and his Lunel grandparents, Guillaume and Marthe, all on top of one another, with his mother and father jammed in last, up against the roof. And it seemed fantastical to Aramon that he was now older than Serge had been when he'd died.

Time, he thought, was so unstable, it was surprising anybody had been able to carve out any rational existence within it at all.

Deep in Aramon's heart lay the knowledge that both their lives — his and Serge's — had been warped and damaged by what they'd chosen to do after Bernadette was gone. But he didn't want to feel that either of them were to blame for it. *Time* was to blame. Time had given them Bernadette and then taken her away, just as it had taken Renée away, long before. *Man that is born of a woman hath but a short time to live.* Time changed the way your body felt and the things it had to do.

It wasn't a thing you could ever talk about, or had ever been able to talk about. Even while he and his father had hoed the onions (in the long-ago days when onions had still earned the family good money) in the hot earth, moving together up and down the rows, while Audrun worked in the underwear factory in Ruasse, they'd been silent on the subject. Only once, right at the beginning, had Serge whispered to him, 'It's perfectly logical, son. There was Renée, but she died, she was punished for what she did, then there was your mother, but she's gone too, she left us. So now . . . there's the other one. It's logical to keep all of this in the family. Quite logical.'

It used to make Aramon black out. The sheer and terrible thrill of going into Audrun's room in the night and doing that. He thought of it as love, the most delirious perfect love he could imagine. It was too much for his body and his mind. Sometimes, afterwards, Serge had to come and pick him off the floor of her room where she'd tipped him, and carry him back to his own bed, slap his cheeks to bring him round, make him drink cognac. '*Allez*,' Serge would whisper tenderly, 'it's all right. You're not dying. You've just done what young men have to do. Go to sleep now.'

154

Then, he would hear Serge walking back down the corridor and going into her room, too, and closing the door and, later, crying out, like a dog. And Aramon didn't care about this, that his love had to be shared. What he minded about, what made him mad, was that she never cried out. All she ever gave him in return for what he did — the *love* he gave her — was her silence.

The years kept passing, like that — Serge and Aramon crying out in the dark for more than fifteen years — until Serge fell ill. Then, on his death-bed, Serge had said to his son: 'I'm going down to Hell, Aramon. I feel it. And it's because of *that*. So you . . . you'd better find a different path now. The mas is yours, and most of the land. Marry some girl. Let Audrun build her own little place. Or your life will go wrong. Do it before it's too late.'

Do it before it's too late.

* * *

Aramon went down to Ruasse (to the other Ruasse that tourists seldom liked to think about) and picked up an olive-skinned whore called Fatima, and fucked her twice a week in her secretive attic room where chiffon scarves were draped over the lampshades and the air was perfumed with body oils and incense.

But what Aramon Lunel did with Fatima never made him black out.

It was never the same as it had been. And then Fatima died. Someone killed her with a knife, there in her hot little scented room, they split her open from her breast bone to her pelvis, and she was taken away, wrapped in plastic sheeting, to the morgue.

Aramon was led into the police station and questioned. (They called it questioning but there didn't seem to be any audible question marks on the ends of sentences.)

You killed this girl.

You stabbed this whore. Fatima. You cut her open.

He told them he wouldn't have bothered to kill her. She didn't mean that much to him. With her, he'd never blacked out.

Blacked out.

This could explain it, then: your loss of memory.

You killed the whore. Then, you blacked out.

The 'questioners' were just stupid, ordinary policemen. How could the intensity of what he'd once felt be explained to people like them? All he kept saying was: 'She's of no account to me. Fatima. I probably never even called her by her name.' And after a long and weary while, after days in police custody, they found another man and accused him of the murder and left Aramon alone. They told him he was 'walking free'. But he knew what they did not know, that after what had happened for fifteen years, he would never be free.

★ ★ ★

There were a lot of family tombs in the cemetery at La Callune. The little graveyard was almost

156

full up. Some of the dead were labelled Heroes of the Résistance, carved in stone. Not Serge, of course. He'd guarded trains and stretches of railway line against Résistance saboteurs. But quite a few of the others. Yet, whenever Aramon went to the graveyard, he found himself alone and it was as though Serge had somehow arranged this, so that the two of them could talk (well, he thought of it as a conversation, even though he knew it was a monologue) and not be overheard by other people visiting their departed relations. 'These villages are full of spies,' Serge had once said to him. 'You can't trust a single soul. Only the family.'

Now, Aramon told Serge that he was confused. He was going to get a pile of money in return for the mas and the land. Four hundred and seventy-five thousand euros! Nearly three million francs! More money than had ever existed in generations of Lunels. But he didn't know where — when he had all this cash in his hands — he was going to go.

'Where should I go?' he asked. '*Where?*'

He longed for Serge to answer. Serge Lunel had been a survivor. Always, this survival had been a close-run thing. He'd narrowly escaped slaughter by the German army in the Ardennes. He'd survived Renée's death by marrying Bernadette. He'd managed to avoid being sent to work in Germany with the S.T.O. by agreeing to a night-time job in Ruasse, guarding trains. And the things that came later: he'd survived his own guilt by making his son his accomplice.

Aramon stared out at the heavy-shouldered

tombs. Everything, he thought, *weighs* so much in this place. The earth. The houses (for the living and for the dead). The canisters of this or that poison you have to carry on your back. The boulders in the path of the river. The thunderclouds filled with rain . . .

He drank because of the weight of things. More and more, the alcohol was making him ill, he knew this, but he couldn't find any substitute, any other way of sliding out from underneath the slab of memories that tried to crush him, crush him with guilt and with love that he could never express.

Often, in his reveries, he was a boy again and Audrun was a little girl, jumping in the dusty courtyard with her skipping rope, with the sun shining on her brown hair. Together, they fed the chickens and the family pig. After heavy rain, they were sent out together, hand in hand, with identical tin buckets, to collect snails.

Sometimes, when they were picking snails near the river and their rubber boots were larded with moist earth and the wet weeds and rushes brushed against their legs, he asked to see her scar, where the surgeons had chopped off her pig's tail, and she lifted her pinafore-dress and showed him her little round tummy, and he stroked it and said he was sorry about teasing her and pretending she'd been the daughter of an SS man. And she said it was all right, she couldn't remember anything about that. And he'd give her some of his snails, so that Bernadette would be proud of her and say: 'Well done, *ma chérie*. You found more than your brother.'

And, at other times, after warm days in April and early May, they stood together in the fields of cherry blossom at dusk, listening out for nightingales, and the white blossom became luminous in the fading light and one evening, when Audrun was still a child, but growing in beauty, beginning to resemble her mother and her dead aunt Renée, Aramon broke off a little branch of it and tucked it behind her ear, and she looked up at him and said: 'Now I'm a princess. Am I?'

Take me there.

That's what Aramon wanted to say to Serge. 'That's the place I want to go. Please, oh please take me there: to the field of white blossom.'

But the dead never responded to any living plea. They could, it seemed, arrange a confidential hour, but then when you whispered your longings to them and asked them to help you, they fell back to being inert and useless: just brittle branches, bare twigs, dust.

★   ★   ★

Aramon walked slowly, painfully back to the Mas Lunel. His feet hurt all the time. There was an ache in his hip. His gut churned with some kind of distress that wasn't quite hunger and wasn't quite sickness, but a mortal unease he couldn't identify. And he wondered whether, when he'd got his great wad of money in exchange for the mas, he wouldn't go in search of some hospital or rest-home and pay them to take him in and take care of him. Were there such places, where you could just walk in the door and be led by the hand to some small but clean room? People said that, in this modern world, everything you could think of existed, provided you could pay for it, so perhaps these existed too? Sanctuaries.

It was the time of year for olive-pruning —
before the summer truly arrived.

Veronica and Kitty had been to a seminar in
Ruasse on how this was supposed to be done.
You cut back the growth only every second year
and, when you did, you had to let the foliage
have air; you had to keep in your mind an
imaginary bird flying into the tree and out again
the other side without pausing in its flight.

The olive grove at Les Glaniques had more
than twenty trees, so Anthony had agreed to help
with the pruning. He enjoyed repetitive tasks.
They calmed his mind. And the feel of the
secateurs in his hand reminded him of pruning
roses with Lal: the bright sound of the cut, the
consoling idea that you were making the plant
strong, the unexpected warmth of spring
sunshine on your face . . . So he felt happy as he
worked. Kitty was satisfactorily far away,
Veronica within easy call. There were no clouds
above them.

The vivid birdsong reminded Anthony of Lal's
garden, too: of a time when the mistle thrush
was a common sight, when scarlet-breasted
bullfinches snickered in the hedges, when you
could hear woodpeckers — those determined
amateurs of DIY — tapping at tree trunks in the
orchard and pheasants squawking in the spinney.

And he thought that here was another reason

to leave England: even as people and property crowded in there, so nature was withdrawing her riches. It was as though the land had tired of the way its variety and complexity kept being ignored by man, and had decided to brand itself with just the few, dull species everybody would recognise. Fifty years from now, there would be only blackbirds and gulls and stinging-nettles and grass.

The beautiful olive branches massed around Anthony's feet. Loving France, he thought as he looked down at them, was going to be easy for him.

★ ★ ★

His mobile rang and it was Madame Besson telling him she had another house for him to see near Ruasse. It had just come onto the market.

Anthony heard himself let out an audible sigh. He knew that he couldn't bear another disappointment so soon after the visit to the Mas Lunel. To have been so near to something beautiful and yet so far from it had enraged him.

He asked Madame Besson if this house was on its own — truly on its own — with nothing to spoil the view, and she said, Yes, it was on top of a hill, with its own drive, its own road that led to it and nowhere else. 'Lonely,' she said. 'Very lonely. But I think that's what you want, Monsieur Verey, n'est-ce pas?'

'Yes,' he said. 'I guess so. Is it stone? Is it beautiful?'

There was a moment's pause and Anthony

could tell that Madame Besson had covered the phone receiver with her hand. Then she came back and said: 'I haven't actually seen it. My daughter went to get the details. She says it's quite nice.'

Quite nice.

It didn't interest him then, if that was all it was. 'Quite nice' was not how Anthony deigned to see his future. Better to have no future than to have that. And he was beginning to be weary of estate agents. They didn't seem to understand who he was — *the* Anthony Verey, who lived in fear of ugly surroundings — and so they were wasting his time.

And yet. He had to go on in his search. He had to try to find it, the place where he could live and be happy. Anthony said to Madame Besson that he would come by on Friday and pick up the keys and get directions to the house. He said he wanted to look at this property on his own.

'Whatever you prefer, Monsieur Verey,' she said. 'I will tell the owners. But it is a very isolated place. I wouldn't like you to get lost.'

★   ★   ★

The night before Anthony went to look at this house, he, Veronica and Kitty were invited to dinner with some French friends of Veronica's near Anduze, Monsieur and Madame Sardi. Veronica had redesigned their garden, made it, they said, 'the true garden of our dreams'. The Sardis' gratitude, Veronica told Anthony, often

163

expressed itself in invitations to fabulous meals.

Their house was solid, grey-stuccoed, turreted, a kind of miniature château, whose style of architecture, Anthony commented as they drove in, didn't suit the region.

'Anthony,' said Veronica sternly, 'you're not going to spend the evening making criticisms, are you?'

'Certainly not,' he said. 'I'm too well mannered. But look at this: why isn't it stone? This stucco belongs in the Loire. Or are your friends barbaric enough to have rendered the stone?'

'Shut up, Anthony,' said Veronica. 'We're going to have a nice time.'

'I didn't say we weren't.'

'Shut up then.'

The Sardis — Guy and Marie-Ange — were people at ease with their wealth. The first thing visitors saw was an impressively large fountain, not dissimilar from the one in front of the White House in Washington, DC, that played a sparkling fan of water into a lily pond, set in the middle of an immaculate gravel turning circle, bordered by Florentine cypresses, topiarised box and pincushions of tenerium and santolina. As they got out of the car, Kitty said: 'I love this garden. The air smells of the *maquis*.'

'That's the whole idea,' said Veronica. And Anthony wondered, with a small frisson of pleasure, whether this didn't sound a bit like a snub. He looked at Kitty, dressed for the evening in a navy silk Nehru jacket and boxy white trousers which made her short legs look even shorter. She was smiling. She didn't appear snubbed. But he remembered with relief that, early tomorrow morning, she was setting off for Béziers, to talk to some gallery owner about her pitiful paintings, and so he and V would be alone for at least twenty-four hours. Snub or no snub, she'd soon be gone. Perhaps he'd even be able find a way of *willing* her to stay away.

The Sardis' guests were greeted, not by Marie-Ange, but by a butler, who offered them flutes of champagne from a silver salver. Taking a grateful sip of the champagne, Anthony immediately caught sight of a marble pedestal on which rested a fine nineteenth-century copy of a Borghese vase, very like the one in the Louvre. He couldn't resist stepping nearer to appraise this. He almost put on his glasses to verify his initial findings ('Possible restoration to rim? Probable value, region of £30,000 . . . ') but restrained himself from doing this, afraid to appear too much like a vulgar auctioneer. Nevertheless, this was how Marie-Ange Sardi found him, gulping champagne from the too-meagre flute, and examining the Borghese vase.

'Ah-ha! Veronica told us that you're an antiques collector,' she said in faultless English, 'and I see you've gone straight to the vase. What d'you think?'

'Oh,' said Anthony, 'good evening, Madame Sardi. I'm so sorry. I just couldn't resist a tiny look . . . '

'No, of course, why not? It is rather special. My husband found it in Florence. It's an 1850s

165

copy of the Borghese vase in the Louvre. I adore the dancing figures, don't you?'

Marie-Ange was a woman in her fifties, well-groomed and slim, but with her skin beginning to suffer the ravages of sun-worship. Anthony made his quick assessment and guessed it was astute. ('Possibly part Jewish, despite the Catholic-sounding name. May have brought Guy Sardi some kind of fortune, to which he then added another one in investment banking, rather like Benita and Lloyd Palmer . . . ')

Anthony now dared to whip out his spectacles and put them on. He longed to touch the vase. 'It's very fine,' he said. 'The satyrs on the handles are such an extraordinary detail, aren't they! So you and your husband are collectors, too?'

'No, not really. We just buy things we like. We've got a lot of Louis XVI furniture. And there may be a few pictures that interest you. We have a couple of Corots down here, but we spend most of the year in our house in Paris, so our best treasures are there.'

Ah, thought Anthony, really deep money, then, the kind of unassailable fortune I should have made — always assumed I would make, until I suddenly became aware that the time for making it had gone. Though he smiled and nodded politely at Marie-Ange, he felt himself squirm, once again, with envy. He wanted to turn round and walk back out into the garden and listen to the birds for a moment and then drive away. But Marie-Ange had put a light hand on his arm. 'Do come and meet Guy,' she

166

said, 'and the others.'

Others?

Oh God. Veronica hadn't warned him this was a dinner *party*. And no doubt, the friends of Guy and Marie-Ange Sardi would all be rich, all be serene in their certainty of a future in which their white linen table napkins would always be starched and enormous, their wine served at the correct temperatures, their chauffeurs at the doors, their clothes lined with silk ... As Anthony turned from the vase to follow Marie-Ange into the *salon*, he felt that same sudden weariness come over him that latterly he experienced in his shop after a day when he'd sold nothing.

Guy Sardi was a tanned and handsome man, a little shorter than Anthony, but with a bearing so confident and upright it made him seem larger than he was. His eyes were still beautiful, with thick, dark lashes. These eyes said: I can seduce at will: men and women of my circle, servants, CEOs of international companies, secretaries, casino croupiers, maids, and even dogs come and try to lick my hands . . .

Sardi's handshake was firm, almost brusque, and made Anthony feel limp and old. Looking at Guy Sardi, imagining how he himself appeared through Sardi's eyes, Anthony thought, How completely absurd it is, my desire to go on living! I was finished a long time ago. Why am I so afflicted with this ridiculous tenacity?

He exchanged a few obligatory sentences about the Borghese vase, then — when his host went to welcome a new guest — started to move

167

to Veronica's side. But, as he approached, he heard her talking in French to a woman he vaguely recognised, who might have been a politician or might have been one of those actresses whose name you never quite remember, but who makes a living out of a thousand small appearances in big-budget films. Anthony assessed that such people could be mortally offended if you didn't recognise them, so he made a sideways sashay towards a waiter going round with a champagne bottle and held out his empty glass.

Over the waiter's shoulder, above a small mahogany spinet ('French, late 18th century . . . with a four octave keyboard with ebony naturals (worn) and ivory accidentals'), he spied one of the Corots. He waited for his glass to brim again and then, relieved by this at least and sipping as he went, moved towards the Corot, his left hand agitating involuntarily upwards towards the pocket where his spectacles resided.

Before he was able to concentrate on the picture, however, Anthony's eye was caught by a black-and-white photograph in a silver frame, standing on its own on the spinet. It was a head-and-shoulders photograph of a young man of astonishing beauty. He smiled at the camera. Juvenile curls flopped over one eye. His sensuous mouth was slightly parted to reveal the tutored, white teeth of an adored and pampered child.

Anthony gaped. He knew that his own mouth had literally fallen open and he closed it quickly. He felt slightly breathless. 'That,' he wanted to whisper aloud, 'is what I mean by beauty. That

168

face epitomises human grace and loveliness to me . . . ' By the young man's just-recognisable resemblance to Guy — particularly the same sleepy eyes, with their long eyelashes — Anthony guessed that this was the Sardis' son. He was about twenty-five. He was wearing an ordinary white T-shirt, probably hadn't really posed for the picture . . . just turned to the photographer and smiled, knowing that what this smile expressed was all the certainty, all the inevitable dazzle of his marvellous future. 'Catch me now,' it said, 'before I soar away and leave you all behind . . . '

Marie-Ange, the ever-vigilant hostess, appeared at Anthony's side. Behind them, the chatter in the *salon* was animated, indicating that more people had arrived, and, in truth, Anthony wasn't sure how long he'd been gazing at the photograph of the young man. He was aware that Marie-Ange might think him rude, or at best slightly weird, to spend this cocktail hour snooping at the Sardi family's personal possessions. But, in fact, her voice was amused and gentle as she said: 'You found Nicolas. I took that picture in the garden here last summer.'

'Your son?'

'Yes.'

'He's very . . . handsome. Beautiful, in fact. He's beautiful.'

Marie-Ange gazed lovingly at the photograph. She reached out and touched the young man's floppy hair.

'He's directing a film at the moment. He's only twenty-four and he's directing his first feature film. Guy and I are rather spellbound.'

'I can imagine,' said Anthony. 'I'm spellbound.'

'Well,' said Marie-Ange. 'Now you must come and meet everyone. Most of our friends are lawyers and bankers, so everybody speaks English.'

Lawyers and bankers.

The world is *so* dull, thought Anthony. So cripplingly tedious. So full of all that you've met a thousand times before and which has never moved you and never will. And still it goes on . . .

Marie-Ange Sardi had her hand on his arm and was leading him towards the noisy group of middle-aged people, guzzling their champagne. He had to let himself be steered away, but he couldn't resist turning one last time to look at the photograph of Nicolas.

Come to me, stammered his heart. *Find me, Nicolas. Give me back my life.*

When you live alone, thought Audrun, when you've lived alone for thirty-four years, you find it difficult to endure the presence of a stranger in or near your house. You can't help but imagine all the wrongdoing of which he's capable.

Audrun made coffee for the surveyor while he went in search of boundary markers. Her mind wasn't on the coffee, but on the surveyor's feet, trudging back and forth. She knew what these feet would do: trample flowers, tread down the shine on the new grass, scuff the gravel, stumble into the vegetable patch, imprint the earth.

Boundary markers.

She told the surveyor, whose name was Monsieur Dalbert, that he wouldn't find any of these. She said he would never find them, never. Because this was not how things had been done.

Once, there had been a byre on this plot, where a grey-brown donkey had been tethered in darkness. Sometimes, during Audrun's childhood, Serge had untethered it and it had stood there, blinking in the daylight, while he put panniers on its back and loaded these up with wood or sacks of onions. Audrun could remember cupping her hands gently over the donkey's poor eyes. Then later, after Serge died, Aramon had told her: 'You can build the bungalow there. All right? Where that useless nag expired. Where the byre collapsed. Use the stones as hard-core.'

Monsieur Dalbert wasn't interested in memory. He was interested in certainty. He said he didn't wish to contradict her in an impolite manner, but there would certainly be boundary markers indicating where her ground ended and Aramon's began. The commune of La Callune would have insisted upon these when permission to build her house had been granted.

Out of her kitchen window, she watched him toiling in the afternoon heat. Sun rays bounced off his bald head. He was a small man, but full of petty cruelty, she could tell, proud of his ability to wound. Audrun crumbled some black earth from the geranium pot on her kitchen window sill and threw it in with the ground coffee because she knew this could have the power to quell her anxiety, to watch the surveyor imbibing geranium compost and never knowing it.

She set the tray of coffee things on the terrace table and waited. The dogs in the pound at the Mas Lunel were braying, scenting the stranger, even at this distance. And no doubt Aramon would be smiling up there in the detritus of his life, smiling as he drank, thinking: Now the last reckoning is about to arrive, the one that chucks Audrun out into the arms of Mother Nature, ha! The one that leaves her with nothing except her sainted forest.

Black earth in the coffee; under the floors, the bones of a dead animal, the mossy stones of the fallen byre . . . If these peculiarities could coexist in time, then other more exceptional things could . . . could what? Well . . . they could suddenly *happen*. For who had imagined that Marilyn Monroe would die like *that*, with her poo-poopy-doo soul fluttering out of her arse while a washing machine turned, while people came and went from her house on Fifth Helena Drive, Brentwood, California, USA in the small hours? But that was the way it was. Apparently.

Back and forth Audrun watched him go, the bald surveyor, staring at the driveway, consulting his bulky papers, laying down his steel measure, straightening up, catapulting the measure back into its housing, searching among weeds and nettles. Back and forth, treading everything down.

Then he strutted back and climbed the three steps to the terrace where Audrun waited and plonked the sheaf of builder's plans on the table. With a jabbing finger, he located the boundary markers on the stiff paper: 'Here, here, here and here.'

Audrun stared at him.

'I can't find them,' Monsieur Dalbert said, wiping sweat from his forehead. 'The markers have either been illegally cut or removed from the ground.'

Audrun said in her mind: I told you. There weren't any boundaries.

'They should not be touched, *ever*,' said Monsieur Dalbert. 'Boundary markers are the property of the commune. Did you know that it is a felony to remove them?'

Felony. A thrilling word.

Audrun wanted to remark how numberless, how diverse might be the crimes to which the word could apply. But there was something in the air, in her breath, in her lungs — a heaviness — which made speaking difficult on this late afternoon.

The surveyor surveyed her over his spectacles. (Another one who considered her mad, no doubt, told by Aramon that she couldn't distinguish north from south, had no idea where one thing began and another ended.) She decided that now she would pour out the coffee, soured with earth, but she found that her arm just stayed where it was, by her side. The surveyor shook his head in an exasperated way, as though the coffee mixed with its little sugaring of compost might have been the thing that had brought him here and now he saw that he wasn't going to get any.

The dogs kept up their whining, their yelping for liberty, for meat, for blood. And Audrun watched Monsieur Dalbert turn his head in the direction of these wild hounds and felt in him a sudden welling-up of anxiety. Yes, *felt it*. As though, for a particle of time, infinitely small, she'd left her own body to inhabit the air this stranger was breathing . . .

. . . and this stepping away, this parting from her *self*, it was as familiar to her as the sound of her heart when she lay in her bed in the darkness. She knew that it signified something — something which wasn't meant to happen any more, but which did happen never the less.

Never the less.

Words. Who knew when they were right ones? Who knew?

Now, he's staring at her, terrified, the man whose name she's already forgotten. He's nothing but this terrified stare, very close to her, with his mouth moving, as though speaking or trying to speak, but all sound has vanished. And then it comes swooping down on Audrun: the void.

*   ★   ★

She woke on the floor of her sitting room, covered by her green eiderdown. Marianne Viala was kneeling by her, holding her hand. Somewhere, just out of sight, was another person, waiting, waiting for time to move on.

In a voice that sounded choked and small, Audrun whispered to Marianne: 'Bernadette used to say that if you live in the south . . . so far south as this, where the mistral blows . . . then events just . . . they just . . . '

'Hush,' said Marianne.

'She used to say . . . you don't mould things to your will.'

'Hush,' said Marianne again. 'Have a sip of water.'

★   ★   ★

Later, she woke in her bed. Her warm little bedside light was on, and this was a comforting thing for which she felt grateful. She knew that something had happened because she felt cold and weak. But what?

She looked around, above the bedclothes, to

see whether she was alone. She felt something acrid come in through her nose, an air that was perfumed with some kind of alteration.

'Well,' said a voice, 'you woke up at last.'

So, Aramon was there. Skinny arse on a hard chair. Cigarette in his hand.

'What happened?' she asked him.

'What d'you think happened? You had one of your fits. You did it on purpose, this time. Didn't you?'

She felt hungry. She wanted to say to him: Make me a broth, with vegetables and marrowbones, like Bernadette used to make when we were children. Lift me up and gently spoon the broth into my mouth, with a hand that's steady and kind. But she refused to ask him to do anything for her. Far better to endure hunger or even thirst than to ask Aramon for any favours.

'Here,' he said. 'Here.'

He stubbed out his cigarette. He bent over her so that he could help her up a little in the bed. She had to close her eyes, because his face so near to hers was a terrible thing to see. She lay back against the pillows. Aramon handed her a glass, half full of water, and she drank. And then he turned away and she saw him standing with his back to her, staring at her room.

'It was never up to much, this place,' he said. 'Was it?'

She drank the water, which was tepid. She understood that she was wearing her flowered overall over a blue blouse, but that there didn't seem to be any skirt underneath the overall. She

176

could feel her naked legs touching the sheet. Aramon turned and sat down on the hard chair near the bed. He drew in his breath and let it out again in a long sigh. 'Demolish it in an afternoon, you could,' he said. 'Walls no thicker than a loaf of bread.'

Audrun tried to think her way back into the day that was passing or had already passed. She believed that she remembered Marianne arriving with one of her famous *tartes au chocolat*, but she couldn't recall whether they'd eaten any of it or not, or whether, even, that had been on a different day.

It felt to Audrun as though she hadn't put anything into her stomach for a long time. And now, through the open curtains, she could see that it was night.

'The thing is,' said Aramon. 'We know where we stand, now. Eh? The survey makes it clear.'

He seemed to be waiting for her to speak, but she couldn't find anything to say because she didn't know what he was talking about.

'I'm calling those agents tomorrow,' he said. 'Tell them to send the English buyer back. If he knows this little dump will soon be gone, he'll pay my price. Then we can all begin again.'

Begin again . . .

This thought went whispering round the shadowy room. Audrun could hear the wind rising, trying to drown it out. Her longing for the marrowbone broth was a raging thing now, she felt so starved of anything good. Aramon lit another cigarette and said: 'Marianne says you can live with her for a bit. I think that's pretty decent of her, don't you? But I don't suppose you can stay there for ever. You have to decide, Audrun: d'you want to build a place in your wood? Or sell up? With what you'd get for the woodland, you might be able to afford an apartment in Ruasse.'

★ ★ ★

At the age of eleven, Anthony was sent away from Hampshire to a boarding school in Sussex. Ever since that day, he'd had difficulty falling asleep at night.

'Verey!' his housemaster, Mr Perkins (known by the boys as 'Polly'), often snapped at morning roll-call outside the refectory. 'You look half dead. Straighten up, boy!'

Anthony had tried to tell Polly that he'd forgotten the trick of how to fall asleep, a trick apparently taken for granted by all the other boys in the dormitory. He watched and heard them perform it, one by one. They turned over and folded their arms around their pillows, or let their elbows lie across their faces, and in moments — in *seconds* — the trick seemed to be accomplished and they sounded blithe in their rest. But he, Anthony, lay in the not-quite-darkness, listening to all the rhythmical breathing and sighing, envying the sleepers with his whole being, longing to cross over to where they'd gone, but unable to do so. Sometimes, he fell asleep just as it got light, or moments before the morning alarm bell sounded at five to seven, or not at all.

178

Verey, you look half dead. Straighten up, boy!

Over the years, Anthony had devised hundreds of different ways of trying to soothe himself into unconsciousness, but this never-ending management of sleep felt to him like some kind of unjust punishment, some miserable penance which, if Lal hadn't sent him away to boarding school, he would never have had to pay.

He sometimes thought that, if his mother were suddenly returned to life, there would be a few things he'd have to berate her for. He'd do it lovingly, of course. He'd hold her hand in his or he'd place her feet gently on his lap and massage them with his long, sensitive fingers, but he'd nevertheless remind her that quite frequently, along the shortish thing that had been her life, she'd committed crimes of thoughtlessness.

Now, in Veronica's spare room after a late return from the Sardis' dinner party, Anthony endured it yet again, that old torturing wakefulness, for which there was never any sure remedy. The sleigh bed felt hard and cramped. Anthony's head ached from drinking too much champagne.

He had a thirst which water didn't seem able to quench.

Images of the beautiful boy, Nicolas, hovered at the edges of his mind. He had an extraordinary longing — not experienced for months — to hold someone, *this* someone, in his arms, and he didn't want to let this feeling evaporate.

He touched himself. He seldom strayed into the traps and delusions of the auto-erotic. This

179

arena depressed him, as though it returned him always and inevitably to the grubbiness of the boarding-school dormitory. But now, Anthony closed his eyes and imagined himself with Nicolas in a spacious hotel suite, in New York City, where the bed was soft and wide and the drapes at the windows heavy and thick. The New York traffic growled and shimmered outside in the street. France and England felt so far away, it was as if there might be no return to either of these places. Nicolas kissed him. The excitement Anthony already felt was intense and it thrilled him to feel such urgent desire once again. He'd been dead, dead in his body for so long, but now he was alive. He laid the precocious boy across the big bed. His young body was tanned and slim and strong. Anthony slowly removed his own clothes, never taking his eyes from Nicolas. The boy held out one arm.

Naked now and not one bit embarrassed by his ageing nakedness, Anthony climbed onto the bed and kissed Nicolas again and then straddled him and knelt above his face. He didn't want to hurt or damage any part of such a dazzling being. Beauty like this had to be respected. All he did was touch the boy's sensual, rosy mouth with his thumb and then Nicolas lifted himself up and Anthony imagined the mouth yearning, open now, like the mouth of an infant yearning for the teat, and it fastened round his cock and began lapping, and in not more than thirty seconds the divine mouth brought him off.

★ ★ ★

Afterwards, he lay very still. He felt as tired as a long-distance runner.

★ ★ ★

He slept and dreamed of Lal's dying. It unravelled in the dream exactly as it had been.

Veronica was away in Italy, on some expensive garden design course, when Lal had at last owned up to her cancer. Lal hadn't wanted her oh-so-healthy daughter alerted. She said she was having what she called 'a little bout of sickness', but promised she would be well again by the time Veronica got back.

Lal was taken to a hospital in Andover. On the morning of her third day in a blank little private room, with her name, Mrs Raymond Verey, on a card next to the door, Anthony had driven down from London to visit her.

It hadn't been far from his thirty-fifth birthday.

The night before, he hadn't slept at all. By the time he arrived in Andover, his body was jumpy with exhaustion.

Lal's skin was waxy and yellow. Into her frail arm dripped some life-prolonging solution. She was drugged on morphine and drifted in and out of consciousness. Anthony sat beside her and read aloud from her favourite book, *Staying On* by Paul Scott. From time to time, he knew that Lal was listening because a smile tugged gently at the corners of her mouth and, when he stopped, she once or twice muttered, 'Go on, darling,' and so he went on:

181

'It was amazing how strong even smaller-built women than Lila could be, and how determined. Their sudden inexplicable whims and preferences in what seemed to him irrelevant matters (for example y-fronted underwear instead of the looser cooler boxer-style trunks) were equally astonishing. It was all part of their charm, of course, not knowing what they'd say or do next, not knowing where you stood with them. Or lay. On the one night he had succeeded in catching Hot Chichanya's eye in Ranpur and been admitted to her room, she had laughed at his underpants . . . '

Then it was lunchtime at the hospital and some nurse plonked something down for Lal, a meal Anthony knew she wouldn't be able to eat, and he left her to go to the cafeteria for some coffee, to try to keep himself awake, so that he could resume his reading of Staying On in the afternoon. But when he got to the cafeteria he realised that he couldn't keep awake another minute and so he went to his car and climbed inside it and fell asleep.

He didn't know how long he slept in the car that afternoon. One hour? Two? He only remembered opening the car door and getting out and seeing a golden sun shining on a low pyrocanthus hedge with fat berries like coral beads, and feeling the beginning of autumn in the scent of things.

When he got back to Lal's hospital room, she was dead.

Her eyes had already been closed by some nurse or doctor, the pillow taken from under her head so that her jaw wouldn't drop open. Her

182

little thin arm was already cooling. And yet
— horrible thing — the meal that had been
brought to her was still there on its plastic tray,
beside Lal's paperback copy of *Staying On*: two
slices of ham going dark at their edges, coleslaw
in a vinegary salad cream . . .

Mixed in with Anthony's feelings of loss was a
rage against the random events which had taken
him out to his car, stuck him there, snoring in a
metal box, when he should have been here, at
Lal's side, breathing with her, breath for breath,
her comforter, the last witness to the completion
of her journey. This dereliction was unimaginably terrible to him. More terrible in its way than
the fact of Lal's dying. Because the crime was so
plain and manifest: he'd deserted his beloved Lal
exactly when she needed him most, and he knew
beyond all certainty that he could never ever let
himself be forgiven.

He tortured himself with the notion that
perhaps she'd even called his name and got no
answer. Perhaps she'd even felt strong enough to
say: 'Go on with the story, darling. Go on about
the boxer shorts. It's such a scream.'

And then she'd waited for the reading to
resume, for the sound of his voice which
consoled her, but nothing was heard, and so she
knew she was alone and that everything was
getting dark.

★　★　★

The sound of a car starting up woke Anthony.
When he got downstairs, he found Veronica

183

alone, making apricot jam, humming as she worked.

Kitty had already left for Béziers.

He sat at the kitchen table and Veronica brought him a fresh croissant and some coffee and then she stared at him in her tender, maternal way. 'Anthony,' she said brightly, 'perhaps this house you're going to see will be the one.'

He shrugged. He put his hands around the coffee bowl. He was glad he was at last alone with V. He was tempted to tell her about his dream of Lal, but knew she wouldn't have any patience with it.

His mobile rang and it was Lloyd Palmer, also sounding breezy. They haven't seen it, Anthony thought, neither V nor Lloyd. They've never glimpsed the face of the old crone in the tapestry, with her lock of black hair hanging loose from the weave . . .

'Lloyd,' said Anthony in a flat voice. 'Good to hear you.'

'What's wrong?' said Lloyd. 'You sound ill, or something.'

Verey, you look half dead. Straighten up, boy!

'No. I'm fine. How's London?'

'It's good. Extraordinary bloody weather! You'd think it was June, not April. Benita's buying Prada swimwear. How's France?'

'It's all right. Hot here, too. I'm going to look at another house today.'

'OK. So you haven't found anything you want to buy?'

'Well, I saw one. It had fantastic potential, but

184

then I discovered it was blighted.'

'What d'you mean, blighted?'

'There was an ugly bungalow in its sightlines.'

'OK, right. QED. Well look, old man, I realise I was a bit tetchy about money the last time we talked. Of course I'm willing to sell shares for you if you want me to. I'll try and pull out the best, but you're still going to take a shit-load of losses . . . '

'Don't worry about it at the moment, Lloyd,' said Anthony. 'If I fall in love with anything, I'll call you.'

They moved on to talking about England. Lloyd said the grass in Kensington Gardens was already going brown in the spring heatwave. He said he was buying Benita a new E-class Mercedes for her birthday. Silver grey. He said he hoped the crack-heads of Ladbroke Grove wouldn't vandalise the bloody thing before she'd done her first thousand miles.

Anthony ended the call. Lloyd, he thought, is a good man, a kind man at heart; he just can't stop himself from sounding smug.

He went back to drinking his coffee and Veronica resumed stirring her apricot jam as she asked him what he wanted for supper.

'Liver,' he answered. 'Let's have liver and mashed potato, like Mrs Brigstock used to make.'

Veronica crossed to him and bent down and put a kiss on his springy hair.

'You have to let go of the past, darling,' she said.

'Why?' he said. 'I like it there.'

Anthony stood in front of the dressing-table mirror in his bedroom and looked at himself. Strong daylight from the nearby window shone on him and he stared at the lines on his forehead and at the narrow little pinched slit that his mouth had become.

He thought about Dirk Bogarde playing Aschenbach in the film of Thomas Mann's *Death in Venice*, getting his hair dyed and lips made up, so that . . . so that *what*? So that the exquisite boy Tadzio would return his gaze for just a fraction longer? So that the evidence of his own mortality wouldn't offend both himself and Tadzio in quite such an awkward and debilitating way?

Anthony saw that the face in the looking glass was much too old to be attractive to Nicolas Sardi. Even if he managed to create a room of exceptional beauty (in a house of exceptional beauty) in which to receive the young man, Nicolas would surely never ever set foot inside it, because he, Anthony, was too flawed and damaged by time to be of interest to him.

He examined his teeth, which were the colour of beeswax candles. Should he pay for some expensive whitening treatment when he got back to London? Or would such a costly step prove to be as vain and pitiful as Aschenbach's hair dye?

He turned away and straightened his back. At least desire had returned.

That was the first step towards something, wasn't it? In his imaginary New York night, he'd felt wonderfully potent and alive.

186

Whenever Aramon went down to the small general store in La Callune in the early morning, which he did perhaps twice a week, he bought a copy of the local paper, *Ruasse Libre*.

Back at the Mas Lunel, he'd make himself coffee, put on his spectacles, spread the paper out on the table, and spend the rest of the morning reading it from cover to cover. If he was lucky, there would be some gripping murder story to spice up all the rest of the mundane content: news of another protest by farmers against the high cost of diesel; the arrival in the region of a genetically modified strain of drought-resistant maize; reports of local fêtes, bullfights, pop concerts, art exhibitions, *boules* championships and car boot sales; surveys of river levels, forest fires, campsite numbers and falling infant-school attendance . . .

It amused Aramon to read how the world still danced about in its whirl of pointless endeavour. It cheered him to imagine the meandering crowds at a car boot sale, buying up mutilated books and brass trinkets and bits of crockery — when they could have stayed at home, like him, and saved their money.

Sometimes, he considered buying a ticket for a bullfight. He used to enjoy the atmosphere of terror, and the ear-splitting brass instruments glinting in the heat. The courage of the bulls, the way they never tired, even when their necks were running with blood, always moved him, somehow. But in recent years, he'd begun to find the matadors ridiculous: their strutting pride, their sequined arses. He now longed for the bull to kill the bullfighter, to see *him* dragged away to a slaughterhouse through the dust . . .

Today, a headline on the front of *Ruasse Libre* caught his eye: *Displacement of local people by foreigners must end, says Mayor*. The article included a graph showing how house prices in the Cévennes had risen in the last ten years, mainly due to '*foreigners*' and quoted the mayor of Ruasse as saying:

> *Enough is enough in our beautiful region. Encroachment has gone too far. The sale of property to non-French nationals must now be closely monitored and possibly made subject to quotas. We do not condone racial discrimination, but we find ourselves now living in an age when our own young people, born in our villages, can no longer afford to buy or build houses here in the land they know and love, because of the invasion by Belgians, Dutch, Swiss and British, in search of second homes. And so I think we have to ask: why should these fortunate people have the right to second homes, while our children are effectively deprived of their right to homes of any kind?*

Aramon read this article several times, until his eyes hurt. Seldom did anything written in *Ruasse*

188

Libre appear to be talking to him — but this was.

He thought about the €475,000 that was out there waiting for him — waiting to release him into a new and blameless life — and he saw that, with one stroke, the interfering mayor of Ruasse might have put his whole future in jeopardy. He banged his fist on the table. 'Idiot!' he barked aloud. 'Arsehole!'

He picked up the telephone and called the agents. He wanted to tell them to send the English art collector back fast, to say that the question of Audrun's bungalow was all settled and taken care of, but he knew that it was no use lying about this. He could lie to Audrun, because she didn't grasp one single thing about how the world worked, but the bossy, know-all agents would surely demand to see the surveyor's report, and there was no report because no boundary markers had been found.

Aramon contented himself with shouting at Madame Besson, asking her why no more purchasers had been to see the house, telling her that a sale was imperative — imperative *now*, this month — before some idiot mayor began interfering with his rights . . . Madame Besson stayed calm and asked him about the status of his sister's house. Was she leaving? Would the bungalow be included in the sale? If the bungalow could be included, she said, then the whole proposition would be very much easier to market . . .

Aramon rubbed his eyes.

'Madame,' he said, forcing himself to become polite, 'I'm almost a hundred per cent sure that my sister will be persuaded to leave. Almost a hundred per cent certain. Unfortunately, the surveyor I employed wasn't able to complete his report because my sister was taken ill while he was there. But I'm going to explain the situation again to her and I think when she understands it properly — particularly when I show her the article in *Ruasse Libre* which could jeopardise my future — she'll definitely agree to leave.'

'Well,' said Madame Besson, 'that would, of course, change the prospects for a fast sale.'

'But what about the price?' said Aramon. 'What could we ask if the bungalow was sold with the mas?'

There was a pause, and Aramon heard the snicker of Madame Besson's cigarette lighter close to the phone. Then, she said: 'I'd need to look round the bungalow — and the land that goes with it. But you'd probably be talking about something close to 600,000 euro.'

600,000 euro!

The wonder in this sum. The salvation in it. For a moment or two, it left Aramon speechless.

'But the other thing I've been thinking about,' said Madame Besson, 'are the vine terraces. I noticed the last time I was there that you hadn't made much progress on these.'

'I *have* made progress!' protested Aramon. 'I'm taking all that in hand . . . '

'The thing is that people find it difficult to imagine what they can't properly see.'

'Yes,' said Aramon. 'I understand. I'm going to work night and day on the terraces. Night and day!'

* * *

It was almost eleven o'clock by the time Anthony picked up the keys and directions to the house from Madame Besson's office. On Madame Besson's desk, a white fan moved the tepid air in a feeble rotation. When she handed Anthony the badly printed photograph and the house description, she said: 'This one, it is very isolated . . . *vous voyez?*'

It was a big stone building that looked dark and lightless in the landscape. On one side of it was a small plantation of umbrella pines, but elsewhere there appeared to be only scrub and stones. The heavy slate roof was lumpy and bowed between the gable ends.

'It looks almost derelict . . . ' Anthony said.

'*Ah, non!*' snapped Madame Besson. 'The owners are Swiss.'

'So why are they selling?'

Madame Besson shrugged impatiently as her phone began ringing and she reached to answer it. 'They told my daughter they don't use it any more,' she said. 'That's all I know.'

Anthony went out to his car, which had become burning hot in the space of ten or fifteen minutes. He sat with the door open, studying the map, and worked out that he had at least twenty miles to drive on a perilous corniche of a road. And he thought that this might be why the owners were giving up the house — because no one came to visit them any more; they didn't want to risk their lives getting there.

Perhaps the Swiss couple had loved the place

191

at first precisely *for* its mountainous isolation, and then . . . a few summers passed and they sat under the umbrella pines and looked out at the valley below and realised that they'd put themselves out of reach of all their friends. And, Anthony asked himself, was this what he really wanted to do? Because here, according to his reading of the road map, even the distance between him and Veronica at Les Glaniques would seem significant. And what would the night feel like in such a place? Or the winter?

He started the car and drove. He felt he had to see the house — just in case the feeling returned, that beautiful feeling of wanting to possess something. But now, suddenly, the route that lay ahead up the mountain made him feel afraid. What if he got lost up there, or the car broke down, or he misjudged a corner and crashed over the edge into the void?

Veronica had packed water for him in a cold-bag. She'd told him the barometer was rising and rising and the heat might suddenly be pitiless up where he was going and if he set off on a walk — which he'd told her he planned to do — he couldn't be sure of finding a river or a spring.

Anthony now felt grateful for the water, for V's unwavering motherliness. But it seemed to him that water wasn't enough: he needed food too, to sustain him in case of an emergency, and he remembered the stall called *La Bonne Baguette* where they had stopped on their way to the Mas Lunel and bought sandwiches. He knew that he'd pass this before he crossed the river, near

192

the village of La Callune, and decided he'd buy at least two sandwiches. With sandwiches and water, he'd be all right. These would be a kind of insurance against the unforeseen.

Here it came now, *La Bonne Baguette*, but Anthony quickly saw that the lay-by where Madame Besson had parked her car on the previous trip was entirely occupied by a tanker-truck. He swore. He was being tailgated by an impatient BMW driver and there was nowhere else to stop. In the ordinary way, he knew he would have resigned himself to being hungry later in the day and driven on, but, suddenly, he saw this getting of a sandwich as a vitally important thing. And there would be no other stall or small café on the road. These hills, as far as he could tell, were empty of every petty amenity. So he *had* to get back to *La Bonne Baguette*.

He slowed down. The BMW kept pulling out, trying to pass. Then Anthony came to a point where the road widened into a bend and provided a narrow hard shoulder of gravel for about a hundred yards, and he dinked the black Renault onto this and came to a noisy stop.

The BMW driver screamed at him as he sped away. Anthony returned the hand insult and climbed out of the car. He inched round it and began the trek back to the sandwich stall.

The sun glinted on rock and road. The narrow space in which he had to walk, between the granite face of the cutting and the oncoming cars, felt so perilously small that he could imagine his feet being run over. His heart was fluttering with panic, and sweat began to slide down the back of his neck, but the idea of going on without his sandwich had now become unthinkable. The sandwich had become the thing that would get him through this day, through whatever lay in wait for him. So he pressed himself close to the rock wall and trudged on. Motorists stared at him — an ageing tourist on foot in a place where nobody was intended to walk. But he didn't care what people thought; he just wanted to get his hands on the sandwich.

And he was here at last. He recognised the stall-holder, a corpulent, tough-seeming man with a stubbled chin. He was chatting to the driver of the tanker-truck. The two men were old friends, it seemed. A joke made them suddenly crease up with laughter and the stall-holder wiped his mouth with a scarlet handkerchief as he turned to give his reluctant attention to Anthony.

'*Alors, Monsieur?*'

Camembert and tomato, he'd chosen last time. He hadn't wanted to risk ham or saucisson, in case these made him ill. (He knew he was fastidious to the point of neurosis, but who cared? He knew a woman who'd died from eating sushi, so why not from salami, improperly chilled?) He surveyed the selection of sandwiches, then pointed again at the Camembert.

'*Deux comme ça, s'il vous plaît, Monsieur.*'

He saw the wide brown hand reach for the sandwiches, each in its cellophane wrapper inscribed *La Bonne Baguette: que c'est bonne!*

And he saw his own hands shaking as he fumbled to pay for them.

★ ★ ★

Back in the car, Anthony turned the air-conditioning down to 16° and waited there for a moment or two, letting the Renault cool, letting his heart rate slow.

Then he set off again and quickly came across the sign to the narrow road that crossed one arm of the River Gardon and branched away to the west, heading for high ground. The road soon enough began the zigzag indicated on the map and Anthony forced himself to stay calm as he steered the Renault into a slow waltz round the impossible turns. On either side of the road were dense firs, now, planted so closely together that nothing grew in the darkness underneath them and Anthony distracted himself from the perils of the road with a memory of these trees from his childhood.

Raymond and Lal and Anthony and Veronica had been driving in Raymond's Rover to a lunch party near Newbury when Lal had caught sight of a Forestry Commission fir plantation and burst out: 'Look at that! Raymond. Children. Just look what they're doing: they're farming trees now. *Frightful!* I think it's absolutely frightful.'

'It's for building materials, darling,' said Raymond. 'For planks and stuff.'

'I don't care what it's for. They shouldn't farm trees like that. They never did in South Africa

195

and we had plenty of planks.'

So then, there had been yet another thing for Anthony to worry about: Lal's eyes alighting on *farmed trees* and her mood suddenly changing to crossness and snappiness and dislike for her adopted country, his only home.

He'd wanted to say something amusing, something that would diffuse her irritation, but he hadn't been able to think up anything amusing and they'd driven on in silence until Veronica — unwisely as it turned out — ventured: 'Ma, you can't really use the word 'farming' in relation to trees. They're Douglas firs, *Pseudotsuga menziesii*, and they're grown in plantations all over Europe.' And Lal had lit a Peter Stuyvesant cigarette with the car lighter and, without turning round, had said quietly: 'Veronica, why are you such an annoying, fat little know-all?'

A dreadful shriek of laughter had broken free from Anthony. He hadn't meant to laugh, because it was terrible, what Lal had just said. *Terrible*. He'd put a hand to his mouth, as though trying to press the inappropriate laugh back into his throat. He hated himself for making such an awful sound and knew that V would be justified in hating him, too. He looked at Veronica, expecting to see her in tears. But she wasn't in tears. She was just looking calmly out of her window at the passing countryside.

Now, as the road unravelled in the high Cévennes, narrowing, twisting, changing direction, its verges here and there littered with evidence of rock falls, Anthony found himself wishing — despite the cruel way his mother had crushed V, despite his inappropriate shriek of laughter — that he was thirteen years old again, driving along a softly undulating B-road in Berkshire, with all his life to come.

★ ★ ★

Veronica was enjoying her solitary day.

She'd bought calves' liver and *lardons* at the *boucherie* and fresh bread from the *boulangerie* and potatoes, vegetables and fruit from her favourite roadside stall, and now all this was safely stowed in the kitchen and she was working on a section of *Gardening without Rain* entitled 'Decorative Gravels'.

It was cool in her study, with the shutters half-closed against the morning sun, but Veronica could just hear and appreciate the sounds of the garden: the sparrows on the wall near the stone bird-bath, the cicadas in the Spanish mulberry outside her window, a tiny breeze rattling the palm fronds.

. . . the type of gravel most favoured for drives and walkways in southern France [she wrote] *is a composite of sand and very small, rounded stones. Its colour is pleasing: it can appear almost white in very dry weather and darkens to a straw shade after rainfall. It is not much used in England, but in France it can be found in the Tuilerie Gardens in Paris and on boules pitches up and down the land.*

197

She looked glumly at this last sentence and knew she had to get rid of 'up and down the land', a phrase so embarrassingly weak, it made her blush. Veronica was well aware that she wasn't a very good writer, but she also knew that the kind of people who'd buy Gardening without Rain probably wouldn't notice this. All they wanted was knowledge and tips and hard information. Yet she always struggled to make her prose as readable as possible, partly to please the publisher's editor, a beauty called Melissa, with whom she was very mildly infatuated. Perhaps, also, she heard Lal's voice somewhere in her head, telling her that her school essays were 'miserably illiterate' and that she'd never get on in the world if she couldn't string proper sentences together.

But she *had* got on in the world. *See me now, Mother. I am happy and I am quite success-ful* . . . The stringing together of words — any incompetence she might have had in this area of endeavour — had turned out not to matter very much at all. Horticulture and colour and form — her understanding of these — had been what mattered.

She decided to ignore '*up and down the land*' for the time being and wrote on:

Gravels, in general, play an important part in the creation of the drought-resistant garden. Where you might be tempted to sow a lawn — that thirsty entity! — think again, and create a gravel space. Consider, even, exotic gravels, such as the black volcanic gravel brought back from Tahiti by Bougainville in 1767. This is an expensive variety, but highly suited to the 'modern' look currently in favour in garden design, where surprising colours (blacks, greys and startling royal blues) can create the unforgettable.

Veronica paused. She felt, suddenly, that her work was going less than brilliantly this morning. 'The unforgettable', for instance, was pathetically wrong; it was just an abstraction hanging there on the end of the paragraph, like an over-ripe fig about to drop off onto Bougainville's wretched Tahitian gravel! She knew that Melissa wouldn't let 'the unforgettable' pass, but again, Veronica couldn't immediately see how she could replace it with something more elegantly formed and firmly attached to the rest of the sentence.

She mused that it would have been very useful to have had Melissa there with her, lying on the cushion-strewn day-bed perhaps, so that she could read everything out to her, sentence by sentence and get from her immediately what she often referred to as 'a titchy bit of editorial input, Veronica'. That way, the chapter on 'Decorative Gravels' would certainly have progressed quite far by the time Kitty returned the following day.

Veronica now looked up. Her gaze fell on the brass carriage clock (an expensive gift from Anthony) on her mantelpiece, and she saw that time had moved on in what felt like a sudden scamper and that it was just before one o'clock.

Kitty had promised to call around eleven, to announce her safe arrival in Béziers, but no call had come.

Veronica picked up the phone and dialled Kitty's mobile. The phone clicked straight to Kitty's abrupt and slightly cross-sounding voicemail: 'Kitty Meadows here. Leave a message please. Thank you. Veuillez laisser un message, s'il vous plaît. Merci.'

'Kitty,' said Veronica. 'It's me. Hope you're all right, darling. Thinking of you and have my fingers crossed about the gallery. I've absolutely got a feeling that they're going to say yes. Almost bought some champagne in the village, but thought this might be tempting fate. Anyway, all's fine here. It's very peaceful on my own and I'm working away on the 'Gravels' chapter. Call me when you have a moment. Lots of love.'

She tried to get back to her writing. She began a sentence about the inadvisability of laying polythene membranes under gravelled spaces to control weeds. *Before making a decision about this*, she wrote, *consider closely the attendant risk of water-logging or flooding during the* crue *season and the* — Then she broke off, suddenly anguished by her failure to reach Kitty.

Kitty's car was old and small. Yet even in this little car she had to drive almost crushed against the steering wheel so that her short legs could reach the pedals. She was a courageous driver, but this image of tiny Kitty buzzing and bumping along the autoroutes, in the jet stream of disdainful Audis and Mercedes, in the annihilating shadows of container trucks, always made Veronica's heart lurch with terror.

She got up from her desk and went out onto the stone terrace. The sun was burning hot on her face and as she began a slow walk round the garden, still green from the wet winter and early spring, she knew that now it was coming back again, the time when much of what was growing here would be at risk once more from drought, that risk only lessened by her vigilance, hers and Kitty's. She walked to the old stone well and peered down into it, holding tightly to the rim. She could see that the water level had already fallen.

⋆ ⋆ ⋆

Veronica ate a slice of *tarte aux oignons* and a salad for her lunch and attempted to return to her writing. She left two more messages for Kitty during the afternoon, but no call came in. She kept telling herself that if Kitty's mobile was still putting out her voicemail, then it — and therefore Kitty — couldn't have been mangled in a car crash.

She wanted the afternoon to pass — so that Anthony would come back and then at least her anxiety about Kitty could be shared with someone — but she also wanted it *not to pass*, wanted it *not to get late*, because then her reasons to be anxious would only multiply, hour upon hour.

She began to feel so paralysed by this conflict with time that she eventually found herself standing completely still in the middle of her

201

kitchen, with no seeming inclination to move in any direction or assign herself any task. Without thinking about it, she started to cry. She knew this was a stupid thing to begin doing and yet, once indulged in, it felt oddly appropriate to the moment. She tore off a strip of kitchen paper and buried her face in this and noted that her tears were warm, almost hot, like blood is hot.

Now the telephone rang.

Veronica blew her nose and ran to it. She felt certain that it was going to be Kitty and already she saw how ridiculous she was, standing there with scalding tears blotching her cheeks for no real reason, and when she said 'Hello', she tried very hard to disguise the choke that was in her voice. But it wasn't Kitty. It was Madame Besson.

'Excuse me for disturbing you,' said Madame Besson in English. 'May I talk with Monsieur Verey?'

'Monsieur Verey isn't here,' said Veronica.

Speaking seemed to release in her a new surge of panic. *Kitty is dead, then. This voice is not hers. Kitty is dead in her crumpled little car . . .*

'Ah,' said Madame Besson. 'OK. I'm sorry to disturb you.'

Veronica understood that Madame Besson was about to hang up and said quickly: 'Is anything wrong, Madame Besson? Did my brother go to see the house?'

Madame Besson cleared her throat. 'He had the keys at eleven o'clock,' she said. 'He told me he would return them by two. But he has not returned them and now I have another couple

202

wishing to see this house.'

'Oh,' said Veronica. 'Well, I'm sorry. I think he planned to go for a walk somewhere up there . . .'

'Yes? But he said he would be back here by two o'clock and it is now almost five.'

Veronica blinked. 'I'll call Anthony,' she said. 'He's got his mobile with him.'

'Thank you,' said Madame Besson. 'I'm leaving the office in half an hour. Please ask your brother to get the keys to me tomorrow morning. I have only the one set and the owners are in Switzerland.'

★ ★ ★

When Veronica dialled Anthony's phone, there was no sound from it.

She tried a second time and it was the same: no beep or tone or buzz or anything. Only silence.

Veronica made mint tea and sat at the kitchen table, sipping it. She had no urge to cry now. She felt sick and hoped the tea would alleviate this. The thought of cooking the calves' liver and the *lardons* made her gag.

When the nausea diminished a little, it was replaced by a feeling of exhaustion and Veronica made her way with slow steps up to her bedroom. She kicked off her shoes and lay down. She stared at the pillow next to hers, the place where Kitty's head always lay. She reached out and clasped the pillow to her and closed her eyes.

* ★ *

When she woke up, she was aware that darkness was beginning to shadow the room, not night yet, but a blue and lonely dusk. Then, she became conscious of a sudden intrusive sound. It was the telephone. Veronica reached out, still groggy from her sleep, and just held the phone to her ear, waiting for whatever news was going to come from it.

'Veronica,' said Kitty's voice. 'It's me.'

Relief surged in, almost as sweet as sexual pleasure. But then anger followed and Veronica began yelling at Kitty: why hadn't she called or sent a text or picked up her phone? Why had she let her go mad with worry? How could she be so selfish and unimaginative?

'I'm sorry,' said Kitty. 'I'm sorry . . . '

'But *WHY*?' shouted Veronica. 'You said you'd call. I left tons of messages. I thought you were *dead*!'

'I'm sorry,' said Kitty again. 'I couldn't call. Or text. I just couldn't.'

'What d'you mean, you just couldn't? And you sound drunk or something. What happened?'

'Nothing happened,' said Kitty. 'That's exactly it. Nothing. So yes, I am a bit drunk. I'm at a hotel.'

'A hotel? What are you talking about? I thought you were going to stay with André and Gilles.'

'Yes. Couldn't face that either . . . I called them . . . '

'Kitty, what in the world — '

204

'Don't make me say it, Veronica. Don't make me say it.'

'Say what?'

'Don't make me say it!'

Veronica was silent. She felt all her crossness subside, cursed herself for not understanding sooner what had happened. Then she said quietly: 'All right. I'll say it. The gallery turned you down.'

Veronica swung her feet off the bed. At the window, now, the sky was darkening all the while. She could hear Kitty crying.

'Kitty,' she said, 'there are other galleries. Are you listening to me? There are hundreds of other galleries we can approach.'

After Kitty had hung up, contrite, consoled a little, promising to get some supper and go to bed, Veronica made her way downstairs and found the house dark and silent. It was near to eight o'clock. She took the calves' liver out of the fridge and unwrapped it and began slicing it. She kept looking up, thinking she heard Anthony's hired Renault coming down the gravel driveway, but no car appeared.

Audrun knew she had to do everything calmly and carefully now, and in the right order.

First, she put all her clothes into her washing machine and set it on a long, hot programme. She tried to stop herself from thinking about that other washing machine, that old American one, turning in the night, long ago on Fifth Helena Drive, but she couldn't prevent this image from coming into her mind.

Next, she ran a bath and washed every part of herself, including her hair, then scrubbed the bath with abrasive cleaner and ran the shower hose round and round the tub until it shone.

When her hair was dry, she tugged on a cardigan and went walking in her wood. She picked some bluebells and took them home and put them into a jar and admired them and breathed their scent. Then, she got into her little rusty car and drove down to the village. She knocked on Marianne's door.

She noticed Jeanne Viala's Renault parked outside the house and she went in calmly and greeted Marianne and her daughter. She recognised on Marianne's face that smile of contentment it wore whenever Jeanne came to visit, and she thought how fine it might have been to have had a daughter — the daughter of somebody she loved. Raoul Molezon had two grown-up daughters by his wife, Françoise, and

Audrun had nobody.

'Don't let me disturb you,' she said. 'I just wanted to come and say a *petit bonjour*.'

'You're not disturbing us,' said Jeanne. 'Come and sit down.'

They embraced each other; this cheek, that cheek, then this cheek again — the threefold greeting the people of the *midi* had always favoured. Then they sat around the kitchen table. Marianne was boiling snails — the delicacy Jeanne asked for whenever she came back to La Callune. Jeanne was thirty now, and dedicated to her job as a teacher in Ruasse. She looked like a younger version of her mother, slim and dark, with a slow, sweet smile.

'How are the schoolchildren behaving themselves?' asked Audrun. 'I don't know any children any more. Tell me what they're like.'

Jeanne Viala unclipped the tortoiseshell comb holding back her hair, then gathered the hair up and fastened it again. In time, Audrun thought, especially if no husband comes along — no man kind enough — Jeanne's face will begin to look severe.

'They're restless,' said Jeanne. 'It's really difficult to get them to concentrate on any kind of lesson for long.'

'I'd heard that said before,' said Audrun. 'I expect it's the city that makes them like that, is it?'

'I don't know. I suppose computer games and television and all those indoor things play a part. And they don't know any history, so they often don't understand what they're looking at. It's

207

shocking, for instance, how little some of them know about this region. They were born here, but they haven't really learned about its past.'

'And yet,' said Audrun, 'its past is so long . . .'

'Exactly,' said Jeanne. 'They haven't, for instance, any true idea how productive the Cévennes used to be. I'm arranging visits to an olive oil factory and to the Museum of Cévenol Silk Production, to learn how the worms were reared, and about the *filatures*, and we're going to visit some working farms.'

'Ah,' said Audrun. 'We could tell them a lot about the farms, Marianne, couldn't we?'

'Yes we could,' said Marianne. Then she got up to stir her snail pot. On the table were the garlic and oil and fresh parsley she'd soon use to make the sauce. Jeanne lit a cigarette and offered the packet to Audrun, who waved it away.

'I bet Aramon still smokes, doesn't he?' said Jeanne with a smile.

'Oh yes,' said Audrun. 'He does. Cigarettes and cheroots. It'll kill him one day . . .'

'I hear he's leaving, anyway.'

'What, Jeanne?'

'I hear he's selling the mas.'

Audrun looked down at her hands on the table. She felt slightly cold in the room, despite the heat under the snail pot and the evening sun at the window. She said: 'Money's all he thinks about now. That's the way he is. Money and drink and cigarettes. But I don't think the sale of the mas is going to go through . . .'

'No?'

Audrun reached out and laid her veined

brown hand on Jeanne Viala's arm. 'There's a crack in the front wall, Jeanne,' she said. 'A structural fault. Raoul came and stuck a bit of render in it and then slapped on that coat of yellow paint and Aramon thinks he can pull the wool over everyone's eyes, but don't tell me a simple survey wouldn't reveal a structural fault. Eh? Would you buy a house with a fissure in the stone?'

'No . . . '

'Aramon should make everything good again, make it sound, but he hasn't done it and he never will. He's always denied the things that are right there in front of his eyes. And so now . . . well . . . it's my opinion that he's going to be disappointed. He won't get that huge sum he's asking. And when that fact comes home to him, he's going to get angry, eh Marianne? He could do something irrevocable.'

Both Marianne and Jeanne looked up and stared at Audrun.

'What d'you mean?' asked Jeanne.

Audrun plucked off a parsley leaf and held it to her nose and smelled its clean, unobtrusive fragrance.

'All I mean is . . . ' she said, 'Aramon was always ungovernable. I should know. He's obsessed now about this particular buyer: some rich English artist type. But I can tell you, that man's not going to buy the Mas Lunel. I'd stake my life on it. And when Aramon wakes up to this fact . . . *Mon dieu!* He's going to curse and rage. He could even do somebody some harm.'

Jeanne exchanged a glance with Marianne.

She took a long drag on her cigarette.

'It'd be sad to sell it to foreigners, anyway,' she said, 'wouldn't it? They say foreigners are taking over all the nice old stone places. I read about it in *Ruasse Libre*. But the mayor has said it has to end.'

'That's right,' said Audrun. 'The mayor's right. Because people from outside don't understand how to care for the land. Everybody thinks these days that it's just houses that matter, but it's not: it's the land.'

There was silence in the room for a moment.

Audrun turned and turned the parsley leaf in her hand and she thought of the drum of her washing machine, still turning.

'If Aramon sells the mas,' said Jeanne Viala, 'where's he going to go?'

'I don't know,' said Audrun. 'You tell me. Where on earth?'

★ ★ ★

Kitty Meadows lay in a hotel room and watched the green neon light of an all-night *pharmacie* winking on and off on the opposite side of the drab street.

She hadn't wanted to spend much money on a hotel and this one, called Le Mistral, was the cheapest she could find, a two-star establishment where the walls were thin and Kitty's bed was narrow and hard. The keening of the hotel elevator kept jolting her awake the moment she closed her eyes. Up and down, up and down it went, carrying people yearning for love or for

210

rest — for the sweet rest that love can give.

At least I'm alone, thought Kitty. Although she was fond of her friends, André and Gilles, she hadn't been able to bear the idea of their pity, their sad smiles concealing smug judgements: 'Sorry, Kitty chérie, but I'm afraid we just *knew* that a gallery like that, with that kind of reputation, was never going to take your work . . . '

Better to be here, in an impersonal hotel room with an annihilating quantity of drink inside her, than to be with them on this night of humiliation. And although Kitty might have liked to be comforted by Veronica, the idea of returning to Les Glaniques and Anthony Verey's undisguised delight in her disappointment was impossible.

In fact, one thing which Kitty couldn't even bear to think about was how that eventual return was to be faced. Since Anthony's arrival, it was as if she'd been prevented from taking any comfort at all from the home she shared with her lover. She'd found refuge in her studio — away from both Veronica and her brother. She was happiest there, alone with her work and her dreams. But now she had to face the agony, not only of returning to live under Anthony's disdainful gaze, but also with something more terrible: coming face to face with the fact that the work she loved doing so much and tried so hard to do well was, when judged by the highest standards, no good.

All right, she'd managed to sell in small galleries and shops, but now a serious establishment had looked at the watercolours and pounced, like a heartless tiger: *I'm sorry, Madame Meadows . . . the Internet photographs of your work did look quite interesting to us, but now that we see the actual pictures . . . your sense of colour is very nice, but there are some shortcomings of technique. So voilà, I just don't think we'd be able to make a sale here . . .*

Kitty lay and shielded her eyes against the maddening *pharmacie* light and told herself that, at least, she'd be able to continue her work for *Gardening Without Rain* — both the watercolours and the photographs. And perhaps, when the book was published, somebody somewhere would think that her illustrations had some merit.

But how ardently — how desperately — she'd longed to be taken on by a reputable gallery! How often had she imagined the brochure that gallery would produce: RECENT WATERCOLOURS *by Kitty Meadows*. And then the fabulous night of the *vernissage* . . . the red 'sold' stickers accumulating . . . the smile of pride on Veronica's face . . . the beautiful money in the bank . . .

Kitty's mobile rang: Veronica's name on the display. Kitty looked at her watch and saw that the time was almost one o'clock.

'Veronica?' said Kitty quietly.

'Sorry it's so late. Were you asleep?'

'No,' said Kitty. 'No chance.'

'OK then, well, listen, darling, something's very wrong.'

Kitty sat up, glad to be distracted, glad to be reminded that there was a world outside her own misery.

212

'Tell me . . . ' she said.

She heard Veronica dragging on a cigarette.

'It's Anthony,' she said, coughing as she exhaled. 'He said he'd be back for dinner. I even asked him this morning what he wanted to eat and he said calves' liver and I went to the *boucherie* and got it. He said he'd definitely be back. But he hasn't come home, Kitty, and it's one in the morning.'

Kitty held the phone close. For a moment, she couldn't speak, so thrilling did she find these words. Cinematic light flooded her brain.

She saw a winding road high up above La Callune and she saw Anthony's hired car sliding too fast into a hairpin bend and then spinning round and flying out into the void and falling and breaking on the rocks below . . .

'Right,' she forced herself to say gravely. 'Have you tried his mobile?'

'Yes. Nothing. Absolutely no sound from it.'

'No voicemail?'

'No sound at all. And the agency woman phoned and said Anthony never returned the keys to the house.'

'Right . . . well, we've got to think what might — '

'I've got a terrible feeling about it, Kitty. There are accidents up in the Cévennes all the time. People drive far too fast and Anthony doesn't know how to manage that kind of corniche. I've just been sitting here waiting and waiting and I keep thinking I see headlights, but it's only cars on the Uzès road. What am I going to do?'

Kitty took a gulp of water and swung her legs

off the bed. The *pharmacie* light kept up its relentless welcoming green flash: *here to help you, here to help you, here to help you* . . .

'We've got to think clearly,' said Kitty, but she was all the while conscious of the alcohol in her blood and the movie of the falling car spooling round in her head.

Anthony Verey dead.

Dead at last.

Kitty wondered whether Veronica could detect in her voice or in her breathing the hectic excitement she was feeling.

⋆ ⋆ ⋆

Kitty breakfasted early and drove home with a headache darkening her vision, like some peculiar clouding of the windscreen glass. She longed for tea and a deep sleep.

She found a police car parked in the driveway at Les Glaniques. Veronica, looking pale and with her hair in a strange tangle, was in the salon, talking to two *agents*, a man and a woman. When they all turned and saw Kitty at the door, Veronica got up and came to her and Kitty put her arms round her and tried to smooth down the tangle of her hair and she heard the *agents* murmuring something to each other in low voices.

'Any news?' whispered Kitty.

'Nothing,' said Veronica. 'No report of a car accident. I suppose that's something.'

'Any theories?'

'Well, one. It's just possible he left the car and

went for a walk and got lost or hurt himself and his phone was dropped and broken. They're going to search with a helicopter,' said Veronica. 'It's on its way now.'

'Good,' said Kitty. 'Good. Easy to get lost up there. But they'll find him.'

Kitty slipped away to make her tea. Her tiredness was now compounded by the wearisome idea that Anthony had escaped death — just like he'd escaped punishment for his vanity and selfishness across sixty-four years. Probably, he'd be back at Les Glaniques by the end of the day. And Veronica would cling to his scrawny neck and tell him how important he was in her life and how she longed for him to be settled in France, and then the days would go on as before, just as before, only without the salvation of her dream of a gallery.

Kitty had imagined the police would leave her alone. She was just 'a friend'. Anthony Verey was nothing to her, and what could she — who had been undergoing her mauling by disappointment at Béziers — know about any accident in the Cévennes? But when she looked up from spooning out her tea, the woman *agent* was standing in the kitchen.

'Just a few questions,' she said. 'You speak French?'

'Yes,' said Kitty. 'Would you like some tea?'

'Tea? *Ah non, merci.*'

It was routine, absolutely routine, said the *agent*, but she just had to verify Kitty's movements in the last twenty-four hours. Had she been anywhere near the hills above Ruasse?

In my mind, I have, Kitty wanted to say. In my mind, I was there. I killed him. I sent his car flying off the corniche. I saw it break apart hundreds of feet below. I saw his blood on the stones.

'No,' said Kitty. 'I was miles away.'

★   ★   ★

When the police left, Veronica lit a cigarette and said: 'Well, I guess all we do is wait, now.'

The heat was rising on the terrace. The geraniums were beginning to look parched.

Kitty thought, I'm waiting too. I'm waiting for you to remember what happened to me in Béziers. I'm waiting for your eyes to fall on me.

She got up and took the cigarette out of Veronica's hand and stubbed it out, and without saying anything led her to the bedroom. She could feel her beginning to resist, to protest, but she, Kitty was determined; she wanted love. No words would do. In fact, she no longer hoped for any words; she needed only speechless desire. And she felt that all the future — hers and Veronica's together — would be determined by what followed in the next few moments.

He told himself that perhaps it was the heat, or the exhausting task of the vine clearance, or both of these, but Aramon's gut was now so devoured by pain that sometimes he had to get down on his knees and then lie curled up on the ground — in the position of a damned foetus — to help the spasm pass. No day went by free of this agony.

His appetite had gone. Sweet things he could bear to suck on — a spoonful of jam, a square of chocolate — and then sit still and wait for the fix of sugar to get into his blood, but even bread, turning to mush in his mouth, made him gag. And the thought of eating meat was now horrifying to him, as if the flesh laid out at the *boucherie* might have been human . . .

'What can I get you, Aramon?' Marcel, the butcher at La Callune, would ask him. 'A bit of veal? Some nice *merguez*?'

Even the smell in Marcel's shop Aramon found disgusting.

'Nothing for me, my friend . . . ' Aramon mumbled. 'Just some bones — for the dogs.'

And then, as he left the shop, he'd hear Marcel talking to other customers about him: 'Lunel's not himself, *pardi*. Is he?'

He sat at his table, sipping *sirop de menthe* and smoking. He wondered whether a cancer was developing in his stomach. He even wondered whether he'd been poisoned. Because this could happen in the modern world. Toxic microbes could enter the food chain or the water supply. You could die slowly, a bit more each day, and never know why.

Other symptoms began to torment him. Sudden dizziness. Everything clawing itself towards darkness. One minute he'd be standing there out in the heat with birds and insects alive all round him, and the next second he was somewhere else — lying by a stone wall, or face down in the earth, with the world gone dumb and the shadows cast by trees falling where they never normally fell.

These strange gaps in the sequence of time . . . he allowed them to remind him of that long-ago era when the things his body did made him black out and Serge would come and slap him alive again, and help him or even carry him to his own bed. He knew there was no connection between the one and the other. Those moments had been willed. He'd opened a door and gone in and the going in had overwhelmed him like nothing else in his life. But none of what was happening to him now was willed. Aramon could see clearly that the *episodes* that blighted his sister's life since that time were now advancing on him.

He considered going down to see the doctor. But the idea of the doctor — eyes staring into his mouth, hands palpating his stomach — made him feel weak. And he knew that if the doctor had bad news for him he wouldn't know how to conduct himself.

★   ★   ★

218

He woke up very early one morning to hear the dogs crying like wolves.

He tugged on his old work clothes and his boots and took his twelve-bore shotgun out of the rack by the door and picked up his cartridge bag and went out. And when the hounds saw him they began clawing in a frenzy at the mesh of the pound.

Aramon reached for two cartridges from the bag and broke the gun to put the cartridges in and saw that there were two spent cartridges in the barrels. Though he kept walking towards the dog pound, his brain jammed itself here, where these cartridges were. He knew that never in his life had he put his shotgun away with two spent cartridges in the barrels.

He opened the gate of the pound and went in, and the stink inside it was so bad it made him retch, and he spat yellow phlegm into the dust. His first thought was that his own condition, his own sickness, had made him less tolerant of the stench of the dog enclosure, but then he looked around him and saw that at the back of the pound was a hound lying dead there in the morning shade, with some of its flesh torn away and flies beginning to settle on two or three bloodstained wounds.

Aramon stood still and stared at this. Then he began to take in the state of the pound and he saw that it was filthy, with excrement everywhere, and that the water troughs were dry and he asked himself when he'd last come here with a bag of bones or even watered the animals. But he couldn't remember.

The dogs were jumping up and clawing at his legs, his groin. He saw in their mouths the foam of thirst. He pushed them away and went to the corpse and grabbed the stiff hind legs and began to drag it through the dust, still carrying his shotgun. Then he looked up and saw Audrun standing there, watching everything, and she held her flowered pinafore up to her face and said: '*Mon dieu*, Aramon, what a stink! What have you done?'

Done? What did she mean? He hadn't done anything. It was only that caring for the dogs had . . . well . . . it had slipped his mind . . .

'I've been out on the vine terraces,' he said, 'working like a savage. And now I've got some illness. I've been poisoned.'

'Poisoned?'

'I could have been. The way my gut hurts.'

'Poisoned by what?'

'Anything. These days, you don't know what's going to finish you off.'

'Nonsense. You talk pure nonsense. Did you shoot the dog?'

'No. Why would I kill a dog?'

'Then it just died, did it? They're all dying of starvation. Look at them!'

Pity for the creatures moved Aramon now. They were blameless. He'd fill their trough with water, drive down to Marcel's for another heap of bones . . .

'It's not my fault,' he said, 'if something's poisoning me. I need help. I told you weeks ago. I can't manage things any more. One man alone . . . what can he do?'

He closed the gate of the pound and the dogs went crazy, clawing at the wire and braying, and Aramon thought: If Serge were alive, he'd flay me for mistreating the dogs. Then he remembered the cartridges in the gun and he was about to say something about this to Audrun, who was following him down towards the house, when she reached into the pocket of her overall and brought out a copy of *Ruasse Libre* and said: 'Did you see this? I came to show you this.'

Aramon let the corpse of the dog fall. Dead things weighed so much; you couldn't lug them far. And the earth was so dry, digging a grave for the animal would take all the strength he had. He turned to face his sister, breathing hard. She held out the newspaper.

'What is it?' said Aramon.

'Look at this picture,' she said.

He didn't have his spectacles with him. He'd just flung on his clothes and picked up the gun. 'I can't see it,' he said.

She'd folded the paper in half and she waved the page in front of his eyes. 'Look!' she said.

He stared at the blurred image. 'Who is it?' he said. 'I can't see a thing.'

She snatched it away and read: '*ENGLISH TOURIST STILL MISSING. Police today renewed their search for Englishman, Anthony Verey, reported missing on Tuesday. Verey, 64, a British Art Dealer, was thought to have been driving his rented car —* '

'Verey?' said Aramon. 'Verey?'

'Yes. Isn't that the man — '

'How could he be 'missing'?'

'I don't know. But it's the same man, isn't it? The one who came here?'

Aramon hefted the gun over his shoulder, reached out for the newspaper. He held the picture very close to his face and slowly, very slowly, his eye focused on an eye. And there was something familiar about the eye, something which sent a shiver through him and he felt this shiver travel the length of his body and go down into his shoes.

'Could be him,' he said. 'If you don't know these hills, you can get lost in them . . . '

'Strange though,' said Audrun, 'that he went missing the day he came back here. Don't you think? Don't you think that's odd?'

The day he came back here.

Aramon lowered the picture and looked around him, not knowing what he was looking for, but knew that he had to keep looking and looking . . . as if there might be something there — in the devastated dog pound, or in the way the holm oaks moved in the hot wind — which would jog his faulty memory. 'Came back here?'

'Yes. On that day . . . '

'What day?' said Aramon.

'Tuesday. The day he went missing.'

'He never came back here.'

He saw his sister shake her head. Shake and shake, as though scolding a child.

'You accuse me of being crazy,' she said. 'Now you're losing your mind. I *saw* you, Aramon. I was ashamed of what a peasant you looked, in your dirty work clothes, next to that smartly dressed person.'

'Saw me . . . ?'

Audrun began to walk away. 'By the river,' she said. 'With Verey.'

'When?' he called, helplessly.

'On Tuesday afternoon. That body stinks, by the way. You'd better bury it pretty fast.'

Aramon looked down at the dead hound. The wounds were in its neck and in its stomach. There were bite marks around them. The flies had returned and were crawling over them. And at his back, the other dogs were still crying and he knew he had to get water to them and he had to clean the pound and bring them food, because to have let animals suffer like this was a terrible thing . . .

'Audrun,' he said, 'help me . . . '

But she just kept walking away.

★   ★   ★

He went in and telephoned Madame Besson. He told himself he wasn't so stupid or made so dumb by pain that he couldn't find a way to sort out at least some of the things that confused him. The phone was answered by Madame Besson's daughter, who told him that her mother was out with a client.

'Verey,' said Aramon. 'That Englishman they say has gone missing. He made one visit to my house, uhn? Not two. He made *one* visit.'

The daughter was silent. After a moment, she said: 'I'm afraid I don't know. You'll have to check with my mother. And I think she has someone else who's interested to see the mas.'

223

'Yes?'

Aramon immediately felt his spirits lift. The huge sums of money promised by the sale entered his brain like music, like the old sweet jazz his father used to play when Bernadette was still living: 475,000 euro . . . 600,000 euro . . . The numbers jived and shimmered. 650,000 euro! Because, Jesus Christ, the house and its land was making him ill now. He was too weary to keep on shouldering such a burden. If it wasn't lifted from him soon, he was going to die.

'I'll ask my mother to call you,' said the daughter.

'When?' said Aramon.

'When she gets in, this afternoon.'

Aramon rolled a cigarette and sat smoking it until the pain in his gut diminished a little. Then he went outside and began digging a grave for the dog. As he raised the pick and brought it crashing down into the earth, he felt the weight and the pain of it, all along his arms and through his shoulder blades.

Veronica lay in the dark.

She thought how strange it was that, when her brother was missing and might be dead, the night could be so quiet. She wanted the world to be out there in a blaze of official light, searching for him. She almost thought she heard him calling to her: *Please help me, darling. I'm trapped. I'm dying . . .*

This was so unbearable that Veronica got up and pulled on her robe and fastened it tightly round her, to cover the scent of sex she could smell on her own body. She went into the kitchen, and drank cold water from the tap, splashed it over her face, and stood there staring at nothing, dismayed by her own behaviour. For what had she done — in the face of the tragedy that seemed to be occurring — other than to call in the police and give them the facts and answer a few questions, and then just let herself go wild with Kitty in bed — the wildest she'd ever been. *Jesus Christ!* Why was human conduct often so shockingly inappropriate? Veronica thought of herself as 'civilised' — a civilised woman, known for her stoicism and her kindness. Now she saw that she was also no better than an animal.

It wasn't that she needed to apologise to Kitty. Not at all. Kitty had played her erotic games with her every step of the way. What Veronica longed to be able to do was erase those hours altogether. They embarrassed and mortified her. She promised herself that she wouldn't let Kitty touch her or even kiss her again until Anthony was found. She owed him this, at least. He was Lal's flesh, Raymond Verey's flesh, just as she was. She owed him — or his memory — a period of sexual abstinence.

Made calm by this decision, Veronica sat down at the kitchen table, pulled a pad and pen towards her and began to make notes.

What to do now? she wrote at the top of the page. Knowing that, really, there was nothing to be done except to wait for news, she also knew that she had to do something. She couldn't just stay quietly as Les Glaniques with Kitty. The voice that cried to her *Help me, help me, darling* had to be heard.

Follow the trail, she wrote.

This felt right. She'd drive to Ruasse, see Madame Besson and get directions to the isolated house Anthony was supposed to be visiting.

She told herself that she, V, would know — somehow, she would know — whether Anthony had been there, or not. There would be some sign of his presence — or of his absence.

Verify, she wrote.

But, after visiting the house, where should she go?

Veronica found a map of the Cévennes and spread it out on the table and stared at the brown contour lines and the snaking yellow of the roads and the black dotted lines of the ramblers' tracks. And she knew what these things represented: a wilderness — one of the last protected wildernesses in Europe. Anthony wasn't the first person to go missing there. The Cévennes hid the bones of countless lost people. Some of these — or so Veronica had been told by Guy Sardi — were German infantrymen, shot by the Résistance in 1944 and buried in the scrub and never named.

★ ★ ★

The telephone rang at 8.15 and woke Veronica, who had gone to sleep with her head on the kitchen table, thinly cushioned by the map.

'Veronica,' said a loud English voice, 'it's Lloyd Palmer, calling from London. I just switched on the news and I'm in total shock.'

For a moment, Veronica couldn't remember who Lloyd Palmer was. Then she recalled a few visits made long ago with Anthony to a house in Holland Park, dinner served by a butler, Palmer's wife wearing the kind of huge diamonds that sent out little daggers of light from her throat. One time, on the way home with Veronica in a taxi, Anthony had told her that, in event of his death, Lloyd Palmer would be the sole executor of his estate.

'I want to help,' boomed Lloyd. 'What a total nightmare. Tell me what I can do. Shall I fly over?'

Veronica waited before answering. This, she told herself, was what she would do in the coming days: consider everything suggested or offered, and then wait before answering.

'Veronica, are you there?' said Lloyd.

'Yes,' she said calmly, at last. 'It's good of you to call, Lloyd.'

'He's alive, isn't he? The radio said he could be 'lost' or stranded. They'll find him, won't they?'

Veronica looked up and saw Kitty at the kitchen door. She was naked. Veronica looked away. She turned her back on Kitty.

'I don't know if they're going to find him,' Veronica said to Lloyd. 'I just don't know . . . '

'Bloody hell,' said Lloyd. 'It's unreal. I spoke to him just a few days ago. D'you think he crashed the car?'

Kitty didn't leave. She stood there, puffy-eyed, barely awake, idly scratching her pubic hair. Veronica took the telephone and went out onto the terrace, where a hot sun was already falling. She closed the door behind her. A voice in her said: This is no one else's business. Only mine. I'm the one responsible for everything and I'll be the one to find my brother.

'Lloyd,' she said, 'it's no use asking me questions, really. I'm absolutely in the dark. Anthony left here in the car, on his way to see a house on Tuesday morning. I packed some water for him in a cold-bag. That's all I can tell you for sure.'

'He wasn't a good driver, was he?' said Lloyd. 'He was always turning round to speak to you, if you were the passenger.'

Passenger.

This lit up a new thought in Veronica's tired mind. Was it possible that Anthony had stopped to pick up a hitch-hiker, or to help someone apparently stranded on a lonely road, and had then been mugged for his wallet and his phone, and for the car itself? Because despite all his sophistication — the *veneer* he'd cultivated over the years — there was a vulnerability about Anthony which seeped through and which would instantly have been apparent to a stranger.

'He wasn't a good driver, no,' said Veronica to Lloyd. 'Or rather, no he *isn't* a good driver. We can't start talking about him in the past tense.'

'Oh God, sorry, absolutely not!' said Lloyd. 'I didn't mean it.'

★ ★ ★

Veronica ran a bath and lay in it, watching a spider perfecting its web in one corner of the bathroom ceiling.

Verification and abstinence. In these words appeared to lie some kind of appropriate resolve. Already, Veronica was preparing herself for the journey to Ruasse and beyond. She was only waiting for Madame Besson's office to open at 9.00.

She heard Kitty come to the bathroom door, but Veronica had locked it. Kitty called softly: 'I've brought you tea, darling.'

Consider everything suggested or offered, and then wait before answering.

Getting no reply, Kitty knocked on the door. 'I've got a cup of tea for you.'

'It's OK,' said Veronica. 'I don't want anything.'

She heard Kitty pause, hesitate. Then walk away.

Veronica felt relieved. And it was at this moment and not before that she concentrated once again on what had happened to Kitty yesterday in Béziers. Veronica asked herself what she felt about it, this rejection by the gallery.

And she knew that it didn't surprise her. It seemed terrible to admit this — almost a betrayal — but Kitty's talent was so small, so almost not there, that it might have been better if it hadn't existed at all.

If it hadn't existed at all, Kitty would have had no unrealistic hopes for it and that part of her which yearned and yearned and never gave up would have given up and been still — thus relieving her, Veronica, of the exhausting obligation to collude with her hopes. Because this was all it amounted to, all the praise she had to heap on Kitty's watercolours — it was no more than dishonest collusion with a lie.

And it wearied her. She saw this clearly now. Kitty's unrealisable dreams were exhausting. They took up too much precious time.

★ ★ ★

Kitty insisted on making breakfast for her: croissant, coffee and melon.

The food made her feel less tired, but when Kitty came to her and put her arms round her, she gently pushed her away. And when Kitty said that she was coming with her to Ruasse, Veronica stood up and said: 'No.'

230

'Yes, I am,' said Kitty. 'I'm not letting you go alone.'

'Well that's OK,' said Veronica coldly, 'because I'm not asking for permission.'

Then she gathered her things and began moving towards the car and Kitty followed her, but Veronica didn't turn round or say goodbye, just got into the car and drove away. As she went, she found herself photographed by two press men, who'd been waiting in the lane, but she set her gaze resolutely beyond them.

★　★　★

As Veronica drove, it affected her as it always did, the beauty of the road to Ruasse: the shimmering of the plane trees, their shadows bisecting the tarmac, the sunflowers, like yellow dolls animated by the wind. She remembered how much she'd been looking forward to finishing her work on 'Decorative Gravels' in *Gardening without Rain* and beginning the chapter entitled 'The Importance of Shade'.

And then she found herself remembering how Lal, brought up in a land of sunshine, had always scorned the idea that anybody needed shade as protection from the sun in England. 'If you've spent your childhood in the Cape,' Lal used to say, 'the words *English summer* are an oxymoron.'

But there had been hot days. Lal exclaimed over them as over a hoard of gold. All her normal tasks were sacrificed to them. In the garden of Bartle House, she'd lie on a cane lounger,

231

wearing a bathing costume or a strapless sundress and white-rimmed sunglasses, pointing herself at the sky. And her skin soon enough turned an obediently sweet honey brown.

The boy, Anthony, would bring out an old tartan rug and put it down on the grass and play with his toy soldiers, positioning them in open formation, moving steadily towards Lal's lounger. When they reached it, he'd make them form a column, then scale the base of the lounger, one by one, to arrive near Lal's feet and as she felt their little bayonets touch her skin, she'd laugh and say, 'Oh no! Not another bridgehead!'

Sometimes, he'd press the soldiers' bodies in between Lal's toes, pretending they were dead and lined up in a mortuary, and hold Lal's feet still as she giggled and squirmed. He told her that her scarlet toenails were the blood of his valiant men.

One time, Anthony stayed too long in the sun, too long on the tartan rug. His face went very red, then pale, then he was sick on the lawn and the doctor was called and he was ill with sunstroke for days and days. But Lal was a careless nurse. She left Veronica to carry up trays of broth, put clean sheets on Anthony's bed. And as soon as Anthony showed signs of recovery, she abandoned them altogether and went to London, to stay at the Berkeley Hotel. 'You'll be *fine*, darlings,' she said. 'Mrs Brigstock will keep an eye. She'll ring if there's any kind of crisis.'

After a few days of this abandonment had passed, Veronica went out into the garden with Anthony, still dressed in pyjamas, clinging to her

232

arm. And she could remember, now, that he kept saying: 'Let's not go into the sun, V. Let's not go into the sun.' So they walked very slowly to the spinney and sat together under the trees.

'I'm on my way!' she said aloud now, her voice strong and purposeful above the throbbing of the car's air-conditioning. 'It's V. I'm coming to find you.'

It was like a poison in her blood, Kitty decided, the 'V' part of Veronica.

It was at the root of every selfish act, every unkindness. Veronica was loving, compassionate and clever; V was none of these things. V was a snob and a tyrant. She was a relic of a vanished time.

Kitty lay down and slept for a while. It had always been her way of trying to overcome misery. But the late morning heat in the room was suffocating and after sweating through a nightmare in which she found herself abandoned by Veronica for ever, she got up and showered and sat in the shade of the terrace, sipping water and eating fruit, and tried to order her thoughts about what was happening.

It wearied her to realise that Anthony's disappearance would be the *only* subject talked about at Les Glaniques from now on. In fact, this was such an exhausting thought that Kitty began almost to wish that the wretched man would suddenly reappear. Scarred a little, of course. Someone who had had to *confront* terror and pain — for once in his pampered life. But alive. And, with any luck, traumatised sufficiently by whatever had happened to him in the Cévennes, to abandon his idea of coming to live in France.

Then, V would revert to being Veronica.

Things would be as they once were . . .

Kitty yawned. Getting Anthony back meant finding him. Kitty judged that the French police might be fairly slow in their search for an ageing English tourist and thought that, after all, Veronica might be right to do some searching on her own.

But it now occurred to her that Veronica was heading to the wrong place. Perhaps only she, Kitty Meadows, had understood that Anthony had already found a house he loved: the Mas Lunel. Until she'd pointed out the ugly bungalow to him, he'd been in a possessive rapture about it. She'd seen it, felt it in him as he stood there surveying the view, at the upper window. He'd been imagining himself installed in that house, lord of the land. And then she'd deliberately spoiled it for him. Had enjoyed seeing his features cloud over with dismay.

But he wasn't a stupid man. He would surely have considered what might be done about concealing the bungalow from view. Even discovered advantages in its being there: told himself that the woman who lived in it might be able to work for him and look after the house when he was away. And then he would have gone back to look at the mas again . . .

It was the scalding middle of the day. The cicada orchestra had reached a discordant pitch. Bees harassed the lavender. Kitty thought that it was really time to go to sleep again, to wait out the heat, wait to think clearly in the relative cool of the evening. But the idea of waiting passively for Veronica to deign to return to her made her cross and sad. Better, she decided, *not* to be here when Veronica came back. Better to climb back into her car and set out on her mission: Kitty Meadows, Private Detective.

★ ★ ★

Kitty's attachment to her small Citröen — a car she felt to be *right* for her short body, her modest aspirations — was at its least affectionate in very hot weather. The car had no air-con. Kitty tried to combat the stifling atmosphere with the breeze from the open windows and with the soaring voice of k.d. lang, given blissful escape by the Citröen's dusty cassette player.

Kitty sang along with k.d. This music, this hard, sexy voice kept her buoyant as far as Ruasse. Then she turned the music off. She knew that from here, she wasn't certain of the road to La Callune, and needed quiet in which to try to remember it. As the road out of Ruasse began to climb and the landscape of the Cévennes encircled her, she felt again the thrill of the idea of Anthony Verey's death. Here, among rock and precipice, among impenetrable forest, his body could lie undiscovered for months — or years. She imagined him hanging, face downwards, his slim ankles in their silk-cashmere socks snagged forever by a tangle of roots, his hair slicked down by rain, hooded by snow. She imagined all the creatures that would come and peck at his flesh, digest it and evacuate it: Anthony Verey turned to dung.

She knew she was on the right road when she

236

passed the sandwich stall, *La Bonne Baguette*. So here she slowed, waiting for the turning to the village of La Callune to come into view.

★　★　★

The overgrown driveway to the Mas Lunel lay higher up, beyond the village, and Kitty found it without difficulty. On her left, exactly as she remembered it, was the bungalow. She let the car slow down, wondering if she might risk stopping and talking to Lunel's sister. But the bungalow appeared closed and shuttered, so she drove on.

The handsome, yellow-painted mas now came into view. Kitty drew the Citröen into some shade and stopped. She sat absolutely still in the car, looking and listening. The shutters of the house were closed, but there was someone at home — Monsieur Lunel, himself? — because Kitty could hear the dogs barking in their pound and an old brown Renault 4 was parked near the front door.

On her right, below the scrubby lawn, was a tall stone barn, also handsome in its dilapidated way. She didn't remember this in the way that she remembered everything else, but now she thought that Anthony would surely have had plans for it — as a garage or a pool house. There was nothing here, he would have realised, that couldn't be *altered in its use*, nothing that couldn't be made to serve his needs. Only the bungalow. He'd seen the bungalow and walked away. But surely she wasn't wrong; the place was beautiful and the problems of the bungalow could be overcome. Anthony would have come back.

Kitty wiped the sweat off her face, ran her hands through her short hair and got out of the car. Something surprised her right away: a foul stench in the air. This, she thought, hadn't been there last time. The air had smelled of the perfumed *maquis*. Now, it had been vitiated. She wondered, did pockets of industrial pollution from factories at Ruasse reach even as far as here, when the wind was right? Or was the smell carried by something else? For the first time since setting out, Kitty felt mildly afraid.

She nevertheless walked boldly towards the house and knocked on the closed front door. As the dogs caught her scent, they began tearing at the sides of their cage. Her fear of them was tempered by pity for their plight. She wondered what Lunel would do with them when the house was sold.

Nobody came to the door. Kitty stood still, looking round her. The stench was strong here and seemed to come from the dog pound. She moved to the right, towards a window whose shutters were not quite closed and, shielding herself from her own reflection, looked in. She could see only fragments of the dark space inside: a kitchen table, a tin basin piled up with dirty washing . . .

Then she heard a movement behind her, turned and gaped as she saw Lunel, a few metres from her, pointing a shotgun at her.

She raised her arms, thinking as she did so: Now I'm going to die because of Anthony Verey.

238

There's no end to the things he asks of the world. *No end*.

'Monsieur Lunel . . . ' she began.

'*Qui êtes vous? Que faites-vous ici?*'

He kept the gun held high, but Kitty saw that his hands which held it were trembling. And he was out of breath, his thin chest rising and falling behind the stock of the gun. He could kill her by accident in the next few seconds.

She summoned a voice to ask him calmly in French to put the gun away, but he didn't move it. He told her he was defending his property, defending it night and day. It was only when she said the word 'Verey' that she saw his expression change. Slowly, he lowered the gun.

'Verey?' he said. 'The Englishman?'

'Yes,' said Kitty. 'I came with him to visit your house.'

'His sister. That it? You're his sister?'

'No. I'm only — a friend. But I just came to ask you — '

'Missing, they say he is. Have they found him?'

'No.'

'Why are you here? He never came back here. He came the one time, when you were all there. Ask the agents. The agents can verify it: he came here just that once.'

Kitty nodded. 'Thank you,' she said politely. 'That's all we were wondering; whether anyone else had seen him on Tuesday. We knew he was very interested in your house, so we thought — '

'Come inside. Use my telephone. You can call Madame Besson. I'm not lying. I never saw Verey again. I would have been willing to sell him this place on very good terms. I wouldn't have been greedy. Look at me. You can tell I'm not a greedy man. And I was talking to my sister about what was to be done with the bungalow . . . '

'Yes. Did you get anywhere with this? Has your sister agreed to sell the bungalow?'

'Not yet. But she will agree. I wanted to tell Verey that — that it could all get sorted out. I expected him to come back, but he never did.'

'You're absolutely sure about that? He didn't come here on Tuesday afternoon?'

Lunel shook his head. 'He never came back,' he said. 'I swear it on my life.'

Kitty now realised that the sweat on her was making her cold. She walked away from the shadow of the house, into the sunshine.

'I'm very sorry, Monsieur Lunel,' she said, 'for disturbing you. I had no right to walk onto your property, but I expect you can understand that we're very very worried . . . '

'He crashed his car, Madame,' said Lunel. 'That's what I think. You English drive on the wrong side of the road. So how do you know which way to steer?'

Kitty smiled. But even in the sun, she was shivering. She longed, now, for the heat of her car, longed to be miles from here. She knew that Private Detective Kitty Meadows would have found a way to look round the house — to see if any clues were buried inside it. But she didn't feel capable of going with Lunel into that darkness. She only wanted to be gone.

She held out her hand and Lunel hefted the gun over his shoulder and took it. She said goodbye and Lunel opened his mouth, as though to say something else, but closed it again, and walked away from Kitty, in the direction from which he'd appeared. Kitty watched him go, then went fast towards the car. She wished she had a bottle of vodka in it. She was in shock and knew she shouldn't be driving until she recovered.

As she opened the car door, she reassured herself that she could stop in La Callune. There would be a café there. She would sit quietly and sip a vodka and tonic until she felt ready for the long drive home. She tumbled gratefully into the driver's seat. She was about to close the car door when she saw something glinting in the grass underneath it. She looked down at this and saw that what she'd thought was a shard of glass was in fact a piece of cellophane. She stared at it. Then, realising what it was, she picked it up. It was a sandwich wrapper from the roadside stall, *La Bonne Baguette*. Kitty closed the car door, glad of the warmth which spread round her, and slowly examined the wrapper. Just visible on its label were the words *fromage/tomate*.

Kitty put the sandwich wrapper into her glove box and started the car.

It took her three turns to manoeuvre it round. The sweat on her hands made the hot steering wheel sticky. She'd drawn level with the bungalow before she realised that she was driving on the wrong side of the road.

She swerved and corrected. Her eye was caught by the sight of a solitary flowered overall, pegged to the bungalow's washing line and moving gently in the rising breeze. Mistral, she thought. It'll come soon, the wind that dries the rivers and yellows the leaves before their time, and lingers . . .

Audrun didn't know why, but all her dreams during this time were happy.

Was it because the thing she'd been waiting for was over? She didn't think so, because it *wasn't* over — not yet, not quite. It was now inevitable, but there was still one more act to be played out. And then, it would be over: it would be at an end.

Here they were, anyway, these dreams of past happiness: of going on a bus to the seaside with Bernadette, singing songs all the way, eating oysters from a tin plate on the quayside, seeing the immensity of the ocean.

And the best dream of all: her dream about the day — just the one in all those years — when Raoul Molezon had been waiting for her when she came out of the underwear factory. She'd almost walked right by him because she never expected him to be there, but he called her name and she stopped. He took her to a café and bought *sirop de pêche* for her and beer for himself. He said to her: 'I've been noticing something, Audrun: you're becoming a beauty. Your mother must have looked just like you look now when she was young.'

A beauty.

Her, a beauty?

She'd felt like crying. Perhaps she had cried. Cried over her *sirop de pêche* in the cheap café because Raoul Molezon had said a wonderful thing.

Then, she told him that the factory was poisoning people. The underwear was made of rayon. As you stitched, you had to pull and stretch the rayon, like skin, and in this skin was a chemical called carbon disulphide which had a bad smell and which could give you eczema and boils or even make you go blind.

And Raoul Molezon had said it was a tragedy that she should be working in such a place, but Audrun could never remember what she'd replied; it seemed to her that there was nothing she could have said, then or ever.

But now she was dreaming, not about the factory or the spots that broke out on her hands and round her nose from the carbon disulphide in the rayon, but only about that moment when Raoul called her a beauty.

Dreams like that refreshed you. You woke in the mornings, not aware of the weight of everything that was wrong, but on the contrary, feeling hospitable towards the day, curious to see what it would bring. And this feeling of optimism could last well into the afternoon; last, sometimes, until the daylight began to fade.

And then, somehow, it vanished. Audrun would look up at the darkening sky behind her wood and feel her hopes for the future flying away.

She'd try to distract herself with the TV. She loved old American crime movies, with terrifying soundtracks. She loved hospital dramas. But best of all, she loved programmes imported from

Japan, where people did the strangest things: they rode horses backwards, they somersaulted through rings of fire, they ate tarantulas, they walked on stilts through snow. Or sometimes they just lay on the ground, not moving, looking up at millions of cherry trees in bloom. And then Audrun would remember Aramon once cutting a branch of white blossom and putting it into her arms and kissing her cheek when she said: 'I'm a princess now. Am I?'

★ ★ ★

Days passed and the river fell. No rain came.

Below La Callune, where the river calmed, the campsites began to fill up. Lessons in kayaking were offered. Tourists put on yellow life jackets, yelping as the frail kayaks bounced and swivelled in the eddies. Barbecue smoke tainted the evening air. Loud music came and went on the ever-changing winds.

Sometimes, Audrun wondered whether the surveyor would reappear, but there was no sign of him, and she didn't care now, because all of that — the question of boundaries and markers — was irrelevant, or would be soon.

For the time being, she avoided Aramon. Sometimes, she glimpsed him trudging off to work on the wrecked vine terraces, noted how he staggered, how his health was failing, day by day. But she didn't go up to the house.

She saw a Dutch family arrive with Madame Besson to look round the Mas Lunel, but they didn't stay long. Their children were terrified of the dogs and kept screaming. The family drove by her bungalow with their faces pointing straight ahead and never turning to look back. And an article in *Ruasse Libre* informed her that property prices were now beginning to fall. 'You see?' she said in her mind to Aramon. 'Those sums of money were daydreams.'

★ ★ ★

Then, Aramon arrived at her door one evening — at that time of day when the beneficial effect of her dreams was running out — and he was pale and could hardly speak. She told him he looked as though he'd seen a ghost and he said: 'I *have* seen a ghost. Come and look in the barn.'

She followed him there. He went ahead, trying to make little galloping steps that soon got him out of breath. She understood that his heart and lungs wouldn't let him run any more.

The heavy doors of the barn were open and they went in. It was dark in there, with the daylight going, but Aramon picked up a flashlight from a shelf and shone it onto the chaos which had accumulated in the huge barn over all the years.

'Look!' he said. 'Look there!'

Something stood there. It was a big, bulky shape, draped with sacking, half concealed by a clutter of old farm utensils, crates, boxes, cement bags and broken domestic tools which had been piled on top of it.

'What's *that*?' said Aramon. 'How did *that* get here?'

Audrun stared blankly.

'There!' Aramon yelled. 'There! Are you blind?'

He walked forwards and lifted some of the sacking so that Audrun could see what was underneath. It was a car.

She moved silently towards it. Aramon watched her reach out, as if about to touch the metal of the bonnet, but then she withdrew her hand. She turned her face towards Aramon and said: 'Whose car is it?'

'I don't know,' he said. 'I don't know . . . ' but then he began to snivel. 'I don't know how it got there, Audrun. I swear. And I swear on my life that I never hurt anybody . . . '

'What d'you mean?' said Audrun. 'What are you talking about?'

He broke down into tears of anguish. He came to her and it was as if he was asking her to put her arms round him and console him, but she held herself apart and said: 'Tell me what you've done.'

'I don't *know*!' he cried. 'I get these blackouts. I wake up in different places. I swear this is the first I've seen of this car, but it could be his, couldn't it? How do I know? I've never laid eyes on his fucking car! I thought they came in the agent's car, didn't they? Didn't they?'

'The first time,' said Audrun. 'The agent brought them the first time, but then, the second time, who knows . . . '

'How did a *car* get into my barn? Jesus Christ! I'm going mad. You have to help me, Audrun. You have to help me!'

Out of her overall pocket, Audrun took a handkerchief (one that had belonged to Bernadette) and gave it to Aramon. He buried his face in it.

'I suppose you killed him, did you?' said Audrun. 'You got in one of your rages and you killed the foreigner because he wouldn't buy the mas, like you killed that whore in Alès long ago?'

'No!' sobbed Aramon. 'Why would I do that? I only saw him that one solitary time . . .'

'You know that's not the truth,' said Audrun.

'It *is* the truth! I called Besson. She confirmed it. She said he only came here once.'

'Once with her. And then the second time . . . on his own. I saw you with him.'

'No! He never came back. I would have remembered. Mary Mother of God, I would have remembered!'

She let him cry. She went boldly to the car and uncovered more of it and they both saw that the bodywork of the car was black.

'God forgive you, Aramon,' she said. 'You killed that poor man. You shot him and tried to hide the car in all this clutter.'

'No!' he sobbed. 'No!'

Aramon let himself fall down. He just collapsed and lay in the dust of the barn floor with his face in his hands. His legs swivelled, like the legs of a baby, trying to crawl.

Audrun stood over him and said: 'Is the body inside?'

'I don't know . . .' he keened. 'Take this away from me! Tell me this isn't happening! Take this away!'

She pulled the sacking off the car windows, dislodging a wooden sieve and a pyramid of discoloured Tupperware containers. She peered inside the car, but it was too dark to see much.

'We'd better call the police,' she said.

He seemed to convulse then, and sat up in the dust and begged her, begged her on their mother's soul not to do that.

'We have to,' she said. 'What else can we do?'

'I'll get rid of it,' he sobbed. 'I know places in the hills. I'll push it off a crag. I'll do it at night. Please, Audrun. Please . . . '

She ignored all this and went back to peering in the car window, shielding her vision from the reflected flashlight.

'Turn the torch off, Aramon,' she snapped.

He grovelled for the flashlight, picked it up and dropped it and it went out and the true darkness of the barn surrounded them. Wrapping her hand in a piece of sacking, Audrun tried the handle of the car door, tugging hard at it, but it wouldn't yield and in the next second an ear-splitting sound came from the car — the burglar alarm — and its indicator lights began a frantic blinking on and off.

Aramon's crying turned to screaming. He put his hands to his ears. He looked like a madman, thrashing about there in the dust.

The gyrations of his body dislodged a clutch of ancient rakes and pitchforks leaning against the wall, and they fell on him, one by one, like the bars of a cage pinning him to the earth.

★ ★ ★

249

She lifted the rakes away from him and found the torch and got its beam to come on and she helped Aramon to his feet. Her hand on his arm felt how thin his body had become. She led him out of the barn into the falling night. The burglar alarm on the car went suddenly silent. Audrun closed the barn doors.

Aramon stopped crying as they made their way up to the mas. The dogs began keening as they approached. Audrun led him into the kitchen and turned on the bar of fluorescent light above the table. She sat him down on a hard chair and poured him a shot of pastis and filled the glass to its brim with cool water from the kitchen tap.

He drank gratefully. His face was muddy with tear-stained dust. Audrun sat beside him and talked to him, quietly, like Bernadette used to talk to them when she scolded them as children, with no need to raise her voice.

'Aramon,' she said. 'Anything like this, it's only a question of time. You can hide things, like you tried to hide the car, but in the end, they come to light. So you've got to try to remember what happened. That's your best hope — to try to recollect. You've never liked doing this, going back over things you wanted to forget, but now you have to, so that you can defend yourself better. Do you understand what I'm saying?'

He was still clutching Bernadette's handkerchief, worn thin by time. He wiped his mouth with this. He nodded.

'The car's locked,' said Audrun. 'So first you have to remember what you did with the keys.

Then we can see whether there's anything inside it . . . '

'It's gone,' he said.

'What's gone? The place where you put the keys? You've forgotten where you hid them?'

'All of it's gone. Did I do something terrible? Perhaps I did, Audrun, perhaps I did, because . . . '

'Because what? Because *what*?'

'Jesus Christ, I found two spent cartridges in my gun! I don't know how they got there. Why would I leave them there? I'd never leave used cartridges in the gun. And what did I use the gun for? I don't *know*!'

He began crying again. Audrun told him to have another pull at the glass of pastis and he gulped this down.

'I think it'll all come back to you,' she said calmly. 'Often, we think that certain things have gone clean from our minds, but then we get some clue — it might be a photograph or the smell of something — and we can put it all back together. I can help you. I think you should sleep now, but when you're feeling better, tomorrow, I can help you fill in some blanks, because, as I keep telling you, I *saw* you that day, with Verey. I saw you from my window . . . '

He turned his pleading face to hers. 'Don't go to the police,' he said. 'You're my sister. Don't betray me.'

She took his hand in hers and held it tenderly against her bony chest.

'It was the money, wasn't it?' said Audrun. 'Verey wouldn't pay your price and you were disappointed. Money makes people insane.'

251

Veronica felt that she was falling into a trance. A trance of sorrow.

In the middle of doing the simplest things, this trance came on. When she sat down to put on her shoes, she sometimes stayed like that, staring at her feet, for minutes on end.

It was June now and very hot. The journalists and photographers who'd clustered near the house after the police announcement had first been made had gone away. *Ruasse Libre*'s references to the case were now in very small print. The *Inspecteur* in charge of the search remarked to Veronica that when someone disappears, the chance of their being found alive diminishes severely after the third day has passed.

'That doesn't mean you can just give up!' Veronica screamed at him.

'*Non, Madame,*' said the *Inspecteur* patiently. 'Of course we're not giving up. We'll find your brother — alive or dead.'

Alive or dead.

What made Veronica's sorrow so hard to bear was the knowledge that she'd loved and protected Anthony all his life — against their father's neglect, against Lal's bad temper, against his own anguished nature — but she hadn't been able to protect him from whatever had happened to him now. In her dreams, he was buried alive

252

and slowly suffocating and she woke up screaming. Kitty tried to stroke and comfort her, but she resisted this, afraid that tenderness would become passion.

She talked to Anthony in her mind. She told him she'd been to the Swiss house. The police had done a cursory search of the place, found nothing unusual and left. But Veronica had seen something which convinced her that Anthony *had* been there on that day. The Swiss couple owned some fine antique French furniture. And here and there, on the dusty surfaces of tables or cabinets there were lines, unmistakably traces left by fingers, and Veronica knew — she knew with absolute certainty! — that these were Anthony's finger marks. 'It wasn't that you were checking for dust, darling,' she said to him, 'were you? It was that you recognised objects of value and you wanted to *touch* them. You wanted to love them for a moment. You wanted to imagine them taking their place among the *beloveds*. I'm not wrong, Anthony, am I? I know I'm not wrong.'

A forensics team was sent to the Swiss house. Yes, indeed, Veronica was informed, there were clearly delineated marks on the furniture. But now, before undergoing further searches at the Swiss house, the team had to see whether they could match these fingerprints with those belonging to Anthony Verey.

The forensics people arrived at Les Glaniques and dusted the surfaces of Anthony's bedroom and bathroom for prints and then they took away Anthony's possessions — took away almost everything that belonged to him — while Veronica stood looking on, seeing the small bit of his life that he'd brought to France being delicately inserted into plastic bags. They even ferreted out his pyjamas, from where Veronica had placed them under his pillow on the day he disappeared, and started to put them into a bag.

'Don't take those,' she said. 'Why do you need those?'

'DNA, Madame,' they said. 'Everything is vital.'

Veronica lay down on Anthony's bed. The smell of him — all the balms and unguents he used — was still on the pillow even though the pillowcase had been taken away.

She remembered how he'd always adored perfume. As a teenager, he'd once been caught sitting at Lal's dressing table, going through all her bottles, one by one, and sniffing the contents. In his hand, when Lal surprised him, was a porcelain pot of vaginal lubricant. Lal took the pot from him and threw it across the room and then hit the side of his head with the back of her hand. She told him he was a grubby and disgusting boy.

This had been during the summer holidays when Lal had brought her Canadian lover, Charles Le Fell, to Bartle House. Although Veronica had long ago guessed that her mother had lovers, it had apparently never entered Anthony's mind, and he told Veronica that, when he thought about what his mother was doing with Charles Le Fell, he wanted to kill him.

'Don't do that,' Veronica said. 'Canadians are quite nice.'

'I don't care,' he said. 'I'd like to kill them both.'

He crept around the house in the night, listening at Lal's door. Charles Le Fell was a very big man, six foot three with wide shoulders and enormous hands, like a bear's paws, whereas Lal was small and delicate, like a springbok. Human behaviour was so stupid, so completely wrong, Anthony told Veronica, if his mother could *choose* that, that hugeness, if she could willingly submit herself to that. And yet, secretly, he wanted to see it. He wanted to open Lal's door and see her naked body being crushed by Charles Le Fell. And then scream. He wanted to stand in his mother's bedroom screaming until he was sick.

He wouldn't talk to Charles Le Fell. At mealtimes, the amiable Canadian tried to make conversation about school, or about the things that were happening in the news, like the launch of the first Russian spaceship, *Sputnik*, but Anthony only mumbled one-word answers and excused himself from the table as soon as his food was eaten.

Lal punished him by refusing to kiss him goodnight any more. She said to him: 'All of that is over. You have to grow up, Anthony. In every way. Or you'll never have a proper life. And you'd better start being civil to Charles or you can spend the Christmas holidays at school.'

'I hate women,' he said to Veronica one night. 'I hate every single woman in the world, except you.'

'I'm not a woman,' said Veronica. 'I'm a horse.'

★ ★ ★

He hated women, and yet . . .

Memories of Anthony's wedding began to chase round Veronica's tired mind.

'Just let that old stuff go,' said Kitty. 'Just get it out of your head, if it upsets you.'

But Veronica felt that it might be there for a purpose. She felt that there was a chance that if she allowed herself to examine it — as one would examine evidence to present to a court of law — then it might give her some new insight into what had happened.

She could see that wedding day very clearly . . .

Lal wearing a gauzy blue dress, but looking tired, suddenly looking older, and in the church turning round and searching the faces of the assembled guests, as though in the hope that handsome Charles Le Fell might reappear and call her his 'Lally-Pally', his 'sweetie-pie' . . .

Anthony, waiting in the front pew for the arrival of his bride, Caroline . . .

Anthony immaculate in a morning suit from Savile Row, his hair still dark then, his face tanned. Beside him Lloyd Palmer (yes, of course it was Lloyd, the best man!), the buoyant, dependable friend. And then suddenly, as the organ music struck up the bridal march and the congregation rustled to their well-shod feet, Anthony bent over, bent almost double, as though he was going to be sick on the flagstones, and Lloyd put a comforting arm round him. Veronica, in the pew behind, wanted to climb

256

over the seat to be beside her brother, but all she could do — hampered as she was by her tight silk suit and her satin high-heeled shoes — was reach out her gloved hand . . .

He wasn't sick. He managed to straighten up as Caroline made her elegant progress down the aisle. But he never looked round to see his bride coming towards him. He held himself rigid and Veronica could see his whole body shaking with fear. He was meant to step out of the pew when Caroline drew level with him, but he didn't move. Caroline and her father waited. The bride's sharp features under the veil turned towards him, her eyes blinking in panic. Her hand, holding the bouquet of lilies, reached out . . .

Lloyd had to nudge Anthony out of the pew and into the aisle beside Caroline. The vicar stared down at them in dismay. Lal whispered to Veronica: 'Something's wrong, V. But what?'

But what?

He got through it. At the reception, he made a speech about love.

But later, when Veronica bumped into him coming out of the hotel cloakrooms, he took her arm and led her away from the party into the garden, where a fountain in the form of a curly-headed cupid pissed water into a lily pond.

'I don't love Caroline,' he said. 'I like her, but that's not the same thing, as we all know very well.'

'It may not matter,' said Veronica. 'It may all be all right in time. Think about arranged marriages. Sometimes, love happens later on . . . '

'Yes,' he said. 'So I've heard. What a wise old thing you are.'

He seemed to be about to return to the wedding reception, but then he caught Veronica's arm and held it in a painful grip as he said: 'This morning, V, I woke up at five and I walked to Chelsea Bridge and I had a set of butchers' weights in a Harrods bag and I began to put them into my pockets . . . '

'What stopped you?' Veronica asked. 'The thought of wasting a bag from Harrods?'

'I'm serious, V. I'm serious.'

'So am I, Anthony. If you wanted to kill yourself, then what stopped you?'

'Not *what*', said Anthony, 'but *who*. A boy. Sixteen or seventeen years old. On the way home from some all-nighter, reeking of everything. And he wasn't even a beauty, but I didn't care. We went to Battersea Park. There are still a few places there where you can't be seen.'

'And if the boy hadn't come by?'

'I don't know. Because why go on? I couldn't answer it and I still can't. *Why?*'

★　★　★

In the night, Veronica woke Kitty and said: 'I've been resisting this. But now I'm trying to face it. I think it's just possible that Anthony committed suicide.'

'Yes?' said Kitty.

'He considered it once before. Maybe more than once. Coming to France was his last throw at his life. I believe it was. And I think he may

258

have understood — up at that lonely house — that it wasn't going to work . . . that everything was over.'

Kitty stroked Veronica's hair. Then she got out of bed and went to the chest of drawers where she kept her mannish underwear. She came back to the bed and held out a crumpled piece of cellophane.

'I found this when I went back to the Mas Lunel,' she said.

Veronica put her glasses on and squinted at the cellophane. 'What is it?' she said.

'Sandwich wrapper,' said Kitty. 'Cheese and tomato. From *La Bonne Baguette*.'

'So?'

'I could be wrong,' said Kitty, 'but it's the same flavour of sandwich that Anthony chose the first time we went there with Madame Besson. And I keep wondering . . . suppose he went back . . . to have another look at the mas . . . '

Veronica stared at the cellophane, turning it over and over in her hands. At last she said: 'We could give this to forensics. But I don't think Anthony went back there. In fact I know he wouldn't have. He'd made up his mind about that place. He knew the bungalow ruined it. Perhaps he thought he'd found it for a moment — his paradise — but then he saw it for what it was: not paradise at all.'

Aramon began praying to his dead mother, Bernadette.

'Help me!' he cried out to her. '*Help me, Maman* . . .'

He knew she couldn't hear him. Or, if she did hear him, if she *did* know what was in his heart and in his mind, then she wouldn't give him any comfort, because she'd also know that he'd long ago put himself beyond her love.

But still he kept imagining her sweet face, calm and tender beside him. She was mending the holes in his own worn-out socks. She handled the darning needle as deftly as a high-class tailor. On her feet, she wore rubber boots, flecked with farmyard mud, to which little bits of damp grass still clung.

He began ransacking the house, looking for the keys to the hidden car.

The pain in his gut made him growl when he had to reach upwards to high shelves or the tops of armoires. He found ancient blankets, bitten to threads by moths. He found Serge's fustian wartime coat with an S.T.O. badge still pinned to the lapel. He found a rolled map of the world, on which Europe looked large and Africa small. He found a selection of shoes and coat hangers and broken lampshades and torches. He knew these things were worthless, but something prevented him from lighting a bonfire and hurling them onto it. So he left them where they were, lying around on the floor in different rooms.

In the nights, he sweated. What he dreaded most was finding the keys.

He told Bernadette that yes, yes he knew he was capable of killing a man. Human life — his own included — hadn't been that precious to him, not after Serge died and everything had had to change, not after what *had* been precious to him was denied him for ever.

In his dreams, he killed Verey. He didn't know why this kept happening, but it did. He shot Verey in the gut. He saw his grey colon come bursting through the flesh of his stomach. Then he rolled the body in a blanket, or in Serge's old coat with the S.T.O. badge still pinned to it, and chucked it in the car. The body was light, almost like the body of a boy.

But when Aramon woke up from these dreams, he still didn't know the truth about what he'd done or not done. The first words on his lips in the mornings were to his dead mother: 'Help me, Maman, help me . . . '

★   ★   ★

Then Madame Besson phoned.

'Monsieur Lunel,' she said brightly, '*j'ai des très bonnes nouvelles*: I have another English family who would like to come and visit the mas.'

Aramon was standing in the kitchen. Five empty pastis bottles adorned the table. On the

261

floor were piles of old farming manuals, mousetraps, broken fishing rods, blackened roasting pans and stained crockery: all the detritus he'd tugged out of cupboards in his terrified search for the keys to the car in the barn. He stared at these objects, bent down and picked up a broken rod with an unsteady hand. Outside, he could hear the mistral tormenting the trees.

'Yes?' he forced himself to say.

'Would today be convenient?' said Madame Besson. 'The clients are in my office with me now. A Monsieur and Madame Wilson. I could bring them up to the mas at about three o'clock this afternoon.'

Now, sweat began to pour down Aramon's forehead and down the back of his neck. It was as though he'd forgotten all about trying to sell the mas, forgotten that more strangers could arrive to poke and pry into the house — and into the barn. And now he saw that he couldn't possibly let anyone come here until he'd got rid of the car . . .

'Monsieur Lunel,' repeated Madame Besson, 'tell me if today would be convenient? I have the Wilsons right here . . . '

'No,' said Aramon. 'Not today. No, I can't . . . '

He heard Madame Besson sniff with irritation. To stop her from suggesting a different day and to stop himself from agreeing to this different day, he pressed the rod across his shoulder — like you press a stick across the shoulders of a dog when you're training it to stay or sit — and he blurted out: 'I've been meaning to call you, Madame Besson. To tell you . . . I'm not well. I'm afraid that I can't have anybody visiting me at the moment.'

'Oh,' said Madame Besson. 'I'm very sorry to hear that . . . '

'I'm confined to my bedroom. The doctor's ordered me to stay there.'

'Oh,' said Madame Besson again, 'well that is . . . very bad luck and I send you my sympathy. Nothing too serious, I hope?'

'Well,' said Aramon. 'Nobody knows. Nobody seems to know . . . '

'I see,' said Madame Besson, then, without a pause, she went on, 'But I must tell you, Monsieur Lunel, that if you want a sale, then I think you should let the Wilsons come today — or tomorrow, when you may be feeling better. They have to return to England on Friday but they are really very interested to see the house. From the pictures and details, they say it sounds exactly what they've been looking for and they've been looking for more than a year now, and also, I don't think the price will be a problem for them, so if there is any way . . . I mean, I myself could conduct them on the tour of the property. *N'est-ce pas?* I could explain about your illness. We would arrange to leave you in peace in your room . . . '

'No,' said Aramon. 'No. Things have happened to me . . . You have to understand. We must set this all aside.'

'Set it aside? What d'you mean by that?'

Aramon looked out of the window and saw

263

yellow leaves flying in the wind, as though autumn were already arriving. He thought of them falling on his parents' stone mausoleum and settling there.

'Cancel the sale,' he said. 'I can't go on with it at the moment.'

★ ★ ★

When Audrun came up to the house the next day, she told him he'd done right.

'Your only hope,' she said, 'is to keep everybody away from here, Aramon. Barricade yourself in. Lie low. Wait till it's all forgotten. All you need to do is get rid of the car.'

He told her he'd been searching for the car keys night and day. He said, 'I swear, I go walking around the house, searching for them in my sleep . . . but I can't find them.'

'Did you look in the chest,' asked Audrun, 'where the old family papers are?'

'I don't know,' said Aramon. 'I don't know where I looked and where I didn't look.'

She took hold of his thin wrist and led him into the salon. She opened the shutters, closed against the midday heat, to let light into the room and she and Aramon knelt down by the chest, side by side.

Very quickly, they came across photographs of Bernadette, and Aramon's agitation seemed to be stilled by looking at these. One black-and-white picture was of Bernadette leading on a rope the donkey who had eventually died in the byre. Both she and the donkey, Audrun noticed,

264

looked skinny, almost starved, and she said to herself that that was the condition you had to bear in the hills of the Cévennes in the middle of the twentieth century: you had to endure hunger. And then she remembered that she herself had endured it as a child and that this had been all right, just part of each day, each week, each month, and it was only the things that had come later that had been unendurable.

After a few moments of lifting out bundles of letters and newspapers, Audrun said: 'You know, we should really go through all these family papers properly. There could be important things in here.'

'Important once maybe,' said Aramon. 'But everybody's dead now. All the news is dead news . . . '

'And the letters?'

Aramon rubbed his eyes. 'Words,' he said. 'Just words.'

Audrun picked up a letter in Serge's handwriting and read aloud: '*My dearest wife, terrible bitter cold these nights and praying it may be kinder at La Callune for yourself and our beloved son, Aramon, and the little girl . . . *'

'*Beloved son?*' said Aramon. 'Did he say that?'

Audrun passed him the letter. 'Yes,' she said. 'Look.'

He fumbled with his spectacles and began reading. He held himself very still. Audrun saw tears begin to slide down the furrows in his cheeks.

'Aramon,' she said gently. 'When you die, who inherits the mas?'

'You do,' he said. 'It's the law. You're my only next of kin left alive. So you get it all — if it's not sold, and if you're still breathing.'

He looked at her kneeling by his side, seeming not to mind that she could see his face all drenched with his sorrow. 'Clean it up, you could,' he said with a hint of a smile. 'Eh, Audrun? Even get your old flame Molezon over to have a proper look at that crack. *N'est-ce pas?* If he can still haul his arse up a ladder.'

She nodded slowly.

Aramon put the letter from Serge aside, and began sifting through the papers remaining in the chest. Then he straightened up.

'The keys aren't in here,' he said. 'I would have remembered putting them in with all this family junk.'

Kitty lay in a hammock under a sickle moon. She stared up at this blade of moon and at the shrapnel of the stars scattered far and wide.

'Heartless!' her mother used to say, glancing up at the darkness above Cromer. 'Never expect consolation from the night sky.'

Kitty made the hammock sway gently. Her head rested on a striped cushion and she'd covered her body with a thin blanket. The garden all around her was almost silent. Now and then, there was a scratch of sound from the cicadas and the scoop-owl let out its anxious exclamation: '*Oh-ooo, oh-ooo!*' But the mistral had died down. The branches of the two cherry trees, where the hammock was suspended, didn't move. No sound came from the house.

Kitty preferred to spend her nights out here now. It was all right to be alone, alone in the darkness, alone in her own little mind. Because she had to hang on to that. She had to hang on to being Kitty Meadows, fifty-eight years old, watercolorist, photographer, lover of women. She had to remind herself that she *was*, she existed, she would go forward into some kind of future, nobody had taken her life.

But she wanted to leave Les Glaniques. She now wanted to leave the place where she'd been happier than anywhere in her life. Leave before her life *was* taken. Because to be cast out as she was from Veronica's love was killing her. Every day, Kitty felt smaller, more ugly, more useless. And she could envisage no end to this. Unless, by some miracle, Anthony Verey was returned to Les Glaniques, returned to his sister . . .

Kitty didn't mind much where she went. She decided she would buy a plane ticket to some destination she'd never imagined visiting: Fiji, Mumbai, Cape Town, Havana, Nashville Tennessee . . . She lulled herself to sleep picturing these places, seeing Fijian war dances, hearing country songs.

But her sleep was strange, as though it didn't quite happen except in short, vivid dreams, and when the sky grew light Kitty just felt surprised that a piece of time had passed without her noticing it.

She lay still in her hammock and looked out at the parched condition of the garden. Birds came down from their night roosts to peck for worms in the grass, but the grass was full of dust and on it was a carpeting of brown cherry leaves, already falling. The lavender flowers, where a few bees still came to search for nectar, had lost all their colour. Leaf-moth was attacking the bays and the laurels, making the leaves blister and curl. Oleander blooms withered and fell.

The well was almost dry. The mayors of all the surrounding villages had agreed together on a hose ban. Vegetables could be watered; nothing else. Not even the dying fruit trees.

'The saddest thing,' Kitty had said to Veronica, 'would be to lose the apricots, wouldn't it?'

'No,' said Veronica. 'There's only one sad

thing. Nothing else feels important to me. Not even the garden.'

Kitty, for once, had pressed on. She'd evoked for Veronica their first summer at Les Glaniques, when they were still discovering what flourished and what died in the garden. And when the apricot trees fruited, they'd found they had the sweetest, most abundant crop they could ever have imagined. They gorged on the juicy, pink-blushed apricots. They made jam and pies and glazed tartlets. Feeding apricots to Kitty in bed, Veronica had said: 'I can hardly remember a pre-apricot world, can you?'

But Veronica halted this retelling of past things. She put her hands up, as though trying to stop a moving train. She said she didn't want to think about all that 'normality'. She said she found any evocation of normality offensive. That was the word she used: *offensive*.

Then, she'd put her face in her hands. Staring at her bent head, Kitty had seen that her hair — the thick head of hair she usually kept clean and shiny — needed washing and she thought that washing Veronica's hair for her might be a consoling thing and so she gently suggested it. But Veronica didn't move.

'My hair's fine,' she said. 'Thank you.'

Kitty walked away. *Gardening without Rain*, she thought, hadn't been a bad title for a book. But Kitty knew now that it was a book that would never be finished.

★   ★   ★

269

Kitty felt the hammock sway slightly. She looked out at the stand of oleanders, blemished by yellowing leaves, and saw them move and she thought, The new misery in my life is like the mistral: it dies down at night and lets me encounter silk-weavers in Mumbai and wind-surfers on the Indian Ocean, and then back it comes with the morning. And there's nothing to be done. The wind sucks away the last drops of moisture from the poor, parched garden . . .

It was still early. Not yet seven. But she heard the telephone ring in the house and held the hammock still, listening and waiting. Lately, the ringing of the telephone had felt to Kitty like the rampaging of a wildcat, something broken free of a cage, intent on damage.

Kitty wondered, should she leave today? Packing wouldn't take long. She could just go to her studio and parcel up some of the watercolours rejected by the gallery in Béziers, be careful to choose the best of these, to try to sell them somewhere when she ran short of money in her new destination. Then fill a small suitcase with clothes and shoes. Put in two photographs: one of Veronica and one of the house. So simple. And by tonight she could be in London or Paris, deciding on her future travel plans, imagining Veronica left to separateness and solitude, to the altered 'normality' she'd apparently chosen . . .

Now she saw Veronica, wearing her white cotton dressing gown, crossing the lawn, coming towards her, carrying a mug of tea, shading her eyes against the strengthening light in the sky.

Kitty pushed back the blanket and swung her legs out of the hammock and jumped down from it. A sparrow was startled out of one of the cherry trees and flew away. Kitty stood waiting.

Veronica handed Kitty the tea.

'He *was* at the Swiss house,' she said. 'They've got matching prints. So we know he was still alive at around lunchtime on that Tuesday.'

'Yes?' said Kitty, looking down at her tea.

'But that's all. It doesn't get us any further.'

Kitty began to sip her tea. 'What about the Mas Lunel?' she asked. 'Did you have the police check the sandwich wrapper I found?'

'No,' said Veronica. 'I don't know what I did with that bit of cellophane. I may have thrown it away.'

Kitty looked at her beloved friend. She thought, I'm no use to her any more. She's tired of the things I say. They stood in silence as the sun crept to the roofline of the house and gleamed on a blue-black starling pecking at the chimney stack, and then Kitty said: 'What I think is best is . . . if I go away.'

Veronica's arms were folded under her breasts. Now, she appeared to tighten her grip on herself, hugging the white robe to her, clutching her forearms with her big, workaday hands. She hung her head.

Kitty waited, but Veronica said nothing.

'I've been wondering where,' said Kitty. 'I guess it doesn't matter much. The world's huge and I haven't seen much of it. Only Norfolk and London. So it's probably time I did . . .'

'It can't be other than it is,' said Veronica,

cutting Kitty off. 'Of course it's *not fair* on you, the way I am. But I can't be any different. Each of us has the past we have.'

Kitty wanted to say, Yes, sure, we each have our own history. But we can *choose* to leave it behind — as I did. We can choose to go forwards and be free.

But Veronica went on talking, not looking at Kitty, but looking at the ground and the fallen cherry leaves. 'In the school holidays sometimes,' she said, 'we went to stay with our cousins in Sussex and they had a huge garden and they knew lots of other children and they'd all get invited over, and we'd make up teams for games, like cricket and rounders. And you'd have to stand in line, waiting to be picked, and what you prayed was that you were going to hear your name early on and then you could feel all proud about belonging to your new team.

'I was OK because everyone knew I was sporty and all that, but Anthony was never picked. He was *always* the last one. He was *always* left there on his own. I can still see it. His bandy little legs. This kid left there by himself because no one wanted him in their team. And I understood it somehow way back then, that I was the only person standing between Anthony and some colossal . . . tragedy. And I swore. I swore I'd never let go. And I never have. So that's just what *is* and I've got nothing more to add.'

Veronica didn't wait for Kitty to speak, sensing no doubt that Kitty was unmoved by the story she'd just told. She turned round and walked away.

Kitty held on to her tea mug. Watched Veronica until she disappeared inside the French windows of the salon. Then she began spinning a globe clockwise in her mind: Morocco . . . Egypt . . . Sri Lanka . . . Thailand . . . Australia . . .

She thought about the vibrant life in these places and how she would go there and become part of it and try to paint the things she saw. She wished, though, that she could just *arrive* somewhere — at some still lakeside jetty, at some clean, inexhaustible expanse of desert — without the lonely torment of the journey.

Aramon bought the newspaper every day now.

Some days, there were photographs of police searching the scrub. Some days, there was nothing about the Verey case — as though it had already been forgotten. Then, the headlines would come creeping back: *VEREY: still no clues. MISSING ENGLISHMAN: police appeal for witnesses.*

All the time, Aramon listened out for a siren, for the arrival of the police.

In the hot nights, sometimes, he believed he could hear the police car coming slowly up the pitted driveway and then stopping at a little distance from the house. He'd hurl himself out of bed and flatten his face to the window, and squint through the half-open shutters. He knew the shape of every shadow the moonlight cast on the terraces. His eye tried to identify each one, with his heart beating like an approaching train, while he held his breath, waiting for the dogs to begin barking. But the dogs stayed silent.

*   *   *

In his dreams, Serge beat him for his neglect of the dogs. His back and his arse were skinned alive.

He went out early one morning, before the

heat came, and opened the gate of the pound and let the dogs out to forage among the holm oaks. Then he began raking up the stinking earth inside the pound. He tied a handkerchief round his face. He trawled all the mess towards him and shovelled it, load by load, into a wheelbarrow and tipped it out into the scrub, scattering it over the dry earth, for the flies and dung-beetles to find.

Then he went down to the lean-to behind the barn where bales of straw were piled up. He knifed open a new bale and began tearing at the straw to load it into the barrow. He felt exhausted. The handkerchief on his face was soaking wet and he tore it off and threw it down. The sun was climbing the hills on the other side of the valley. Get it done, Aramon told himself. Spread the straw, fill the water trough, whistle for the dogs, pen them in. Take a drink of pastis to calm your heart. Then sleep . . .

He piled up the straw and pushed the barrow back to the pound. He wheeled it in and tipped the straw out and took up his pitchfork, to begin spreading it around over the newly raked earth. Then he felt the sun's heat strike him and he paused in his work. As he straightened up, his eye fell on something glinting in the soil in the far corner of the pound.

He stood the fork against the barrow and walked over to where the object lay. He bent down. He reached out and picked up a set of car keys.

★ ★ ★

275

The things that had to be done then . . . they made Aramon faint with terror.

He knelt in the pound, clutching the keys, smelling the clean straw, wishing he had the life of a dog, blameless and uncomplicated. From his afflicted lungs came an agonised keening sound, barely human.

He left everything the way it was, his task unfinished, the water trough unfilled, the gate of the pound open, the dogs loose among the oaks, sniffing for the scent of wild boar.

He looked in the direction of Audrun's bungalow. He could see his own washing on her drying line, everything still in shadow down there, and motionless, with no wind to move it. He dreaded seeing Audrun standing there, watching him. And he thought, If I postpone the things I've got to do, she'll arrive and find me and she'll see whatever is in the car and then everything will be lost.

He made his way to the barn. His walk was limping and crabbed, as though he were trying to dodge his own shadow. He held the keys bunched in his hand, so tightly they dug into his palm.

He inched the old barn doors open and went in and it was cold in the barn and the sweat on him seemed to turn to ice. He stared at the car, draped in its sacking, piled up with crates and boxes. He felt unable to move.

Suppose it really was there, the body of Anthony Verey, rotting in the hired car?

Aramon wanted to cling to something. Almost wished he could die right there, just fall onto the floor of the barn and cease to be. Because this thing had come into his life and blighted it. It had no name. There was no name he could give it because he didn't know what it was that he'd done.

To make himself move towards the car, he had to imagine that Serge was behind him, Serge with his belt, whipping him on.

Go on, boy. Go on and open the door . . .

He pressed the lock release button on the key fob. Lights flashed on the car.

Now you'll see what's waiting for you, waiting in the darkness . . .

He did it in one movement, reaching out and grabbing the handle and pulling the door, dislodging an empty apple crate, which crashed down beside him.

Immediately, it leapt at him, a foul stench in the car, and he cried out and slammed the door shut again.

He stood there, with his eyes closed, his breathing so fast and laboured that his chest burned with pain. To his dead father, he whispered, 'Take it away. Take it away from me . . .'

Then he heard a movement at the barn door: a scuffling and whimpering.

And he knew that some of the dogs had followed his scent and found him. And so an idea came to him: let the dogs find it. Let the starving dogs feast their eyes on it, let them tear it apart and eat it up . . . and then it will be gone and I'll never have to see it . . .

With his back turned to it, Aramon opened the car door again, opened it wide and then began calling to the dogs and they whimpered in response.

He shuffled to the door as fast as he could and opened it and they came bounding into the barn, three dogs, and clawed at him and he pushed them towards the car, knowing that smell was the sense that powered all their actions and that they would go straight to it, to that stench, and begin whatever it was their animal brains commanded them to do.

He went back to the open door, taking gulps of the fresh air. He heard the dogs' claws clattering and sliding on the bodywork on the car. One of them began barking. Then they were quiet and he knew they were in the car now, following the smell, and he waited for the frenzy to start.

Time seemed to stretch and tease Aramon. Outside, cicadas and bees were stirred from sleep as the sun warmed them. A buzzard turned in the blue sky. That's the world, the real world, thought Aramon longingly, and the black car is not part of it, but only part of some dark nightmare that I can't understand.

★ ★ ★

He sat at his kitchen table, gulping pastis.

There had been no dead body in the car.

The stench that had momentarily filled the air had come from a half-eaten and now putrid Camembert and tomato sandwich, which even the dogs had left alone.

Aramon had made himself open the car boot, but there had been nothing in the boot except a pair of binoculars and a floppy hat and an

278

insulated bag containing a bottle of water. He closed and locked the car, with the sandwich still inside, because he couldn't bear to touch it. He called to the three dogs and walked out with them into the sunshine, with the car keys in his pocket.

Now, what occupied his mind as he gulped his pastis was how to make the car disappear.

He'd seen plenty of old films on TV where people succeeded in pushing cars off cliff tops, in setting fire to them, or drowning them in a lake. But, they were always found in the end. There was always some charred or broken version of the car which came to light. Those movie scenes were exciting precisely because you knew that, no matter what the murderers did, the cars would be found.

Murderers.

Was he one of them?

Aramon knew that trying to get rid of the car was beyond him. He was too weak, too ill, to contemplate any kind of action in regard to it. He knew that it'd just sit there in the barn. It wouldn't move from there. He'd pile straw over it, to mask it from sight. He'd put a strong padlock on the barn doors. That was the best he could do.

He climbed his stairs, unsteady after the pastis. He went into the room which had once been Audrun's room, and which neither he nor she ever visited. The shutters were closed and the room felt cold. Aramon took the car keys out of his pocket and stuffed them away under Audrun's mattress.

Audrun began measuring the river levels.

She went out at first light, when the valley was still deep in shadow.

She didn't need a notched stick or a knotted rope; she measured with her eye. She remembered Raoul Molezon once telling her: 'The wind sucks up the water. The mistral especially. It's thirsty for the river.' Audrun's heart galloped to see how fast the river was going down.

She watched the TV weather forecasts. She saw the temperatures indicated in red: 38°, 39°, 41° . . . The kind of heat in which people died. They suffocated in airless apartments, or contracted sunstroke, or expired from dehydration, or were burned alive in forest fires, trying to rescue their animals or their possessions. No end in sight to the heatwave, said the forecasters. No respite from water shortage, despite the wet spring. All leave for the region's fire-fighters cancelled, the *canadair* planes put on twenty-four-hour alert. Infernos feared in the Cévennes.

Infernos feared.

For fifteen years — until it ended, until Serge ended it by dying — there had been an inferno inside Audrun. Fifteen years. Her youth burned away inside her, in agony, with no one to tell, no one to come to the rescue. Not even Raoul Molezon. Because how could she tell him — tell any man — about that shame, that *branding*?

She couldn't. Not even when Raoul came to meet her outside the rayon factory that day, came courting her in fact, buying that glass of *sirop de pêche* while he drank his beer and told her she was beautiful. She felt that she loved him, but she was too disgraced and shamed by what she'd done to risk showing him what was in her heart.

Put the girdle on, Audrun.

So sweet it is, that bit of your pussy I can see underneath it.

See what it does to me? See?

Your brother's the same. Big as a snake, he gets. Eh?

We can't help it. It's your fault for being who you are.

She thought Raoul loved her. On that day, he seemed to caress her with his tender brown eyes. She longed to reach out and touch his hair, his mouth. But she knew it was impossible. Everything was impossible and so she had to say it: 'Don't come to meet me again, Raoul. It's better if you don't.'

And he'd looked so sad, it was unbearable.

It's your fault for being who you are.

★ ★ ★

A car stopped outside her gate. She stood at the window of her kitchen, peeling white onions for her supper, watching.

Two middle-aged strangers got out and looked all around them. Then the man began walking towards her door, while the woman hung back, as though embarrassed or afraid.

Audrun rinsed her hands and took off her flowered overall and smoothed her skirt and went to the door very calmly, and the man stared at her; an agitated kind of look.

'Can I help you, Monsieur?' she said.

He was a foreigner. He spoke French, but with some ugly accent or other. He said he'd been told by agents in Ruasse that there was a mas for sale beyond La Callune — the Mas Lunel — but the agents wouldn't bring him here, because apparently the vendor had changed his mind, so he . . . he and his wife . . . had decided to drive up and take a look for themselves . . . just in case . . .

Audrun stared at the foreigners. There was something about the man, a kind of worn and lean look, which reminded her of Verey.

She smiled at him. 'The Mas Lunel belongs to me,' she said.

'Oh,' said the man. 'We were told there was a Monsieur — '

'My brother,' said Audrun. 'He works the land. It suits me to let him live up there. I prefer my small modern house, you see.'

'Yes, I see. But is the mas still for sale? We love the proportions of it, the outlook . . . Our name is Wilson. This is my wife . . . '

The anxious woman stepped forward and held out her hand and Audrun took it. Then she said sweetly: 'My situation has changed. This happens unexpectedly in life, *n'est-ce pas*? So I've decided not to sell. The house has been in my family for three generations. So now I'm going to restore it. Perhaps I'll end my days there? Who can say?'

They looked crestfallen. They asked if she could be persuaded to change her mind.

'No,' she said. 'Other things have changed, but my mind will not change.'

They both turned and stared longingly at the mas and Audrun could see it in their eyes, a will to possess it. They said they'd been looking at houses in this part of France for a long time and tomorrow they were leaving for England . . .

Audrun contemplated their ordinariness. She wondered how these colourless, mute people had made so much money that they could waltz down to the Cévennes and buy themselves a second home. And she thought, I don't know how money is made. I've never known. All Bernadette had was what we grew on the terraces or what we could exchange for the things we grew; all I had was what I earned in the underwear factory, and all I have now is my little state pension — that, and what I can grow in the *potager*.

'I'm sorry,' she said. 'Nothing here is for sale.'

★　★　★

The Wilsons drove away. The moment they'd gone, Audrun saw Aramon limping down the drive towards her. He looked like a scarecrow, with his trousers held up at the waist by a piece of string and his hair dirty and wild.

'Who were those people?' he asked. 'What did they want?'

283

Audrun looked away from him. She knew she could make him sweat by saying they were friends of Verey's, but at that moment Marianne Viala appeared at Audrun's gate.

Marianne kissed Audrun. Then she turned to Aramon and said: 'You don't look well, *mon ami.*'

'I'm not well,' he said. 'Something's poisoning me. I may have to go to the hospital.'

'You *should* go,' said Marianne. 'And you shouldn't drink, Aramon, if your stomach's not right . . .'

'Who were those people?' shouted Aramon again. 'Tell me who they were.'

'Foreigners,' Audrun said. 'They just stopped to ask the way.'

'The way to where?'

'To Ruasse.'

'Ruasse? Their car was facing in the wrong direction.'

'Yes,' said Audrun. 'I set them on the right road.'

He stood there, twisted up with fear. At the corner of his mouth was a fleck of white foam. Marianne Viala looked at Audrun questioningly, then reached out and laid a hand on Aramon's arm.

'You should take better care of yourself, Aramon,' she said. 'But listen, I've got a favour to ask you.'

Aramon's eyes darted left and right, left and right, and Audrun knew what thought those darting eyes hid: *Don't ask me favours. I'm too ill, too tired, too frightened, to grant them.*

'Yes?' he said. 'Well?'

'Jeanne wants to bring her class up here tomorrow, after they've visited the Museum of Cévenol Silk Production at Ruasse. She's bringing packed lunches for the kids and she wants a nice shady spot for their picnic, so I thought about your lower terraces — if you didn't mind them on your land. It's only a small class and — '

'On my land?' he said. 'Where, on my land?'

'I said: on your lowest terrace, the grassy plateau below the vines . . . '

'I can't have kids poking about on my property. I told you, I'm not well. I can't have the worry of it.'

'They won't 'poke about'. They're just going to eat a picnic.'

'Kids. I can't endure that . . . '

'You can have the picnic on the other side of the road,' said Audrun quietly. 'On my land. Near the wood.'

'Oh,' said Marianne. 'But I thought . . . if Aramon didn't mind . . . they could combine the picnic with looking at the dry-stone walling of the terraces. They might do some drawing, and — '

'No!' said Aramon, and he threw Marianne a look of anguish. 'I don't want anybody near anything. I'm tired of strangers. I want to be left alone!'

Aramon turned away from them abruptly and began his slow walk, *hobbledehoy, hobbledehoy,* back towards the mas, and in silence the two women watched him go.

When he was out of hearing, Marianne said:
'Is he dying?'

'Well,' said Audrun. 'Let's say that time's
caught up with him.'

Time.

A flickering out of each and every moment before it had been properly lived — as though time were a whirlwind, a mistral, blowing everything to kingdom come — this was what Anthony Verey had had to contend with for years — ever since his business had begun to fail. Then, sitting in his back office, that morning in spring, he'd caught sight of the black silk thread hanging from the Aubusson tapestry, that black thread escaping from the head of the malevolent witch, and he'd held it between finger and thumb and understood at last what waited for him: *death unfurnished*.

★ ★ ★

And so a certain day had arrived.

On this inevitable day, Anthony found himself sitting on a mahogany-framed armchair ('Probably French, c.1770. With padded cartouche back. Arms and seat on cabriole legs') and he was looking around at a handsome room in an unfamiliar, lonely house, with a view of empty sky at every window.

His gaze settled and moved on, settled and moved on. The room was aesthetically pleasing — there was nothing ugly in it. But it was here in this place, in this almost-beautiful room, sitting on this expensive chair, upholstered in charcoal-grey-and-white damask, that Anthony Verey felt it pinching and pulling at his frame: *final defeat.*

He sat very still. So still, he could hear the thud of his own heart. The room had a high beamed ceiling, painted a soft shade of blue-green. Near him, was a tall stone *cheminée* ('Modern. Sandstone. In the English Georgian style. Simplified lines and moulding') and in the fireplace a half-burned piece of wood, resting on a pile of ash.

With his dispassionate, collector's eye, with some distant part of himself still alive in this present, Anthony admired the room, its proportions, its flicker of grandeur, its place in a house that stood so alone. For a little while, he was able to distract himself from his feelings of collapse by imagining the Swiss couple who'd put this room together: lawyers or professors, educated people, a couple with a full address book which connected them, perhaps, to many different worlds. People on whom life had smiled. And yet they'd hung on to their souls. They weren't vulgar. They weren't afraid of silence.

But then, when a certain amount of time had passed, they'd understood what Anthony understood: that this house *exposed* them in too terrible a way. It sat too high on a pitiless plateau, unguarded, unprotected — with a precipice at its feet. The wind bent the pines planted to give it shade and shelter, bent them and bowed them.

The trees were still just alive. They clung to

288

the stony soil, still, clawed into it with their obstinate roots, but they couldn't shield the house or its occupants. The dome of sky held everything here in its grip. Here, at night, you'd find no retreat from the icy stars. The universe would reach down to you. And everything that you'd been, tried to become, hoped fondly yet to be: all this, in its folly and delusion, would be revealed to you — as though there were no decency or honour in any of it.

Perhaps you could light a fire in the grate, huddle near it, grasping at small comforts: wine and memory. But always, round and round you, would expand the void. You'd see yourself as though from a vast height: the way you crawled from one purpose to the next, endlessly starting and giving up, endlessly hoping and repenting, endlessly lost . . .

Anthony gripped the arms of the chair. He looked down at the charred log on the mound of ash. He could no longer hold on to his musings about the Swiss couple. What came instead to his desolate mind was an image of Lal, tripping into this spacious room, always so light on her feet, wearing perhaps that lavender dress she'd worn the day she climbed the ladder to his tree-house and eaten brandy snaps filled with whipped cream . . .

He looked up. Yes, there she came, his beloved Lal, insubstantial as candyfloss, and then something caught her eye: the sight of the half-burned piece of wood on the dead ashes and she skipped over to it and knelt down in front of it and said: 'Oh, do look, darling! Doesn't that silly old stick remind you of someone? What a scream, hey? *A stick!* Doesn't that remind you of you?'

Despite the insult (or was it only a joke? With Lal you never really knew), Anthony longed for his mother to stay with him. In his reverie, he got up from the chair and took her hands and then put his arms round her and held her close to him and buried his face in her golden hair and said, 'Stay with me, Ma. Please. Don't leave me in this place.'

'Oh, all right, darling,' she said. 'All right. I'll stay. If I must. I'll hold on to you.'

But she escaped from his arms and went back to the fireplace and knelt by it, and then she did something awful: she crawled onto the mound of ash, and lay down, lay down in the ash, holding the half-burnt log close against her breast.

'Don't, Ma . . . ' said Anthony.

There was ash in her hair, in the folds of her dress, on her slender legs, on her naked feet. He reached down, to try to pull her up, but she wouldn't be moved.

'Ma . . . ' he pleaded. But she lay there, laughing, clutching the stick. She just lay there laughing her silvery laugh and said: 'I've got you now, Anthony. See? That's what you always wanted, wasn't it? I've got you close to me!'

He begged and begged her: 'Ma, get up. You're covered in ash. Please . . . '

But she'd never heard a single thing he'd said in his whole life. And she couldn't hear him now.

★ ★ ★

Anthony walked slowly round the room, trailing his fingers over the surfaces of furniture that he admired, but found this admiration tempered, as though even these — these *beloved* kind of things — held no importance for him any more.

He went outside. He was awed by the vast bowl of hills that spread round him, from horizon to horizon. The wind was so strong that the car was rocking where it stood on the gravel driveway. And he thought, If I walked to the edge, the northern edge of the plateau, where the mistral pulls hardest against gravity, I'd only have to wait a few moments before I'd be hurled away. I'd be pitched into the darkness where, soundless, voiceless, Lal lies waiting.

And then it would be over.

It would be over.

There would be no more dallying and flirting with the future, in any of its ever-changing, ever-mutating versions. I would simply be lifted up by the wind and thrown down on a bed of ash.

And I would accept.

★   ★   ★

Jeanne Viala settled herself and the children in Audrun's little field, close to the oaks that grew at the edge of the wood.

The class had been attentive and well behaved in the Museum of Cévenol Silk Production. Even Jo-Jo, with his short attention span, had seemed to be interested in the exhibits and all the children had completed quite good drawings

291

of the different stages of silkworm-rearing: the incubating of the eggs in pouches secreted against the human body; the spreading of the worms in the *magnaneries*; the devices used to keep rats and ants at bay; the gathering of mulberry leaves; the *montada* of the grown worms, five centimetres long, into the sprigs of heather; the spinning of the cocoons; the boiling alive of the emerging moths inside the cocoons as the threads were unwound . . .

Only the Parisian girl, Mélodie, had seemed unhappy. Her drawing, reluctantly undertaken, had consisted of dark lines up and down and across the page. When Jeanne Viala asked her what this was meant to be, Mélodie had replied in a strangled voice: '*Les flats*. All the dead worms.'

And then, in the middle of the picnic, which was so pleasant under the great dark trees — such a happy moment, in fact that Jeanne would have liked to share it with her new boyfriend, Luc, who worked for the Fire Service — Mélodie had got up and run off, without permission, without even looking back when Jeanne called her.

Jeanne had decided to let her go. She knew these terraces. The child couldn't come to any harm. The land lay well below the road. The way to the river was impassable because, for years now, Aramon Lunel had ignored the directives of the commune on river-bank maintenance. And Jeanne didn't want to leave the whole group, to go running after one child. She hoped Mélodie would soon reappear. Jeanne had packed bottles of cherry Yop for dessert and she would tempt her with one of these to sit down again.

The other children stared at Mélodie as she ran off. Stared and stared.

'She didn't like the silkworms,' said Magali. 'All she likes is dancing class and *violin*!' And the others laughed at this, and Jo-Jo burst out: 'She thinks she's better than us, just because she used to live in Paris, silly cow.'

'Stop it, Jo-Jo!' said Jeanne. 'I won't tolerate that kind of talk.'

'She's a Jew, anyway,' mumbled Stéphanie. 'Hartmann's a Jewish name.'

'*What* did you say, Stéphanie?' said Jeanne.

'Nothing . . .'

Jeanne Viala set down her bottle of Evian water. She held up her hands in an embracing gesture. 'Listen, everybody,' she said. 'Please everybody stop talking and listen to me. Jo-Jo, that includes you. Now I want to remind you that in this country we are a tolerant people. You know what tolerant means? It means that we accept people into our community and into our hearts, no matter what their background is, or their religion, or what city they've come from. And this means — please listen very carefully — this means that we don't *bully* anybody or call them names. Is this understood? I would really like to know that you've all understood this.'

The children were silent, every one. Jeanne shook her head in a sorrowful way. 'The way Mélodie Hartmann has been treated in this class is . . . disappointing. Her home was in Paris. There's nothing wrong with that. She's trying to adapt to her new surroundings. But you're not giving her the chance — '

'She doesn't 'adapt', said Magali. 'She just keeps telling everybody how brilliant her school in Paris was.'

'She's homesick, that's all,' said Jeanne. 'If you'd all make an effort to be more friendly to her, her homesickness would disappear. So, as from today, I want you all to make a resolution. Are you listening? Stéphanie? As from today, I want to see kindness shown to Mélodie. All right? Real kindness. Let her into your games. When she gets lost, help her. OK? I really hope everybody is understanding this?'

Some of the girls nodded. Mostly, the boys turned away and looked blank.

'Can we have the Yops now?' said the youngest girl in the class, Suzanne.

Jeanne waited. She wanted something more from the children than this. She had bad dreams about the way the Parisian girl was being treated. She thought of poor Audrun Lunel and Marianne saying, 'When lives are blighted young, Jeannette, sometimes you just don't quite recover, and that's a true tragedy.'

Jeanne began to take out the cherry Yops from the cold-bag. 'Before I give these to you,' she said, 'I want to hear from each one of you that you've heard what I've said. Say it please. 'There will be no more bullying of Mélodie Hartmann.''

It was on its way to the hand of the first child, the little bottle of Yop . . . it was on its way but didn't reach the hand, didn't elicit from the child any words . . . because it was then that Jeanne and the children heard the screams.

Jeanne dropped the bottle and sprang to her feet. All the children's faces turned and looked down towards the edge of the field. Jo-Jo and his friend André jumped up in hectic excitement. 'What's that, Miss? What's that?'

'Wait here,' Jeanne said firmly to the group. 'Wait here and don't move. Jo-Jo and André, sit down on the rug please. Nobody go from here, right? Stay exactly where you are. Promise me? Magali, give out the Yops.'

The screams kept on. Jeanne Viala began to run towards them. She ran faster and faster, but soon she could feel her heart cramping, like the heart of an old woman, as she forced her legs to carry her across the sloping field. She cursed herself. What kind of teacher sat back and allowed a child to wander off on her own from a country picnic?

And . . . *oh God* . . . which way had the child gone? The screams had suddenly stopped as Jeanne reached the edge of the field. Should she go straight on, into the pasture that led to the river, or turn left? She looked at the ground, to see if any tracks were visible, but nothing showed up in the dry grass, only the red-backed crickets jumping and the dry heads of hemlock burning up in the sun.

She began calling: 'Mélodie! Mélodie!' But now everything around Jeanne seemed infected with a colossal silence. The loudest thing was the beating of Jeanne's own heart. She kneaded her chest, felt her white blouse sticking to her body. Luc, she wanted to cry, help me . . . '

Then she made herself think rationally: try one direction, then another. Keep calling. Everything's up to you now.

She stumbled on, shouting out the child's name, telling her she was on her way, she was coming, it was all right . . . She pushed through a rusted iron gate into the pasture. She thought that in the damp pasture, there might be footprints she could follow, but when she got into the meadow she saw that the grass here was brown and parched too, and it was lumpy and her feet in her white canvas shoes were twisted this way and that and she almost fell, but recovered herself and ran on, going towards a spindly clump of ash, beyond which was the river bank.

She was out of breath now, in the colossal heat, struggling with the tussocks of dead grass. She stopped for a moment. What could she hear?

Nothing. A bird of prey calling, a buzzard or a kitty-hawk. And then . . . yes . . . something else . . . the sound of the river. She went on in that direction, through the ash grove, and was grateful for the dappled shade of the spindly trees, shielding her from the sun, just for a moment. The river was louder now. But between the ash trees and the river bank were briars and nettles. Surely, the child couldn't have pushed her way through those?

Jeanne stopped again. She was about to turn round and make her way back up the pasture when she saw that what she'd taken for nettles weren't in fact nettles, but those plumed dark weeds that hugged the shingle banks of the

Gardon in a few shady corners, where snakes sometimes made their nests, in places the fishermen avoided.

And then she saw that, at one spot, a clump of these weeds had been flattened. Perhaps she'd chosen the right path after all? She followed where the tracks led, imagining the child's little feet treading all this down, careless of snakes in her misery, just rushing on, away from the bullying Jo-Jo and the sneering girls, fighting her way through the rank weeds . . .

Jeanne arrived on a shingle bank and saw the river trying to rush steadfastly on, but slowing, slowing almost as she watched it, the way it did every summer when no rain fell after the month of April. But her gaze didn't linger on the water. She began searching for footprints in the shingle. The stones were coarse and slippery, but nearer the water's edge there was a grey beach and she walked down to this and thought she saw tracks going left, towards the river bend.

'Mélodie . . . Mélodie . . . ' she began calling again, knowing her voice wasn't loud any more. She felt exhausted, as though she'd walked from Ruasse to La Callune, uphill all the way, with cars rushing by her and the road edge scarred with fallen rocks. 'Oh please, please let me find her,' she said. 'Please let her be alive . . . '

Jeanne rounded the bend. Immediately, she saw the child, naked except for a little pair of red-and-white briefs, lying on a boulder in the middle of the river. She lay on her back, with her legs overhanging the boulder, gravity threatening to pull her body down at any moment into the water. Strewn about on the shingle beach were the clothes she'd been wearing for the outing.

Cold now. Jeanne was suddenly cold. And the thought of wading into the icy water was unbearable. *Oh God* . . . if only Luc were here to gather the child into his arms, to frighten away the stranger who might be hiding anywhere along the river line . . . But sometimes, Jeanne knew, there is no one, no Luc, no Marianne, no one. You're alone and what you have to do is to go on. And whatever is going to happen, is going to happen . . .

Jeanne kicked off her canvas shoes, remembered her mobile phone in the pocket of her jeans and stuck it inside one of the shoes. She walked into the river and felt the chill eddy round her calves. She clung to rocks to steady her progress on the slimy, stony river-bed. 'I'm here now,' she kept repeating out loud. 'I'm here now. I'm here now . . .'

And she was almost there. She reached out. She said the child's name again: Mélodie. She touched one of the little smooth legs, the toe dangling almost into the water. She held it tight. Then she pressed herself against the boulder and gathered the child to her. Mélodie still lay across the stone, but she was held now, held in Jeanne Viala's arms. Her eyes were closed. Her mouth open. But Jeanne could feel her heartbeat and her breathing.

She shook her and cried out to her, told her she was safe now. And to her ecstatic relief Mélodie opened her eyes. And Jeanne felt the

298

child's thin arms go round her neck and cling to her.

Jeanne cradled her and rocked her, letting the boulder still take the weight but holding her as close as she could while she readied herself to carry the child back across the water.

'What happened?' she said softly. 'Are you hurt? Did someone hurt you?'

But the little girl couldn't speak. She opened her mouth, but the sounds that came out weren't words, only a low melodic moaning.

Make her warm, Jeanne instructed herself. Carry her to the bank. Get her clothes on. Get help. Call Luc. Tell him to send an ambulance. Call Maman to come and be with the children.

Now, she had to lift Mélodie, take the whole weight of her and somehow turn and, without slipping and falling, make her way to the shingle strand. Without letting go of the child, Jeanne looked all around her, to determine the safest pathway through the water.

Beyond the boulder was a deep pool. Jeanne Viala had a flicker of memory about pools like this, where she'd once paddled and swum with her father when he was alive and he would try to tickle a trout for supper from under the overhanging stones.

She stared at the green pool. There were fish in this one, she suddenly saw. But dead: the white bellies of two dead fish floating on the surface of the water. But, strangely, not borne away by the current . . . as though they were still attached to something below the water line . . . *not fish at all . . .*

Jeanne gagged. She looked away. Shivering, clutching the girl, she felt her stomach keep rising. She tried with all her will to keep the sickness down, but she couldn't. Her body convulsed and she vomited up her sandwich. Flecks of this regurgitated food spattered Mélodie's arm. Then the water bore it away, towards the green pool, towards the white soles of the feet of the drowned body and the thin funnel of tissue, like scarlet smoke, drifting up from the depths, where the head must lie.

So now it arrived.

Audrun knew it was the last storm of her life and when it was over, if she survived it, everything would be altered, and she would be free. It came flying in to La Callune on a late afternoon, when the sun was still hot and the sky empty and blue.

First, Audrun heard the wailing of an ambulance, then she saw a posse of police cars gathering on the road. She began to count the police officers: five, six, seven . . . and she thought, I may have to say it seven times or more, over and over again, the same thing, the same statement.

She went to her bedroom and changed her clothes, putting on a clean cotton dress and brown sandals she'd bought at the market in Ruasse.

She tidied her hair. She could hear the police radios coughing and shrieking like zoo animals. It was all exactly as she'd imagined it would be, as though she'd seen it in a film — in hundreds of films, as she sat alone in her chair on winter afternoons, with her crocheted rug over her knees and the light from the television the only light in the room — and these films had also shown her something else: they'd taught her how she, the innocent witness, should behave.

She half expected Aramon to come running

down to her bungalow, blubbing with terror, but he didn't appear. So she knew what he was doing: he was hiding. Anywhere he thought was safe: in a wardrobe with his old clothes and his shotgun; in the attics; in the spinney of holm oaks behind the dog pound. As though he believed, if he curled up like a hedgehog, he'd become invisible . . .

★ ★ ★

The day was sliding towards sunset when the first policeman knocked at Audrun's door. Another man was with him, dressed in plain clothes, the kind of man who, in the TV movies, is the one to piece everything together.

This man — unlike the mere *flics* — is always given a tainted private life: a failing marriage or a drink problem or an incurable sadness of heart; the things that make film-characters human and real.

So Audrun knew that it was to him that she should address everything — in a voice that faltered just a little (because of the shock of it all), but in a sequence that was logical. And this man would be kind to her and patient and would listen while the *flic* took notes . . .

His name was Inspecteur Travier. His age was about forty and he was good-looking. He sat down in Audrun's kitchen, which was tidy and clean.

'The body of a man has been found in the river,' he announced gravely.

Audrun gasped. Her wait to hear these words

now felt unbearably long, as if it had lasted years and years. She clutched at the bodice of her cotton dress.

'Drowned?' she forced herself to ask in a breathless voice. 'Not one of the fishermen from our village?'

'No. We're ninety per cent certain the body is that of the missing English tourist, Anthony Verey.'

'*Pardi*!' exclaimed Audrun. 'I read about that in the papers. So he was in the river! Did he slip and fall? The river can be so treacherous, unless you know it . . . '

'The cause of death has yet to be determined,' said Travier, 'but we have reason to believe, from a wound found in the gut, that a crime was committed.'

'*Pardi*!' said Audrun again, and she got up to snatch a glass from beside the sink and filled the glass and began gulping the water.

Travier waited. Out of the corner of her eye, Audrun saw the *flic* watching her closely, but Travier just waited patiently, looking quietly round the room. When Audrun sat down again, Travier cleared his throat and said, 'It's on record that on the 27th of April, Monsieur Verey came up here, to look round the house known as the Mas Lunel — '

'I'm sorry,' said Audrun. 'Oh I'm sorry but I can't talk at the moment. I can't catch my breath. This news is so shocking. Who found the body?'

'A young woman, Madame. With a party of schoolchildren. In fact, one of the children was the first on the scene.'

'*Ah non!*' Audrun burst out. '*Mon dieu,* the things that happen . . . '

'I know,' said Travier, as if replying to Audrun's hidden thoughts. 'Terrible.'

Audrun kneaded her bony chest with her hand, as though massaging her heart. When she'd allowed her breathing to calm a little, Inspecteur Travier said: 'Are you all right? May I ask you just a few questions?'

'*Mon dieu, mon dieu,*' said Audrun. 'You know, I met that poor man. I saw him living . . . '

'You met him when he came up here to look round the Mas Lunel?'

'Yes.'

'The Mas Lunel is your family home?'

'It *was* our family home. Aramon — my brother — inherited it when our father died. But now it's got too much for him — keeping the house ship-shape, and all the land . . . He's older than me. His health isn't good . . . '

'So he decided to sell it?'

'He hoped for money, Inspecteur. Lots of money. It's the scourge of our modern world, everybody wanting to be rich. We were never rich in this family, we just got by. I don't know what's got into Aramon's head.'

Inspecteur Travier paused. He rested his chin on his hand. Audrun sipped more water as Travier asked, 'It was on that day, was it, that Monsieur Verey came with agents from Ruasse, to look round the house?'

'I don't know,' said Audrun. 'Days and dates. I don't know . . . Oh God, I keep thinking about

304

that poor child who found the corpse! A thing like that could disturb you for life, couldn't it? It could haunt your dreams.'

'She'll be given counselling. She will be helped to forget. Now, could you confirm to me when you first saw Monsieur Verey?'

'It probably was at the end of April. But I can't remember the date. I don't keep a calendar. I haven't got very much to write on it.'

'I understand. But you think that you did definitely see him on that occasion?'

'Yes.'

'And can you tell us, was he alone, except for the estate agent?'

'No. On that occasion, he was with his sister, I think, and another friend and the agent. And then the second time — '

Audrun cut herself off, put a hand to her mouth. Silence descended on the small room. Travier, who had those same intelligent blue eyes that characterised so many of his movie counterparts, exchanged a glance with his constable, and then these captivating blue eyes of his narrowed and gazed at Audrun with thrilling attention.

'Tell me about that 'second time',' he said.

Audrun shook her head. 'I can't be sure,' she said. 'I shouldn't say things I can't be sure about . . . '

She hung her head. Both men watched her closely. She laid her hands one beside the other on the patterned oilcloth, on the little space where she ate her countless solitary meals and took her pills and sometimes just sat motionless, waiting for her life — her real life, in which she would feel safe — to begin. Then she drew in a deep breath and it came to her attention how sweetly the air of her tiny kitchen was scented by the presence of these two men still in the prime of their lives.

'The second time,' said Travier. 'You say you can't be sure about it, but you thought you saw Verey again, didn't you?'

'I think it was him,' said Audrun hesitantly. 'I couldn't swear to it. I saw a man walking up to the mas,' she said.

'By himself?'

'Yes. I looked out of my window and saw him — his back view. I didn't think anything about it, except that Monsieur Verey had decided to come back. I didn't come out to talk to him. I just saw him walking towards the house on his own. Then, a bit later on, I was looking out of my other window, in my sitting room, and I saw him — the man I saw — crossing the road with Aramon . . .'

'Aramon, your brother?'

'Yes.'

The constable wrote and wrote. Travier's face was now very near to Audrun's. Despite the blue eyes, there was something about him which reminded her of Raoul Molezon, long ago. She found herself wondering whether Travier had ever bought *sirop de pêche* in a café in Ruasse, for a girl dear to his heart.

'After that,' he said, 'did you see this man again?'

'No,' said Audrun.

'Are you sure? Are you absolutely sure? You didn't catch a glimpse of them both, coming back from the river?'

'No. That was the last time I saw him.'

'And your brother? When was the next time you saw him?'

Audrun took another gulp of her water. 'I can't remember,' she said.

'So you didn't see *him* coming back from the river?'

'No.'

'When d'you think you saw him again — Aramon?'

'I don't know. I told you, my memory's not good for dates and times. It'd be a few days after that. I think it might have been when he found a dead dog in the pound.'

'A dead dog?'

'Yes. He was upset. He's fond of the dogs — his hunting dogs. But he went out one morning and there was a dead animal. He was very upset.'

'He hunts wild boar with dogs?'

'Yes. There's a syndicate in La Callune.'

'So he keeps a shotgun?'

'Oh yes. Don't worry, he's got a licence. We don't know why the dog died. But it was very upsetting for Aramon. And . . . I think it was on that day that I showed Aramon the picture of Monsieur Verey in the papers. I said to him, 'Wasn't that the man who came here?' And he got very agitated. But I think he was mainly still concerned about the dog and how to bury it in the hard ground.'

The constable stopped writing and he and

Travier looked at each other. Audrun knew there were *words* in this look. In films, looks were often substituted for words, because movies tried to be true to life, to how things actually unfolded — in patches of silence, in wordless darkness . . .

Travier stood up now. He walked back and forth the length of the small kitchen. Back and forth with his hands in his pockets. Then he stopped and said: 'Mademoiselle Lunel, did your brother reach any agreement with Monsieur Verey about the sale of the house?'

'No,' said Audrun, 'He thought Monsieur Verey was going to buy it — for quite a large sum — but then he changed his mind.'

'Who changed whose mind?'

'Monsieur Verey. He changed his mind — that's what my brother told me. Maybe he'd found another house. And Aramon was — '

'Yes?'

'Well, I think he was very disappointed. It was a large sum. He'd thought he was going to be rich.'

Travier sat down again and he reached out to Audrun, as though to take one of her hands in his, but she held herself apart, folded her hands in her lap. She imagined the film director saying to her: 'No, no. Don't let him take your hand, Audrun. Remember you're innocent. *Innocent.* The innocent don't betray weakness. On the contrary, they demonstrate that they've got no need of special kindness.'

But Travier nevertheless spoke in a kind voice when he said: 'Let me ask you, Mademoiselle Lunel, do you think your brother bore any

308

animosity towards Verey?'

Audrun stared at Travier, held his gaze. 'Are you asking me,' she said, 'if I think he could have harmed him?'

'Yes. I'm asking you if you think your brother has anything to do with the death of Anthony Verey.'

Now, she began to cry. It wasn't difficult.

It never had been difficult. To summon tears, she only had to think about Bernadette. It wasn't even acting. It was just Bernadette calling to her from her chair in the sunlight, where she sat stringing beans, with a colander in her lap.

Audrun put her head in her hands and let her head shake from side to side and she felt the gentle touch of Inspecteur Travier's hand come gently to rest on her shoulder.

'I'm sorry,' he said, 'to ask you such a terrible question. You don't have to answer it. You don't have to — '

'I'm afraid for him!' Audrun burst out. 'He has blackouts. He does things and then can't remember them. Poor Aramon! His memory's all gone. I'm so frightened for him!'

She sobbed for a long time and her own crying sounded beautiful to her and full of harmony.

★   ★   ★

The policemen didn't stay long after that, as she knew they wouldn't.

They walked back to one of the cars on the road and the radios roared with staccato sound all down the valley. Audrun stayed out of sight, in the shadow behind the window, watching and waiting, and the sun went down and the light became grey and flat.

In this grey light, she saw them come past her door: twenty or thirty armed officers.

Far too many, she thought. Far too many for what's needed.

She opened her door a crack and stood watching, without moving.

The armed men moved slowly and quietly, fanning out onto the grass in front of the Mas Lunel. Travier was with them. A police van waited.

As the dogs caught the scent of them — of so many human bodies all at once — they began braying and howling and Audrun wondered whether Aramon wouldn't — in one last act of defiance — let the dogs loose on the policemen. She could hear their claws scrabbling against the wire of the pound.

She craned her neck to see. Three of the officers had broken off from the group and were going towards the barn, as the others crept silently onwards towards the mas. Audrun's mind stayed for a moment with those headed for the barn. She could hear them breaking the new padlock Aramon had fitted, tugging open the doors . . .

And she thought that at first, even with the flashlights they carried, they might not see it, because the vaulted dark space of the barn was so huge and because she'd succeeded so well with her camouflage . . . but then, in a matter of moments, they'd find it . . .

Driving it in there — a car so much larger and

more powerful than her own little machine — had caused her anguish. It had been the worst moment of all. Her heart had fluttered pathetically, like a bantam's heart. Her hands had begun to sweat, inside her rubber gloves. She'd stalled the Renault on the driveway, had had to rev the engine loudly when it re-started, all the while petrified that Aramon would see or hear what she was doing and then everything — *everything* — would be lost. But nobody came. No other car had gone by on the road.

And once the Renault was in place — with the horrible sandwich locked away inside — and Audrun had begun the task of draping the car with sacking and laying on the sacking a wild collection of objects broken and abandoned by Aramon over time, she'd exalted in her own cunning. People thought she was stupid. Just because she hadn't been able to have a proper life with a husband she loved, they thought she had no idea how the world worked. But now she asked herself: how many of them could have done what she'd done? How many could have done this and felt such exaltation in their hearts?

★   ★   ★

Later, the police van passed her door, with its lights a burning yellow in the darkness. And Audrun knew Aramon was inside it. She imagined the police cell where he'd be taken and his old scarecrow head tumbling down on some comfortless bed and his face, cross-eyed with confusion, staring out at the unfamiliar room.

Veronica was driven to the hospital morgue in Ruasse.

She'd been told on the telephone that forensic identification had already been done conclusively from DNA samples; she wouldn't be forced to identify her brother; those days of putting relatives through this agony were — in very many cases, such as this one — past.

But Veronica knew that until she'd seen Anthony, until she was sure that the world wasn't lying to her, she'd never believe that he was dead. And then she'd probably go mad. She'd sit at her window, listening for his car. She'd grow old sitting and listening there. She'd keep his room dusted, the sheets aired. She'd never rest in her delusion that, one day, he'd walk in through the door.

Now, she was looking down at a grey and bloated corpse, an assemblage of decayed and stinking flesh, its features gone, half-zippered into a waterproof bag.

It could be anyone . . . she wanted to say. It's certainly not Anthony. He was a lean man. His hair was strong and springy. His hands were delicate . . .

But she saw that it was him.

Pity for him swelled in her like the long slow movement of a symphony, pity boundless and deep.

312

There was a little room where she was taken to recover. She sat on a hard sofa. A mortuary assistant brought her water. In England, she thought, it wouldn't have been water, it would have been tea, but she didn't care.

None of these small details mattered one jot — and never would again.

* * *

She didn't know where to go then or what to do. Above her, all around her, she thought about the life of the hospital going on. Doctors and nurses rushing from ward to operating theatre, to recovery room, to ward again, trying to overcome suffering, trying to save lives. And the patients so touching in their belief that suffering would be overcome, their lives saved! Forgetting that in the end, every battle is lost. Every single one.

The young mortuary assistant, a student in his twenties, had stayed with Veronica. He knelt beside her, holding her hand. Over his green overalls, he wore a green plastic apron, scrubbed violently clean.

'I know,' said Veronica to this young man, 'that there are things I should be doing. Lots and lots of things. But I just can't imagine what they are.'

He shook his head, encased in a soft gauzy cap. 'You will remember these things later, Madame,' he said gently.

'I don't know if I will,' said Veronica. 'I feel my mind has . . . just . . . more or less melted away.'

313

'This is normal,' said the mortuary assistant. 'Absolutely normal. It's the shock. Now, can you get to your feet? I'll take you to the police car and they will drive you home.'

'What's your name?' asked Veronica in a tender, motherly voice.

'Paul,' said the boy.

'Paul,' repeated Veronica. 'That's a very nice name. Easy to remember. I like it when that is the case.'

★   ★   ★

So many things to do . . .

But she did nothing. She knew this was lamentable.

She sat on the terrace, watching leaves fall. She sat so still that she lost almost all the feeling in her feet. Then she got up and limped to her room and lay down, unable to hold herself upright any more. She covered herself with the sheet and the blue-and-white bed cover and closed her eyes.

She knew that crying was one of the things she should be doing, but this felt like an impossible demand, the kind of stupid, insensitive demand Lal might have made — Lal, or some stranger who didn't know her properly and who would never know her, would *never ever* know how it felt to be Veronica Verey, alive in the world . . .

She wondered whether, in fact, she'd never do anything again, except lie there in her room at Les Glaniques. Just lie there unable to move, like someone in a ghastly play by Samuel Beckett, in which nothing ever happened. It seemed very likely.

She tried to think of all the things she *might* do, but none of them attracted her. She remembered that when the vet had had to be summoned to put Susan down, she'd run into the spinney behind Bartle House and taken a stick and charged round and round and round, whacking the trees. She'd kept on running until the stick broke, then she'd found another stick and kept hitting and hitting until she had no more breath in her lungs and had to fall over and let her face come to rest on a pillow of moss.

Now, she admired from a distance the girl who had done all this charging about. She could imagine the high colour it had brought to her cheeks.

She thought it all admirable and right, for that adorable little pony. But as she lay on her bed, the idea of any bodily movement made Veronica feel so tired that she seemed to sink right down into the mattress, as if it were as deep and soft as a quicksand. Breathing felt exhausting.

★   ★   ★

Perhaps she slept. She wasn't sure.

She could see now that the room was dark and she could hear something going on, a sound she was meant to recognise, but she couldn't recognise it.

It belonged in a different life.

After some time, she decided the sound might have been the telephone ringing, but she

315

couldn't think of anybody she wanted to talk to. She was glad of one thing: that she was alone. She thought that in this loneliness there was a kind of dignity and peace.

★ ★ ★

Her memories came tumbling towards her, like sprites, like characters escaping from a story, holding hands and running fast. *'Look at us! Look at us! We're alive!'*

An evening when . . .

. . . she and Anthony sat alone in the kitchen at Bartle House, eating cereal. Lal had gone out to dinner. She, Veronica, would have been fifteen and Anthony twelve or thirteen. All they had to eat for supper was the cereal. Anthony went to the fridge and opened it and saw that it was filled with bottles of champagne and with dishes of dressed game and fish, waiting to be cooked for a party Lal was giving for her smart Hampshire friends the following night.

'Nothing's ever for us,' he said. 'I don't know why.'

'Yes you do,' said Veronica.

'You mean she doesn't care about us?'

'She doesn't *love* us.'

He sat down and stared at the cereal, half eaten in a blue bowl. Then he overturned the bowl and let the milk and cornflake mush seep into the tablecloth. He pushed it about with his hands. Veronica got up and came to him and put her arms around him. She kissed the top of his head.

'I love you,' she said. 'And I always will. I promise I always will.'

'I know, V,' he said.

★   ★   ★

Had she kept her promise?

There had been times of dereliction, months when she didn't call him or even think much about him, particularly after she'd met Kitty Meadows. For she saw it clearly now: Kitty had always wanted to separate her from Anthony, always wanted to destroy the feelings she had for him — as though they'd been sexual feelings and posed a threat. So, in a sense, Kitty was responsible for his death . . .

This felt like a coherent thought: *Kitty is responsible.*

And Veronica decided that it might always feel like that to her, that Kitty Meadows had sent Anthony to his death. Someone else, some crazed, unhappy stranger had shot him — for being an English tourist? For a reason which would always feel unreal to her. But Kitty was the one who'd wanted him dead. She was the one who'd been too obtuse to see the truth of what Anthony and his sister felt for each other and so, out of inappropriate jealous feelings, she'd willed his end.

The telephone rang again but Veronica didn't move.

★   ★   ★

In the night, she woke up and thought she heard rain.

But she knew that sometimes, you couldn't tell: was it rain or was it just the wind changing direction, breathing differently through the trees?

It went on, this sighing sound. On and on. She half wanted to get up, just to see if the rain had come, if all the weeks of drought were ending. But then she realised that she didn't care about this either. Let the garden die.

Because what is a garden? A piece of ground changed temporarily by artifice, requiring inordinate attention. An attempt at creating some baby 'paradise' to console you for all the other things that will never be yours.

And then a new thought came: *There should have been a child.* Mine or Anthony's, it wouldn't have mattered which. There should have been someone to whom all of what we've tried to do could now be given.

Someone *beloved* at last.

Fire came to the hills behind La Callune.

A thoughtless rambler discards a cigarette.

A dry leaf begins to burn . . .

The mistral chivvied the flames across the skyline. The wind blew from the north and the fire, gorged by pine resin on the high tops, paused for a moment, then changed direction and began an assault on the valley.

The air was filled with smoke and with the wailing of the fire trucks. Marianne Viala came panting up the road to Audrun's bungalow and the two elderly women stood by the gate, watching. They'd watched it before, year upon year: Cévenol fire in all its heartless grandeur. They'd seen the sky turn black. They'd seen the vinefields greyed and choked with ash. They'd seen power lines explode. But never before had they seen it come straight towards them like this, straight towards the Mas Lunel on the veering wind.

Marianne clutched Audrun's hand. The fire-fighters struggled up the steep terraces with their heavy hoses.

'The *canadairs* are on their way,' said Marianne. 'Luc called Jeanne and she rang me. The *canadairs* will put it out, Audrun. They're at the coast now, refuelling with water.'

Audrun stared up. What fascinated her about fire was the way it appeared so alive. In its crackling and spitting, she could almost hear its boast: *The earth is mine, the tinder-dry earth has always been mine.*

In contrast to the tireless, boastful fire, Audrun felt like a shadow. She knew she was faltering on the edge of one of her *episodes*. She knew she ought to go and lie down, now, before it began. But she was trying to fight it off this time. She clung to Marianne, with her head lowered, her vision concentrated on the ground at her feet. Sometimes, it could be fought like this, with her concentration on the earth, with her will alone.

When she next looked up, Raoul Molezon was there, his pickup on the driveway. She heard Marianne say to him: 'She's not well, Raoul. She's going to go . . . '

But there was no time to think about this. Audrun herself knew that there was no time. She felt the touch of Raoul's hand on her arm. 'The dogs,' he almost shouted at her. 'I'm going to set the dogs free.'

'The dogs?'

'You can't let the dogs be burned alive!'

He began to run towards the mas and Audrun thought how sweet a thing it was that Raoul Molezon could still run fast, like a boy. She broke away from Marianne and tried to run after him, not because he was still beautiful to her, but because he was right, the dogs had to be saved — those poor animals she'd kept alive with offal and bones since Aramon had been driven away in the locked and guarded van.

But she also understood, as she ran, that if the

dogs needed saving, then there were other things at the Mas Lunel that had to be saved too.

Audrun could hear Marianne trying to call her back, but she hurried on.

She knew she looked awkward, attempting to run. One of her feet seemed to kick out in the wrong direction and she kept stumbling. But she had to reach the house before the firemen swarmed in and prevented her. Because all that remained of Bernadette was in the house. The sink where she'd peeled potatoes. The bed where she'd slept. The table where her elbows had rested . . .

Raoul was at the pound. Audrun saw him slide open the bar of the gate and the dogs clawed and pressed on each other to come out into freedom and then ran round in frenzied circles and pissed and defecated with joy and confusion. Only one dog remained in the pound, lying in the dry mud, its eyes open in a terrified stare, but its voice mute. Raoul went into the cage and took this dog in his arms, to bring it out, and Audrun thought, Raoul Molezon is a good man and always was a good man . . .

But she went on by him and up to the house. She pushed open the door of the Mas Lunel, the heavy door splintered by the police, that would no longer close. She stood in the kitchen which, when Aramon had left, when the *gendarmes* had finished their searches, she had scrubbed to the bone, throwing out everything he'd owned: all his half-broken gadgets and contrivances, every domestic item he'd ever laid his hands on. The kitchen no longer smelled of him. It smelled of

321

caustic soda and beeswax polish. The old brass taps on the sink shone in the sunlight. The blackened oak table was slowly returning itself to a sweet whiteness.

And Audrun thought that if fire was going to come now to destroy it all . . . now, when everything was scoured and renewed, beginning its journey back to what it had once been . . . she thought that this didn't seem right. She said it aloud: *This isn't right.*

She began to push the heavy table towards the broken door, to try to get it outside to save it from the fire, but then she saw that the table was too wide to go through the door, even if she could have lifted it. So, with the table jammed against the door, she just stood behind it, like a shopkeeper, as though waiting for customers to arrive. She knew this was stupid, this standing still behind the table: it achieved nothing. But she couldn't think what else she was supposed to be doing. She could smell the fire, coming closer, but had no idea how it could be fought off. When she fell, she fell with her head on the table and her arms outstretched.

★ ★ ★

Sometimes, when an *episode* came, there was darkness, walled in and complete, and no memory of anything afterwards. Other times, there were visions in that darkness, visions that took on sound and substance like an old-fashioned slide-show beginning, or even a film . . . and bits of these visions would be remembered . . .

The sky is huge and filled with light: a wide screen of sky.

Audrun is standing under that sky, stringing up her runner beans, when she sees the black car go driving past her and stop outside the mas.

The Englishman — Verey — gets out and knocks at the door, but there's no one there. Aramon is out on the vine terraces, with his secateurs and his canisters of weed-killer and his bread and beer for lunch.

Audrun stops her work. She likes the thrill of it, suddenly, that she's here alone with the English tourist and can do what she wants with him. The land is hers — should all have been hers, every centimetre of it — and he's trespassing on it and she can taunt Verey with whatever comes into her mind.

She removes her green rubber gloves and puts them in the pocket of her overall. She walks quietly up the driveway, taking Verey by surprise. He's a nervous man, she can tell. He reminds her of a puppet, long and limp.

She introduces herself as Aramon's sister, owner of the bungalow. He gives her a disdainful look ('the bungalow owner . . . the one I'd like to obliterate . . . ') then he remembers he has to be polite, so he shakes her hand. He tells her he's come back to look at the mas again. He gestures at the land around them. 'It's beautiful,' he says. 'And I love the silence here.'

She opens the door of the mas and leads him in. He walks slowly round the house. His glance is directed most of the time towards the rafters of the high ceilings. She's silent, following him from room to room, watching every move his body makes. She knows that he's imagining himself as the owner of the Mas Lunel, and she thinks how, if Bernadette were here, she'd smile her sweet smile and say quietly to him, 'No, I'm sorry, Monsieur, but I'm afraid you're wrong about that. This is my house.'

They go into Audrun's old room. Audrun hangs back, standing at the door. Verey opens wide the shutters and the room is flooded with sunlight and the sunlight falls on Audrun's bed and on the chest of drawers where she used to keep the disgusting girdles, hidden under her own sad clothes.

Verey opens the window and leans out. He raises his arms, as though to embrace the view down the valley. Then he turns to Audrun and says in his faltering French, 'If I bought the house . . . which I think I am going to do . . . would you work for me? I'm going to need somebody to keep everything clean . . .'

She stares at him, at this stranger in her room. She pictures herself getting down on her hands and knees, scrubbing floors for him, working till she's too old to work any more, lying exhausted in her bungalow, trapped behind the wall this man has built to keep her out of sight. And then she sees it come towards her — exactly as she knew it would one day — the idea that will set her free.

★ ★ ★

Audrun and Verey are walking towards the river now. Their progress is slow because Verey seems to need to walk very carefully over the tussocky ground. Grasshoppers jump round their feet and he tries vainly to flit them away with a broken stick.

Audrun has Aramon's shotgun slung over her shoulder.

As they left the house, she took the rubber gloves from her overall pocket and put them on and then she snatched the gun from the rack. Delicately, she inserted two cartridges into the firing chamber, admiring their perfect fit.

'Herons,' she said, as she hefted the gun.

'Herons?' said Verey.

'Yes,' she said. 'Devil birds, we call them.'

She didn't know whether this Englishman understood all of what she was saying, but she thought that this didn't really matter.

'There are still fish in the river,' she went on. 'Trout and grayling. When I was a child, we used to eat a lot of river fish. But the summers are too dry now. The fish die in shallow water because they don't get enough oxygen and then the herons come. They're like vultures. The herons just stand and wait and pounce. They're taking what's left of the fish in the Gardon. So they have to be culled.'

'Culled?' said Verey.

'Killed,' she said.

'Ah, yes. I see.'

'Whenever we go as far as the river,' she said, 'we always take a gun.'

As she and Verey came out of the mas into the

325

sunlight, she glanced away to the left, to the path leading to the vine terraces — just in case Aramon had decided to stop work and come back to the house. But there was no sign of him. Recently, toiling over his vines, he'd reminded her of a character in an old fairy tale, trying to spin straw into gold. But now she'd understood the terrible covenant he was trying to make: if Verey bought the mas, her brother wouldn't need to struggle with the vines, or indeed with anything at all ever again; into his hands would be placed all the gold he could ever wish for: more than his diseased frame would be capable of carrying.

★ ★ ★

Audrun and Verey go down through the ash grove where the leaves are yellowing and flying in the wind. Verey asks Audrun whether she would mind if — once the mas belonged to him — he planted a fast-growing cypress hedge in front of her bungalow.

A fast-growing cypress hedge.

The kind of thing a man contrives to block out what he can't bear to look on . . .

Audrun's hand tightens around the stock of the gun. She says sweetly, 'I understand about privacy, Monsieur Verey. There's nothing more precious. I, of all people, understand this.'

The Englishman nods and smiles. Audrun's noticed in Ruasse that many of the *Britanniques* seem vulgar and rude, but Verey's a courteous man. And he wants to make a beautiful garden, he tries to tell her. His sister is going to help him, his adored sister, who's a professional garden designer. 'It will be my last project,' he says, '*ma dernière . . . chose . . .* '

'Yes?' she says with interest. 'Well, it's good to have something to hope for in the future.'

Down they go, side by side, through the lower pasture, then along the impenetrable, overgrown bank of the river to where, about a hundred yards further east, there's a narrow pathway made of stones. This pathway to the river, emerging opposite a deep pool, is a secret, Audrun tells Verey. It was laid down long ago by her father, Serge. He made it for his use alone, but sometimes he brought her here . . . He carried the heavy stones, one by one, with his own bare hands and pressed them into the earth.

'History . . . ' says Verey. 'This region is very full of history.'

'Yes,' she says, 'You're right, Monsieur. We have difficulty forgetting.'

★   ★   ★

For a few moments, there's darkness now, a void.

Then, as if seen down a long, silent tunnel, Verey's face stares mutely at Audrun, his blue eyes, his sunburnt lips. He shows no surprise. His mouth doesn't open in a cry. It's almost as though he's already accepted what's going to happen, as though he were just murmuring to himself: *So this is it after all. This is the way it ends . . .*

Verey falls backwards. Blood bursts around

327

him and the crimson droplets hang there in the sunlit air. It's almost beautiful.

Then he lies in the water, with only his legs sticking out onto the little beach of shingle. This sight fills Audrun's field of vision. It enthrals her. It is, she thinks, a thing almost perfected.

She lays the gun aside and moves slowly towards the body. She bends down and extracts Verey's car keys from the pocket of his trousers and places them carefully on a flat stone. The air all around her is suddenly silent.

Blood flows into the water; skeins of blood floating free and away in the bubbling torrent.

A thing perfected.

She takes off her overall and her skirt and blouse and her shoes. Then she modestly removes her nice white cotton underwear (not any hideous pink garment made of carbon disulphide from the old factory at Ruasse!) and walks naked into the river. All she wears are the green gloves. She pulls Verey's body towards her. She swims on her back, holding him under his arms, as though saving his life.

Now, she's swimming in the deep pool, where she played as a girl while Bernadette pounded her washing on the stones. The cold of it is sweet and pure. And she knows that in the depths of the pool — if you dare to dive down to where there's almost no light, to where weeds like flat eels spring up from the river-bed — is a rock cavity, where, on very hot days, she would wedge a heavy ceramic jar, a jar made in the *poteries* of Anduze, a jar that was almost round but not quite.

Audrun takes a breath, submerges herself. She takes the body down with her, held in her arms. She reaches out to find the hollow in the rock.

As she jams Verey's head into the cavity, hearing the skull crack as the rock scrapes it, as she binds the neck round and round with long fronds of weed and knots them and re-knots them, she remembers that, usually, there was lemonade in this jar, or sometimes *sirop de menthe*, but now and again, perhaps once or twice a year, for no reason that Audrun could determine, the jar was filled with cider. And when they drank it, all the world seemed sweet to them.

The child, Mélodie, lay in her room.

This isn't my room, she thought. Not my real room. My room was in Paris. From my window, I could just see the tip of the Eiffel Tower. At midnight sometimes, I'd get out of bed to watch it prickling with light.

Her mother sat on the bed and held Mélodie's hand. She told her that tomorrow she was going to be taken to see a counsellor and the counsellor would help her come to terms with what had happened to her at the river.

'I don't know what 'come to terms' means,' said Mélodie.

'It means,' said her mother, 'that in time you'll be able to forget it.'

'No, I won't,' she said. 'I'll never be able to forget it.'

★　★　★

The counsellor was a calm, forty-year-old woman whose name was Lise.

Lise occupied a small room above a doctor's surgery in Ruasse. She sat very still, with her hands held in her lap. In Lise's presence, away from her mother and father, Mélodie felt that it was all right to be angry. She told Lise how she'd been taken away from what she called her 'lovely life' and stuck in this other life, which was disgusting, where you had to keep your eyes closed for most of the time because there were so many things in it that you didn't want to see.

'What things don't you want to see?' asked Lise.

'Insects,' said Mélodie.

'Yes. What else?'

'Everything,' said the child. 'Everything. I want to not see *everything!*'

Lise allowed a long silence to come into the room. At the window was a venetian blind and the sun, Mélodie noticed, fell in peculiar, jerky stripes onto the floor and she thought, This is all wrong, too. Nothing is how it's meant to be in this place.

'Mélodie,' said Lise, when this silence was over, 'do you sometimes see the man's body in the river?'

'It wasn't a man,' said Mélodie, 'it was nothing.'

'I think it was a man. A drowned man.'

'No!' screamed the child, 'it was nothing! It was just a *thing* like a dead snake. It was all white and slimy. It was a gigantic silkworm!'

Mélodie began crying. She put her face in her hands.

Lise sat very still on her chair. She said gently: 'That man you saw had been killed. Another man had shot him. People die in the world. It's terrible but it's what is and so we have to accept it. Sometimes they die violently, like that person died. But then, after that, they're at peace, at rest. And he's at rest now, the man you saw in the river. He's absolutely at peace. And I'd like

331

you to try to imagine that peace, Mélodie. How d'you think it might feel?'

She couldn't answer. She thought words like 'peace' were meaningless.

Her own head was crammed with horror. It was so full of it, her skull was going to burst and then stuff would come out of it and slide down her neck or down her face and then the children in the school would stick their fingers into the stuff and run away and pretend to be sick.

Yuk! You're disgusting, Mélodie!

Look at your head, Mélodie! You've got ca-ca coming out of your brain.

Lise leaned forward and gave Mélodie a tissue.

The little girl crumpled the tissue in her hand and threw it on the floor. She smeared her hands with her own tears and snot and held them up for Lise to see.

'This is what everything looks like now,' she said. 'Like this *merde*.'

★ ★ ★

She refused to go to school.

She heard her parents whispering about this in the early evening.

'It doesn't really matter, at her age.'

'It's nearly the end of term anyway.'

'By September, let's pray she's all right.'

She went to where they were standing, drinking wine in the kitchen whose walls were made of stone — drinking their wine as though nothing had happened. She ran at them and began beating at her father with her fists. The long-stemmed glass was jolted out of his hand and shattered on the tiled floor. Her mother tried to grab her, but she fought her off, fought them both with her fists and with her will, that could be as hard and black as the body of a scorpion.

'Take me home!' she screamed. 'Take me home!'

'*Ma chérie*,' said her mother, 'this is your home now . . . '

It wasn't. It wasn't. *It wasn't.* It would never be her home. It would never protect her.

'I want to go home, to *my home*!' she cried louder, still trying to hit out at them with her fists and kick them and butt them with her head.

'*Mon dieu*, Mélodie, that's enough . . . '

It wasn't enough. Nothing would ever be enough. Not until she got it back: her room with its soft white carpet and its blue-and-white wallpaper, patterned with shepherdesses and fluffy blue sheep. And her walk to school, past the florist's shop and the pâtisserie and the optometrist's on the corner, to the school gates where her friends — her real friends — waited for her. Until then, until she got it all back, no matter what she did to punish her parents, it would never be enough.

⋆ ⋆ ⋆

Jeanne Viala arrived one afternoon.

Mélodie was lying on the sofa watching daytime TV, holding her Barbie doll to her top lip, letting the feel of Barbie's silky hair against her skin soothe her into a kind of exhausted half-sleep. But when her mother showed Jeanne Viala into the room, the sight of her — of the one person who cared about her in that school, the person who had carried her away from the river in her arms — she flung her doll away and got up and ran to her and pressed her head against Jeanne's breast.

Jeanne's arms went round her and held her close. The child's mother slipped out of the room. Mélodie began crying, but it wasn't the kind of crying which made her more and more angry; it was the kind that felt beneficial, like gulping some medicine you couldn't describe. And then the child understood that Jeanne was crying too and that this was how they needed to remain, holding tight to each other and crying until they were unable to cry any more.

Eventually, Jeanne wiped Mélodie's tears and her own, and they sat down on the sofa and Jeanne picked up the doll and smoothed its golden hair.

'I came to ask,' she said after a moment or two, 'would you like to go with me to Avignon one day? It's a big city. A beautiful city, with lots and lots of people, like Paris, and it isn't very far away.'

Mélodie nodded. She hadn't known any proper cities were nearby. She'd thought that what surrounded them for miles and miles beyond Ruasse were rocks and trees and rivers and flies.

'I thought we could go to hear an afternoon concert,' said Jeanne. 'I know you used to play the violin — and you will again, because I'm going to find you a teacher. Do you think you'd like to go to a concert?'

'Yes,' said Mélodie.

'Good. I'll get some tickets. Then, after the concert, I thought . . . if you wanted to . . . we could find a nice café and go and have cakes and chocolate milkshakes. Just the two of us. You and me. If it's OK with your parents. What d'you think?'

Mélodie reached over and took her doll out of Jeanne Viala's hands and once again pressed Barbie's golden hair against her top lip.

'When can we go?' she said. 'Can we go tomorrow?'

On an October afternoon, Veronica stood in the graveyard of the Church of St Anne's at Netherholt, Hampshire, holding Anthony's ashes in a plastic urn.

It was one of those rare, sunlit days when the countryside of southern England seems to be the most beautiful place on earth. The graveyard was bordered by a dark yew hedge. Beyond this, to the east, was an old, majestic beech tree Veronica had known since childhood. Its leaves glinted amber in the brilliant light. Behind the church was a green meadow, where two bay horses were grazing.

Veronica was standing now beside two men she hardly knew: the vicar of Netherholt and Anthony's friend and executor, Lloyd Palmer. The three of them were staring silently down at Lal Verey's headstone, commissioned by Anthony.

Lavender Jane (Lal) Verey
Beloved mother
Born Johannesburg 1913 —
Died Hampshire 1977

At the foot of the slab which covered Lal's grave was a small, freshly dug hole. Here, the remains of Anthony would be placed — deep down in the earth, not *beside* his mother, but resting at her feet.

This had been his wish, his will. But for a while, it had looked as though his will couldn't be accommodated. The graveyard at Netherholt was full, Veronica had been informed. Her brother would have to go into the 'overspill' cemetery behind the village hall.

Overspill.

Veronica knew that Anthony wouldn't care for this word, any more than he'd care to lie in the vicinity of the Netherholt village hall, a low, brick building which was host to drunken weddings, children's tea parties, Bingo nights, amateur dramatics and (it had been known to happen) illegal raves. Anthony wanted to be near Lal — as near as it was possible to be — and that was that.

Lloyd had saved the day. 'I'll sort it,' he'd told Veronica blithely. 'The Church of England loves to make a ding-dong about everything, but the only thing to remember when they do is that all their little parishes are practically bankrupt. Leave it to me, Veronica.'

How much had Lloyd Palmer paid to get permission to bury Anthony's ashes here? Veronica didn't ask. But the vicar of Netherholt had quickly said that yes, after all, if it was . . . erm . . . just a question of . . . erm . . . a small receptacle, not a coffin, then space could perhaps be found 'between the rows'.

And so here they were, with Anthony clutched against Veronica's bosom, and Lloyd wearing a black cashmere overcoat and a red cashmere scarf, and the vicar shivering just a little in his cotton surplice, holding a prayer book.

337

'Shall I start?' the vicar asked anxiously. 'Are you ready?'

'Yes,' said Veronica. 'Please do start.'

The familiar words fell into the cool but sunlit air. ' . . . *Man that is born of a woman hath but a short time to live . . . He cometh up, and is cut down, like a flower; he fleeth as it were a shadow . . . Earth to earth, ashes to ashes . . . '*

The voice of the vicar was soft, not unpleasing. On the breeze, Veronica could *smell* ash: leaves and twigs being broken down to dust and smoke on a garden bonfire. And she thought, All of this feels right. It's where Anthony and I began. It's home.

But then, when the moment came to put the urn into the muddy hole, she couldn't do it, she couldn't let go. Lloyd and the vicar waited silently, with their heads bowed. She hugged the plastic jar. She kept thinking, I loved him too. He belongs to me, too, not just to Lal . . .

She held the urn out in front of her and the sun fell onto the lid, painted with copper-coloured lacquer, and gave it a burnished sheen, like an antique saucepan. She saw Lloyd raise his head and look at the urn and then up at her face.

'Anthony,' she said aloud, in as strong a voice as she could manage, 'this is what you would have called a 'ghastly moment'. Letting go. But I'm going to do it. When I think about it, I probably should have let you go years and years ago, but I never did. I loved you far too much.'

She paused. She knew that her voice sounded strangely loud in the still air.

'You're at Netherholt,' she went on. 'OK, darling? I know you can't see it or feel it. I know you're nowhere, really. But this was the place you wanted to be. The beech tree's still here. And the sun's shining. And I'm putting you by Ma's feet. It's the best we can organise. I don't think you'll mind. I expect you'll remember better than I do that she always wore absolutely brilliant shoes . . . '

Veronica half wanted to go on, to say something more portentous, but she found that she just stopped there and then she knelt down and put the jar in the ground. At her side, she discovered that Lloyd Palmer was crying. He blew his nose loudly, then gathered up a fistful of damp earth and threw it onto Anthony's urn.

'Bye, old sod,' he said. 'Happy times.'

★　★　★

Veronica and Lloyd walked beyond the church-yard to the meadow where the horses grazed. Above the distant combes, rain clouds were shading the sky. Lloyd and Veronica stood leaning on a wooden fence. Then, in a gesture that was second nature to Veronica, she held out her hand to the horses and immediately saw their heads go up.

They stood still, ears pricked, regarding her. She loved that moment, when she spoke silently to a horse and it seemed to listen. And now they came to her, ambling slowly across the shining field, and as they got near to her, the scent of them — the scent of living horses, which, to

Veronica Verey, was more consoling than any other scent — reached her and held her in its spell.

'Good girls,' she said. 'Lovely girls . . . '

She took off her black gloves and touched the hard, warm heads of the bay horses, rubbing and caressing their noses, each in turn. At first, they trembled imperceptibly, still wary of the stranger. Then Veronica felt all their anxiety vanish and they came nearer to her still, and one of them rested its head on her shoulder and her arm went round its neck.

'Good lord,' said Lloyd. 'Love at first sight!'

Veronica smiled. 'They were always my thing, horses,' she said. 'I used to love my pony Susan far more than I loved my mother.'

'It figures,' said Lloyd.

Then he blew his nose again and stuffed the handkerchief away in his pocket and said, 'What are you going to do, Veronica?'

'Do? You mean, with the rest of my life?'

'Yes. I know it's none of my business, but you will come into quite a bit of money, once we get probate . . . '

Veronica stood still, caressing the horses, loving the warmth of them, their breath on her neck. She wondered whether, after so much time, she could be taught to ride again.

'I don't know . . . ' she said. 'I've never loved anything very passionately. Only gardens. And horses.'

She looked up at the sky. The sun was still shining on Netherholt, but rain was falling on the combes and she thought how beautiful these

340

things were in their proximity, the sunlight and the drift of rain.

'I thought I was happy in France,' she said. 'But now, after everything that's happened . . . I don't know whether I really was. I think I just made myself believe I was.'

'Happiness,' said Lloyd, with a sigh. 'It's what Anthony and I talked about the last time I saw him. The near impossibility of ever hanging on to it for more than five minutes. He told me he thought he'd only been happy once in his life.'

'What? Drinking from Ma's tits when he was a baby?'

'Almost. He said he made a tree-house . . . '

'Ah, the tree-house! And he invited Ma for tea?'

'Yes. He said it was the most perfect afternoon of his life.'

Veronica began to stroke the ear of the horse whose head rested on her shoulder.

'Did he say that?' she said.

'Yes. He said everything was completely beautiful.'

'Yup? Well you know, Lloyd, it wasn't, in fact. It wasn't beautiful. The tea may have been perfect — made by Mrs Brigstock, no doubt. And Anthony and Ma may have had a nice conversation up there in the tree. But on the way down, climbing down the ladder, Ma slipped and fell. She hurt her back very badly. And after that day, she was always in pain. Till the day she died. The pain was always there. It might even have been the thing that brought on her cancer.'

Lloyd re-knotted his expensive scarf, as if he suddenly felt cold.

'Anthony just cut that bit out of his mind,' Veronica went on. 'He literally forgot about it. If you ever reminded him, he always told you you were wrong. He succeeded in convincing himself that Ma's fall was on a different day — somewhere else. Because he couldn't bear to think that he was in any way responsible.'

★ ★ ★

Lloyd and Veronica drove back to London in Lloyd's silver Audi. Rain slicked the grey motorway.

Suddenly tired, Veronica rested her head against the soft black leather upholstery and dozed as the darkness came on.

Half asleep and half awake, she remembered the strict, unvarying routine she'd followed when she was a girl and cared for Susan. It was like a High Mass, she thought, with each stage followed in exactly the same way, morning after morning, with nothing missed or bungled, nothing out of time or out of place:

Wake up at six.

Look out of the window to check the weather. Long for sun in summer, rain in spring, snow or hard frost in winter: everything in its right season.

Pull on old clothes: Aertex shirt, jeans, sweater, boots, riding hat.

Go down the stairs, quiet as the tooth fairy. Unlock the back door.

342

Inhale the first scent of the morning air. Feel like running, running all the way to the stables.

Open the stable door and hug Susan and breathe in the smell of her and talk to her and give her a handful of oats.

Rope halter. Lead Susan out. Tie her to post.

Get the shovel and start mucking out. Twenty minutes average time.

Hose down the stall. Lay out clean straw. Lay it thick and soft.

Fill the water trough.

Saddle up. Girths properly tightened and correct. Lead Susan to the paddock. Sun up now, or nearly up in deep winter. Or rain.

Trot twice round the paddock, then just dig gently into Susan's broad flanks to start the rocking canter. The most comfortable canter any horse ever perfected: rock-and-rock, rock-and-rock, easy and lovely. The trees and the fencing waltzing by.

And as they waltz by, see the two plumes of breath, mine and Susan's, telling me that we're alive, alive, alive, *alive* . . .

★   ★   ★

Veronica shifted in her luxurious car seat.

She realised she must have slept for a few moments because she'd been having a dream, not about Susan, but about Kitty.

In the dream, Kitty had sent her an invitation to a forthcoming show: *Recent Work by Kitty Meadows.* On the invitation card was a reproduction of Kitty's watercolour of the

343

mimosa blossom. Reduced to a surface no wider than a few inches, this painting looked deft and accomplished, and Veronica now wished, for Kitty's sake, that these things could have been true: that there could have been a one-woman exhibition, that the mimosa watercolour could have been perfectly achieved. But she knew that neither was the case.

What had arrived instead at Les Glaniques, before Veronica had left for England, was a postcard from Kitty, postmarked Adelaide. On the front was a picture of Kitty, smiling, wearing a white T-shirt and blue dungarees, and holding in her arms a koala bear. Underneath this, Kitty had inscribed the caption: *At least somebody loves me!*

Veronica had looked at the photograph for a long time, and at Kitty's backward-sloping writing and imagined Kitty, alone in an Adelaide hotel room, smiling as she wrote it, proud for a moment of her sorrowful little joke.

Then Veronica had torn up the card and thrown it away.

★ ★ ★

Veronica reached for her handbag and took out a peppermint and put it into her mouth.

'All right?' said Lloyd.

'Yes,' said Veronica. 'You're a very good driver, Lloyd. Do you want a Tic-tac?'

Lloyd refused the mint. Veronica was silent for a moment, then she said suddenly: 'You know, I've been thinking: gardening in southern France

344

is really, really arduous. I can't grow any of my favourite things, it's far too arid.'

'I can imagine.'

'More and more often, I have dreams about English flowers; sweet peas, peonies, forget-me-nots . . . '

Lloyd turned off the Mozart concerto that had played softly, in a repeating loop, since they'd left Hampshire.

'Come home,' he said. 'Sell up in France and buy a house here. Benita can help you decorate it, if you want her to. Make a divine garden, Veronica. Think of primroses and cowslips and daffodils and trellises of blowsy roses . . . '

'Yes,' she said quietly. 'I think that's what I'd like. Just that: an English garden and a paddock for a horse. Or is that terribly selfish?'

'I can't see why,' said Lloyd. 'When life is so bloody short.'

Audrun woke up in a dark room.

She was lying in a bed, but she knew this wasn't her own bedroom in the bungalow. So where was it? She could smell something acrid, as though the walls might be damp. Was she in a prison cell?

She tried to sit up. But there was a pain in her chest which grew stronger, deeper as she moved. It pushed her back down again, pushed her violently, like an old enemy, standing at her bedside.

Her hand groped to her breast-bone and kneaded the scant flesh there. She thought that all she could do was wait: wait for someone to come into the room, or for a light to be switched on. Then, she would know . . .

If this was prison, it was very quiet. No sound of doors closing or opening. No screams. No footfalls. Or were there noises all around her that she couldn't hear? Was the silence inside herself? She tried whispering her own name aloud: Audrun Lunel. She thought she heard it, but it sounded timid and far away, like a shy schoolkid reluctantly reciting her name at morning roll-call.

★   ★   ★

So much of her life had been like this: waiting in darkness, without moving. She was practised in this submission.

346

But waiting for what, this time? Except for the strangely scented air she was being forced to breathe, there didn't seem to be any clues about what was going to happen.

She began searching her memory.

Had the handsome detective come back and arrested her? Had the poor traumatised child, Mélodie Hartmann, or even Jeanne Viala, remembered something and whispered it in his ear — something nobody else knew?

Or had he himself, Inspecteur Travier, seen what remained hidden to everybody else — in the way that his movie counterparts so often glimpsed with their sky-blue eyes the obscure pathway to the truth?

Audrun had no recollection of any arrest. The last thing she could remember was standing near the road with Marianne and seeing fires in the hills and being told the *canadairs* were coming to put them out. But what had happened next? Had the planes arrived? Did the water come cascading down onto the trees? Did she walk back to her bungalow and close her door and sit down in her chair? And then?

I'm sorry, Mademoiselle Lunel. I'm sorry to disturb you again, after all the anxiety about the fire, but I wonder if I can ask you a few more questions . . . ?

Did he say these words? They sounded familiar. Did he arrive with the same constable, the note-taker?

Just a few more questions.

This won't take very long. I only want to clarify a couple of things . . .

347

He'd been so nice, so polite. But it was the violent, angry things you remembered in your heart and in your body, not the conversation of gentle people.

★ ★ ★

To be confined in a prison: Audrun thought that there would be nothing more terrible. She wanted to remind the charming detective, in case he didn't know: 'I already lived through that, when I was young. From the age of fifteen to the age of thirty — through all the 'best' years of my life — I understood what it was to be in prison. Two prisons, in fact. The underwear factory, breathing carbon disulphide; my room, stinking of my brother and my father. All I wanted was to die.'

I'm sorry, Mademoiselle Lunel, I do sympathise, but what you've told me alters nothing. I'm arresting you for the murder of the Englishman, Anthony Verey. You have the right to remain silent . . .

She'd be driven away in a police van and thrown into a cell. And there she'd remain, for ever, with the stink of strangers all around her, just like at the factory — as though, after all, she'd never escaped from that.

She began to cry. She had difficulty catching her breath. Her tears were hot on her skin and made runnels into her hair. Then a voice in the darkness said: 'Hey, shut up, will you? People need their sleep in here.'

'Where am I?' said Audrun. But no one answered.

Light came.

Light above her, not from any window, but from harsh fluorescent rods, suspended from a high ceiling. And she felt some movement at her side. She turned her head and saw a young nurse standing by her, holding her wrist to check her pulse. Behind the nurse, a green curtain hung lifeless, shrouding whatever lay beyond it.

A hospital.

The nurse was Armenian. Or Algerian. Her hand was warm.

'What happened?' Audrun said to the pretty Algerian nurse, but she just smiled and laid Audrun's wrist down and went away, drawing the green curtain behind her.

A male orderly with a kind old face brought her breakfast — a cup of coffee and a stale croissant and a tiny blob of jam. The orderly helped her to sit up in the hospital bed so that she could eat it.

'What happened to me?' said Audrun.

'You're all right,' said the orderly. 'You're going to be all right. Want some sugar in your coffee?'

She tried to eat and drink. She found swallowing difficult. She thought that if she got a bit stronger, she might remember what had happened.

★ ★ ★

She slept and woke, slept and woke. Pissed in a bed-pan, holding on to the nurse. Slept again,

349

her chest tight and aching. The light above her never changed.

Then she saw Marianne at her bedside. Marianne looked pale and tired and wore a cross expression on her face.

'How are you?' Marianne asked in a flat voice.

'I don't know,' said Audrun. 'My chest hurts. I don't know what happened. Did the *canadairs* arrive?'

Marianne half turned away, seeming to draw in a long breath. Then she looked at Audrun and said: 'It's gone. I had to come and tell you. Someone had to tell you straight to your face. It's gone.'

'Gone?'

'Yes.'

'I don't know what you mean, Marianne.'

'The Mas Lunel. The fire took it. Parts of the walls are still standing, but they're black, absolutely blackened. It seemed to split open in the middle. I've never witnessed anything like that in my life! The heat made the stones just . . . *explode*.'

Audrun said nothing. She closed her eyes. In her mind, now, she saw something new: Raoul Molezon running, running towards the dog pound, calling out that he was going to save the dogs. And she was following him, she was trying to run, too. But she didn't follow Raoul to the pound; she opened the damaged front door of the mas and went inside and stood in the kitchen, which was dark, with all the shutters bolted against the heat.

She laid her arms across Bernadette's oak

table, which she'd been trying so hard to return to bare wood, to scour to perfect whiteness. Then, she began tugging and pushing at the heavy table. Her arms and back ached.

She knew she was too light to lift up this ancient piece of furniture, too weakened by time. But she wasn't going to give up. She was Audrun Lunel. She was going to save what remained of her mother — all the things Aramon had tried to despoil, but which now belonged to her; she was going to bring everything out before the fire came. She remembered that she could hear shouting in the hills above and the barking and wailing of the dogs, but she took no notice of these sounds . . .

'You were very lucky,' said Marianne curtly. 'Raoul Molezon risked his life to get you out.'

'Risked his life?'

'Yes, he did. You'd wedged the front door shut somehow. Raoul slammed at it with his shoulder, but it wouldn't move. The fire was terribly near and jumping from tree to tree. The firemen told him to come away, but he wouldn't. He helped one of the fire-fighters tear the door off its hinges. He carried you out.'

Audrun looked at Marianne, whose expression was still stern, but she didn't care. She didn't care at all. She couldn't prevent a smile from spreading across her face at the thought that Raoul Molezon had risked death to save her.

'He was always a good man,' she said. 'Always.'

351

Aramon Lunel was incarcerated in a prison above Ruasse while he waited for his case to come to trial. He knew that the trial was far away in time and that its outcome could be foretold, so he seldom thought about it.

He attempted to live his life one day at a time.

The prison buildings had once housed a regiment of the French Foreign Legion. They were cold in winter, but strongly built of stone. Aramon had been allocated his own cell. It was prison policy to keep murderers and sex-offenders separated from petty felons. It had been stated by the governor that men who had taken lives, or blighted lives for ever, should be made to endure a certain degree of loneliness. But Aramon was impervious to this. He knew that he'd been lonely for thirty years.

The walls of his cell were painted white. The room had a small window, protected by an ironwork grille. Through the criss-cross of the grille bars, Aramon could see down the steep valley to the roofs of the town: the tilting, red-grey tiled roofs and boxy chimney flues of old Ruasse, the blank corrugations of the retail sheds, the water towers and TV masts of the high-rise blocks in the cheaply constructed 1970s suburbs they still called 'new'.

In one of these blocks, the girl Fatima had lived and died, and Aramon sometimes found himself thinking about her: the way she'd draped scarves over her lampshades, the better to conceal the shabbiness of her room; the way she tried to turn him on by rotating her belly. From time to time, he wondered whether — after all — he *had* killed her. Killed her for her fat, gyrating stomach. Killed her for not being the person he loved.

Fatima, the belly-dancing whore. He had no recollection of slitting open her body from sternum to pelvis. None. But then, he had no recollection of shooting Anthony Verey in the gut, either. He'd thought at first that it would all come back to him, that moment by the river. It would come streaming into his mind like a motion picture and then he would *feel it*, feel in his being that he'd taken a life. But time went on and this didn't happen. There was no motion picture, no feeling: only fog and darkness.

It had been suggested to him by his lawyer, Maître de Bladis, that his mind had 'blanked out' the terrible things that he'd done. Some killers, de Bladis had opined, found their feelings of horror and guilt 'too terrible to be borne'. They managed to achieve 'absolute mental suppression of their crime' — and he was almost certainly one of them. He was subsequently informed that he had the right to psychiatric help, if he should request it.

★   ★   ★

His cell was four metres long by two and a half metres wide. It contained a wooden bed, narrow

353

and low to the ground. The single pillow was surprisingly soft. Under the window, stood a wooden table and chair.

In the corner of the cell nearest the door were a lavatory and a washbasin, both cracked and stained, but serviceable. And in the night, when he needed to empty his bladder, Aramon often thought how convenient — how almost *enjoyable* — it was to have this WC just a few paces from his bed.

Sometimes, he didn't even bother to stand up, but just crawled to the toilet bowl (which was also set low to the ground) on his knees. Then he'd go back to his bunk and listen for the dawn outside the window and often sink into dreams of being a boy again, toiling along the onion rows before the sun came up behind the hills of La Callune.

When he'd first arrived at the prison, they'd put him into the hospital, because he couldn't keep his food down. He told the prison doctors that he thought he had stomach cancer. They showed towards him a surprising degree of sympathy and kindness. His body was scanned. He was informed that there was no cancer, only two bleeding ulcers.

'That figures,' Aramon said. 'I could feel that, *pardi*: that bleeding inside. I think that's been going on a long time.'

He was put on a special alkaline diet. His cigarettes were taken away for a while. And when he came out of the prison hospital, he felt almost well again, well enough to stand up straight, well enough to crack a few jokes at mealtimes or in the exercise yard or in the wood shop where he worked making pallets.

He made friends with another murderer, an old Somali man called Yusuf, who had an infectious, high-pitched laugh. Yusuf claimed he couldn't remember his crime, either. The police had told him there was more than one, but he'd long forgotten what they were or why he might have committed them. He said to Aramon: 'It doesn't matter what they were. I may have been wicked a long time ago, I may even have slit a man's throat, or the throats of more than one man, but God has forgiven me. He has given me rest from toil. He has given me shelter in my old age. And now He's giving it to you, too.'

Shelter in my old age.

This thought made Aramon smile. It also made him take a certain pride in his cell. He cleaned it with care. At the Mas Lunel, he'd allowed everything to go to hell, not caring — not really noticing — if the place stank, until it all got too disgusting and too complicated to be endured and he'd had to send for Audrun to sort it out.

Here in prison, he disinfected his lavatory bowl three times a week. He stretched the bed-sheets tight. He wished he had pictures or photographs to tape to the walls: views of places where he'd never been and never would go and which would therefore ask nothing of him. Niagara Falls. Mount Etna. The Great Wall of China. Venice. A lake in Somalia, where, Yusuf told him, men fished for eels under a crimson sunset. These pictures, he thought, would give his mind a resting place: somewhere to dwell.

★ ★ ★

Many of the inmates of the prison were young men — Caucasian French, Somalis and North Africans, staying mainly in their own ethnic groups.

At mealtimes and in the yard, all the groups strutted and bragged and cursed. Sometimes, there were bloody fights and these amused Aramon. He could remember what it was like to be twenty years old and full of fury. But he admitted to Yusuf: 'I wouldn't want to be young again. It's too exhausting.'

One day, a group of young white men gathered around Aramon in the exercise yard and one of them, a boy called Michou, said to him: 'We heard you're the guy who wiped out that *rosbif*. The one in the newspapers, who went missing. Is that true?'

Aramon was leaning against the wire fence, smoking. The air was cold, under a leaden sky. He looked down at the expectant faces, and his pride, his manhood wouldn't let him tell these youths that he didn't know whether he'd been Verey's killer or not.

'Yeh,' he said. 'That's me.'

The boys began tittering. Michou's friend, Louis, said: 'You shot away his pallid face? Uhn?'

Shot away his pallid face . . .

Aramon said in a strong voice: 'He'd promised me money. A lot of money for some land. We had a deal. You see? He tried to back away from it.

356

Cunt. He tried to cheat me. But nobody cheats a member of the Lunel family!'

'What did it feel like? *Blaff!* One foreigner less! Pretty fucking good, uhn?'

'It felt all right,' said Aramon.

'Did you knock his head off with the first shot?'

'Not his head,' said Aramon. 'I shot him in the gut.'

He was about to brag that he'd killed Verey with one shot, but then he remembered: *two* spent cartridges in the firing chamber and he stammered, 'I thought I'd get him first time, but my hands were shaking. I had to fire the second barrel.'

'What, and then his guts spilled out?'

'Yeh.'

'You did OK,' said Michou. 'Foreigners are vermin. More and more each fucking year, swarming over us, like rats. And they just help themselves to what belongs to us. They try to cheat us all the time. You did good, old man.'

After that, this group — Michou, Louis and three others — began to 'look after' Aramon, out of *respect*, they told him. They began by procuring extra cigarettes for him, and pornographic magazines. At his request, they managed to find him a colour photograph of Niagara Falls, which he taped to the wall above his bed and stared at for long hours at a time. He knew that, in recent years, his life had had about it an absence of wonder.

★ ★ ★

357

One day, in the yard, Michou told him he was looking tired, asked him, why didn't he try the other stuff, the beautiful stuff that took all your sorrows away?

'The 'beautiful stuff'?'

'Yeh. Coke. Crack. Whichever. Even Smack if you think you can handle it. Easy to get. Easy.'

'How would I arrange it?' Aramon asked.

Michou said this was easy, too. Deals were always done on the outside. Certain of the guards 'facilitated' it, because their own pay was so stingy. Easy as farting.

Aramon told Michou he would think about this. But really, he didn't have to think about it very long. Because this was what he ached for — had ached for, for most of his benighted life — the drug that would make the world seem wonderful.

Yusuf warned him not to do it, not to go anywhere near it. He warned him he would be putting fetters on himself, selling himself into slavery.

But Aramon had already begun dreaming about it. He clung to his soft pillow and conjured in his mind a substance of perfect whiteness which would allow him to feel what he'd felt long ago, before Bernadette died.

The thing she had sometimes, on summer evenings, described as happiness.

Snow fell on the charred ruins of the Mas Lunel.

Audrun, wearing her rubber boots and her old red coat, stood alone in the landscape and found herself wishing that the snow would go on falling and falling until all the contours and edges of the building were blurred, and the mas became indistinguishable from all that existed around it: a small mound or hill among the greater hills.

She loved the whiteness of everything. Even the raw air she loved.

And the silence. This more than anything.

★ ★ ★

When the snow melted and the remains of the mas appeared again, in all their blackened ugliness, Audrun had to keep the blinds of the bungalow windows pulled down and barely ventured out of her door, so terrible did the proximity of this *thing* appear to her.

When she realised she'd once again become a prisoner of her loathing, she called Raoul Molezon. She offered him pastis, which she served with cheese crackers. She told him she wanted him to demolish the Mas Lunel.

'Demolish it? And then what?' said Raoul.

Then what?

She remembered her father boasting about

selling the stones when he'd torn down the two wings of the mas, long ago.

Then what?

'Then it will be gone,' she said. 'And the land will recover.'

Raoul was silent for a moment. Audrun noticed that he'd dropped a few cracker crumbs on his tartan shirt. Men, she thought, seldom see what's been dropped or spilled or just abandoned. They just hurry on . . .

'I've got a better idea,' said Raoul. 'With the insurance money, I could rebuild it for you. It would take a bit of time, but — '

'Insurance money!' said Audrun. 'Aramon won't see a cent of that. It's tied up in the courts. Insurers don't want to pay out to a murderer if they don't have to! Who can blame them?'

Raoul nodded. He sipped his pastis, with his face lowered. The word 'murderer' seemed to have disconcerted him.

After a while, Audrun said, 'I think it's better if the house is gone, Raoul. Better for me. Better for the land. Couldn't you just bring a bulldozer? I can pay you for the work. And you can salvage the stones.'

Raoul was silent again for a moment, then he said: 'What does Aramon want?'

'Who knows?' said Audrun. 'But it's of no importance. Aramon's going to die in prison. They say he'll get thirty years. He'll never set foot on this hillside again.'

★   ★   ★

360

Raoul arrived with his demolition team at the end of February. The days were grey and cold.

Audrun made coffee for the men. She reminded Raoul of her instruction to take away everything, drag it all away, every last stone and tile, every floor joist, every ancient run of piping, every piece of flaking plaster.

'What I want to see when you've finished,' she said, 'is flat ground. I don't want there to be anything left above the earth.'

Raoul told his men to go on up to the mas, but he stayed behind, sitting at Audrun's kitchen table, with his hands round his coffee bowl. His brown eyes looked not at Audrun, but down into the bowl.

'Audrun,' he said, 'I've been wanting to say this. I should have said it the last time I was here. I'm sorry for everything that's happened. We all are. Everybody in La Callune. We want to help you in any way we can.'

Audrun looked at him, the still-handsome man she could so easily have loved, if her life had been differently constructed, and felt towards him a sweet tenderness she knew time would never diminish.

'Thank you, Raoul,' she said. 'I'm sorry for Jeanne, too. That it had to be her to witness such a terrible thing . . . I'm sure nobody ever imagined that. And the little girl from Paris . . . on their picnic . . . '

He shook his head, as if to say that wasn't what he wanted to talk about. He moved the bowl round and round on the oilcloth. He still wouldn't look at Audrun, although she sensed

361

that he had something else to say.

'I know . . .' he began, 'I know . . . that when we were young, your life was made very difficult by . . . by certain things that — '

Audrun stood up straight away, pushing her chair away so violently that it fell over with a crash.

'A life is a life,' she said emphatically. 'I never dwell on the past. Never! Which is why it's going to be better for me when the Mas Lunel is gone. And look at the time, Raoul. Hadn't you better get started? They've forecast rain this afternoon.'

He stood up. He took his gloves out of the pocket of his work coat and slowly put them on. He nodded and went out.

★ ★ ★

Built over years, it was demolished in days.

True to Audrun's orders, Raoul and his men left nothing standing above ground. When their work was finished, where the Mas Lunel had been, there was only a rectangular declivity in the earth.

Audrun walked round and round this declivity, a clay and limestone wound, fancifully zippered together by the stitching of the bulldozer tracks. The shallow rectangle appeared far smaller than the house itself had been and there was about it, thought Audrun, an embarrassing pointlessness, as though, in the end, the beautiful hillside above La Callune had been dug out and levelled and terraced to no purpose. And this thought tore at Audrun's heart, tore at her sacred memory of Bernadette, standing at her sink or at her ironing table, keeping watch.

But then, hearing a blackbird singing in one of the holm oaks, Audrun remembered that spring was coming and that the seasons would bring their own, more kindly alteration. In the ruts left by the bulldozer tracks no less than on the bare mud and limestone, tiny particles of matter would accrue, swept down by the rain and the wind: filaments of dead leaves, wisps of charred broom. And in the air, almost invisible as spring came on, would be specks of dust, grains of sand, and these would slowly turn and fall and settle among the detritus, making a bed for the spores of lichen and moss. In one season, the scar of the Mas Lunel would begin to heal.

About this, she was not wrong.

Later, in the autumn gales, in the drenching rains falling under Mont Aigoual, berries and seeds would fall onto the lichen and take root. Box and bracken would begin to sprout there, and in time, in not much time . . . wild pear, hawthorn, pine and beech would spread their branches . . .

About all this, she was not wrong.

She knew her beloved land. What would begin to grow all around her, as the seasons passed, was virgin forest.

★ ★ ★

Spring came slowly, reluctantly, with cold squalls of rain and morning frost and nights when the wind seemed bent upon hurling the roof off the bungalow.

And then everything quietened. The sun was suddenly warm. In Audrun's wood, aconites and dog's-tooth violets pushed up in the new grass. The sound of the cuckoo was heard.

She drove her car down to Ruasse and parked in the square and walked up through the old town to the prison. She hadn't known she was going to do this. But some sudden feeling of . . . what could she call it? Kindness? Some sudden calm in her prompted her to dress herself in her Sunday clothes and drive down to Ruasse, and then to walk up the steep cobbled road to the prison and ask at the gate to see her brother, Aramon Lunel. She was there almost before she realised it. After she'd said his name, clouds gathered above the town and a light rain began to fall.

She went in and the stone walls of the old Foreign Legion barracks closed around her. The guards looked at her with interest. She was Lunel's first and only visitor, aside from his lawyer. She was told to wait. She'd brought an awkward package with her, wrapped in newspaper, but this was taken away.

She sat on a hard bench and listened to the sounds of the prison. After a while, the newspaper package was returned to her and she was shown into the long empty space reserved for prison visits, set out with tables and chairs, as though for some school examination. The room was deserted except for Audrun and an elderly prison warder, on whose features was etched a melancholy of the most profound kind.

'Do you know my brother?' Audrun asked.

The warder nodded.

'Is he . . . is he able to *endure*?' she asked.

The warder shrugged. 'He'll never be well,' he said. 'His ulcers were treated, but they still bleed . . . '

'And . . . in his mind . . . how is he in his mind?'

As Audrun said this, a lock turned, then the door opened and Aramon came into the room. He wore his prison uniform: grey trousers, blue shirt, grey pullover. And in these clothes, thought Audrun, he looked better dressed than he'd been for a long time. His face was freshly shaved, his hair cut and washed. Prison had cleaned him up.

A second warder led him to the table where Audrun sat, then withdrew. He and the elderly prison officer walked away and kept guard by the door.

Aramon stood with his hands by his sides, looking at Audrun. Behind her, she heard the rain fretting against the narrow windows. Aramon sat down. He put his hands flat on the scarred wooden table that separated them.

'Normally,' he said, 'I don't get any visitors.'

'No?' said Audrun. 'Well, you're used to being alone, aren't you?'

She noticed that the soreness in his eyes had gone and he smelled of strong soap, not alcohol. His look was hectic and bright, as though some recent news had excited him.

'You don't have to feel sorry for me,' he said.

'I don't feel sorry for you,' said Audrun.

365

'I have a room of my own,' he said. 'Painted white. Well, it's a cell, not a room, but I think of it as my little room. I have my own toilet and washbasin.'

'Good. That's nice.'

'And a picture of Niagara Falls on the wall.'

'Yes?'

'I like waterfalls. There used to be falls in the Gardon, high up near Mont Aigoual, in the winter-time, after the snows. Remember?'

'Yes.'

'They won't let me frame my picture of Niagara. Stupid idiots. They don't let me have glass — in case I cut my wrists, *pardi*! But I don't feel like cutting my wrists. I'm all right.'

'I'm glad you are.'

'I told you, you don't need to pity me. I take pride in my cell. I keep it tidy. Not like up at the mas. Uhn? I couldn't keep track of things up there. Even on the land, I couldn't keep pace with the work. I'm better off here.'

'Are you?'

'I tell you I am. Like you're better off in your bungalow, Audrun. I told you that when Father died: a little small place you can keep clean . . .'

She cut him off by reaching down and lifting up the bulky package she'd brought and placing it in front of him on the table.

'I brought you this,' she said.

'What is it?' he asked. 'I'm not allowed to have my own things.'

'It's not a 'thing',' she said.

His labourer's hands began unfolding the newspaper wrapping. They worked slowly,

366

tentatively. But eventually what lay revealed on the table in front of him was a branch of white cherry blossom.

Audrun watched him. Aramon lifted his hands, as though afraid to touch the branch, but his eyes, so strangely bright, stared down at it in wonder. He seemed — with his whole expression — to drink in the scent and sweetness of the flowers. Then, he gathered it up and buried his face in it and began to cry.

Audrun stayed very still on her chair. She glanced over at the warders and took in some expression of alarm on their faces, but it wasn't Aramon's weeping that was agitating them. Indeed, they didn't seem to have noticed this, but were instead staring at the rain, which was now beating harshly on the windows. She heard one of them comment that it was getting dark in the room, even though it was only mid-afternoon.

She stayed still, letting Aramon cry like a boy, letting the storm-darkness gather round them from moment to moment. She saw Aramon's shallow chest moving up and down as the weeping caught at his breath. Then he looked at her and said: 'Why did you bring this? Why?'

'Well,' she said, 'I suppose, when I saw it, I thought . . . I thought about you and me as we once were. In the days when we were kind to each other.'

He laid the branch down and put his head in his hands. His crying gathered in intensity and now the two warders approached, both looking anxious, and the older man laid a hand on

Aramon's shoulder.

'*Allez*, Lunel,' he said. 'Don't make yourself sick. Let's take you back to your cell now.'

'Madame,' said the other officer, 'I regret your visit is at an end.'

Audrun stood up obediently, but Aramon suddenly reached out and grabbed hold of her hand. 'I'm sorry!' he stammered. 'I've been wanting to say it! *I'm sorry!* You were my princess . . . that's all. You were my princess and I couldn't find any other. You were my princess for all time!'

There was a silence in the room, disturbed only by the sound of the rain on the glass. Audrun said nothing, but nevertheless gently covered Aramon's hand with hers and held it in a tender grip for a moment before it was torn from her, as the warders led her brother away.

The door opened and closed and Audrun heard the lock turn and she knew she was alone. She looked down at the branch from the cherry tree, left where it was on the table, and she saw how the white blossoms remained luminous and bright, when everything around them was becoming indistinct.

Acknowledgements

Extract from *Salad Days* reproduced by permission of The Agency (London) Ltd 1954 © Julian Slade.

Extract from *Staying On* by Paul Scott, copyright © 1977 Paul Scott, published by William Heinemann. Reproduced by permission of David Higham Associates on behalf of the author.

Drawing of mulberry leaf by Nicole Heidaripour.

We do hope that you have enjoyed reading this large print book.

Did you know that all of our titles are available for purchase?

We publish a wide range of high quality large print books including:
Romances, Mysteries, Classics
General Fiction
Non Fiction and Westerns

Special interest titles available in large print are:
The Little Oxford Dictionary
Music Book
Song Book
Hymn Book
Service Book

Also available from us courtesy of Oxford University Press:
Young Readers' Dictionary
(large print edition)
Young Readers' Thesaurus
(large print edition)

For further information or a free brochure, please contact us at:
Ulverscroft Large Print Books Ltd.,
The Green, Bradgate Road, Anstey,
Leicester, LE7 7FU, England.
Tel: (00 44) 0116 236 4325
Fax: (00 44) 0116 234 0205

Other titles published by
The House of Ulverscroft:

THE ROAD HOME

Rose Tremain

Lev is on his way to England to seek work, so that he can send money back to eastern Europe to support his mother and little daughter, but he finds himself struggling with the mysterious rituals of 'Englishness', and the fashions and fads of the London scene. Gradually, as Lev improves his command of communication and culture, he begins to recognise what it is that he wants, above all, to do with his working life. But by then he is no longer certain where 'home' is . . .

THE COLOUR

Rose Tremain

Mid-nineteenth century: Joseph and Harriet Blackstone, along with Joseph's mother Lilian, emigrate from Norfolk to New Zealand, in search of new beginnings and prosperity. But the harsh land near Christchurch where they settle threatens to destroy them almost before they begin. When Joseph finds gold in the creek, he guiltily hides the discovery from his wife and mother and is seized by a rapturous obsession with the voluptuous riches awaiting him deep in the earth. Abandoning his farm and family, he sets off alone for the new gold-fields over the Southern Alps, a moral wilderness where many others are violently rushing to their destinies.

INVISIBLE

Paul Auster

1967 to 2007 — three people's lives — three different perspectives . . . In New York City, in the spring of 1967, twenty-year-old Adam Walker is an aspiring poet and student at Columbia University who meets the enigmatic Frenchman Rudolf Born and his silent and seductive girlfriend, Margot. Before long, Walker finds himself caught in a perverse triangle that leads to a sudden, shocking act of violence that will alter the course of his life . . .

THE BETRAYER

Kimberley Chambers

Maureen Hutton's life has never been easy. Married to an alcoholic and stuck on a council estate in East London, she scrimps and saves to bring up her three children alone. Despite her family's involvement in murder, the underworld and drug addiction, over four decades, Maureen sticks by her brood through thick and thin. But then the unforgivable happens. Maureen is told a terrible secret which threatens to rip her family apart. She can't say anything. She is too frightened of causing a bloodbath. The only thing Maureen can do is get rid of the betrayer, before it is too late.

THE PRODIGAL SISTER

Laura Elliot

Scared and pregnant, fifteen-year-old Cathy Lambert ran away from her Dublin home. Settled in New Zealand with her new son Conor, she believed the secret she carried would never be revealed . . . When Rebecca Lambert's parents died she took responsibility for her younger sisters. Now, she is still haunted by fears she hoped she'd conquered. And mother of three Julie Chambers is determined to recapture the dreams of her youth. Meanwhile Lauren Moran embarks on a love affair that threatens to destabilise her fragile world . . . Anxious to make peace with her three sisters, Cathy invites them to her wedding. And their journey together through New Zealand, towards their reunion, forces them to confront the past as the secret shared histories of the Lambert sisters are revealed.

FOOLISH LESSONS IN LIFE & LOVE

Penny Rudge

When eager-to-please, accident-prone Taras Krohe ambles into an English public school — on a puzzling scholarship, with his funny foreign name, no father, but an over-protective Bukovinian mother — disappointment beckons. A decade later, Taras and his mother are still living off their benefactress, Mrs Bartlett, in a cramped South London flat, while Taras's promising job has warped into a Kafkaesque nightmare. His truculent Russian girlfriend has decamped with a ponytailed aesthete. And when Mrs Bartlett dies, eviction looms. Now even the easygoing Taras must show his mother he's a man and uncover the secret behind his family's plummet into disaster. However, she's determined to wrestle her little pourchi away from the dangerous influences his search reveals, and it's not certain who will come out on top . . .